D0950379

THE INHERITANCE

Also by Megan Lindholm

Harpy's Flight
The Limbreth Gate
The Windsingers
Wizard of the Pigeons
The Luck of the Wheels
The Reindeer People
Wolf's Brother
Alien Earth
Cloven Hooves
The Gypsy (with Steven Brust)

Also by Robin Hobb

The Rain Wilds Chronicles
Dragon Keeper
Dragon Haven

The Soldier Son Trilogy
Shaman's Crossing
Forest Mage
Renegade's Magic

The Tawny Man Trilogy
Fool's Errand
Golden Fool
Fool's Fate

The Liveship Traders Trilogy
Ship of Magic
Mad Ship
Ship of Destiny

The Farseer Trilogy
Assassin's Apprentice
Royal Assassin
Assassin's Quest

MEGAN LINDHOLM

THE INHERITANCE

AND OTHER STORIES

ROBIN HOBB

HARPER Voyager
An Imprint of HarperCollins*Publishers*
www.harpervoyagerbooks.com

This book is a work of fiction. The characters, incidents, and dialogue are drawn from the author's imagination and are not to be construed as real. Any resemblance to actual events or persons, living or dead, is entirely coincidental.

HarperCollins books may be purchased for educational, business, or sales promotional use. For information please write: Special Markets Department, HarperCollins Publishers, 10 East 53rd Street, New York, NY 10022.

First Harper Voyager trade paperback edition published 2011.

Harper Voyager and design is a trademark of HCP LLC.

Designed by Paula Russell Szafranski

Library of Congress Cataloging-in-Publication Data has been applied for.

ISBN 978-0-06-156164-1

11 12 13 14 15 OV/RRD 10 9 8 7 6 5 4 3 2 1

For Fred, in our fortyish year

Contents

PREFACE

Behind every story a writer writes, there is the story of how the writer came to the tale. In the introduction to each story in this collection, I hope to share a bit of what went on in my mind and in my life that prompted each story.

It is also true that behind every book, there is a story. This one is no exception.

I began my writing career when I was eighteen years old, as an aspiring children's author. I was newly married and living in a small village called Chiniak on Kodiak Island. The population was small, the local business was a combination gas station and convenience store that kept fitful hours, and initially there was little for me to do other than keep my small house trailer tidy and take long walks on the beach with my dog, Stupid. I had long known that I wanted to be a writer, so I borrowed a small portable electric typewriter from my sister-in-law, bought a ream of paper and some carbon papers, large brown envelopes for my SASEs (self-addressed stamped envelopes for rejection slips!), and a copy of *Writer's Market*. I was soon submitting short works to various children's magazines such as *Humpty Dumpty, Jack and Jill,* and *Highlights for Children,* in addition to many tiny magazines with very small circulations. In the beginning, rejection slips far outnumbered sales, but with each contact with the editorial world, I was learning.

By the time ten years had passed, I had realized that writing for children was hard work, much harder than simple words and linear plots had seemed at first glance. Trial and error had taught me that there was a corollary to the famous "Write what you know" advice. That was, "Write what you love reading." I had long been passionate about fantasy and science fiction, but equally daunted at the prospect of trying to compare my work with the tales from the writers I lionized. But by my midtwenties, I was venturing out with submissions to "fanzines," the small-press homemade magazines of the genre. Some were little more than mimeographed or Xeroxed pamphlets while others had ventured into glossy pages and illustrations. They were my proving ground as a writer, and I will forever owe a debt to magazines such as *Space and Time,* and editors such as Gordon Linzner.

When I began writing SF and fantasy for adults, I initially wrote as M. Lindholm. I was very happy with that sole initial in front of my surname. In 1978, I submitted a story to Jessica Amanda Salmonson that I hoped she would consider for her small-press magazine *Fantasy and Terror.* To my shocked delight, she wrote back saying that she would like to use it for her forthcoming feminist fantasy anthology, to be entitled *Amazons!* But she felt strongly that women writers needed to declare themselves as female. She urged me to put a name rather than an initial in my byline. I wrote back to her that I'd never been fond of my given name, Margaret, and that the nicknames such as Maggie,

Peggy, Marge, and so on had never really felt like my own, either. I added, almost as an afterthought, that Megan was not so bad.

Months later, when the book came out, I was a bit astounded to see that I had a new byline. Megan Lindholm it was. I confess to having mixed feelings about it, then and still. A year or two later, when the first Ki and Vandien book, *Harpy's Flight,* sold to Ace Books, I realized that without my intending to I'd made an important decision. Since the story in *Harpy's Flight* featured the same characters as "Bones for Duluth," the story in *Amazons!,* I would have to use the same byline. Without giving it much thought, I'd become Megan Lindholm.

And Megan Lindholm I would remain for many years.

Leap forward in time yet another decade and a bit more. It was a time of change in my life. I had recently switched to a new US publisher, my career-shifting agent Patrick Delahunt had passed me on to a new agent, Ralph Vicinanza, and I was writing a story of a type I'd never attempted before. This was to be a big fantasy, on an epic scale, and written from the first-person point of view of a young man. I was writing in a style that I felt was completely different from any I'd ever used before. Perhaps it was a time to make a complete break with the past. The idea of changing my pseudonym greatly appealed to me. Although I remained very fond and proud of my works as Megan Lindholm, the drama of adopting a "secret identity" was irresistible. I jumped at the chance to become Robin Hobb.

My editors, my agent, and I all agreed that the change presented an opportunity for me to break out of my "Megan Lindholm" voice and tell a big compelling story in a very lively way, one that I hoped would reach new readers. I hadn't realized that I had begun to feel bound by what readers might expect of a Megan Lindholm book until I stepped away from that name. I wrote with a depth of feeling that I didn't usually indulge. When *Assassin's Apprentice* by Robin Hobb was first published, I spent weeks with my nerves in a knot, wondering how this new series by a "new author" would be received.

The results were beyond my wildest hopes. I will never know how much the name change had to do with the success of *Assassin's Apprentice* and the other Hobb books that followed it. I don't think there's a way to quantify that. But it felt absolutely wonderful to have reached a wider readership. And for several years, I played my cards very close to my chest, concealing that Megan Lindholm and Robin Hobb were one and the same. I attended conventions as Megan Lindholm, and while I was there, I did not speak about my work as Hobb. I did not do any readings or signings for the initial Farseer books.

Beyond my agent and publishers, only two people knew the secret. One was Steven Brust, my collaborator on *The Gypsy*. I think Steve enjoyed keeping the secret, and he did it very well, for which I will always be grateful. The other person was Duane Wilkins of University Book Store, Seattle. I'd known Duane for years at that point. He'd been instrumental in helping my career as Megan Lindholm, supporting me with signings and readings as he did many, many fledgling SF and fantasy writers in the Seattle area. One night I received a call from him. He mentioned he hadn't seen me in a while, and we talked about various forthcoming books and what he thought of them. Then he brought up *Assassin's Apprentice.* It was very gratifying to hear him say nice things about the book I couldn't openly acknowledge as mine. But then he proceeded to say that he could tell it wasn't a first effort by any writer. And that he had noticed some stylistic resemblances. I kept my mouth shut. But then he asked me, directly, and there is no lying to old friends.

And Duane, too, kept the secret intact for me.

Of course, the information eventually leaked out, in drips and drops, and finally I did a *Locus* interview with Charles Brown in which I admitted that yes, Robin Hobb and Megan Lindholm were both my pseudonyms.

But to this day, they remain separate writers in my mind. They may use the same battered keyboard, the one with the letters worn off the buttons. They share office supplies and an assistant, and even do very similar online updates. But they are not the same author, but rather two writers with different styles, issues, and choices of tale. I think each writer continues to attract a different readership, though some readers tell me they enjoy stories by both writers. Even today, when I get a story idea, I immediately know if it belongs to Lindholm or Hobb, and the story is written accordingly. Robin tends to hog the word processor with her big books, but Megan has continued to write and publish shorter works.

This is the first time that a selection of stories by both pseudonyms has appeared in one volume. The Lindholm stories are, if you will, the inheritance that Hobb built upon. The styles and the subject matter differ from name to name, but if you check the DNA, you will find the shared genetics and the common fascinations.

There are old stories here, written when Megan Lindholm was first establishing herself, as well as new tales by both authors. Robin still tends to sprawl in her storytelling, so while she takes up as many pages, there are fewer stories by her in these pages.

To those readers who are encountering one (or both) of my bylines for the first time, welcome! And thank you for taking a chance on a "new" writer. And for those readers of Lindholm or Hobb who are taking the opportunity to acquire some of these stories in a more durable form, thank you, I hope you will not be disappointed.

THE INHERITANCE

PART I

MEGAN LINDHOLM

A Touch of Lavender

The old question "Where do you get your story ideas from?" still has the power to stump me. The easy, and truthful, answer is "Everywhere." Any writer will tell you that. An overheard conversation on the bus, a newspaper headline read the wrong way, a simple "what if" question—any of those things can be the germ that grows into a story.

But for me, at least, there is one other odd source. A stray first line. I may be driving or mowing the lawn or trying to fall asleep at night, and some odd sentence will suddenly intrude. I always recognize these sentences for what they are: the first line of a story that I don't yet know.

In the days before computers figured into writing, I would jot those butterfly lines down on a piece of scrap paper and keep them in my desk drawer, with other stray ideas. I knew they had to be captured immediately or they would flutter off forever. The line "We grew up like mice in a rotting sofa, my sister and I" came to me at a time when

I had just moved into a house that possessed just such an item of furniture. It was a smelly old sofa, damp and featuring a green brocade sort of upholstery. It came with the used-to-be-a-chicken-house house that my husband and I purchased with my very first book advance from Ace Books. My advance was $3,500 and the run-down house, on almost four acres of choice swampland (oh, wait, we call those "wetlands" nowadays and preserve them!) cost us the whopping sum of $32,500. The payment of $325 a month represented a $50 saving over what we had been paying in monthly rent! And we could keep chickens for eggs. Such a deal!

From the attic, I could look up and see sky between the cedar shingles that were the roof. A brooder full of chickens was parked in the bathroom. (Buff Orpingtons for you chicken connoisseurs.) We regarded those twenty-five half-fledged layers as a value-added feature of the house, much better than a spare room. A spare room can't lay eggs! There were no interior doors in the house, and some of the windows didn't close all the way. We tore up the rotted carpet and lived with bare ship-lap floors. There were no shelves in the noisy old refrigerator; we cut plywood to fit and inserted it. The only heat came from a woodstove. It was thus a mixed blessing that the yard was dominated by an immense fallen cedar tree. My ax and I rendered it into heat for the house for that first winter, one chop at a time.

A week after we bought it, at the end of March, Fred said good-bye and went off to fish the Bering Sea, leaving me there with my faithful portable Smith-Coronamatic, three children under ten years old, an overweight pit bull, and a tough old cat. I would not see my husband again until October. We were impossibly broke when he left, and I knew that somehow I had to hold it together until after the end of herring season when he would finally get paid. We borrowed money from his sister to buy a can of paint because my daughter could not stand the lavender walls left her by the previous tenant of her bedroom. The bathroom chickens got older and began to lay eggs. It was mend-and-

make-do time. Smelly and mice infested or not, the couch and other abandoned furnishings were what we had. I felt a bit bad for the mice when I evicted them. They'd been cozy and safe there, despite the run-down surroundings. Vacuumed, cleaned by hand, and with an old bedspread tossed over it, the rotting sofa became the main seating in the living room.

Somewhere in the back of my mind, I suppose it occurred to me that my children were now much like those mice had been. Tough as things were, we now had a place to call our own. And, I hoped, my kids had good folks who would see them through.

Did the lavender walls have anything to do with the story that would be written, years later, and feature that opening line? Who knows?

It's all grist for the writing mill.

We grew up like mice nesting in a rotting sofa, my sister and I. Even when I was only nine and she was an infant, I thought of us that way. At night, when she'd be asleep in the curl of my belly and I'd be half falling off the old sofa we used as a bed, I'd hear the mice nibbling and moving inside the upholstery beneath us, and sometimes the tiny squeakings of the newborn ones when the mother came to nurse them. I'd curl tighter around Lisa and pretend she was a little pink baby mouse instead of a little pink baby girl, and that I was the father mouse, curled around her to protect her. Sometimes it made the nights less chill.

I'd lived in the same basement apartment all my life. It was always chill, even in summer. It was an awful place, dank and ratty, but the upstairs apartments were worse, rank with urine and rot. The building was an old town house, long ago converted to four apartments upstairs and one in the basement. None of them were great, but ours was the cheapest, because we had the furnace and the water heater right next to us. When I was real small, three or so, a water main beside the building broke, and water came rising up in our apartment, maybe a foot deep. I woke up to my stuff floating beside me, and the old couch sucking up water like a sponge. I yelled for Mom. I heard the splash as she rolled out of bed in the only bedroom and then her cussing as she waded through the water to pick me up. Her current musician took the whole thing as a big joke, until he saw his sax case floating. Then he grabbed up his stuff and was out of there. I don't remember seeing him after that.

My mom and I spent that day sitting on the steps down to our apartment, waiting for the city maintenance crew to fix the pipe, waiting for the water to go down, and then waiting for our landlord.

He finally came and looked the place over and nodded, and said, hell, it was probably for the best, he'd been meaning to put down new tiles and spraysulate the walls anyway. "You go ahead and tear out the old stuff," he told my mom. "Stack it behind the house, and I'll have it hauled away. Let me know when you're ready, and I'll send in a crew to fix the place up. Now about your rent . . ."

"I told you, I already mailed it," Mom said coldly, looking past his ear, and the landlord sighed and drove off.

So Mom and her friends peeled up the cracking linoleum and tore the Sheetrock off the walls, leaving the bare concrete floor with stripes of mastic showing and the two-by-four wall studs standing bare against the gray block walls. That was as far as the remodeling ever got. The landlord never hauled the stuff away, or sent in a crew. He never spraysulated the walls, either. Even in the summer the walls were cool and misty, and in winter it was like the inside of a refrigerator.

My mom wasn't so regular about paying the rent that she could raise a fuss. Most of the folks in our building were like that: pay when you can, and don't stay home when you can't, so the landlord can't nag at you. The apartments were lousy, but complaining could get you kicked out. All the tenants knew that if the landlord had wanted to, he could have gotten a government grant to convert the place into Skoag units and really made a bundle. We were right on the edge of a Skoag sector and demand for Skoag units was increasing.

That was back when the Skoags were first arriving and there wasn't much housing for them. It all had to be agency approved, too, to prevent any "interplanetary incidents." Can't have aliens falling down the steps and breaking a flipper, even if they are pariahs. These outcasts were the only link we had to their planet and culture, and especially to their technology for space travel that the whole world was so anxious to have. No one knew where they came from or how they got to Earth. They just started wading out of the seas one day, not all that different from a washed-up Cuban. Just more wetback aliens, as the joke went. They were very open about being exiles with no means of returning home. They arrived gradually, in groups of three and four, but of the ships that brought them there was never any sign, and the Skoags weren't saying anything. That didn't stop any of the big government people from hoping, though. Hoping that if we were real nice to them, they might drop a hint or two about interstellar drives or something. So the Skoags got the government-subsidized housing with showers that worked and heat lamps and carpeted floors and spraysulated walls. The Federal Budget Control Bill said that funds could be reapportioned, but the budget could not be increased, so folks like my mom and I took a giant step downward in the housing arena. But as a little kid, all I understood was that our place was cold most of the time, and everyone in the neighborhood hated Skoags.

I DON'T THINK it really bothered Mom. She wasn't home that much anyway. She'd bitch about it sometimes when she brought a bunch of her friends home, to jam and smoke and eat. It was always the same scene, party time, she'd come in with a bunch of them, hyped on the music like she always was, stoned maybe, too. They'd be carrying instruments and six-packs of beer, sometimes a brown bag of cheap groceries, salami and cheese and crackers or yogurt and rice cakes and tofu. They'd set the groceries and beer out on the table and start doodling around with their instruments while my mom would say stuff like, "Damn, look at this dump. That damn landlord, he still hasn't been around. Billy, didn't the landlord come by today? No? Shit, man, that jerk's been promising to fix this place for a year now. Damn."

Everyone would tell her not to sweat it, hell, their places were just as bad, all landlords were assholes anyway. Usually someone would get onto the Skoag thing, how it was a fine thing the government could take care of alien refugee trash but wouldn't give its own citizens a break on rent. If there'd been a lot of Skoags at the café that night, Mom and her friends would get into how Skoags thought they were such hot shit, synthesizing music from their greasy hides. I remember one kid who really got worked up, telling everyone that they'd come to Earth to steal our music. According to him, the government knew it and didn't care. He said there was even a secret treaty that would give the Skoags free use of all copyrighted music in the United States if they would give us blueprints of their ships. No one paid much attention to him. Later that evening, when he was really stoned, he came and sat on the floor by my sofa and cried. He told me that he was a really great musician, except that he couldn't afford a good synthesizer to compose on, while those damn Skoags could just puff out their skins and make every sound anybody had ever heard. He leaned real close and told me that the real danger was that the Skoags would make up all the good music before he even got a chance to try. Which I knew was dumb. While Skoags can play anything they've ever heard, perfectly, no one had ever heard them play anything original. No one had ever heard them play Skoag music, only ours. I started to tell him that but he passed out on the floor by my sofa. Everyone ignored him. They were into the food and the beer and the music. All my mom's parties were like that.

I'd usually curl up on one end of the sofa, face to the cushions and try to sleep, sometimes with a couple necking at the other end of the sofa and two or three musicians in the kitchen, endlessly rehearsing the same few bars of a song I'd never heard before and would never hear again. That's what Mom was really into, struggling musicians who were performing their own stuff in the little "play for tips" places. She'd latch on to some guy and keep him with her aid check. She'd watch over him like he was gold, go with him every day, sit by him on the sidewalk while he played if he were a street musician, or take a table near the band if he was working cafés and clubs. They'd come home late and sleep late, and then get up and go out again. Sometimes I'd come in from school and find them sitting at the kitchen table, talking. It's funny. The men always looked the same, eyes like starved dogs, and it seems like my mom would always be saying the same thing. "Don't give up. You've got a real talent. Someday you'll make it, and you'll look back at them and laugh. You've really got it, Lennie (or Bobby or Pete or Lance). I know it. I can feel it, I can hear it. You're gonna be big one day."

The funny part is, she was always right. Those guys would live with us for a few months or a year, and suddenly, out of the blue, their careers would take off. They'd be discovered, on a sidewalk or in a café, or picked up by a band on its way up. They'd leave my mom, and go on to better things. She never got bitter about it, though she liked to brag to other women about all the hot ones she'd known "back when they were nothing." Like that was her calling in life, feeding guitar humpers until someone besides her could hear their songs. Like only she could keep the real music flowing. One night she brought home a disc and gave it to me. It was called *Fire Eyes,* and the guy on the front had dark hair and blue eyes, like me. "That's your daddy, Billy Boy," she told me. "Though he don't know it. He took off before I knew you were coming, and he was on a national tour by the time you were born. Look at those pretty, pretty eyes. Same as you, kid. You should have heard him sing, Billy. I knew he had it, even then. Even then." I think that was the first time I ever saw her sit down and cry. I'm still not sure if she was crying over my dad leaving us, or something else. She didn't cry long, and she went to bed alone that night. But the next night she brought home a whole pack of musicians from some open mike. By next morning, she had a new musician in her bed.

Sometimes during a party, if Mom was really stoned, or safe-sexing someone in the bedroom, I'd get up in my pajamas and make for the food, stuffing down as much as I could and hiding a couple of rice cakes or a handful of crackers behind the sofa cushion. I knew the mice would nibble on it, but hell, they never took much, just lacing around the edges. I figured they didn't do much better than I did anyway. If I was really lucky, there'd be some girls in the group, and they'd fuss over me, telling me how my big blue eyes were such a surprise with my dark hair, and giving me gum and Life Savers from their purses, or maybe quarters and pennies. Like people in sidewalk cafés feed sparrows. If my mom caught me, she'd get mad and tell me to get to sleep, I had school tomorrow and didn't I want to make something of myself? Then she'd smile at everyone like she was really saying something and go, in a real sweet voice, "If you miss school tomorrow, you miss music class, too. You don't want that to happen, do you?" As if I gave a shit. She was always bragging that I had my daddy's voice, and someday I was going to be a singer, how my music was my life, and that the school music lesson was the only way she could get me to go to school.

Dumb. Like singing "Farmer in the Dell" with forty other bored first graders was teaching me a lot about music. Music was okay, but I never understood how people could live for it like my mom did. She'd never learned to play any instrument, and while she could carry a tune, her voice was nothing special. But she lived for music, like it was air or food. Funny. I think the men she took in might have respected her more if she'd been able to create even a little of what she craved so badly. I could see it in their eyes, sometimes, that they looked down on her. Like she wasn't real to them because she couldn't make her own music. But my mother lived music, more than they did. She had to have it all the time; the stereo was always playing when she didn't have an in-house musician of her own. I'd be half asleep watching her swaying to the music, singing along in her mediocre voice. Sometimes she'd just be sprawled in our battered easy chair, her head thrown back, one hand steadying a mug of tea or a beer on her belly. Her brown eyes would be dark and gone, not seeing me or the bare wall studs, not seeing the ratty couch or scarred cupboards. Music took her somewhere, and I used to wonder where. I thought it was dumb, the way she lived for a collection of sounds, for someone else's words and notes.

I KNOW THE day my life changed. I was about three blocks from home, partway into the Skoag sector, listening to some Skoags on a street corner. Not listening, really, so much as watching them puff their greasy skins out until they looked like those stupid balloon animals Roxie the clown used to make for my Head Start class. Then when they were all puffed out, membrane ballooned over corally bone webs, they'd start making music, the skin going in and out just like speaker cones on really old speakers. They reminded me of frogs, because of how their throats puffed out to croak, and because of the wet green-yellow glints on their skins.

I kept a safe distance from them. Everyone did. From the Don't Do Drugs sessions at school, I knew what the stuff on their skin could do to me. I'd seen Skoag gropies, wandering around bald-eyed, hands reaching to grope any passing Skoag, to get one more rush even if it deafened them. Skoag gropies were always getting killed, squashed by cars and trucks they could no longer hear, or dreaming themselves to death, forgetting to eat or drink, forgetting everything but groping a fingerful of Skoag slime. But there were no gropies around these Skoags, and because they all still had crests, I knew they were new to Earth. Skoags usually lost their crests pretty fast in our gravity. One of these Skoags had the tallest crest I'd ever seen, like a king's crown, and purple like a deep old bruise.

There was a mixed crowd around the Skoags. Inlander tourists who'd never seen a Skoag before, taking videos, making tapes. Locals panhandling the tourists, sometimes pretending they were passing the hat for the Skoags. Older boys and a few girls, just hanging out, calling the Skoags dirty names to shock the tourists, making out with a lot of tongue. And a few kids like me, skipping school because the sun was shining and it wasn't too windy and we didn't feel like doing the weekly pee-in-the-bottle thing. The Skoags played for us all.

They'd been playing all morning, the usual Skoag set. They did "Happy Trails to You," and "Horiko Cries," and "When You Were Mine," and then "America the Beautiful." That was the weirdest thing about Skoags, how they'd pick up any music they fancied, and then play it back in any order. They'd started "Moon over Bourbon Street" when I saw my mom coming.

She and Teddy had gone to pick up her aid check that morning. But Teddy wasn't with her, and I knew from her face that another musician had moved out. I was glad in a selfish way, because for the next few days there'd be regular meals on the table, and more food, because the check would only be feeding us two, and Mom would talk to me twice as much as usual. Of course, she'd make sure I actually got up and went to school, too, but that wasn't much price to pay. And it wouldn't last long before she'd hold another party and reel in a new musician.

So I was determined to enjoy it while it lasted. So I ran up to her, saying, "Wow, Mom, you should hear this purple-crested one play, he's really something." I said that for about four reasons. First, so she wouldn't have the chance to ask me why I wasn't in school, and, second, to show that I wasn't going to notice that jerk Teddy was gone because he wasn't worth her time. Third, it cheered her up when I acted like I was interested in music. I think she always hoped I really would be like my father, would grow up to be a singer and redeem her, or justify her life or something. And fourth, because the purple-crested one really was something, though I couldn't have said why.

"You playing tourist, Billy Boy?" my mom asked me in her teasing way that she used when it was only she and I together again. And I laughed, because it was dumb the way the tourists from inland came down to our part of Seattle to spy on the Skoags and listen to them jam. Anybody who'd lived here ignored them the way you ignored supermarket music or a TV in a store window. All you ever heard from a Skoag was the same thing you'd heard a hundred times before anyway. So what I said was sort of a joke, too, to make her laugh and take the flatness out of her eyes.

But Teddy must have been better than I'd known, because her smile faded, and she didn't scold me or anything. She just stooped down and hugged me like I was all she had in the world. And then she said, very gently, as if I were the adult and she were the little kid explaining something bad she'd done, "I gave him our check, Billy Boy. See, Teddy has a chance to go to Portland and audition for Sound & Fury Records. It's a new label, and if things go like I know they will, he'll be into the big money in no time. And he'll send for us. We'll have a real house, Billy, all to ourselves, or maybe we'll get a motor home and travel across the country with him on tour, see the whole United States."

She said more stuff but I didn't listen. I knew what it meant, because once one of her guys had stolen both checks, her Career Mother Wage and my Child Nutrition Supplement. What it meant was bad times. It meant a month of food-bank food, runny peanut butter on dry bread, dry milk made up with more water than you were supposed to use, generic cereal that turned into sog in the milk, and macaroni. Lots and lots of microwaved macaroni, to the point where I used to swallow it whole because I couldn't stand the squidgy feeling of chewing it anymore. I was already hungry from being out in the wind all morning, and just thinking about it made me hungrier. There wasn't much food at home; there never was right before the aid check was due.

I just went on holding on to Mom, hating Teddy, but not much, because if it hadn't been Teddy, it would have been someone else. I wanted to ask, "What about me? What about us? Aren't we just as important as Teddy?" But I didn't. Because it wouldn't bring the money back, so there was no sense in making her cry. The other reason was, about three weeks before, Janice from upstairs had sat at our kitchen table and cried to Mom because she'd just given her little girls away. Because she couldn't take care of them or feed them. Janice had kept saying that at least they'd get decent meals and warm clothes now. I didn't want Mom to think that I wanted food and clothes more than I wanted to stay with her.

So I wiped my face on her shirt without seeming to and pulled back to look at her. "It's okay, Mom," I told her. "We'll get by. Let's go home and figure things out."

But she wasn't even listening to me. She was focused on the Skoags, actually on the one with the big crest, listening to "Moon over Bourbon Street" like she'd never heard it before. It sounded the same as always to me, and I tugged at her hand. But it was just like I wasn't there, like she had gone off somewhere. So I just stood there and waited.

My mom listened until they were done. The big purple-crested Skoag watched her listen to them. His big flat eye spots were pointed toward her all the time, calm and dead and unfocused like all Skoag eyes are. He was looking over the heads of the tourists and hecklers, straight at her.

When the song was finished, they didn't go right into another song like usual. Purple stood there, watching my mother and letting the air leak out of his puffers. The other Skoags looked at him, and they seemed puzzled, shifting around, and one made a flat squawk. But then they let their air out, too, and pretty soon they were all empty and bony, their puffer things tight against their bodies again. My mom kept staring at the Skoag, like she was still hearing music, until I shook her arm.

"I'm coming," she said, but she didn't. She didn't even move, until I shook her arm again and said, "I'm hungry."

Then she jerked and looked down at me finally. "Oh, my poor little kid," she said. She really meant it. That bothered me. I thought about it while we walked home. I wasn't any more selfish than any kid is, and kids have a right to be selfish sometimes. So I walked along, thinking that she really did know how awful this month was going to be and how much I hated squidgy macaroni, and she probably even knew that the sole was coming off my sneaker. But she'd still given the check to Teddy. And that was a hard thing for a kid to understand.

So we went home. Mom switched on the stereo and went right to work. She was real methodical and practical when there wasn't a musician to distract her. She sorted out what groceries we had and organized them in the cupboard.

Then she went through all the pockets of her clothes and dug inside the chair and got together all the money we had. It was ten seventy-eight. Then she sat me at the table with her, like I was one of her musicians, and told me how she was going to get us through the month. She explained that if I went to school every day, I'd get the free morning milk and vita-roll, and free hot lunch on my aid ticket. So I'd be mostly okay, even if there wasn't much for dinner. We'd get through just fine. After all, we were pretty tough, weren't we? And couldn't the two of us beat anything if we just stuck together? And were we going to let a month of crummy groceries knock down tough guys like us? All that stuff. But suddenly, in the middle of the pep talk, she got up and knelt by her stereo. She twiddled the knobs, frowning. "Signal's drifting, or something. Damn, that's all I need. For this to drop dead on me now." She tried about three different stations, then snapped it off. "Lousy speakers," she complained to me. "Everything sounds tinny."

It had sounded okay to me, but I didn't say anything. Instead, I sat still and watched her take out a pot and run water and take things from the cupboards for dinner.

We had oatmeal for dinner, and toast with peanut butter melting on it. Mom gave me the last of the brown sugar for my oatmeal. "Good grains and protein in this meal," she said wisely, as if she had planned it rather than scraped together what we had left. I nodded and ate it. It wasn't so bad. At least it wasn't macaroni.

That evening Mom sat at the table, reading a paperback that Teddy had left and wearing his old sweatshirt. I guess she felt pretty bad. Every so often, she'd turn on the stereo and fool with it for a while, then shake her head and snap it off. She'd read a little longer, and then she'd get up and turn the stereo on again, searching through the stations, but never finding what she wanted. In between, I was listening to the building sounds, spooky at night. The water heater in the utility room was growing and gurgling through the wall. I was coloring a Don't Do Drugs handout from school, wishing they'd given me more than three crayons. I wanted to color the spoon and syringe silver. Yellow just wasn't the same.

Mom had just snapped the radio off for about the twelfth time. In the quiet I heard a sound like someone dragging a bag of potatoes down our steps. Mom and I looked at each other. She lifted her finger to her lips and said, "Shush!" So I sat perfectly still, waiting. There came a slapping sound against the door, and whatever was slapping pushed against it too. The door thudded against the catch.

My mom's dark eyes went huge, scaring me more than the noises outside the door. She went to the kitchen and got our biggest knife. "Go to my room, Billy Boy," she whispered. But I was too scared to move. Like a monster movie, when the music screams and you know they're going to show you something awful, but you can't look away. I had to know what was outside. And Mom was too scared to make me obey. Instead she crept a little closer to the door, holding the knife tight. "Who's out there?" she yelled, but her voice cracked.

The pressure on the door stopped, and for a moment all was silent. Then there was a sound, sort of like a harmonica wedged in a trumpet, and someone blowing through it anyway. It was a silly cartoon sound, Doofus Duck smacked with a rubber mallet, and my mom looked so startled that I burst out laughing. It was a dorko noise. Nothing scary could make a sound like that. Then a voice spoke, a low, low voice, like cello strings being rubbed slowly.

"That is my name on my world. But humans call me Lavender."

"The Skoag?" Mom asked, but I was already past her and undoing the flimsy dead bolt on the door. I had to see it. It was so impossible for a Skoag to be outside our door at night that I had to see it was real. "Billy!" Mom warned, but I dragged the door open anyway.

The Skoag was there. The same purple-crested one we had listened to earlier. Only he looked a lot smaller with all his bladders deflated, not much bigger than my mom. He was wearing a sort of pouch thing on his front, and in it was a brown grocery sack, a bouquet of flowers wrapped in green tissue paper, and a skinny brown liquor store bag. He was draped in the transparent plastic robe Skoags were supposed to wear in human dwellings. His skin glistened through it in the watery streetlamp light like oil on a puddle, iridescent and shifting. His fat little flippers waved up and down slowly, like a fish underwater. His murky blue eye spots fixed on my mother.

She stared back at him. She still had the knife in her hand, but she had forgotten it. She crossed her arms, a closing, denying gesture. "What do you want?" she demanded, in the scared stubborn voice she kept for the landlord.

A little bladder above his eyes pulsed with his cello voice. "To come in."

"Well, you can't," she said, at the same time as I asked, "How did you get down the steps?"

"With great difficulty," he pulsed at me, but there was a violin squibble above the cello that made his answer a sort of joke. I grinned at him; I couldn't help it. He'd noticed me. He'd answered my question before he paid attention to what my mom had said, and he'd answered it in the way one buddy might kid with another. I felt two feet taller.

He looked back at Mom, waiting.

"Go away," she told him.

"I cannot," he said, all cello again. "Earlier today, I heard you listening to us. I think. My companions tell me it was not so, that I am tricking myself because I want too badly. But I am not deceived. I have hope only. I have brought gifts. Flowers and wine for you, as is fitting, and food for your child, who said he was hungry. May I come in?"

She just stood there, staring at him. A car shushed by in the rainy street outside, and the wind gusted, blowing cold air down our steps and in past the Skoag. And still they both just stood there, waiting for something.

"I love you," the cello thrummed, and the sound swelled, like a big warm wave washing through our apartment. The sound didn't end with the words, it went on with musiclike embroidery on the edges of the thought. I listened to it pass and fade, and then the silence came behind it, separating us again. The silence seemed unbearable.

"Come in," said my mother.

So Lavender came to live with us.

EVERYTHING CHANGED.

Everything.

Within just a few days, the neighbors stopped knowing us. I'd walk down the streets, and rocks would bounce around me, but I'd never see who'd thrown them. The radio was never turned on again. There was real food, every day. Mom stopped looking at street musicians and haunting the open mikes. The street people called her ugly names, and our mailbox got ripped off the wall in the upstairs lobby. I got into so many fights at school that the principal said I had to stay in at recesses for the rest of the year. After that, I was left totally alone. I didn't care. Because I had Lavender at home.

Every day I went to school, because Lavender said I should. It would be important later, he assured me, and that was enough for me. Every day I came home and slid down the ridged ramp that had replaced our steps. And Lavender was always waiting for me to come home, even if my mother wasn't there. Always before, Mom's musicians had tolerated and ignored me, treated me like a cat or a houseplant, a semiannoying creature that lived in my mother's house. Not Lavender. He knew I was there, and he was glad. He made me important. We would have a snack together, he rubbing his sludgy porridge through a membrane on his chest, me munching cookies and milk. Then I had to show him every single paper I'd brought home, read aloud from every library book I'd checked out. All I did amazed him. But mostly we'd talk and laugh. His laugh reminded me of a giant grasshopper chirring. Once he told me that Skoags had never laughed before they came to Earth, but the idea of a special sound made just to show happiness was so wonderful that now it was the first thing that all exiles were allowed to do. Each Skoag got to make up his own kind of laugh. He said it like it was some big favor for them. Then he told me that my laugh was one of the best ones he'd ever heard. That first day, when he'd heard my laugh in the street, he'd known that anyone who could create so marvelous a sound had to be very special indeed. And then he laughed my own laugh for me to hear, and that set me laughing; and we laughed together for about ten minutes, in harmony, like a new kind of song,

Looking back, I know he didn't understand much of basic human needs. Because he learned mostly from me, he had a seven-year-old boy's idea of what was important. Food he understood, and he always made sure there was plenty of it, though he tended to buy the same kinds over and over again. He loved bright, simple toys that moved, yo-yos and tops and plastic gliders, marbles and Super Balls and Frisbees. I'm convinced he thought that flowers were essential to my mother, and he filled our little apartment with graceful glass vases full of them. I never thought to ask for anything more than what he brought and I know my mother never did. She was too used to giving to learn taking easily. Still, Lavender tried to provide for us. I remember the day I came home and found him cautiously touching his flippers to the protruding nails and scabs of Sheetrock on the two-by-four wall studs. "This pleases the Mom?" he asked me.

"No. It's really ugly. But it's all we've got," I told him. A wrinkling ran over his deflated bladders, a gesture I had learned was like an excited grin. "This would please the Mom?" the cello thrummed, and he began pulling yards and yards of stuff out of his belly pouch. Shiny like plastic, but soft like fabric, and so thin you could crumple up a square yard of it in your fist. He began fastening it to the wall, in graceful drapery, and as it fell straight, the room warmed with both color and heat, the musky basement smell faded, and a gentle light suffused the room. Then we hid in the closet until my mom came home and was surprised by it. "Oh, Lavender, you cover up all the rough edges of my life," Mom told him. For a long time, I thought she meant the wall studs. He could make the hanging different colors, and he adjusted it almost daily, though I never asked how. If I had, he would have told me. I just didn't ask.

He told me anything I wanted to know. I knew more about Skoags than any of the "experts" of that time. Anything I asked him, he answered. I knew that they had been exiled to our world because they sang in public, and that was not permitted in their home world. I knew that they sang only other people's music, because making up new music was something only a holy leader could do. The Earth Skoags were religious rebels, sort of like the Pilgrims. They believed singing was so worshipful that Skoags should do it all the time, everywhere, and that everyone should do it, not just priest-Skoags. On their own world, that was heresy, and anyone caught at it had to choose between exile or "a most unfortunate happening." For a long time I didn't know what he meant by that. A lot of what he told me was puzzling. Lavender kept trying to explain to me that singing was a circle, and that if one sang well enough to make the perfect music, it would create the one that would close the circle. My mom, he said, was "Close. Almost the end of the circle. The one, but not quite." I never understood what he meant, but it was very important to him. A day didn't pass without him trying to make me understand. There just weren't human words for the Skoag ideas. It worried him very much. It was the only hole in our communication. He told me other stuff, like how some Skoags had long, articulated flippers like my fingers, and how they were dehydrated for their space journeys, and how they thought of humans as "half sexed" because we weren't self-fertile. Anything I asked, he answered. But if I didn't ask, he didn't bother me with it. I never asked him if he had come to end his people's exile, or if he were a very important Skoag on his world or how their spaceships operated. Or he would have told me. But I didn't ask.

In the long evenings, Lavender made music for us, playing anything we wanted. He knew every song my mother ever asked for and could do them in any artist's style. She would sit on the end of my couch, my feet warm against her, listening raptly while Lavender played until I fell asleep. Mornings I would waken to his slaps on the door and run to let him in. He'd be laden with cereal and milk and fruit and a packet of his own gruelly food, and always fresh flowers for Mom. He'd play back to me all the new sounds he'd heard in the night city, not just the music that drifted out from the bars, but seagulls crying over the bay, and the coughing of winos and the barking of dogs. It was always hard to go to school. I was sure they had fun without me all day at home, but to please Lavender, I went.

Life was good. There was food and talk and warmth at home, and that's all most kids ask. But on top of all that, I had Lavender. The value of that is too great to tell. For over a year, the world was as good as it could possibly be.

One day my mother touched him. By accident. I know, because I was there when it happened. So simple, so stupid. She slipped on the kitchen floor, reached out to steady herself and caught Lavender's flipper. Lavender's bare flipper tip, shining with Skoag slime, caught my mother's hand, steadied her, and transported her to ecstasy. Her face changed, she cried out, a simple "oh" like a kid seeing his first Christmas tree, and sat down on the kitchen floor. She just sat and smiled. Lavender gently pulled his flipper free of her grip, but it was too late. His dark blue eye spots fastened on me.

"You didn't do it on purpose," I told him. "It wasn't your fault." But my heart was shaking my whole body.

A scant second later, Mom was standing up, saying, "I'm all right. Don't be upset, Lavender. Stop flapping like that. Billy, don't stare, I'm fine." She caught at the edge of the kitchen table, sat down in one of the chairs. "Shit. What a rush!" she said a moment later, and then sighed. And got up from the table and went to the stove and started stirring the spaghetti sauce again. And that was that. *Whew,* I thought as my mind darted to my Don't Do Drugs book at school. *I'm glad Mom didn't turn into a Skoag gropie.*

But, of course, she did.

At first she never touched Lavender when I was around. And kids don't notice gradual changes. I'd get home from school, and she'd be sitting at the table, humming to herself. It got harder to get her attention. More and more, she told me to fix my own supper. At first she'd tell me what to cook, but later she'd just wave at the fridge. After a while, Lavender learned about frozen dinners and bought them for us. One day when I got home, I found that Lavender had replaced our little aid-issued microwave cooker with a more elaborate one. I cooked all the meals from then on. But even then, I didn't catch on.

If I suspected anything, it was only that Mom and Lavender were growing closer. That first night he had said he loved her. That had never seemed strange to me. I loved my mom, a lot of musicians had said they loved her, so why shouldn't a strange Skoag standing on the doorstep say it? I never doubted it was true, and

I don't think Mom did either. Lavender never missed a chance to show how important "the Mom" was. Not just the flowers, or the way he played whatever she wanted him to play. It was the way he respected her in a way no one else ever had. He made her listening as important as his playing.

And it started being more and more important. Now when he played for her at night, he'd stop, sometimes in the middle of the music, and say, "Is that it? Is that right?"

"No," she'd say, and he'd deflate with despair.

Or, "Almost," she'd say, and hum a bit to herself, a swatch of music nothing like what he'd been playing, but he'd say, "I think I hear," and try again.

And if she said, "Yes, yes, that's it," he'd play the piece over and over again, while she sat and nodded and smiled. Slowly she changed. She didn't care about her clothes anymore, and she seldom went outside. She got fat and bought big men's shirts from the secondhand store to cover her belly. She became fussy about her hair, brushing and combing it like a fussy fiddler tuning his strings. Her voice changed, becoming dreamy and muffled, the ends of her words blunting. Sometimes when I got home from school, she'd be sitting at the table, dreaming with her eyes open. I'd talk to her but get no response until Lavender came to stand beside her. Then she'd focus on me, and answer my questions in a sweet, dreamy voice.

It was easier to talk to Lavender instead. He always knew everything anyway, and Mom was so happy and dreamy that I didn't worry about anything being wrong. She wasn't like the filthy, skinny Skoag gropies in the schoolbook. She was clean, and shining with health and dreams, plump and pretty. About then I found out Lavender didn't always leave at night anymore, but sometimes lay on the bed beside her, with Mom gripping his flipper all night, her head pillowed on his plastic-coated body. So I should have known she was a Skoag gropie, right, and realized she was stone deaf. How could I? I was a kid, she didn't look like a gropie, and even if she ignored me a lot, she was still my mom. And she still listened every night to Lavender's playing.

Even I was enchanted by his music. Mom no longer asked for stuff by titles, and I had never cared what he played. What had mattered to me was that he was playing for me as well as for Mom. That last bit of special attention at the end of the day was what mattered to me. But slowly that changed, as the music he played changed. He started playing a lot of stuff I didn't know. Some of it was dreary and mournful, and sometimes the words were in a different language. Sometimes it was full of strings and campfires, and sometimes it sounded like brass challenges and steel replies. But sometimes the music was so strange and wonderful it made the hair stand up on my arms and legs and tickled the back of my neck. I began to understand how my mother could live for music. Some of the music he played made my heart want to dance outside my body, pulled me from my sofa to sit beside Lavender's fat, calloused feet-flippers, hypnotized me with joy. And some of it made me cry, isolated stinging tears because I could almost, but not quite, tell what the music was about.

That had to be Lavender's music. No one else could have made up such music, music that knew me so well. It had to be his original music. But Skoags weren't allowed to make their own music. Unless they were priest-Skoags, composing for the temples.

In February, the first package came for Lavender. It was at the bottom of the ramp when I got home, and I picked it up and took it into the house. Just a little flat black plastic box. "Look what I found," I said as I came in the door, and Lavender came immediately and took it from me.

"For me," he told me. "A message." His cello strings quivered unnaturally as he slipped it into his pouch. I never saw him open it, and he didn't speak of it again, just asked to see my school papers.

There were three more after that, or perhaps four. Always at the bottom of the ramp when I got home from school, and always Lavender took them. One day it started raining on my way home and when I got to our house, there were flipper prints outlined on the ramp, leading to the flat black box. So Skoags left them. I wondered why the Skoags were sending him messages instead of just talking to him.

The last message box was silver, not black. Lavender held it for a long time, just looking at it. Then the muscles around his eye spots moved and he looked at my mom for a long time. She knew something about those message boxes, and it wasn't good. I wanted terribly to know what it was, but I was too frightened to ask. Silence wrapped me so tightly it cut into me like wires. I went to Mom, and she held me against her fat stomach and stroked my head like I was a baby. Then she gave me a gentle push and pointed to the door. I was to go outside.

"I'm not a baby anymore," I said angrily, knowing I was being shut off from something.

"No," said Lavender. He moved a slow flipper, and Mom let go of me. "You certainly aren't. You are old enough to be trusted with important things." He paused, then the cello thrummed rapidly. "Billy Boy. I have made the other Skoags very angry by being here with you. They demand I come back to them and live as they wish me to live. I cannot. Tomorrow I will go to tell them that. There may be . . ." the cello sighed wordlessly, then went on, "a great unpleasantness for me. A most unfortunate happening, perhaps. Until I come back, I will rely on you to take care of the Mom." He turned slowly until he faced my mom again. "That is all there is to say. Billy does not need to leave." She bowed her head, accepting his wishes. He spoke no more about it but went about the apartment tunelessly humming and adjusting the wall hanging from pale mauve to a sky blue.

That evening he played long, wordless songs with lots of strings and high-pitched wind instruments. I fell asleep to music like seagulls crying after a storm.

The next day when I got home from school, Lavender wasn't there. Mom was sitting at the table. She didn't even look up until I slapped my schoolbooks down in front of her. Then she looked up with eyes as flat and dark as Lavender's eye spots. Her face was like the day she'd given Teddy our check, but a thousand times worse. "Billy," she said, in a low swollen voice like her mouth was packed with marshmallows. She reached for me, to pull me near, but the palms of her hands were scarred with iridescence, like the pictures in the Don't Do Drugs textbook. Suddenly I couldn't let her touch me. My mind tagged and rejected the truth. I pulled back, feeling betrayed, knowing something was terribly, terribly wrong. "Lavender!" I cried, but no cello sawed an answer. I looked again at my mom, at her scarred hands and her deaf loneliness. I saw what he had done, but his not being here, now, was worse.

"Don't hate him," Mom said, in her slow, sticky voice. "We had to do it, Billy. We couldn't help ourselves. And some day it's going to be all right."

She couldn't have known how bad it was going to get. All that long empty evening, she'd shiver suddenly and then wrap her arms around herself and cock her head as if seeking for a sound. I sat on the couch and watched her and tried to imagine her loneliness. My mother cut off from music, from all sound. As kind to seal off her lungs from air. But he loved her, he loved me; he couldn't leave her empty like that and me alone, and he wouldn't just go away. I watched her digging her fingers into her ears like she was trying to claw out a stopper. Her nails came out with tiny shreds of dry skin and scabby stuff. She wiped at her ears with pieces of toilet paper, and they came away pink. It was awful to watch. But the worst was the sound of flippers on the ramp, and the heavy slap at the door. The worst was me jumping up, believing that Lavender had come back and everything was going to be all right. I ran to the door and dragged it open for him, and he fell halfway into the room.

It was a terribly clattery sound, his fall, but he didn't cry out. My mom didn't make a sound as she went to him. I stood clear of them both, watched her roll him over.

I screamed when I saw what they had done to him. The remains of his bladders fluttered in feeble rags, and a pale yellowish stuff oozed from the torn edges. They had slashed them all, every sound membrane on his body. He tried to speak, but made only a ridiculous sound of flapping curtains and newspapers blowing down the street, a terrible fluttering of ripped drumheads. My mother knelt over him and lifted his flippers and pressed them to her cheeks. Even now, I don't believe it was the act of a junkie trying for one last rush. There was terrible wisdom and love in her eyes as his shining iridescence ate into her skin and marked her. His tattered membranes fluttered once more and then hung still.

I ran out of the apartment and down the streets. They were shiny with rain, shining like his skin, and wet like the dripping stuff from his wounds. I ran as far and fast as I could, trying to run away from those terrible moments to a place where it hadn't happened. I don't know who called the police or the ambulance or whoever it was that came and took the body away. I know it wasn't my mom. She would have sat there forever, just holding his flippers while his music faded.

I came back in the gray part of morning. A man and a woman were waiting for me. They wore long overcoats and stood, as if sitting in our chairs might make them dirty. An outline was chalked on the floor, and they wouldn't answer any of my questions. Instead, they asked me questions, lots of them. Had the Skoags killed

Lavender? Why? Did I see them do it? Did my mom help them do it? Why had a Skoag been living with us? Had he ever tried to touch me? But the anger inside me wouldn't let me answer their questions. "Where's my mom?" I demanded each time, and finally they put me in a car and took me to the Children's Home and left me there.

The women at the Children's Home all wore gray pants and white shirts. They all called me "honey." They gave me two pairs of pants, two shirts, underwear, socks and shoes, and a bath. They threw away all my own stuff. Then they showed me a bed with a brown blanket on it in a row of beds with brown blankets and told me the bed and the box at the foot of it were mine.

The next day, more people came to talk to me. Nice people, with kind voices and gum and Life Savers. A lady told me my mommy was sick but was in a place where she'd get better soon. But she said it like really my mom was very bad and had to stay somewhere until she was good again. They told me the Skoag was gone and I didn't have to be afraid anymore. I could tell about it and no one would hurt me. They told me the best way to help my mom was to answer all of their questions. But their voices sounded like creaking cage doors and iron gates swinging in the wind. I knew that talking to them wouldn't help Mom. So when they asked me questions, I always said I didn't know, or I answered the opposite of what was true. I contradicted myself on purpose. I said Lavender was my father. I said my mom was his secretary. I said I was going to throw up. Then I did, trying to make it hit their shoes. After three days they left me alone.

After that I had to go to school classes each day with the other Home kids and special anti-substance-abuse classes for the kids of junkies. I got beat up nearly every day. The bigger kids called me "Billy Bun, the Skoag fucker's son." One of the kids had a checkstand newspaper with a picture of my mom on the front and big black print that said, SKOAG'S LOVE SLAVE WITNESSES RITUAL EXECUTION!!! GROPIE CONFESSES, "THEY KILLED HIM FOR LOVING ME!" I hit that kid and grabbed the paper and tore it up, and the playground lady said I was an animal not fit to associate with other children. I had to stay in for three recesses. Which was fine with me. That night I got out of bed and went down to that kid's bunk and pissed on the foot of it. So he got in trouble for wetting his bed. I learned fast.

A very long time went by. Probably it was only a month or two, but it seemed forever. My real life had ended, and someone had stuck me in this new one. I felt like I was someone else, that both Lavender's life and Lavender's death had happened to someone I knew, some dumb little kid who hadn't seen his mom was a junkie and his friend was her pusher. I'd never be that stupid again. The counselor told me that I must always remember that none of it was my fault. I was only a child, and I couldn't have done a thing about my mother's decision to become a Skoag gropie. They worked real hard at taking away my guilt and replacing it with bitterness toward my mom, who had ruined my life. But then a spring day came, and I looked out the classroom window and saw a lady with a coat and hood and gloves and a scarf wrapped around her face. I didn't recognize her, so I just went back to arithmetic. At recess they let her take me home.

Things are simple when you're a kid. So simple and so awful. I accepted what happened and the aftermath, just kept on day after day, and nothing surprised me because I never knew what to expect. So I wasn't shocked to find that our door had been busted in, and someone, our neighbors or the street kids, had trashed the place. The smeared chalk outline was still on the floor, with piles of human shit all over it. Lavender's wall hangings were dead brown tatters, and his flowers were a moldering mess of brown stems and petals and broken glass on the table. The cupboard doors had been ripped down, the microwave was gone, and my couch smelled like urine. Food had been thrown around and mouse droppings were everywhere.

Mom picked up a kitchen chair and set it on its feet and brushed off the seat. She took off her coat and scarf and gloves and put them on the chair, baring her scars so matter-of-factly that they didn't shock me. They were part of her now, like her fat belly and dark eyes. She picked up a scrap of paper off the floor and wrote down a list of cleaning supplies and cheap food and gave me some money. Then she picked up our old broom.

No one bothered me on the way to the store. The checkout man stared at me for about two minutes before he rang up the stuff. Coming home, I passed a Skoag on the street, a big fat one, and he turned and started following me. But all Skoags are slow, and I ignored the way he tooted for me to come back, he wanted to be my friend, he had candy for me. I just hurried, going through alleys until I lost him.

I got home, and the place looked almost normal. Most of the mess had been scraped into brown sacks for me to shuttle out to the Dumpster. The chalk lines were gone, and as if that was some kind of undoing magic, I half expected to see Lavender come out of the bedroom, or to hear his cello thrumming. Instead there was silence, and the crisp brown tatters of his wall hangings dangled over the edges of a garbage sack.

I stood there and the silence filled me up, made me as deaf and isolated as my mother. Welling up with the silence came the sudden grief of knowing he was really dead. I sat down on the floor and started crying and calling out, "Lavender, Lavender!" Mom kept right on trying to put the cupboard doors back on, using a table knife for a screwdriver, and I kicked my feet and slapped my hands on the hard cold cement and screamed until someone upstairs started pounding on the floor with a broom handle. I guess

Mom felt the vibrations. She came and held me until I stopped crying, and said I was okay. But I wasn't. I knew just how alone I really was. My pain was like an invisible knife stuck in me that no one could see to pull out. I knew my mother was hurt just as badly, and there was nothing I could do to help her, either. That was when I decided to forgive her for the awful thing she had done to me, for making Lavender go away.

We found a rhythm in our days, a steady beat that kept us living. Mom became a very good housekeeper, mostly to fill her time. Everything was cleaned up, and she pieced back together the broken stuff. She saved from each aid check until we could buy an economy microwave and have hot foods again. She mended all my clothes and sewed things from my outgrown stuff. Every two weeks she'd put on her gloves and scarf and go after her aid check, but I did all the shopping. I went back to school. I got beat up every day on the playground. Then I stole a baseball bat from school and lay in wait for the kid who had done it and really worked him over. The third time a kid beat me up, and then got bushwhacked, the other kids made the connection. They left me alone. They knew they could hit me at school, but sooner or later the price for doing it was higher than anyone wanted to pay. So I got by. I'd still see the fat Skoag outside the grocery store, and he'd call to me, but I outran him. So no one bothered me. The silence of my home spread out and wrapped me up. No one talked to me much, and that seemed fitting. What better way to mourn Lavender's passing than with silence? I was nine years old, and the best part of my life was over.

Mom got fatter and slower. I thought she was going to die. She moved like an old, old woman and sat like she was blind as well as deaf. Once a week an aid lady came, with pamphlets about how not to be a Skoag gropie, and Don't Do Drugs coloring books and balloons and crayons for me. She'd give Mom a signed slip, and Mom had to turn it in to get her aid check. The aid lady was younger than Mom and wore gray pants and a white shirt. I secretly believed she was from the Children's Home and might take me back there. She always made me show her my hands, and every week I had to pee in a bottle for her, even though everyone knows that Skoag slime won't show in a pee test. She left signing booklets for my Mom, but she didn't want them. So I took them and learned to sign dirty words to the kids at school.

And Lavender was never there.

That's how it would hit me; I'd be going along, doing a math page or signing out something about someone's sister or folding up my blanket or getting a drink of water, and suddenly I'd notice, all over again, that Lavender wasn't there. It always felt like someone had suddenly grabbed hold of my heart and squeezed it. I looked all through the house one day, trying to find one thing that he had touched, one thing he'd given to us that we still had. But there was nothing. It was like he'd never existed, and the silence was like he'd never made music.

One May day I came home from school and Mom had a baby. She hadn't warned me, so it was a big shock to find her lying in bed with this little pink thing dressed in a nightgown made from one of my old T-shirts. I knew someone had helped her from the neatly folded towels by the bed, and the gray box of paper diapers. More aid stuff. My mom's fat stomach was gone, and I felt really dumb for not knowing she had been pregnant. I saw pregnant women in the streets all the time, but it had never occurred to me that my mom could get that way. I knew, too, that she couldn't get a baby unless she'd done it with somebody. And the only one who'd been living with us . . .

Mom wasn't saying much, just watching me as I looked at the baby. What fascinated me the most was those tiny little fingernails she had, thin as paper. I kept staring at her hands.

"Go ahead," Mom finally said. "You can touch her. She's your little sister, Billy. Put your finger in her hand." Her voice dragged like an old tape, and she sounded really tired.

"Is it . . . safe?" I asked. But she wasn't watching my mouth, so she didn't know I'd said anything. I went and got my school tablet. On it I printed, very carefully, IS SHE PART SKOAG ON HER SKIN? Then I took it back into Mom's bedroom and handed it to her.

She read it and crumpled it up and threw it across the room. Her mouth went so tight it was white around her lips. It scared me. She'd never been mad at me while Lavender was around, and since he'd died, she'd been too beaten to be angry at anything.

"Shit!" she said, and the word came out with hard edges, sounding like she used to. She grabbed my wrist, and I could feel the hard slickness of her Skoag scarred palms. "You listen to me, Billy Boy," she said fiercely. "I know what you been hearing. But you knew Lavender, and you damn well know me. And you should know that we . . . that we loved each other. And if he'd been a human and we could have had a baby together, we'd have done it. But he wasn't, and we didn't. This baby here, she's all mine. One hundred percent. It sometimes happens to women who get hooked on Skoag touch. They call it a self-induced pregnancy. This baby's a clone of me. You understand that? She's the same as me, all over again. Only I'm going to make sure she comes out right. She's going to be loved, she's going to have chances. She's not going to end up in a dump on aid, with no . . ." Her voice got more and more runny, the words souping together. She let go of my wrist and started crying. She lifted her hands and curled her fingers toward the tight skin on her palms and held them near her face but not touching it. Her tears trickled into the flipper scars that her final touching of Lavender had left on her face. Her crying woke the baby up, and she started crying, too. Her little face got red and her mouth gaped open, but no sound came out. Then my mom said to her, in the most terrible voice I've ever heard, "Baby, what'd you come here for? I got nothing to give you. I got nothing to give anyone." And she rolled over and turned her back on her.

I stood there, watching them, thinking that any minute Mom would turn back and pick her up and take care of her. But a long time passed, and Mom just lay there, crying all shaky, and the baby lay there, all red and crying without sound.

So I picked her up. I knew how; I used to hold Janice's baby before she gave her kids away. I held her against my chest, with her head on my shoulder so it wouldn't wobble. I carried her around and rocked her, but her face stayed red and she kept breathing out through her mouth, really hard. She didn't make any sound when she cried, but I thought maybe newborn babies didn't cry out loud. I thought she might be hungry. So I went in the kitchen and I checked the refrigerator, to see if Mom had bottles and government aid formula in plastic envelopes like Janice used to have. And there was, so I warmed one up in the microwave until the plastic button on it turned blue to show it was the right temperature. Then I sat down and put the bottle in her wide open mouth. But she acted like she didn't even know it was there and kept up her unhearable screaming.

I sat down on the couch with her on my lap. Her little legs were curled up against her belly. I looked at her red wrinkly feet and her teeny toes. My old T-shirt looked dopey on her, and I wished I had something better for her to wear. Maybe she was cold. So I pulled a corner of my blanket up over her. Her mouth stayed open and her face stayed red. I really wished I had a suck-on thing to stick in her mouth. But I didn't. So I started rocking her on my lap and singing this song Janice used to sing to baby Peggy, about a mockingbird and a pony cart and all sorts of presents the baby would get if she'd be quiet. And right away she closed her mouth and went back to being pink instead of red. She opened her eyes that she'd squinched shut and looked right at me. Her eyes were kind of a murky blue. I looked into them and I knew Mom had lied. Because she looked at me just the way Lavender used to, when I didn't know if he was looking at my face or at something inside my head. I knew she was his, and as long as I had her, he wasn't really gone. This baby was something he'd touched, something he'd left for me to hold on to and keep. Part of him for me to keep.

I suddenly felt shaky and my throat closed up so tight I couldn't breathe or sing, but she didn't seem to mind now. She just kept looking up at me and I kept looking at her, and I wondered if this was what Lavender had meant about closing a circle. Because I knew she was loving me as much as I loved her. It was as important as he had said it was. I held her until her eyes closed, and then I carefully lay down on the couch with her on my stomach and my blanket over us. Her face was against my neck, breathing, and every now and then her mouth would move in a wet baby kiss. Before I fell asleep, I named her Lisa, from an old song Lavender used to sing about Lisa, Lisa, sad Lisa, Lisa.

After that, she was more my baby than Mom's. Coming home to her was like coming home to Lavender. I meant that much to her. She was always crying and wet when I got home. Mom never seemed to notice when she needed changing, and even if she hadn't been deaf, she wouldn't have heard this baby cry. So I'd clean her up and feed her and hold her and rock her. And I'd sing to her. She liked that the best. She was just like my mom that way. I got the idea of tuning the stereo to an all-music station and leaving it on for her when I had to go to school in the morning. Since our place had been trashed, the stereo always had a background sound like cars going by on a wet street, but Lisa didn't care. I'd put her down in the morning and turn on the stereo for her, and she'd still be happy when I got home from school. She slept with me at night, since I was afraid she'd fall out of Mom's bed. But my couch was perfect, because I could put her between me and the back of it, and she'd be safe all night long, just as safe as the little mice nesting inside it.

A new pattern came into my life. I was taking care of things, taking care of the Mom, just like Lavender had told me, and taking care of him, in the form of Lisa. Mom didn't have to do much at all. She got her checks and kept the house clean. I took the checks to the store and got food and sometimes a few extra little things for Lisa. She loved anything that made a noise, rattles, bells—anything. The only time Mom got mad was when I spent seven dollars on a stuffed lamb with a music box inside it. She yelled at me in her mushy voice, because to get it I had to buy tofu instead of hamburger and skipped getting margarine and eggs and jam. But it was worth it to watch Lisa wave her little fists excitedly every time the lamb started playing.

After four or five months, I noticed Mom wasn't keeping the house as clean. She still swept and stuff, but not like before, and I was doing almost all the cooking. Something had gone out of Mom and left her flat, something more than just a baby coming out of her stomach. I think she had expected more, had thought that Lisa was going to be better, somehow. Disappointed was how she acted at first, and then later, uninterested. I felt mad about it, and I'd try to make her pay more attention to Lisa. I'd take her to Mom and show her how Lisa was learning to smile, or how she could sit on her own. But it didn't do any good. Mom would hold her awhile and look at her, and then she'd go set her down on the couch, without even making sure she couldn't roll off. She never talked to Lisa or played with her. And after a while I knew she never would. So I started loving her even more, to make up for Mom not loving her.

It got harder as Lisa got bigger. Summer went okay, but by the time school started again, it wasn't safe for me to leave her all day. I tried putting her in a cardboard box while I was gone, but it was hard to find ones that were strong enough. She'd get hold of the edges and try to stand up, and I was afraid she'd fall. She was eating more, too, so even if I left a bottle inside her box for her, she'd still be really hungry when I got home. Mom didn't notice her at all, and of course she couldn't hear Lisa's silent crying. Mom didn't seem to notice much of anything. She'd tidy up the house each day, and then just sit at the table. Late at night, she might put a scarf around her face and go out for a walk. But that was about all she did, and it didn't make me feel any safer about leaving Lisa all day. So after Christmas I just didn't go back to school and no one ever noticed.

When I think about those days, with Lisa starting to be a real person and all the time we had together, they're almost as good as the days with Lavender. Lisa's eyes turned brown, but they never lost that Lavender look, where she could look right through me while I rocked her to the music. Her hair was dark like Mom's, but curly at the back of her head, and she was almost always smiling. I hated dressing her in stuff made from old T-shirts. The stuff was too small, and Mom hadn't made her any new clothes. So I asked the aid lady who came about once every two months then, and she told me where I could get baby clothes that rich people gave away. She gave me slips for Lisa and me and Mom and helped me write down the right sizes on them. That aid lady wasn't too bad.

On Monday I took the slips and Lisa and went, using my aid pass to ride the bus. Everyone on the bus thought Lisa was cute and kept calling her honey and touching her hands or bouncing her feet. She was real good about it. One old lady who sat beside us part of the way gave me a five-dollar bill and told me to buy my little sister something with it. She was really nice. When she got off the bus, she kept saying, "Bye-bye, sweetie. Bye-bye," like she expected Lisa to say something. "She doesn't talk," I told her, and the old lady just smiled and said, "Oh, she will pretty soon. Don't you worry."

It was the same at the clothes place. A lady at the counter kept talking to Lisa, saying, "You such a sweet thing! You such a good girl, aren't you?" Lisa would smile, but never make a sound.

"She's shy, isn't she?" the lady said. "I bet she babbles her head off at home."

"Yes, ma'am," I said, and then felt bad for lying when the other lady came back with three bags of clothes for us. They showed me the stuff they'd picked out for Lisa, little dresses with lace and a new blanket and a chiming rattle that Lisa grabbed right away. Lisa's bag was the fullest of all, probably because she was so cute.

I should have felt good going home. But the bags were heavy, and it was hard to carry them and Lisa. There was another baby on the bus, making fussy angry noises. It sounded awful, but I wished Lisa could do that. Her being quiet at home had never worried me, but now I was thinking, she won't always be a baby at home, and what then?

I got off the bus with the heavy bags, and Lisa was wriggly. It was getting dark and starting to rain and I had eight blocks to go. I felt like I couldn't take another step when the fat Skoag bounced out of an alley right in front of us.

"Hello, little boy!" he honked.

"Stuff it up your ass!" I said back, because I was really scared. Even if I dropped all the clothes, I couldn't run with Lisa. In the dark and the rain I might fall on top of her and kill her. I squished her close to me, hoping the Skoag wouldn't see Lavender's eyes, and kept walking. Maybe if I just kept walking, he'd leave us alone.

But his flipper feet kept on slapping the wet sidewalk beside us.

"I've got something for you," he said, and I got even scareder, because that was just like the guy in the *Okay to Say No* book at school.

"Stuff it up your ass," I said again and walked faster. One of the bags tore, and I wanted to cry. I'd have yelled for help, but it was dark and there was no one on the streets. This close to home, even if I did yell for help, no one would want to come.

"Boy," he tootled softly. "It has been hard to find you, for it was commanded that none should speak of it. Every time I speak to you, I put myself in danger of a most unfortunate occurrence. Please take these and free me of a heavy promise."

Lisa was wriggling in my arms, trying to get a better look at the tootling voice. She kicked out and one of my bags went flying. Before I could grab it up, he took a package from his pouch and dropped it into the bag. Plastic baggies, taped together, but I couldn't tell what was inside them. I stood still and stared through the dark at him. I was scared to pick up the bag because I didn't want to get close to him and I didn't know what he'd put in it. Drugs, maybe, something I'd get arrested for having. But it was the bag with Lisa's clothes in it, the ones I'd gone through all this for.

"What's that?" I demanded, trying to sound tough.

"One for each of your months. Green trading paper, what is the word for it? Money. For you to take care of the Mom."

"Lavender." I said his name, knowing there was a connection but not figuring it out yet.

"Silence!" the fat Skoag honked, and he sounded like a scared Volkswagen. "To speak the name of a blasphemer is to invite a most unfortunate occurrence."

"But . . ."

"My task is done, until your next month begins. Next time I

call, do not run away. This task is heavy and I would call back the promise, if I had known what would befall the one who asked. Go away quickly, before I am seen with you."

He waddled off like a frightened duck. I managed to snag up the fallen bag. All the way home, my heart was banging against my lungs. I felt like I'd seen Lavender's ghost, that he was still around somehow, looking out for us. I kept wondering about the money in the bag. Not how much it was, or what I'd use it for, but what Lavender had been thinking when he made the fat Skoag promise. If he'd known he was going to die, why'd he go to the Skoags who killed him, why didn't he go to the police or something, or even just come home and ignore those message boxes?

Somehow I got Lisa and the bags down the ramp and managed to turn the doorknob without dropping anything. When I got inside, there was only one light burning and Mom wasn't there. I didn't know if she'd gone looking for us because it was so late or just gone out on one of her night walks.

Some things you just have to do first. So I changed Lisa and got her a bottle and put one of the new nightgowns on her and put her in a cardboard box with her bottle, the chiming rattle, and the new blanket. She looked so sweet, all done up in new stuff that it was suddenly worth all I'd gone through. I turned the stereo to some soft music and she settled down.

Then there was time to think, but too much to think about. The package in Lisa's bag was money, little rolls of it in plastic baggies. I opened it carefully and threw the bags away, even though the slime on them was dried, and dry Skoag slime isn't dangerous. Each baggie was the same, five ten-dollar bills. I unfolded every single one, looking for a note, or some sign from Lavender to help me understand why he had left us and let someone kill him. But there was only money.

I wrapped the money in one of Lisa's old nightgowns and stuffed it down into the couch. I wasn't giving it to Mom. Lavender had left it for me, because he knew I would buy the right things with it. I already knew I was going to get Lisa a playpen so she didn't have to crawl on the cold cement anymore. And fresh, real bananas instead of dried banana flakes that always looked like gray goop.

I went over to her box and looked in at her. She looked back at me, her legs curled up on her tummy and helping hold the bottle, one little leak of milk trickling down her cheek. I reached down and wiped it away, but she smiled at my touch and more milk trickled out of the corner of her mouth. Her dark Lavender eyes looked at me and through me, and for a second he was there, like any moment his cello voice would fill the room.

But Lisa had no voice.

And that was another thing to think about.

She could hear, that was for sure. So why didn't she make noises like other babies? I took her bottle away and tried to look in her mouth. She sucked on my finger, but when I tried to open her mouth, she got mad. Finally, she opened it herself, in one of her silent screams. I looked in, but if there was anything wrong in there, I couldn't see what it was. I looked until she was all red and sweaty from her soundless crying. Then I gave her the bottle back and rocked her to make up for being mean. And I thought.

Lisa was asleep and I was bedded down beside her, nearly falling off the couch now because she'd grown so much, when Mom came back in. She didn't turn on any lights or say anything; she just came in and went straight to her room, making a little humming sound as she went.

And I lay there on the couch and I knew. I knew what she'd gone out for.

God, I was mad.

I lay there and shook with anger and being scared. Because she was going to blow us all up. I wanted to get up and go into her room and scream at her. But she wouldn't hear me, and if I held up a note, she'd just ignore it. I could go to her and tell her everything, about the money from Lavender and the new clothes and Lisa not being able to talk, and she wouldn't even care. She'd only go on with her idiot humming and staring. Because she didn't care, and probably never had, not about anything except her damn music.

She wasn't stupid. She'd keep the house clean and dress decent and pick up her aid checks. She didn't want to be a Skoag gropie in the streets. She'd sneak out by night, find Skoags standing outside the clubs listening to the music, and touch one. I knew it as plainly as if I'd seen it. That was what mattered to her, a press of Skoag flesh. She didn't care that if the aid worker caught her with slimy hands, they'd take Lisa and me to some children's home. I remembered what it was like. I could imagine Lisa there, her silent crying going ignored, growing up not able to tell anyone when someone was mean to her. They'd put her with the other ones they called "special" in a big room with a lot of baby toys and ignore her. I'd never see her and she'd forget about me. I'd lose the only thing Lavender had left me. Because of Mom.

I watched Mom the next day, hoping I was wrong. But the signs were there, in the rhythmic way she swept the floor, her chin nodding to the unheard beat. She was groping Skoag slime. It was such a slutty thing to do. I had thought that her touching Lavender had been because they loved each other. Now she seemed like a whore to me, someone who'd touch any Skoag just to make music in her head. I hated her.

The next day I went out to the secondhand store. I bought Lisa a stroller, a playpen, and a piece of carpet to go in the bottom of it. And one of those suits with the feet and a hood. It took me two trips to get everything home.

When my Mom saw all the stuff, she tried to ask me where

it had come from. But I just ignored her and her mashed potato voice. She grabbed hold of my arm and shook me. "Biw-wweee! Wherr aw thisss-tuff frum? Huh?"

That's what she sounded like. I grabbed her hand off my arm and turned it over and pried her fingers open. The Skoag scars were shiny and wet in the cracks. She jerked away from me.

"I don't have to tell you anything," I said as she held her hands to her chest. I didn't yell it. I just said it real clearly, making sure she could see my mouth move. I picked Lisa up and took her to the couch. I started playing patty-cake with her, ignoring Mom. After a while, Mom started going, "Hub. Huh-uh-uh! Hub!" She sat down and put her scarred hands over her scarred face and rocked. After a while I realized she was crying. I didn't go to her. I remembered Don't Do Drugs at school, and I knew it was true, that junkies don't have friends, don't love, don't care about anything but their next fix. No one can afford to love a junkie. So I did what the books said. I ignored her. And that was the day I was ten years old.

I took control of things. I found the sign language booklets that the aid lady had left, and I started making Lisa sign. Simple stuff at first. Hold up your arms to be picked up. Finger in the mouth for bottle. Nod your head for stereo turned on. It was harder for me than for Lisa. Because I knew what she wanted, but I couldn't give it to her until she signed, no matter how she cried. I'd make the sign and then I'd take her hands and make the sign. But after a while, I had to make her sign for herself. She cried a lot. But finally, she started doing the simple signs. By the time she was two, we were on the ones in the pamphlet.

Things went okay for a while. Mom was careful about her habit. None of the aid ladies caught on to her. She was always home when they visited, and the place was tidy. Once, I came back from the store and found her giving Lisa a bath in the sink. But it was only because the aid lady was there. It was just a trick to have her hands busy, and if the aid lady saw the wetness in the cracks of her palms, she'd think it was bathwater. Lisa was splashing water all over and smiling like it was normal for Mom to take care of her. I set the groceries on the table and said, "Hi, Mom," like we were a happy little family. Mom kept on sponging Lisa, and finally the aid lady said she had to go, but she was glad that things were going better for us.

As soon as she left, I got a towel and took my Lisa and dried her carefully. Lisa kept signing for "cookie" while I was drying her and dressing her while she was kicking and wriggling. Mom gave her one, and it wasn't until I got her shoes tied and set her on the floor that I realized what that meant. It made me madder than her using Lisa's bath to keep the aid lady from checking her hands. I found the sign booklets on her nightstand. I carried them out and slapped them down on the kitchen table. Mom was watching me.

"These are mine," I told her, making my lip movements plain. "Leave them alone."

"Bwee," she said pleadingly, and I could see how big and purple her tongue was getting inside her mouth. It made me feel sick and sad and sorry, for Lisa and myself, mostly. That big purple tongue was a withdrawal symptom for a Skoag gropie; it meant she'd been down for more than forty-eight hours. I thought about her washing Lisa, keeping her back to the aid lady. Hiding. She'd still been hiding from the aid lady; it was just a different way from the one I'd figured. She was still using us.

She wasn't getting her slime. I didn't know why, but I knew it was dangerous for us. She wouldn't be able to last. Before long, everyone would know. It hit me. I'd have to take care of it. One more thing for me to handle to keep Lisa safe. It made me angry and at the same time, hot and satisfied because I'd been right about her; she was just going to drag us in deeper and make it all harder. I'd been right to stop caring about her, because she was just going to hurt us if we let her be important to us.

Everything was getting harder. They'd tracked me down for school, and now I had to get there an hour earlier for remedial math. Which meant leaving Lisa with Mom for even longer. And Lisa was walking, so if you left the door open she'd head up the ramp and out onto the sidewalk. I'd sit in school and wonder if Mom had gone out to finger some Skoags and left the door open and Lisa had toddled out and been hit by a car. Or worse, just wandered off and I'd go home and call her but she wouldn't be able to answer . . . My imagining made school hours torture.

I'd race home each day, and each day Lisa would be okay. Every few nights Mom would go out, and I didn't know what to hope for. That she'd score some slime and come home hummy, but easy to spot as a gropie? That she wouldn't get any, but then she'd be trying to sign to Lisa and showing off her withdrawal? Maybe that she wouldn't hear a delivery van coming down the alleys?

It all came together one night when I went to get another envelope from the fat Skoag. The streetlamp was glinting off his skin, and flashing off his voice membrane each time it swelled like a khaki neon light. He was holding out the envelope in a plastic-mittened flipper, but I said, "I need a favor."

"No," he tooted. "No favors." He flapped the envelope at me frantically. He looked toward the alley mouth, but there was nothing there. I took a breath.

I said calmly, like I was sure of it, "You promised Lavender you'd look out for me and the Mom."

"Yes. I bring you the money, every time."

"Yeah. Well, that's good, but not enough. I need you to come to my house, twice a week, late at night."

"No." He said it fast, scared. Then, "Why?"

"Yes. You know why."

He rocked on his flippers like a zoo elephant. "I can't," he tootled mournfully. "Please. I can't. Take the money and go. Dangerous for me."

"Dangerous for me if you don't. And you promised Lavender."

"I . . . Please. Please. Once a week. Wednesday night, very late. Please."

He shoved the envelope into my hand. I watched him rock. If I demanded it, he'd come twice a week, but he'd hate me. Or he'd come once a week and think I'd let him off easy. "Okay," I said, settling for the second one. I might need something else someday, and once a week would hold Mom together.

He came late Wednesday. It startled me awake, his flippering down the ramp and then slapping the door. Mom had stayed in, looking at her hands and sighing, and gone to bed around midnight. It was two A.M. when the fat Skoag showed. I'd gone to sleep, thinking he wasn't going to come. Odd. Just the sounds of him coming down the ramp and me opening the door like I used to for Lavender made my heart pound. Like maybe I'd open the door and somehow it would be Lavender standing there, gently waving his flippers and waiting for me.

But it was only the fat Skoag. He was pressed into the darkest corner of the stairwell, staring up at the sidewalk. As soon as I opened the door, he scuttled in and pushed it shut.

"Quickly," he said, pulling off a plastic mitten. "Quickly, please, and then I will go."

"This way," I said, and led him into my mother's bedroom.

She wasn't asleep. She was lying on her back, staring at the ceiling. The bed, wedged in a corner of the small room, was a tousled wreck. Some movement of air as we came into the room turned her eyes to us. She stared at us, between dreaming and awake, and suddenly she sat up and screamed "Lavender!"

The word came out crisp and hard and real, like she used to

talk. Then she saw it wasn't him and she broke. She made this horrible laughing-crying sound. The fat Skoag freaked when she screamed and waddled frantically for the door, but I was closer, and I slammed it and put my back to it. "No," I said, gripping the knob. "You don't leave until she's touched you."

His eye spots went flat and dead. He turned and slowly walked toward the bed. Her hysterics trailed away in broken sobs. I watched her face, her shock fading and being replaced by horror as the fat Skoag came closer. "No," she said, clearly, and then, "Nooh. Nooh." She backed up on the bed, pressing into the corner. "Noooh. Doanwanis. Goway. Bwee. Pease. Trynstob. No." But when the Skoag held his flipper out, she suddenly lunged across the bed and gripped it like a handful of free lottery tickets. She held on and her body jerked in little spasms, like the kid at school who had fits. Her eyes went back and she threw her head way back on her neck and her tongue came out. I felt sick and dirty, like I was watching her have sex with someone, or watching a doctor work on guts. But I couldn't look away. The Skoag stood there until her hands slid away. They were thick with his slime and iridescent in the darkness. The stuff was thick, like the goop she used to rub on my chest when I was little and had a bad cold. She crumpled over onto her side. I pulled the blankets back up over her. As I let the Skoag out, I wondered why I had bothered to do that.

"Remember," I said, as he waddled up the ramp. "Next Wednesday. It's important. And you promised Lavender."

I was thinking that Wednesday was about right, because the aid lady always came on Thursdays or Fridays, and Mom would still look okay when she got here. The fat Skoag paused on the ramp.

"For Lavender," he said, like brass trumpets coming from a far hill. "Only for him would I do this thing. Only for him."

I knew then that the fat Skoag was close to hating me tonight, and that it didn't have to have been that way. If I hadn't demanded this, he might have become my friend. I watched the fat Skoag leave and felt pimpish and sly and small for trading on his loyalty to Lavender. But I had to, to keep Lisa safe. Sometimes the only thing I was sure of was that Lavender had entrusted Lisa to me. I went back to bed, curling up around Lisa. I fell asleep hoping that the things I did to protect her wouldn't stain her.

So that's how it went. The fat Skoag came once a week. Mom stayed slimed and happy. The aid lady never suspected a thing. I went to school enough to keep everyone happy and took care of Lisa. Lisa grew. She turned into a little kid. On Saturdays we'd bus over to Gasworks Park. I'd push her on the swings or we'd watch the fancy kites people fly there. I kept her away from other kids, so she wouldn't be teased about being mute. When some mommy would say hello to her, or say, "My, such pretty hair," I'd step in and say, "She's real shy. And my mom says don't talk to strangers." Then I'd take her away and buy her ice cream. No one expects kids to talk while they're eating.

She was three when the message came. The radio was always on for Lisa. Classical music made her close her eyes and sway, or suddenly shiver. Jazz made her hyperactive. If I wanted her to go to sleep, it was good old rock and roll. I should have heard about it. But I never listened to the news or wasted food money on a newspaper. So I scowled at the check-out guy when he shoved a *Seattle Times* into my brown bag.

"I ain't paying for that," I told him.

"On the house, kid," he told me. "I figure you got a right to know, it being your Skoag and all."

He'd never talked about Lavender before that. He'd treated me decent while Lavender was alive, and he'd never given me a bad time about shopping there after Lavender died. Not like the Laundromat where they threw me and our laundry out because they didn't want "Skoag slime clogging the drains." Anyway, he turned right away to the next customer so I knew he didn't want me to say anything. I headed home.

After I got dinner cooking, I unfolded the paper, wondering what I was supposed to look at. The headlines jumped at me. SKOAG PLANET CONTACT CONFIRMED. I read slowly, trying to understand it. The story said the rumors were confirmed, without saying what they were. The big deal was the Skoags officially sending a message to Earth, planet to planet. The newspaper went on about the sending technology being based on stuff we knew but hadn't thought about using together, and stuff like that. I had to sort through the whole paper to find the last few lines. They scared the hell out of me. Sources wouldn't say what the message had been, but didn't deny it had to do with the ritual murder of a "highly placed Skoag exile in Seattle."

I didn't know the microwave had buzzed until Mom set food in front of me. I looked up, and Lisa had already finished eating. I hated it when Mom did stuff like that. Like she was pretending she was a good little mommy, taking care of her kids instead of a Skoag gropie who didn't give a damn. In the drug classes at school, they called that "ingratiating behavior" and said junkies and alkies used it to fool their families into thinking they were changing, especially if the families were close to sending them to a cure station. It didn't fool me. I crumpled up the paper and gave it to Lisa to play with and ate dinner.

Two nights later, the man came. Maybe he thought no one would notice a gray government sedan pulled up in front of a slummy house at midnight. I heard someone nearly fall down the ramp, and when he knocked, I opened the door on its chain.

"Yeah," I said, but my stomach was shaking. Skoag slime dependency wasn't supposed to show up in pee tests. That's what all the kids said, and I'd always believed it was true, but what if they'd changed the test and knew from Mom's pee that she was a gropie?

But I tried not to let any of that show on my face as I stared out the crack at the government man.

"I have to come in," he said, whispery. "I have to talk to your mother."

"Too bad," I said, being tough. "She's deaf. You can write it down, or you can tell it to me, but you can't talk to her."

"I can sign," he said nervously, echoing with his fingers.

"She can't," I said, and started to close the door.

"Please," he said, not quite shoving his foot in the crack, but leaning on the door to keep it open. "It's about the dead Skoag. Lavender. And it's important, kid."

We stared at each other.

"Look, kid," he finally said. His voice came out normal, not whispery, but real tired. "I can come back with cops tomorrow and kick this door in and drag you out. It's that important. Or you can let me in now, and we'll keep this quiet."

My mom reached past me and undid the chain, and the man came in. I hadn't even known she was awake. She looked awful, with her scarred face shining in the streetlamp light leaking in the door. All except for her hair, which was as pretty as ever. She clicked on the light and shut the door behind him. He looked around and said, "Oh, Jesus Christ." It was the first time I'd ever heard a grown man say it like a prayer. Then he sat down at our table and started signing to my mom.

He wasn't an aid man, or a drug man, but a real high-up government man. The second surprise was that my mom signed back to him. I suddenly remembered I hadn't seen the signing books around in a while. Probably in her room. Ingratiating behavior. I wondered what she'd been signing to Lisa while I was away at school each day. Then I forgot that and paid attention to what he was saying. He talked out loud as he signed, like it helped him keep his place or something.

"Lavender's . . . people . . . are very angry . . . about his death. He was . . . important Skoag (the sign for Skoag was to put your fingers on your forehead and make your hand do push-ups, like a pulsing membrane). Not exile . . . but like a priest . . . or civil rights worker."

He went on about how important Lavender had been, how he had come in the hopes of reconciling the exiles and instead he started sharing their beliefs, and then went further than they did. It didn't match what Lavender had told me, but I kept my mouth shut. The heart of it was that news of his death had finally reached his home planet, and a lot of Skoags were very upset. The way he said it, I didn't know if the message had just taken that long to get there, or if the exiled Skoags had kept killing Lavender a secret. But I still kept my mouth shut. Anyway, the planet Skoags were going to send someone to look into it, and our government had agreed to cooperate fully. Including letting the Skoags talk to my mom and me. I felt like telling him it was up to us whether we met the Skoags. But I didn't. He went on about how this was a real opportunity for humans to establish diplomatic relations with the Skoag planet, and it might be our first step toward deep space, and the United States could lead the way, and all that shit. Then he suggested the first thing we'd have to do was move.

That's when I opened my mouth. "No," I said, firmly, and was surprised when my mom repeated it, "No," very clear.

He talked a lot about why we had to move. The Skoag ambassador or whatever was coming, probably within two or three years. (I was surprised they didn't know exactly when, but they didn't.) And we had to be somewhere nice, so the United States wouldn't be embarrassed, and somewhere safe, so no terrorists would try to kidnap us or kill us, and somewhere more official, where advisers could tell us what to say to the Skoags.

He was still explaining at four in the morning, when Mom

stood up, said, "NO" very emphatically, and then walked back to her bedroom and shut the door.

He stared at the door. Then he sighed and rumpled up his hair. "This is a big mistake," he said. And he shook his head. "A damn big mistake that we're all going to hate remembering. You're going to blow it for all of us, kid, for the whole damn human race. Shit. Well, I guess we work around it, then."

So he left.

For a while I lay awake, wondering if there really was danger, if our neighbors would turn on us or terrorists would bomb us. But then I decided that at least terrorists wouldn't try to take Lisa away from me and put her in special school or a home while they treated Mom for being a gropie. That would happen for sure if they moved us, because there'd be no way to hide Mom's addiction. That was why Mom said no, too. She was afraid of losing her Skoag slime source. As for me, I could never leave the only place I'd ever shared with Lavender. I stared at the spot where he'd died. The chalk marks were years gone, but I could still see them.

The government man was trickier than I thought. A month later our neighborhood was picked for Facelift Funding. All owners were given eighteen months to upgrade or lose the funding. So our walls got spraysulated and paneled, and they foamed the floor and put in carpet-heat and a tiny insta-hot unit under the sink. Then the old furnace room became part of our apartment, as a second bedroom.

The whole neighborhood changed. They jackhammered up squares of sidewalk and put in skinny little trees, and all the buildings got new siding. They hauled away the trash heap from behind the building, including our old linoleum. They put in a tiny fenced play yard, with organo-turf and big plastic climbing toys. They put flower boxes around the streetlamps. I hated it. They were trying to cover us up, trying to say, these aren't poor people living in their own trash, these are nice folks like in the readers at school. The daddies and mommies have jobs, they go to church, and their kids drink white milk and eat brown bread. I hated it, but Lisa loved it. She kept picking the flowers and bringing them to Mom. Mom always put them in a vase, just like Lavender's flowers. Sometimes I wanted to smash it.

I came home from school one day, and a moving van was just pulling away. Scared the hell out of me. Had Mom decided to move after all? Had she kidnapped Lisa and left?

But she was there. "Govamin," she said disgustedly, and stood there like there was no place to sit.

All our old stuff was gone. Even the cupboards and fridge were different, and the cooker was huge, with hot beverage taps on the side. My couch was gone, the friendly smell of mice gone with it. The new one matched the fat chair beside it. The stereo was about as big as a loaf of bread, but it was a real wall shaker. There was a vid-box, a keyboard console, and a minidish. Guess the government wanted us to look good.

The new bedroom had twin beds with a dorky little screen between them, like I hadn't been bathing Lisa since she was born. Lisa was bouncing on her bed already, looking like a kid in a catalog. I caught her as she jumped, and for just a second, as she came down in my arms, she looked just like Mom. Exactly. Same hair, same eyes, and I knew it was true, she was Mom's clone and would look just like her when she grew up. Except that her hands and cheek would never be scarred. I set her down and she ran to Mom and hugged her around the knees. And we stood there and looked around, like there was no place left for us.

So they thought they changed us, so we wouldn't shame the United States when the Skoag came. But they didn't change the fat Skoag's secret Wednesday visits, or Mom's blank humming. The chalk lines were still there, and I could see them right through the carpet. And our neighbors still didn't talk to us.

We waited. One year. Two years. More Skoags came but not the Skoag we waited for. Three years. Someone wrote a big article in the paper that the whole thing about a Skoag ambassador coming had been a scam, a hoax. The fat Skoag told me the truth. He'd come. He'd talked to the ones that killed Lavender. And he'd agreed it had been necessary. He hadn't wanted to talk to humans at all.

The carpeting got worn spots, and Lisa scribbled on the new paneling and Mom couldn't get it off. Four years. Graffiti on the buildings, and beer bottles in the flower beds. We forgot about the government and the government forgot about us.

Lisa was seven, nearly eight. We were walking home after a day at Gasworks Park. I was worrying because a letter had come from the school. Someone had turned us in, had reported that a child in our home was being deprived of an equal education. If Lisa didn't go to school, they'd cancel the aid checks. We couldn't get by without the aid checks. I didn't know what the hell to do. I was thinking about running away with her. I was fifteen, nearly old enough to get work somewhere.

A bunch of Skoags were jamming on the corner, same old thing. I kept walking. I never listened to Skoags anymore. I was a block past them before I realized Lisa wasn't with me. I ran back, but it was too late.

All she was doing was listening. Eyes big, lips parted, listening like she always listened to music. The Skoags were playing some old Beatles thing. There were a few tourists, a few hecklers, the usual mix, and the Skoags were playing and Lisa was listening.

Then all of a sudden they stopped, their membranes all swelled out, and they all looked at her. Colors washed through their crests, bright colors, and they started making a sound, an incredible sound like Jesus coming in the sky on a white horse to save us all. It got louder and louder. Skoags started coming out of buildings, flipping down the sidewalks, and as soon as they came, they started making the sound, too, and colors started racing through their crests. They surrounded Lisa, pushing to get closer, all making the sound. It was a glorious Alleluia sound, and Lisa loved it. She glowed, and her eyes were huge. I shoved my way in there. I grabbed her hand and I dragged her out of there, past Skoags who reached for us with shining flippers. I snatched her up and ran all the way home and locked the door behind us.

The next day our street was packed so full of Skoags that cars couldn't pass. Silent Skoags, standing and swaying on their big flat flippers, but not making a sound. Staring at our building. Copters flew over, and the film was on television, but the news people had no idea what was going on, they just "urged inhabitants of the affected neighborhood to stay inside and remain calm while officials determine what to do."

It lasted for two days. The streets packed with Skoags, our door locked, and my heart hammering the whole time until I thought my head would blow up. Suspecting, almost knowing.

On the third day, I woke up to a sound like birds harmonizing with the rush of ocean waves and the laughter of little kids. The sound had been part of a very good dream I was having, so when I woke up and still heard it, I wasn't really awake. Then I realized what had wakened me. A smaller set of sounds. A chair being pushed across the carpet to the door. The chain being undone. I jumped out of bed.

The street was empty, almost. There was only a gray government sedan, and the same government man who had come four years ago. And a big, big Skoag, with a tall purple crest. He was singing the harmonizing bird song, and Lisa was walking straight toward him. She was smiling and her hair was floating on the wind. Like a dream walker. Then the Skoag opened his mittened flippers to her, and she began to run.

I screamed her name, I know I did, but she didn't seem to hear me. The Skoag picked her up, and I was still running down the street as they all got in the car. The government man gunned it and they were gone.

And that's the end of the story. Almost.

Mom was standing in the doorway, crying. The tears went crooked where they met her scars and flowed around them.

"Go after her!" I screamed. "Get her back. They just took her."

"No." She said each word carefully, signing them for emphasis: "They didn't take her. She wanted to go. She had to go. She shouldn't have to come back, not just for us."

"You can't know that!" I yelled. "How can you say that?"

She looked at me a long time. "Because I heard it," she signed slowly, silently. I watched her scarred fingers move, the wonder that flooded her face. "I heard it, and it called me. But it wasn't for me, not the me that's here. It was for the other me, the one you made. The one you made for them. The circle closer. The one who listens so well that she has no need to speak. The me done right. But this me heard it and knew how bad she wanted to go."

Then Mom went back in her room and closed her door.

Nothing happened after that. The fat Skoag never came back, and Mom never went through withdrawal. I guess the last song was enough to last her forever. I never went to school again, and the government people never came to ask about us. They never came to tell us anything either. There were no write-ups in the paper, no news stories about a little girl stolen by the Skoags. No one ever asked why Lisa never came to school. No one ever asked just how much one little girl is worth to the government. Or to a Skoag with a purple crest.

But the next month Boeing got a huge government contract

that put half of Seattle back to work, and the papers were full of news about the breakthrough design that could give us the stars. So I didn't need it spelled out. Do you?

The world gets the stars, the Skoags get Lisa, and I get nothing. Lisa's gone, and with her every touch of Lavender. It was a hard thing he asked of me, but I did it. I looked after the Mom. The Skoags can go back home now. Every day, there are fewer of them on the streets. They always bow to my mom and me. They no longer sing, but all their crests ripple with color. Sometimes I wonder if Lavender even knew what he was asking.

Or maybe all he meant was that I should look out for Mom, and the rest of it was just an accident. I don't know.

Mom and I still live here. Next month I'll be eighteen. I'll have to register with the aid office as an adult, and with the job office for training. Mom's Career Mother checks will stop and she'll have to get job training or lose all her aid. I'll have to move out, because aid receivers aren't allowed to let other adults share their homes. Mom will probably get a smaller place.

That's too bad. Because just last night, as I was falling asleep on the couch, I heard a mouse, nibbling inside there.

It's been a good home, really. I had good folks.

Silver Lady and the Fortyish Man

This story was written in 1988 as a fortieth birthday present for my husband, Fred.

Since the early 1970s I'd had an agreement with my husband. He didn't read my fiction. He didn't read it in draft form or before I sent it out. He didn't even read it after it had been published. It was a wall we'd put in place after we realized that we simply knew each other too well. I could shrug off criticism from any other reader, but not from him. He was simply too good at putting his finger unerringly on exactly my greatest doubt.

Writing fiction, my friend, is a game of sleight of hand that a writer plays with her- or himself. The writer takes key events, dazzling pains, gasping joys, and unutterable boredom and weaves them into a story that is always, inevitably, about the writer's own life. The trick is to write it in such a way that the writer does not know he or she is merely holding up a very large and distorted mirror of the writer's life. It is my opinion that the only way writers can serve up their own steaming entrails on a platter and not know they are offering their own vital essence to the world is by disguising it.

And I was never able to disguise it well enough from Fred. He would read a story, a story that wasn't about me or us or any time or place we had ever lived, and then he'd say, "Oh, yeah, I remember that day. That was awful, wasn't it?"

And suddenly I'd see the roots of my own tale. And be unable to even finish polishing the story, let alone put it out there for sale. There were two choices for me. I'd either have to give up being a writer or ask Fred not ever to read anything I wrote. I chose the second alternative, and to this day, he has kept his word. The sole exception is this story, "Silver Lady and the Fortyish Man." It was written for him, as a gift, and he read it. And had the great good sense to not point out exactly where and how it intersected with my reality.

I do think that every freelance writer reaches a point at which he or she says, "If I quit trying to write fiction and just spent those hours working for someone else for minimum wage, I'd come out dollars ahead." I know I certainly have, and more than once. In the speckled years of my writing career, I've served pizza, pulled beers, delivered the US mail, sold consumer electronics, managed an electronics store, and yes, worked as a salesperson in the ladies' clothing department of a Sears store. And at times like that, when a writer is not writing, sometimes someone else believing in you is what it takes to put the world back on track.

And thereby hangs a tale . . .

It was about 8:15 P.M. and I was standing near the register in a Sears in a substandard suburban mall the first time the fortyish man came in. There were forty-five more minutes to endure before the store would close and I could go home. The Muzak was playing, and a Ronald McDonald display was waving at me cheerily from the children's department. I was thinking about how animals in traps chew their legs off. There was a time when I couldn't understand that type of survival mechanism. Now I could. I was wishing for longer, sharper teeth when the fortyish man came in.

For the last hour or so, salespeople had outnumbered customers in the store. A dead night. I was the only salesperson in Ladies' Fashions and Lingerie, and I had spent the last two hours straightening dresses on hangers, zipping coats, putting T-shirts in order by size and color, clipping bras on hangers, and making sure all the jeans faced the same way on the racks. Now I was tidying up all the bags and papers under the register counter. Boredom, not dedication. Only boredom can drive someone to be that meticulous, especially for four dollars an hour. One part boredom to two parts despair.

So a customer, any kind of a customer, was a welcome distraction. Even a very ordinary fortyish man. He came straight up to my counter, threading his way through the racks without even a glance at the dresses or sweaters or jeans. He walked straight up to me and said, "I need a silk scarf."

Believe me, the last thing this man needed was a silk scarf. He was tall, at least six feet, and had reached that stage in his life where he buckled his belt under his belly. His dark hair was thinning, and the way he combed it did nothing to hide the fact. He wore fortyish-man clothing, and I won't describe it, because if I did you might think there was something about the way he dressed that made me notice him. There wasn't. He was ordinary in the most common sense of the word, and if it had been a busy night in the store, I'd never even have seen him. So ordinary he'd be invisible. The only remarkable thing about him was that he was a fortyish man in a Sears store on a night when we had stayed open longer than our customers had stayed awake. And that he'd said he needed a silk scarf. Men like him *never* buy silk scarves, not for any reason.

But he'd said he needed a silk scarf. And that was a double miracle of sorts, the customer knowing what he wanted, and I actually having it. So I put on my sales smile and asked, "Did you have any particular color in mind, sir?"

"Anything," he said, an edge of impatience in his voice. "As long as it's silk."

The scarf rack was right by the register, arranged with compulsive tidiness by me earlier in the shift. Long scarves on the bottom rack, short scarves on the top rack, silk to the left, acrylics to the right, solid colors together in a rainbow spectrum on that row, patterns rioting on that hook, all edges gracefully fluted. Scarves were impulse sales, second sales, "wouldn't you like a lovely blue scarf to go with that sweater, miss?" sales. No one marched into a Sears store at 8:15 at night and demanded a silk scarf. People who needed silk scarves at 8:15 at night went to boutiques for them, little shops that smelled like perfumes or spices and had no Hamburglars lurking in the aisles. But this fortyish man wouldn't know that.

So I leaned across the counter and snagged a handful, let my fingers find the silk ones and pull them gently from their hooks. Silk like woven moonlight in my hands, airy scarves in elusive colors. I spread them out like a rainbow on the counter. "One of these, perhaps?" I smiled persuasively.

"Any of them, it doesn't matter, I just need a piece of silk." He scarcely glanced at them.

And then I said one of those things I sometimes do, the words falling from my lips with sureness, coming from God knows where, meant to put the customer at ease but always getting me into trouble. "To wrap your tarot cards, undoubtedly."

Bingo, I'd hit it. He lifted his eyes and stared at me, as if suddenly seeing me as a person and not just a saleswoman in a Sears at night. He didn't say anything, just looked at me. It was like having crosshairs tattooed on my forehead. In exposing him, I had exposed myself. Something like that. I cleared my throat and decided to back off and get a little more formal.

"Cash or charge?" I asked, twitching a blue one from the slithering heap on the counter, and he handed me a ten and dug for the odd change. I stuffed the scarf in a bag and clipped his receipt on it and that was it. He left, and I spent the rest of my shift making sure that all the coat hangers on the racks were exactly one finger space apart.

I had taken the job in November, hired on in preparation for the Christmas rush, suckered in by the hope that after the New Year began I would become full-time and get better wages. It was February, and I was still getting less than thirty hours a week and only four dollars an hour. Every time I thought about it, I could feel rodents gnawing at the bottom of my heart. There is a sick despair to needing money so desperately that you can't quit the job that doesn't pay you enough to live on, the job that gives you just enough irregular hours to make job hunting for something better next to impossible. Worst of all was the thought that I'd fashioned and devised this trap myself. I'd leapt into it, in the name of common sense and practicality.

Two years ago I'd quit a job very similar to this one, to live on my hoarded savings and dreams of being a freelance writer. I'd become a full-time writer, and I loved it. And I'd almost made it. For two years I skimped along, never much above poverty level, but writing and taking photographs, doing a little freelance journalism to back up the fiction, writing a story here, a story there, and selling them almost often enough to make ends meet.

Almost.

How the hell long can anyone live on almost? Buying almost new clothes at the secondhand store, almost fresh bread at the thrift store, almost stylish shoes at the end-of-season sales. Keeping the apartment almost warm, the dripping, rumbling refrigerator keeping food almost cold, telling my friends I was almost there. Almost writing the one really good story that would establish me as a writer to be reckoned with. I still loved it, but I started to notice little things. How my friends always brought food when they came to visit, and my parents sent money on my birthday, and my sister gave me "hand-me-downs" that fit me perfectly, and, once, still had the tags on.

This is fine, when you are twenty or so, and just striking out on your own. It is not so good when you are thirty-five and following your chosen career. One day I woke up and knew that the dream wasn't going to come true. My Muse was a faithless slut who drank all my wine and gave me half a page a day. I demanded more from her. She refused. We quarreled. I begged, I pleaded, I showed the mounting stacks of bills, but she refused to produce. I gave her an ultimatum, and she ignored me. Left me wordless, facing empty white pages and a stack of bills on the corner of my desk. One of two things happened to me then. I've never decided which it was. Some of my friends told me I'd lost faith. Others said I'd become more practical. I went job hunting.

In November, I reentered the wonderful world of retail merchandising to work a regular nine-to-five job and make an ordinary living, with clockwork paychecks and accounts paid the first time they billed me. I'd leapt back into salesmanship with energy and enthusiasm, pushing for that second sale, persuading women to buy outfits that looked dreadful on them, always asking if they wanted to apply for our charge card. I'd been a credit to the department. All management praised me. But no one gave me a raise, and full-time hours were a mirage on the horizon. I limped along, making almost enough money to make ends meet. It felt very familiar. Except that I didn't love what I did. I was stuck with it. I wasn't any better off than I had been.

And I wasn't writing anymore, either.

My Muse had always been a fickle bitch, and the moment I pulled on pantyhose and clipped on an "I Am SEARS" tag, she moved out, lock, stock, and inspiration. If I had no faith in her power to feed me, then to hell with me was the sentiment as she expressed it. All or nothing, that was her, like my refrigerator, either freezing it all or dripping the vegetable bin full of water. All or nothing, no halfway meetings.

So it was nothing, and my days off were spent, not pounding the keys, but going to the Laundromat, where one can choose between watching one's underwear cavort gaily in the dryer window or watching gaunt women in mismatched outfits abuse their children. ("That's it, Bobby! That's it, I absolutely mean it, you little shit! Now you go stand by that basket and you hold on to it with both hands, and don't you move until I tell you you can. You move one step away from that basket and I'm going to whack you. You hear me, Bobby? YOU *Whack!* GET YOUR *Whack!* HANDS ON THAT *Whack!* BASKET! Now shut up or I'll *really* give you something to cry about!") I usually watched my underwear cavorting through the fluff-dry cycle.

And so I worked at Sears, from nine to one, or from five to nine, occasionally getting an eight-hour day, but seldom more than a twenty-four-hour week, watching income not quite equal outgo, paying bills with a few dollars and many promises, spacing it out with plastic, and wondering, occasionally, what the hell I was going to do when it all caught up with me and fell apart.

DAYS PASSED. NOT an elegant way to express it, but accurate. So there I was again, one weekday night, after eight, dusting the display fixtures and waiting for closing time, wondering why we stayed open when the rest of the mall closed at seven. And the fortyish man came in again. I remembered him right away. He didn't look any different from the first time, except that this time he was a little more real to me because I had seen him before. I stood by my counter, feather duster in hand, and watched him come on, wondering what he wanted this time.

He had a little plastic container of jasmine potpourri, from the bath and bedding department. He set it on the counter and asked, "Can I pay for this here?"

I was absolutely correct as a salesperson. "Certainly, sir. At Sears, we can ring up purchases from any department at any register. We do our best to make things convenient for our customers. Cash or charge?"

"Cash," he said, and as I asked, "Would you like to fill out an application for our Sears or Discover charge card? It makes shopping at Sears even more convenient, and in addition to charging, either card can be used as a check cashing card," he set three Liberty Walking silver dollars, circa 1923, on the plastic countertop between us. Then he stood and looked down at me, like I was a rat and he'd just dropped a prefab maze into place around me.

"Sure you want to use those?" I asked him, and he nodded without speaking.

So I rang up the jasmine potpourri and dropped the three silver dollars into the till, wishing I could keep them for myself, but we weren't allowed to have our purses or any personal cash out on the selling floor, so there was no way I could redeem them and take them home. I knew someone would nab them before they ever got to the bank, but it wasn't going to be me, and wasn't that just the way my whole life had been going lately? The fortyish man took his jasmine potpourri in his plastic Sears bag with the receipt stapled on the outside of it and left. As he left, I said, "Have a nice evening, sir, and thank you for shopping at our Sears store." To which he replied solemnly, "Silver Lady, this job is going to kill you." Just like that, with the capital letters in the way he said it, and then he left.

Now I've been called a lot of things by a lot of men, but Silver Lady isn't one of them. Mud duck. More of a mud duck, that's me, protective coloring, not too much makeup, muted colors in my clothes, unobtrusive jewelry if any at all. Camouflage. Dress just enough like anyone else so that no one notices you, that's the safest way. In high school, I believed I was invisible. If anyone looked at me, I would pick my nose and examine it until they looked away. They hardly ever looked back. I'd outgrown those tricks a long time ago, of course, but *Silver Lady*? That was a ridiculous thing to call me, unless he was mocking me, and I didn't think he had been. But somehow it seemed *worse* that he had been serious; it stung worse than an insult, because he had seemed to see in me something that I couldn't imagine in myself. Stung all the sharper because he was an ordinary fortyish man, run of the mill, staid and regular, potbelly and thinning hair, and it wasn't *fair* that he could imagine more about me than I could about myself. I mean, hell, I'm the writer, the one with the wild imagination, the vivid dreams, the razor-edged visions, right?

So. I worked out my shift, chewing on my tongue until closing time, and it wasn't until I had closed my till, stapled my receipts together, and chained off the dressing room that I noticed the little box on the corner of my counter. Little cardboard jewelry box, silver tone paper on the outside, no bag, no label, no nothing, just the silver stripes and Nordstrom in elegant lettering on the outside. A customer had forgotten it there, and I shoved it into my skirt pocket to turn it in at Customer Convenience on my way out.

I went home, climbed the stairs to my apartment, stepping in the neighbor's cat's turd on the way up, got inside, cleaned off my shoe, washed my hands five or six times, and put the kettle on for a cup of tea. I dropped into a chair and got jabbed by the box in my pocket. And the "oh, shit, here's trouble come knocking" feeling washed over me in a deep brown wave.

I knew what would happen. Some customer would come looking for it, and no one would know anything about it, but security would have picked me up on their closed circuit camera inside their little plastic bubbles on the ceiling. This was going to be it, the end of my rotten, low-paying little job, and my rent was due in two weeks, and this time the landlord wanted all of it at once. So I sat, holding the little silver box, and cursing my fate.

I opened it. I mean, what the hell, when there's no place left but down, one might as well indulge one's curiosity, so I opened it. Inside were two large earrings, each as long as my thumb. Silver ladies. They wore long gowns and their hair and gowns were swept back from their bodies by an invisible wind that pressed the metallic fabric of their bodices close against their high breasts and whipped their hair into frothy silver curls. They didn't match, not quite, and they weren't intended to be identical. I knew I could go to Nordstrom's and search for a hundred years and I'd never find anything like them. Their faces were filled with serenity and invitation, and they weighed heavy in my hand. I didn't doubt they were real silver, and that someone had fashioned them, one at a time, to be the only ones of their kinds. And I *knew,* like *knowing* about the tarot cards, that the fortyish man had made them and brought them and left them, and they were for me.

Only I don't have pierced ears.

So I put them back on the cotton in their little box and set them on my table, but I didn't put the lid back on. I looked at them, now and then, as I fixed myself a nutritious and totally adequate Western Family chicken pot pie for dinner and ate it out of the little aluminum pan and followed it with celery with peanut butter on it and raisins on top of the peanut butter.

That evening I did a number of useful and necessary things, like defrosting the refrigerator, washing out my pantyhose, spraying my shoes with Lysol spray, and dribbling bleach on the landing outside my apartment in the hopes it would keep the neighbor's cat away. I also put my bills in order by due date and watered the stump of the houseplant I'd forgotten to water last week. And then, because I wasn't writing, and the evening can get very long when you're not writing, I did something I had once seen my sister and two of her girlfriends do when I was thirteen and they were seventeen and rather drunk. I took four ice cubes and a sewing needle and went into the bathroom and unwrapped a bar of soap. The idea is, you sandwich your earlobes between the ice cubes and hold them there until they're numb. Then you put the bar of soap behind your earlobe to hold it steady, and you push the sewing needle through. Your earlobes are numb, so it doesn't hurt but it is weird because you hear the sound the needle makes going through your earlobe. On the first ear. On the second ear, it hurt like hell, and a big drop of blood welled out and dripped down the side of my neck, and I screamed "Oh, SHIT!" and banged my fist on the bathroom counter and broke a blood vessel in my hand, which hurt worse than my ears.

But it was done, and when my ears quit bleeding, I went and got the earrings and stood before the mirror and threaded their wires through my raw flesh. The wires were thin, and they pulled at the new holes in my ears, and it couldn't have hurt more if I'd hung a couple of anvils from my bleeding earlobes. But they looked beautiful. I stood looking at what they did to my neck and the angle of my jaw and the way they made the stray twining of my hair seem artful and deliberate. I smiled, serene and inviting, and almost I could see his Silver Lady in my own mirror.

But like I say, they hurt like hell, and tiny drips of my blood were sliding down the silver wires, and I couldn't imagine me sleeping with those things swinging from my ears all night. So I lifted them out and put them back in their box and the wires tinged the cotton pink. Then I wiped my earlobes with hydrogen peroxide, shivering at the sting. And I went to bed wondering if my ears would get infected.

THEY DIDN'T, THEY healed, and the holes didn't grow shut, even though I didn't keep anything in them to hold them open. A Friday came when there was a breath of spring in the air, and I put on a pale blue blouse that I hadn't worn in so long that it felt like new again. Just before I left my apartment, I went back and got the box and went to the bathroom and hung the silver ladies from my ears. I went to work.

Felicia, my department head, complimented me on them, but said they didn't look, quite, well, professional, to wear to work. I agreed she was probably right, and when I nodded, I felt their pleasant weight swinging on my ears. I didn't take them off. I collected my cash bag and went to open up my till.

I worked until six that day, and I smiled at people and they smiled back, and I didn't really give a damn how much I sold, but I sold probably twice as much as I'd ever sold before, maybe because I didn't give a damn. At the end of my shift, I got my coat and purse and collected my week's paycheck and decided to walk out through the mall instead of through the back door. The mall was having 4-H week, and I got a kick out of seeing the kids with their animals, bored cats sitting in cages stuffed full of kitty toys, little signs that say things like, "Hi, my name is Peter Pan, and I'm a registered Lop Rabbit," an incubator full of peeping chicks, and, right in the middle of the mall, someone had spread black plastic and scattered straw on top of it, and a pudgy girl with dark pigtails was demonstrating how to groom a unicorn.

I looked again, and it was a white billy goat, and one that was none too happy about being groomed. I shook my head, and I felt the silver ladies swing, and as I turned away, the fortyish man stepped out of the Herb and Tea Emporium with an armful of little brown bags. He swung into pace beside me, smelling like cinnamon, oranges, and cloves, and said, "You've just got to see this chicken. It plays tic-tac-toe."

Sure enough, some enterprising 4-H'er had rigged up a board with red and blue lights for the *x*'s and *o*'s, and for a quarter donation, the chicken would play tic-tac-toe with you. It was the fattest old rooster I'd ever seen, its comb hanging rakishly over one eye, and it beat me three times running. Which was about half my coffee money for the week, but what the hell, how often do you get the chance to play tic-tac-toe with a chicken?

The fortyish man played him and won, which brought the rooster up to the bars of the cage, flapping its wings and striking out, and I found myself dragging the fortyish man back out of beak range while the young owner of the rooster tried to calm his bird. We just laughed, and he took my elbow and guided me into a little Mexican restaurant that opens off the mall, and we found a table and sat down. The first thing I said was, "This is ridiculous. I don't even know you, and here I find myself defending you from irate roosters and having dinner with you."

And he said, "Permit me to introduce myself, then. I am Merlin."

I nearly walked out right then.

It's like this. I'm a skeptic. I have this one friend, a very nice woman. But she's always saying things like, "I can tell by your aura that you are troubled today," or talking about how I stunt my spiritual growth by ignoring my latent psychic powers. Once she phoned me up at eleven at night, long distance to me, collect, to tell me she'd just had a psychic experience. She was house-sitting for a friend in a big old house on Whidbey Island. She was sitting watching television, when she clearly heard the sound of footsteps going up the stairs. Only from where she was sitting, she could (she says) see the stairs quite clearly and there was no one there. So she froze, and she heard footsteps going along the upstairs hallway and then she heard the bathroom door shut. Then, she said, she heard the unmistakable and noisy splashing of a man urinating. The toilet flushed, and then all was silence. When she got up the nerve to go check the upstairs bathroom, there was no one there. But . . . THE SEAT WAS UP! So she had phoned me right away to jar me from my skepticism. Every time she comes over, she always has to throw her rune chips for me, and for some reason, they always spell out death and disaster and horrendous bad fortune just around the bend for me. Which may actually prove that she's truly psychic, because that fortune had never been far wrong for me. But it doesn't keep me from kidding her about her ghostly urinator. She's a friend, and she puts up with it, and I put up with her psychic-magic-spiritualism jazz.

But the fortyish man I didn't know at all—well, at least not much, and I wasn't going to put up with it from him. That was pushing it too far. There he was, fortyish and balding and getting a gut, and expecting me to listen to him talk weird as well. I mean, okay, I'm thirty-five, but everyone says I look a lot younger, and while only *one* man had ever called me Silver Lady, the rest haven't exactly called me Dog Meat. Maybe I'm not attractive in the standard, popular sense, but people who see me don't shudder and look away. Mostly they just tend not to see me. But at any rate, I *did* know that I wasn't so desperate that I had to latch on to a fortyish man with wing-nut ideas for company.

Except that just then the waitress walked past on her way to the next table, laden with two combination plates, heavy white china loaded to the gunwales with enchiladas and tacos and burritos, garnished with dollops of white sour cream and pale green guacamole, with black olives frisking dangerously close to the lip of the plate, and I suddenly knew I could listen to anyone talk about anything a lot more easily than I could go home and face Banquet

Fried Chicken, its flaking brown crust covered with thick hoarfrost from my faulty refrigerator. So I did.

We ordered and we ate and he talked and I listened. He told me things. He was not *the* Merlin, but he did know he was descended from him. Magic was not what it had been at one time, but he got by. One quote I remember exactly. "The *only* magic that's left in the world right now is the magic that we make ourselves, deliberately. You're not going to stumble over enchantment by chance. You have to be open to it, looking for it, and when you first think you might have glimpsed it, you have to will it into your life with every machination available to you." He paused. He leaned forward to whisper, "But the magic is never quite what you expect it to be. Almost but never exactly." And then he leaned back and smiled at me and I knew what he was going to say next.

He went on about the magic he sensed inside me, and how he could help me open myself up to it. He could feel that I was suppressing a talent. It was smooth, the way he did it. I think that if I had been ten or fifteen years younger, I could have relaxed and gone along with it, maybe even been flattered by it. Maybe if *he* had been five or ten years younger, I would have chosen to be gullible, just for the company. But dinner was drawing to a close, and I had a hunch what was going to come after dinner, so I just sort of shook my head and said that nothing in my life had ever made me anything but a skeptic about magic and ESP and psychic phenomena and all the rest of that stuff. And then he said what I knew he would, that if I'd care to come by his place he could show me a few things that would change my mind in a hurry. I said that I'd really enjoyed talking to him and dinner had been fun, but I didn't think I knew him well enough to go to his apartment. Besides, I was afraid I had to get home and wash my hair because I had the early shift again tomorrow morning. He shrugged and sat back in his chair and said he understood completely and I was wise to be cautious, that women weren't the only ones distressed by so-called date rapes. He said that in time I would learn that I could trust him and someday we'd probably laugh about my first impression of him.

I agreed, and we chuckled a little, and the waitress brought more coffee and he excused himself to use the men's room. I sat stirring sugar and creamer into my coffee, and wondering if it wouldn't be wiser to skip out now, just leave a little note that I had discovered it was later than I thought and I had to hurry home but that I'd had a lovely time and thank you. But that seemed like a pretty snaky thing to do to him. It wasn't like he was repulsive or anything; actually he was pretty nice and had very good eyes, dark brown, and a shy way of looking aside when he smiled and a wonderful voice that reminded me of cello strings. I suppose it was that he was fortyish and balding and had a potbelly. If that makes me sound shallow, well, I'm sorry. If he'd been a little younger, I could probably have warmed up to him. If I'd been a little younger, too, maybe I would even have gone to his apartment to be deskepticized. But he wasn't and I wasn't and I wouldn't. But I wasn't going to be rude to him either. He didn't deserve that. So I sat, toughing it out.

He'd left his packages of tea on the table and I picked one up and read it. I had to smile. Magic Carpet Tea. It smelled like orange spice to me. Earl Grey tea had been renamed Misplaced Dreams Tea. The scent of the third was unfamiliar to me, maybe one of those pale green ones, but it was labeled Dragon's Breath Tea. The fortyish man was really into this psychic-magic thing, I could tell, and in a way I felt a little sorry for him. A grown man, on the slippery-slide downside of his fortieth birthday, clinging to fairy tales and magic, still hoping something would *happen* in his life, some miracle more wondrous than financing a new car or finding out the leaky hot-water heater is still under warranty.

It wasn't going to happen, not to him, not to me, and I felt a little more gentle toward him as I leaned back in my chair and waited for him to return.

He didn't.

You found that out a lot faster than I did. I sat and waited and drank coffee, and it was only when the waitress refilled my cup that I realized how long it had been. His coffee was cold by then, and so was my stomach. I knew he'd stuck me with the check and why. I could almost hear him telling one of his buddies, "Hey, if the chick's not going to come across, why waste the bread, man?" Body-slammed by humiliation that I'd been so gullible, I wondered if the whole magic thing was something he just used as a lure for women. Probably. And here I'd been preening myself, just a little, all through dinner, thinking that he was still seeing in me the possibility of magic and enchantment, that for him I had some special fey glow.

Well, my credit cards were bottomed out, I had less than two bucks in cash, and my checkbook was at home. In the end, the restaurant manager reluctantly cashed my paycheck for me, probably only because he knew Sears wouldn't write a rubber check and I could show him my employee badge. Toward the end he was even sympathetic about the fortyish man treating me so badly, which was even worse, because he acted like my poor little heart was broken instead of me just being damn mad and embarrassed. As I was leaving, finally, let me get out of here, the waitress handed me the three little paper bags of tea with such a condescending "poor baby" look that I wanted to spit at her. And I went home.

The strange part is that I actually cried after I got home, more out of frustration and anger than any hurt, though. I wished that I knew his real name, so I could call him up and let him know what I thought of such a cheap trick. I stood in front of the bathroom mirror looking at my red eyes and swollen runny nose, and I suddenly knew that the restaurant people had been seeing me more clearly than I or the fortyish man did. Not Silver Lady or even mud duck, but plain middle-aged woman in a blue-collar job with no prospects at all. For a moment it got to me, but then I stood up straight and stared at the mirror. I felt the silver ladies swinging from my ears, and as I looked at them, it occurred to me that they were probably worth a lot more than the meal I had just paid for, and that I had his tea, to boot. So maybe he hadn't come out of it any better than I had; these earrings hadn't gotten him laid, and if he had skipped out without paying for the meal, he'd left his tea as well, and those specialty shop teas don't come cheap. For the first time, it occurred to me that things didn't add up, quite. But I put it out of my mind, fixed myself a cup of Misplaced Dreams tea, read for a little while, and then went to bed.

I dreamed about him. Not surprising, considering what he'd put me through. I was in a garden, standing by a silver bench shaded by an arching trellis heavy with a dark green vine full of fragrant pink flowers. The fortyish man was standing before me, and I could see him, but I had the sense that he was disembodied, not really there at all. "I want to apologize," he said, quite seriously. "I never would have left you that way voluntarily. I'm afraid I was magicked away by one of my archrivals. The same one who has created the evil spell that distresses you. He's imprisoned me in a crystal, so I'm afraid I won't be seeing you for a while."

In this dream, I was clad in a gown made of peacock feathers, and I had silver rings on all my fingers. Little silver bells were on fine chains around my ankles. They tinkled as I stepped closer to him. "Isn't there anything I can do to help you?" my dream self asked.

"Oh, I think not," he replied. "I just didn't want you to think badly of me." Then he smiled. "Silver Lady, you are one of the few who would worry first about breaking the enchantment that binds me, rather than plotting how to break your own curse. I cannot help but believe that the forces that balance all magic will find a way to free us both."

"May you be right, my friend," I replied.

And that was the end of the dream, or the end of as much as I can remember. I awoke in the morning with vague memories of a cat batting at tinkling silver chimes swinging in a perfumed wind. I had a splitting headache. I got out of bed, got dressed, and went to work at Sears.

For a couple of days, I kept expecting him to turn up again, but he didn't. I just kept going along. I told Felicia that I couldn't live on the hours and pay I was getting, and she told me that she was very disappointed with the number of credit applications I was turning in, and that full-time people were only chosen from the most dedicated and enthusiastic part-timers. I said I'd have to start looking for work elsewhere, and she said she understood. We both knew there wasn't much work of any kind to be had, and that I could be replaced with a bored housewife or a desperate community college student at a moment's notice. It was not reassuring.

In the next three weeks, I passed out twenty-seven copies of my résumé to various bored people at desks. I interviewed for two jobs that were just as low paying as the one I already had. I found a fantastic job that would have loved to hire me, but its funding called for it to be given to a displaced homemaker or a disadvantaged worker. Then I called on a telemarketer telephone interviewing position ad in the paper. They liked my voice and asked me to come in. After a lot of pussyfooting, it turned out to be a job where you answered toll calls from heavy breathers and conversed animatedly about their sexual fantasies. "Sort of an improvisational theater of the erotic," said my interviewer. She had some tapes of some sample calls, and I found myself listening to them and admitting, yes, it sounded easy. Best of all, the interviewer told me, I could work from my own home, doing the dishes or sorting laundry while telling some man how much I'd like to run a warm sponge over his body, slathering every nook and cranny of his flesh with soapsuds until he gleamed, and then, when he was hard and warm and wet, I'd take him and . . . for six to seven dollars an hour. They even had pamphlets that explained sexual practices I might not be familiar with and gave the correct jargon to use when chatting about them. Six to seven dollars an hour. I told the interviewer I'd have to think about it and went home.

And got up the next day and defrosted the refrigerator again and swept the carpet in the living room because I was out of vacuum bags. Then I did all the mending that I had been putting off for weeks, scrubbed the landing outside my apartment door and sprayed it with Cat-B-Gon, and thought about talking on the telephone to men about sex, and how I could do it while I was ironing a shirt or arranging flowers in a vase or wiping cat turds off my shoe. Then I took a shower and changed and went in to work at Sears for the five-to-nine evening shift. I told myself that the work wasn't dirty or extremely difficult, that my coworkers were pleasant people, and that there was no reason why this job should make me so depressed.

It didn't help.

The mall was having Craft Week, and to get to Sears I had to pass all the tables and people. I wondered why I didn't get busy and make things in the evenings and sell them on the weekends and make ends meet that way. I passed Barbie dolls whose pink crocheted skirts concealed spare rolls of toilet paper, and I saw wooden key chains that spelled out names, and ceramic butterfly wind chimes, and a booth of rubber stamps, and a booth with clusters of little pewter and crystal sculptures displayed on tables made of old doors set across sawhorses. I slowed a little as I passed that one, for I've always had a weakness for pewter. There were the standard dragons and wizards, and some thunder-eggs cut in half with wizard figures standing inside them. There were birds, too, eagles and falcons and owls of pewter, and one really nice stag almost as big as my hand. For fifty-two dollars. I was looking at it when I heard a woman standing behind me say, "I'd like the crystal holding the wizard, please."

And the owner of the stall smiled at her and said, "You mean the wizard holding the crystal, right?" and the woman said, in this really snotty voice, "Quite."

So the owner wrapped up the little figurine of a wizard holding a crystal ball in several layers of tissue paper and held it out to the woman and said, "Seventeen seventy-eight, please," and the woman was digging in her purse and I swear, all I did was try to step out of their way.

I guess my coat caught on a corner of the door or something, for in the next instant everything was tilting and sliding. I tried to catch the edge of the door-table, but it landed on the woman's foot, really hard, as all the crystal and pewter crashed to the floor and scattered across the linoleum like a shattered whitecap. The woman screamed and threw up her hands, and the little wrapped wizard went flying.

I'm not sure if I really saw this.

The crystal ball flew out of the package and landed separately on the floor. It didn't shatter or tinkle or crash. It went Poof! with a minute puff of smoke. And the crumple of tissue paper floated down emptily.

"You stupid bitch!" the woman yelled at me, and the owner of the booth glared at me and said, "I hope to hell you have insurance, klutz!"

Which is a dumb thing to say, really, and I couldn't think of any answer. People were turning to stare, and moving toward us to see what the excitement was, and the woman had sort of collapsed and was holding on to her foot, saying, "My God, it's broken, it's broken."

I knew, quite abruptly and coldly, that she wasn't talking about her foot.

Then the fortyish man grabbed me by the elbow and said, "We've got to get out of here!" I let him pull me away, and the funny thing is, no one tried to stop us or chase us or anything. The crowd closed up around the woman on the floor like an amoeba engulfing a tidbit.

Then we were in a pickup truck that smelled like a wet dog, and the floor was cluttered with muddy newspapers and Styrofoam coffee cups and wrappers from Hostess Fruit Pies and paper boats from the textured vegetable protein burritos they sell in the 7-Eleven stores. Part of me was saying that I was crazy to be driving off with this guy I hardly knew who had stuck me with the bill for dinner, and part of me was saying that I had better get back to Sears, maybe I could explain being this late for work. And part of me just didn't give a shit anymore; it just wanted to flee. And that part felt better than it had in ages.

We pulled up outside a little white house and he turned to me gravely and said, "Thank you for rescuing me."

"This is really dumb," I said, and he said, "Maybe so, but it's all we've got. I told you, magic isn't what it used to be."

So we went inside the little house and he put the tea kettle on. It was a beautiful kettle, shining copper with a white-and-blue ceramic handle, and the cups and saucers he took down matched it. I said, "You stuck me with the bill at the restaurant."

He said, "My enemies fell upon me in the restroom and magicked me away. I told you. I never would have chosen to leave you that way, Silver Lady. But for your intervention I would still be in their powers." Then he turned, holding a little tin canister in each hand and asked, "Which will you have: Misplaced Dreams or Forgotten Sweetness?"

"Forgotten Sweetness," I said, and he put down both canisters of tea and took me in his arms and kissed me. And yes, I could feel his stomach sticking out a little against mine, and when I put my hand to the back of his head to hold his mouth against mine, I could tell his hair was thinning. But I thought I could hear wind chimes and scent an elusive perfume on a warm breeze.

I don't believe in magic. The idea of willing magic into my life is dumb. Dumb. But as the fortyish man had said, it was all we had. A dumb hope for a small slice of magic, no matter how thin. The fortyish man didn't waste his energy carrying me to the bedroom.

I never met a man under twenty-five who was worth the powder to blow him to hell. They're all stuck in third gear.

It takes a man until he's thirty to understand what gentleness is about, and a few years past that to realize that a woman touches a man as she would like him to touch her.

By thirty-five, they start to grasp how a woman's body is wired. They quit trying to kick-start us and learn to make sure the battery is charged before turning the key. A few, I've heard, learn how to let a woman make love to them.

Fortyish men understand pacing. They know it doesn't have to all happen at once, that separating each stimulus can intensify each touch. They know when pausing is more poignant than continuing, and they know when continuing is more important than a ceramic kettle whistling itself dry on an electric burner.

And afterward I said to him, "Have you ever heard of 'Lindholm's Rule of Ten'?"

He frowned for an instant. "Isn't that the theory that the first ten times two people make love, one will do something that isn't in sync with the other?"

"That's the one," I said.

"It's been disproved," he said solemnly. And he got up and went to the bathroom while I rescued the smoking kettle from the burner.

I stood in the kitchen, and after a while I started shivering, because the place wasn't all that well heated. Putting my clothes back on didn't seem polite somehow, so I called through the bathroom door, "Shall I put on more water for tea?"

He didn't answer, and I didn't want to yell through the door again, so I picked up my blouse and slung it around my shoulders and shivered for a while. I sort of paced through his kitchen and living room. I found myself reading the titles of his books, one of the best ways to politely spy on someone. *Theories of Thermodynamics* was right next to *The Silmarillion.* All the books by Carlos Castenada were set apart on a shelf by themselves. His set of Kipling was bound in red leather. My ass was freezing, and I suspected I had a rug burn on my back. To hell with being polite. I went and got my underwear and skirt and stood in the kitchen, putting them on.

"Merlin?" I called questioningly as I picked up my pantyhose. They were shot, a huge laddered run up the back of one leg. I bunched them up and shoved them into my purse. I went and knocked on the bathroom door, saying, "I'm coming in, okay?" And when he didn't answer, I opened the door. There was no one in there. But I was sure that was where he had gone, and the only other exit from the bathroom was a small window with three pots of impatiens blooming on the sill. The only clue that he had been there was the used rubber floating pathetically in the toilet. There is nothing less romantic than a used rubber.

I went and opened the bedroom door and looked in there. He hadn't made his bed this morning. I backed out.

I actually waited around for a while, pretending he would come back. I mean, his clothes were still in a heap on the floor. How he could have gotten redressed and left the house without my noticing it, I didn't try to figure out. But after about an hour or so, it didn't matter how he had done anything. He was *gone.*

I didn't cry. I had been too stupid to allow myself to cry. None of this made sense, but my behavior made the least sense of all. I finished getting dressed and looked at myself in the bathroom mirror. Great. Smeared makeup and nothing to repair it with, so I washed it all off. Let the lines at the corners of my mouth and the circles under my eyes show. Who cared? My hair had gone wild. My legs were white fleshed and goosebumpy without the pantyhose. The cute little ankle-strap heels on my bare feet looked grotesque. All of me looked rumpled and used. It matched how I felt, an outfit that perfectly complemented my mood, so I got my purse and left.

The old pickup was still outside. That didn't make sense either, but I didn't really give a damn.

I walked home. That sounds simpler than it was. The weather was raw, I was barelegged and in heels, it was getting dark, and people stared at me. It took me about an hour, and by the time I got there I had rubbed a huge blister on the back of one of my feet, so I was limping as well. I went up the stairs, narrowly missing the moist brown pile the neighbor's cat had left for me, unlocked my apartment door and went in.

And I still didn't cry. I kicked off my shoes and got into my old baggy sweat suit and went to the kitchen. I made myself hot chocolate in a little china pot with forget-me-nots on it, and opened the eight-ounce canned genuine all-the-way-from-England Cross & Blackwell plum pudding that my sister had given me last Christmas and I had saved in case of disasters like this. I cut the whole thing up and arranged it on a bone china plate on a little tray with my pot of hot chocolate and a cup and saucer. I set it on a little table by my battered easy chair, put a quilt on the chair, and got down my old leather copy of Dumas's *The Three Musketeers.* Then I headed for the bathroom, intending to take a quick hot shower and dab on some rose oil before settling down for the evening. It was my way of apologizing to myself for hurting myself this badly.

I opened the bathroom door, and a stench cloud of sulfurous green smoke wafted out. Choking and gasping, I peered in, and there was the fortyish man, clad only in a towel, smiling at me apologetically. He looked apprehensive. He had a big raw scrape on one knee, and a swollen lump on his forehead. He said, "Silver Lady, I never would have left you like that, but . . ."

"You were teleported away by your archrival," I finished.

He said, "No, not teleported, exactly; this involved a spell requiring a monkey's paw and a dozen nightshade berries. But they were *last* year's berries, and not potent enough to hold me. I had a spell of my own up my sleeve and . . ."

"You blasted him to kingdom come," I guessed.

"No." He looked a little abashed. "Actually, it was the 'Incessant Rectal Itch' spell, a little crude, but always effective and simple to use. I doubt that he'll be bothering us again." He paused, then added, "As I've told you, magic isn't what it used to be." Then he sniffed a few times and said, "Actually, I've found that Pine-Sol is the best stuff for getting rid of spell residues . . ."

So we cleaned up the bathroom. I poured hydrogen peroxide over his scraped knee and he made gasping noises and swore in a language I'd never heard before. I left him doing that and went into the kitchen and began reheating the hot chocolate. A few moments later he came out dressed in a sort of sarong he'd made from one of my bedsheets. It looked strangely elegant on him, and the funny thing was, neither of us seemed to feel awkward as we sat down and drank the hot chocolate and shared the plum pudding. The last piece of plum pudding he took, and borrowing some cream cheese from my refrigerator, he buttered a cabalistic sign onto it.

Then he went to the door and called, "Here, kitty, kitty, kitty."

The neighbor's cat came at once, and the ratty old thing let the fortyish man scoop him up and bring him into my living room, where he removed two ticks from behind its ears and then fed it the plum pudding in small bites. When he had done that, he picked it up and stared long into its yellowish eyes before he intoned, "By bread and cream I bind you. Nevermore shalt thou shit upon the threshold of this abode." Then he put the cat gently out the door, observing aloud, "Well, that takes care of the curse you were under."

I stared at him. "I thought my curse had something to do with me working at Sears."

"No. That was just a viciously cruel thing you were doing to yourself, for reasons I will never understand." He must have seen the look on my face, because after a while he said, "I told you, the magic is never quite what you think it to be."

Then he came to sit on the floor beside my easy chair. He put his elbow on my knee and leaned his chin in his hand. "What if I were to tell you, Silver Lady, that I myself have no real magic at all? That, actually, I climbed out my bathroom window and sneaked through the streets in my towel to meet you here? Because I wanted you to see me as special?"

I didn't say anything.

"What if I told you I really work for Boeing, in Personnel?"

I just looked at him, and he lifted his elbow from my knee and turned aside a little. He glanced at his own bare feet, and then over at my machine. He licked his lips and spoke softly. "I could get you a job there. As a word processor, at about eleven dollars an hour."

"Merlin," I said warningly.

"Well, maybe not eleven dollars an hour to start . . ."

I reached out and brushed what hair he had back from his receding hairline. He looked up at me and then smiled the smile where he always looked aside from me. We didn't say anything at all. I took his hand and led him to my room, where we once more disproved Lindholm's Rule of Ten. I fell asleep curled around him, my hand resting comfortably on the curve of his belly. He was incredibly warm and smelled of oranges, cloves, and cinnamon. Misplaced Dreams tea, that's what he smelled like.

And that night I dreamed I wore a peacock feather gown and strolled through a misty garden. I had found something I had lost, and I carried it in my hand, but every time I tried to look at it to see what it was, the mist swirled up and hid my hand from me.

In the morning when I woke up, the fortyish man was gone.

It didn't really bother me. I knew that either he would be back or he wouldn't, but either way no one could take from me what I already had, and what I already had was a lot more magic than most people get in their lives. I put on my ratty old bathrobe and my silver ladies and went out into the living room. His sarong sheet was folded up on the easy chair in the living room and the neighbor's cat was asleep on it, his paws tucked under his chin.

And my Muse was there, too, perched on the corner of my desk, one knee under her chin as she painted her toenails. She looked up when I came in and said, "If you're quite finished having a temper tantrum, we'll get on with your career now."

So I sat down at my machine and flicked the switch on and put my fingers on the home row.

Funny thing. The keys weren't even dusty.

Cut

And here is yet another of my stories that gets a bit too close to the bone.

Some stories, I feel, are written because the writer has a point to make. The writer knows something, or thinks he or she knows something, and intends to inflict that knowledge on the reader. At their worst, those stories turn into polemics or badly disguised fables with the moral shouting at the reader from the final paragraph.

I hope and pray that I do not do that.

Rather, I like to think (and please don't disabuse me of this notion!) that I write stories because I have a question. Not the answer, mind you, but just the question. The question at the core of this story is, Who owns the body? Is my body my own, to modify with tattoos and piercings? May I color my hair or shave it off, enlarge my breasts, or starve myself into bony submission?

And if the answers to all those questions is, Yes, you may, then at what point is society allowed to interfere with what I do? At what point do those decisions belong solely to me? When I am twenty-one or when I am twelve? May I make those sorts of decisions for my child, for religious or aesthetic reasons? Now we are on shakier ground, are we not? Do you immunize your child, straighten his teeth, correct a club foot, radiate his cancer, and circumcise him?

Or not?

Patsy sits on a bar stool at my breakfast counter. She is sipping a glass of soy milk through a straw. I glance at her, then look away at my rainforest cam on the wall screen behind her. My granddaughter had an incisor removed so that she could drink through the straw with her mouth closed. She claims it is more sanitary and less offensive to other people. I don't know. It offends the hell out of her grandmother.

"So. SATs next week?" I ask her hopefully.

"Uh-huh," she confirms, and I breathe a small sigh of relief. She had contemplated refusing to take them, on the grounds that any college who wanted to rate her on a single test score was not her kind of place anyway. She swings her feet, kicking the rungs of her stool. "I'm still debating Northwestern versus Peterson University."

I try to recall something about Peterson, but I don't think I've ever heard of it. "Northwestern's good," I hedge. As I set a plate of cookies within her reach, I notice a bulge in the skin on her shoulder blade just above the fabric of her tank top. An irritated peace sign seems to be emblazoned on it. "What's that? New tattoo?"

She glances over her shoulder at it, then shrugs. "No. Raised implant. They put a stainless steel piece under your skin. Works best when there's bone backing it up. Mine didn't come out very good. Grandma, you know I can't eat those things. If the fat doesn't clog up my heart, sugar will send me into a depression and I'll kill myself."

She nudges the plate away. I smile and take one myself. "I think that's a bit of an exaggeration. I've been eating chocolate chip cookies for years."

"Yeah, I know. And Mom, too. Look at her."

"Doesn't it hurt?" I ask, nodding at her implant. I evade the topic of her mom. It is not that I expect my granddaughter to always get on with my daughter. It is that I don't want to be wedged into the middle of it.

My gambit is successful. "This? No. A little slit in the skin, then they free the skin layer from the tissue underneath it, slide in the emblem, put in a couple of stitches. It healed in two days, and now it's permanent. Besides, women have always been willing to suffer for beauty. Inject collagen into your lips. Get breast implants. Have your ribs removed to have a smaller waist."

I give a mock shudder. "I never went in for those sorts of things. I think God meant us to live in our bodies the way they are."

"Yeah, right." She snorts skeptically and picks up a cookie crumb, then licks it off her finger. I catch a brief glimpse of her tongue stud. "You made Mom wear braces on her teeth for two years. She's always telling me what a pain that was."

"That was different. That was for health as much as for appearances."

"Oh, let's be honest, Gran." Patsy leans forward on her elbow and fixes me with her best piercing glance. "You didn't take her to an orthodontist because you were worried she couldn't chew a steak. She told me the kids at school were calling her 'Fang'."

I wince at the memory of my twelve-year-old in tears. It had taken me an hour to get her to tell me why. Katie was never as forthcoming as her own daughter is. "Well, appearance was part of it. It was affecting her self-esteem. But straight teeth are important to lifelong health and—"

"Yeah, but the point it, it was plastic surgery. For the sake of how she looked. And it hurt her."

I feel suddenly defensive. Patsy is going over all this as if it is a well-rehearsed argument. "Well, at least it's more constructive than some of the ways you hurt yourself. Tattoos, body piercing, tooth removal. It worries me, frankly, that so many people can damage their bodies for the sake of a fad."

"Hardly a fad, Gran. People have been doing it for thousands of years. It's not just that it looks good, it makes a point about yourself. That you have the will to make yourself who you want to be. Even if it means a little pain."

"Or a lot of infection."

"Not with that new antibiotic. It kills everything."

"That's what worries me," I mutter.

I take another cookie. Nothing betrays my amusement as Patsy absentmindedly takes one and dunks it in her milk. She slurps off a bite, then says with a full mouth, "I've been thinking about getting cut myself."

"Cut?" The bottom drops out of my stomach. I'd seen it on the netnews. "Like a joint off your little fingers like that one group of kids did? To express solidarity with one another." An almost worse thought finds me. "Not that facial scarification they do with the razor blades and ash?"

She laughs aloud and my anxiety eases. "No, Granma!" She hops off her stool and grabs her groin. "Cut! Here, you know."

"No, I don't know."

"Circumcision. Everyone's talking about it. Here." While I am still gaping at her, she takes her net link from her collar and points it at my wall screen. My rainforest cam scene gives way to one of her favorite links. I cringe at what I see. Some net star in a glam pose has her legs spread. Larger than life, she fills my wall. Head thrown back, hair cascading over her shoulders, she is sharing with us her freshly healed female circumcision. Symmetrical and surgically precise are the cleanly healed cuts, but all I can see is the absence of the flesh that should be there. I turn away, sickened by the slick pink scars, but Patsy stares, fascinated. "Doesn't it look cool? In the interview, she says she did it to get a role. She wanted to show the producer her absolute commitment to the project. But now she loves it. She says she feels cleaner, that she has cut a lot of animal urges out of her life. When she has sex now . . . here, I can just play the interview for you—"

"No, thanks," I say faintly. I tap my master control, and the screen goes completely blank. After what I have just seen, I could not bear the beauty of the rainforest cam with the wet dripping leaves and the calling birds everywhere. I take a breath. "Patsy, you can't be serious."

She clips her link back onto her collar and pops back onto her stool. "You know I am, Granma. At least you aren't going all meltdown like Mom did."

"She knows you want to do this?" I can't grasp any of it, not that some women do this voluntarily, not that Patsy wants to do it, not that Katie knows.

Patsy crunches down the rest of her cookie. "She knows I'm going to do it. Me and Ticia and Samantha. Mary Porter, too. We'll be like a circumcision group, like some African tribes had. We've grown up together. The ceremony will be a bond between us the rest of our lives."

"Ceremony." I don't know when I stood up. I sit back down. I press my knees together because they are shaking. Not to protect my own genitals.

"Of course. At the full moon. The midwife who does it has this wonderful setting; it's an open field with these big old rocks sticking up out of it, and the river flowing by where you can hear it."

"A midwife does this?"

"Well, she used to be a midwife. Now she says she only does circumcisions, that this is more symbolic and fulfilling to her than delivering babies. But she is medically trained. Everything will be sterilized, and she uses antibiotics and all that stuff. So it's safe."

I suppose I should be relieved they are not using broken glass or old razor blades. "I don't get it," I say at last. I peer at my granddaughter. "Is this some sort of religious thing?"

She bursts out laughing. "No!" she sputters at last. "Granma! You know I don't go for that cult stuff. This is just about me taking control of my own life. Saying that sex doesn't run me, that I won't choose a man just because I'm horny for him, that I'm more than that."

"You're giving up sexual fulfillment for the rest of your life." I state it flatly, wanting her to hear how permanent it is.

"Granma, orgasm isn't sexual fulfillment. Orgasm isn't that much better than taking a good shit."

I smile in spite of myself. "Then you're sleeping with the wrong boys. Your grandfather—"

She covers her ears in mock horror. "Don't gross me out with old-people sex stories. Ew!" She drops her hands. "Sexual fulfillment—that's like code words that say women are about sex. *Women need sexual fulfillment,* like it's more important than being a fulfilled person."

We are arguing semantics when what I want to tell her is not to let some fanatic cut her sweet young flesh away from her body. Don't let anyone steal that much of you, I want to say. I don't. I suddenly understand how grave this is. If I become too serious, she won't hear me at all. She is poking me, trying to provoke me to act like a parent. I hold myself back from that futile abyss. Reasoning with her won't work. Get her to talk, and maybe she will talk herself out of it.

"Have you any idea how much it's going to hurt? Well, I'm sure she'll use an anesthetic for the surgery, but afterward when you're healing—"

"Duh! That would defeat the whole purpose. No anesthetic. It would go against the traditions of female circumcision throughout the world. Ticia and Mary and Sam and I will be there for each other. It will be just women sharing their courage with other women."

"Female circumcision was invented by men!" I retort. "To keep women at home and subservient to them. To take away a precious part of their lives. Patsy, think about this. You're young. Once done, you can't go back."

"Sure you can. At the midwife's site, there's a link to a place that can make you look like you did before. Here." She is fiddling with her net link. I press the Off on my master control again.

"That's appearance, not functionality."

"Are you sure?"

"Yes. And you should know that much before you get into this. I can't understand how that woman can do this to girls." The parent part is getting the better of me. I clamp my lips down.

Patsy shakes her head at me. "Granma! It has always been women doing it to other women, in all the cultures. Look." She reaches over to push my master button back On. "Here's a link to her website. Go look at it. She has all the historical stuff posted there. You like anthropology. You should be fascinated."

I stare at her, defeated. She is so sure. She argues well, and she is not stupid. She is not even ignorant. She is merely young and in the throes of her time. Patsy will do this if she is not stopped. I don't know how to stop her. Her words come back to me. Women doing it to other women. Women perpetuating this maiming. I try to imagine what she must be like. I can't. "I'd have to meet her," I say to myself.

Patsy brightens. "I hoped you would. Look. On her site, my link is the Moon Sisters. Our password is Luna. Because we chose the full moon. There's pictures of us, and the date and time and place. You're invited. Mary wanted to have a webcam on the ceremony, but we voted her down. This is private. For us. But I'd like you to be there."

"Will your mom be there?"

Again her snort of disbelief. "Mom? Of course not. She gets all worked up whenever I talk about it. She threatened to kill our midwife. Can you believe that? I asked her if she ever bombed abortion clinics when she was a kid. She said it wasn't the same thing at all. Sure it is, I told her. It's all about choice, isn't it? Women making their own sexual choices." Her beeper chimes and she leaps from the stool. "Wow, I've got to get going. Big date with Teddy tonight."

I make my last stand. "How does Teddy feel about this?"

She shakes her head at me. "You just don't get it, Granma. It's not about Teddy. It's my choice. But he's excited. After this, if I have sex with him, he'll know it's not because I'm horny at the moment, but because I want to give that to him. And I think he's excited because it will be different. Tighter because of how she sews us up. You know men."

She doesn't wait for an answer from me, which is good, because right now I am sure that I don't even know women, let alone men. As soon as she is out the door, I phone Katie. In a moment, I see her in the corner of my wall screen, but she does not meet my eyes. She is looking past me, at something on her own wall screen. I stare for a moment at my beautiful talented daughter. By a supreme effort of will, I don't shriek, "Circumcision! Patsy! Help!" Instead I say, "Hi, whatchadoing?"

"Sorting beads from the St. Katherine site. It's fascinating. You know my beadmaker from the Charlotte site? Well, I'm finding her work here, too. They're unmistakably hers from the analysis. Which means these people traded over a far greater area than we first supposed."

"Or that the trade network was greater." I have to smile at her. She is so intent, her eyes roving over the screen as she continues working. When she is enraptured in her archaeology like this, she suddenly looks eighteen again. There is that fierceness to her stare. I am so proud of her and all that she is. She nods her agreement. I know she is busy, but this is important. Still, I procrastinate. "Do you ever miss actually handling the beads and the artifacts?"

"Oh. Well, yes, I do. But this is still good. And the native peoples have been much more receptive to our work now that they know all the grave goods will remain in situ and relatively undisturbed. The cameras and the chem scanners can do most of the data gathering for us. But it still takes a human mind to put it all together and figure out what it means. And this way of doing it is better, both for archaeology and anthropology. Sometimes we're too trapped in our own times to see what it all means. Sometimes we're too close, temporally, to understand the culture. By leaving all the artifacts and bones in situ, we make it possible for later anthropologists to take a fresh look at it, with unprejudiced eyes." She glances up at me and our eyes meet. "So. You called."

"Patsy," I say.

She clenches her jaw, takes a breath, and sighs it out. The intent eighteen-year-old anthro student is gone, replaced by a worried, tired mom. "The circumcision."

"Katie, you have to stop her!"

"I can't."

"You can't?" I am outraged.

She is weary. "Legally, her body is her own. Once a child is over fourteen, a parent cannot interfere in—"

"I don't give a damn about legal—" I try to break in, but she continues doggedly.

"—any decision the child makes about her sexuality. Birth control, abortions, adopting out of children, gender reassignment, confidential medical treatment for venereal disease, plastic surgery—it's all covered in that Freedom of Choice Act." She gives me a woeful smile. "I supported that legislation. I never thought it would be construed like this."

"Are you sure it covers things like this?" I ask faintly.

"Too sure. Patsy has forced me to be sure. Shall I forward all the web links to you? She has, in her typical thorough way, researched this completely . . . at least in every way that supports her viewpoint." She shrugs helplessly. "I gave her a set of links to websites that oppose it. I don't know if she looked at them at all. I can't force her."

I realized I have my hand clenched over my mouth. I pull it away. "You seem so calm," I observe in disbelief.

For an instant, her eyes swim with tears. "I'm not. I'm just all screamed out. I'm exhausted, and she has stopped listening to me. What can I do?"

"Stop her. Any way you can."

"Like you stopped Mike from dropping out of school?"

Even after all the years, I feel a pang of pain. I shake my head. "I did everything I could. I'd drop your brother off at the front door, I'd watch him go into the school, and he'd go right out the back door. Battling him was not doing anything for our relationship. I had to let him make that mistake. I stopped yelling at him in an effort to keep the relationship intact. At least, it saved that much."

"Exactly," Katie says. She stares past me at her screen, but I have broken the spell. She can no longer forget her daughter's decision in wonder at some ancient beadmaker's work. "I was quite calm last night. I told her that all I asked was that she always remember the decision was hers and that I completely opposed it. 'Fine,' she said. 'Fine.' At least this way, she'll come back here after the damned ceremony. If she gets an infection or doesn't stop bleeding, at least I'll know about it and can rush her to the hospital."

"Can you legally still do that?" I ask with bitterness that mocks, not her, but the society we live in.

"I think so." She stops speaking and swallows. "Pray, Mom," she begs me after a moment. "Pray that when the other girls scream, she loses her courage and runs away. That's my last hope."

"It's a slim one, then. Our Patsy never lacked for guts. Brains, maybe, but not guts." We smile at each other, pride battling with despair. "Once she's said she'll do a thing, she won't back down no matter how scared she is. She'll let that woman cut her up rather than be seen as a coward by her friends."

"It's the baby I feel sorry for," Katie says suddenly.

"Baby?" All the hair on my body stands up in sudden horror.

"Mary's baby. She decided to have her baby done; the midwife is doing the baby first."

I didn't even know Mary had a baby. She is only a year older than Patsy. "But she can't! She has no right to make a decision like that, to scar her daughter for the rest of her life!"

Again the bitter smile makes Katie a sour old woman I don't know. "It's the flip side of the Freedom of Choice Act. The compromise Congress made to get it passed. Under the age of fourteen, a parent can make any choice for the child."

"It's barbaric."

"You had Mike circumcised when he was three days old."

That jolts me. I try to justify it. "It was a different time. Almost all boys were circumcised then. Your dad and I didn't even think about it, it was just what you did. If the baby was a boy, you had him circumcised. They told us it made it easier to keep the baby clean, that it helped prevent cancer of the penis, that it would make him like all the other boys in the locker room."

"They do it without anesthetic."

I am silent. I am no longer sure if we are talking about Mary's baby girl, or my own tiny son, all those years ago. I remember tending to the fresh cut on his penis, dabbing on petroleum jelly to keep his diaper from sticking to it. I am suddenly ashamed of myself. I had not hesitated, all those years ago. I had charged ahead and done what others told me was wise.

Just like Patsy.

The silence has stretched long and said more than words. "She invited me to be there," I say quietly. "Do you think I should go? Is that like giving my approval?"

"Go," Katie pleads quickly. "If it all goes wrong, you can rush her to a hospital. She won't tell me where it is, and I won't ask you to betray that confidence. But be there for her, Mom. Please."

"Okay," I say quietly.

Katie has started to cry.

"I love you, baby. You're a good mom," I tell her. She shakes her head wildly, tears and hair flying, and breaks the connection.

For a time I stare at my rain forest. Then I get up. There is a backpack in the hall closet. I go to the bathroom and begin to put things in it. Clean towels. Bandaging. I shudder as I put in the alcohol. I try to think what else. There is a spray antiseptic with a "nonsting, pain-relieving ingredient." Feeble. What else should I take, what else?

I draw a breath and look in the mirror. Katie's face is an echo of mine, made perfect. Patsy, I see you in my green eyes and almost cleft chin. They are mine, the daughter of my body and my daughter's daughter. Born so soft and pink and perfect. I make my arms a cradle and wish they were both still mine to hold and protect.

I grope up behind the towels and take it down. Shining silver, it slips from the holster. There is a horsie on the handle. Fred always loved Colts. There is a dusty box of ammunition, too.

I am suddenly calm. Don't be afraid, baby. Not my baby, not Mary's baby, no one's baby need fear. Granma is coming. No one's going to cut you.

I think for a moment of what a mess I'm going to make of my life. I think of the echoes that will spread out from one bullet, and

I wonder how Patsy and her friends will deal with it, and what it will do to Katie. Then I know I am too close to any of it to understand. Maybe we should just leave the midwife's body where it falls. In situ. Perhaps in a hundred years or two, someone else will know what to make of it all.

The Fifth Squashed Cat

Oh my, this one is one of those stories that has so many roots in different parts of my life that it's difficult for me to remember where it began. Certainly it owes much to my days of working in a restaurant. And to many road trips taken in vehicles held together with string and prayers. There is a nod to the friendships that are based not on mutual interests but on proximity and need. Not to mention those mornings after a full moon when some stretches of rural highway seem to be partially upholstered in small furry bodies.

But I think the biggest influence on this one is a small pet peeve I have with many fantasy tales. In so many of them, the main character discovers that he or she is the chosen one, the one gifted, for no particular reason, with the ability to do magic. The protagonist receives the gift and becomes the hero. Or heroine. In the worst of these stories, the magic and the mantle of being the hero is bestowed without effort by or cost to the protagonist.

Herewith, my protest to such tales.

"That's the fourth squashed cat we've passed today," Cheryl observed as the left front wheel bumped gently. I didn't trust myself to reply. I was trying to remember why driving cross-country to New Mexico with Cheryl had seemed like a good idea. Had working at Ernie's Trucker Inn really been that bad? The grease. The noise. The rude customers. Ernie's flatulence. The peepholes poked through the wall from the men's room to the ladies' room that Ernie would "repair" by poking full of wet paper towels. The witty way Cheryl would shout, "Hey, Sheila! Drop another order of chicken tits in the fryer. This guy's no leg man." Watching her turn back and simper at some infatuated trucker while I tried to fix six orders at once. All of that had added up to make me believe there must be a better job somewhere.

Chicken tits. I pulled irritably at my seat belt. Resettled, I focused my eyes down the endless stretch of rainy afternoon freeway. So I had quit my job, to drive to New Mexico, where it was warmer and maybe there would be better work. That much made sense. But why had I chosen to take someone who thought "chicken tits" the epitome of humor? Why hadn't I realized that the same person would find counting squashed cats an exercise in higher mathematics?

"Hey, where are the Cheetos? I know we had nearly a full bag back here somewhere. You eat them while I was asleep?"

"No, Cheryl, I didn't eat your Cheetos." Nor your Ding-Dongs, Nerds, Twinkies, not even your Jalapeno and Sour Cream Flavored Pork Rinds. God only knew how I had resisted them, but I had.

She had twisted around and was hanging into the backseat, rummaging for food. I glanced over at her and saw only a pair of blue-jeaned cheeks. She continued to rustle papers and toss unwanted items to the floor. Reminded me of a black bear ransacking a garbage can.

"You sure you didn't eat my Cheetos?" she asked again, a small whine slinking into her voice. "'Cause remember, when we bought them, you said you didn't like them, and I said, 'Okay, I'll eat them, then,' and you said okay. Remember? 'Cause I don't think it's fair if you ate them like that, after you said you didn't like them. If you'd said you'd liked them, I woulda bought two bags and then there would have been enough for both of us. But you said you didn't . . ."

"Cheryl," I said in a level, reasonable voice. "I didn't eat your crummy Cheetos."

"Well, jeez, don't get all bent out of shape about it." She dived deeper into the wreckage in the backseat. "I just wanted to, you know, ask . . ." Her rear end pressed against the ceiling of the car. I wondered what passing motorists thought she was doing.

It was then that I saw the hitchhiker. He was carrying a backpack with a green sleeping bag strapped to the bottom of it, and his worn felt hat was dripping water off the brim. He wore old green fatigue pants and a red checked wool jacket and high-laced hiking boots. The hair that stuck out from under his hat was gray. He was hoofing along the side of the road, his querying thumb stuck out almost like an afterthought. I like that, when hitchhikers are walking while they hitch. I never pick up the ones who just stand there with their thumbs stuck out. They're too much like beggars. I like the ones who look like they're determined to get somewhere, whether you help or not. I hit the turn signal and tapped the brakes to get a station wagon off my bumper before I swerved to the shoulder of the road. Cheryl gave a squeal of distress.

"What are you doing?" she demanded, plopping back into her seat.

"Giving a guy a lift," I muttered.

A big grin was splitting his weathered old face as he jogged toward us. I was impressed. The guy had to be at least seventy. Gutty old man, hitching his way somewhere at that age.

"Well, you didn't even ask me! I don't think that's a good idea; I mean, all that stuff you read in the paper, he might have a knife or be an escaped convict or anything. Sheila, pull out quick before he gets here. I never pick up hitchhikers."

I ignored Cheryl, something I was getting better and better at doing. She folded her arms across her chest and started that huffy breathing she always did when she was pissed. Used to drive the truckers crazy, big boobs bobbling up and down like corks in a swell. Didn't bother me at all. By this time the hitchhiker was standing outside her door, but she wasn't moving. He grinned at me and tried the back door on her side of the car. It was locked, and she didn't move to unlock it. I unlocked the one on my side. He came around right away and opened the door and pushed Cheryl's junk over to make room for himself. He squished in with his backpack on his lap. As soon as he slammed the door, I pulled back onto the freeway. I glanced in the mirror, but all I could see was backpack and hat.

"So where you headed?" I asked. Cheryl was still huffing.

"Where you going?" he asked in return.

"New Mexico," I said, swerving slightly to miss some bloody fur on the road.

"Sounds good to me," he said.

Cheryl muttered, "That's the fifth squashed cat we've passed today."

"Actually, that looked more like a coon to me, missy. Didn't ya see that ratty kind of tail it had? More likely a coon. Dead cat, its tail don't look like that lessen it's been rained on a lot, and it hasn't rained all that much yet today. Besides, that one looked near fresh. Cat's tail don't look like that until it's been out there, oh, two, three days. Probably a coon. Dumb old thing. Nothing dumber than a roadkill."

About then I was thinking there were at least two things dumber than a roadkill. Possibly three, if you counted the person responsible for getting both of them into the same car.

"You see any Cheetos back there?" Cheryl asked him, her voice brightening. Nothing like shared interests for bringing people together. I heard the sounds of dedicated rummaging, and Cheryl turned, presenting cheeks once more. Great. Well, maybe they'd occupy each other and leave me alone.

"Here they are!" announced the old man, and handed her the bag after helping himself to a generous handful. Cheryl flopped back into her seat again and thrust the bag into my face.

"Here, Sheila, you want some?"

"No." I pushed her hand away and she sat back. The crackle of cellophane and the rhythmic grinding of teeth filled the car. "Why are you going to New Mexico?" I asked the old man. Anything to cover Cheryl's feeding sounds.

"Me? I thought you were going to New Mexico."

"Well, yeah, we are, but when you got in, I thought you said you were going to New Mexico too."

"No." The old man had a cheerful, hearty voice. Nothing old about the way he sounded. "No, I don't think I said that at all. I think I said, 'Sounds good to me.' That's what I said. And it does. New Mexico. 'Bout time those Mexicans got a fresh start somewhere. Maybe in New Mexico they'll do things a little better. Their biggest mistake, I always thought, was in having Mexico so close to Texas. Bound to be a bad influence. Glad they got a new place now."

I forced a chuckle at his humor and then glanced at the rearview mirror. His eyes were blue and calm as a summer sky. Not joking. I couldn't think of anything else to say.

"Hey. Hey, missy. Did you say that was the fifth dead cat you passed today?"

"Yeah. Only if that's a coon like you say, then it's only the fourth." Cheryl sounded disappointed.

"Yeah?" The old man sounded incredibly pleased. "Well, that's good, really, actually, that's good. Fifth dead cat you see is always the lucky one. When we get to number five, now, you just pull over and I'll show you a thing or two about a number five squashed cat. Thing most of you young folk don't know nothing about."

I really wished the radio was working. Maybe I'd check the fuse box at the next gas stop. Maybe it was only a blown fuse and there was an alternative to listening to a dialogue about dead cats.

"Why's it got to be a number five dead cat?" Cheryl was asking earnestly.

"Well, it just does, that's all. You can work it out any way you like. Crystals, pyramids, channeling, or tarot. No matter how you compute it, it always comes out to a number five dead cat. And if you don't believe me, just have your aura checked. Number five, every time." The old man chuckled happily. "Guess I'm just lucky, throwing in with you and having you folks be on cat number four already. Know how long it usually takes me to pass five dead cats on foot? Days, sometimes. Days! And an old man like me, it's hard for me to go days between number five squashed cats. Gimme a few more of them Cheetos things, missy."

Cheryl obligingly passed the bag back to him.

"Only fifty-two more miles to the California border," I observed brightly as my contribution to the conversation.

"There's some Kool-Aid Koolers back there in little boxes, if you want," Cheryl offered. "Would you pass me one, too?"

The Cheetos bag and a little waxed box of Kool-Aid were passed forward. Sensitive as I am, I realized they were ignoring me. Childish as I am, I felt piqued by it. "Wait a minute," I interrupted loudly. "How do you know which cat is the fifth one? Doesn't it all depend on when you start counting?"

"It sure does!" The old man was delighted. "And I'm real glad you saw it right off, like that. Only the fifth dead cat will work, and it all depends on when you decide to start counting them. Ain't that real Zen, now?"

I didn't think it was Zen any more than I thought it was tapioca pudding, but I didn't say so. The conversation lagged.

Cheryl jabbed her straw into the grape box, took a long gurgling sip, and suddenly choked.

"Omigod!" she exclaimed, pointing down the road. "What's that?"

"Something dead," I muttered, changing lanes.

The old man craned his head forward. "Cat for sure! Look's like a calico, but it might be a Persian with real good tire tracks. Hit the brakes, kid, this here's pay dirt!"

"You've got to be kidding," I said, not even easing up on the gas.

"Please. You've got to!" The old man's hand closed on my shoulder and squeezed like a vise as Cheryl began bouncing up and down on the seat, squealing, "Please! Please, Sheila? Please stop, I wanna see it. It'll only take a second. Come on, Sheila, be a sport!"

So I pulled off on the shoulder, more out of concern for my car's shocks than for any curiosity. Besides, it was the only way to get the old man's grip off my shoulder. I hate being touched by strangers. And the old man was definitely a stranger, and getting stranger all the time. Maybe if I stopped, I could leave him with his dead cat. I wished I could leave Cheryl, too, but she was paying half the gas and it was her cousin in New Mexico we were going to stay with until we got jobs. So I pulled my old Chevette over and cut the engine.

Cheryl and the old man were out before I got the car into Park. I leaned back in my seat. I wasn't getting out. I'd seen dead cats before. Their little mouths are always open, fangs bare, neat pink tongues curled, as if making a final snarl at death. I like animals. Seeing dead ones always gives me a sense of loss, of waste. Tiny little lives, flame bright and candle brief, snuffed out. Probably had been someone's pet.

I glanced in the rearview mirror and nearly gagged. The old man had found a piece of cardboard by the roadside and had coaxed most of the cat's body onto it. The hindquarters were dangling. Obviously everything in the cat's middle was crushed. He was using a stick to poke the rest of it onto his improvised stretcher. Cheryl trotted back to the car and jerked open a back door. Her eyes were wide, her face pink.

"Get in," I said softly. "And let's get the hell out of here. Just push his stuff out the door."

She reached in and grabbed his backpack and unstrapped the top flap. She dug into it, pulling out a single-burner hiker's stove, and then an aluminum pot.

"What are you doing?" I demanded. "Just drag the whole thing out."

"What? No. This is all we need. Oh, and Dougie says it would look better if you got out and acted like you were changing the tire or looking under the hood. Okay?"

She didn't wait for an answer, but stepped away from the car and nestled the stove down into the gravel of the ditch and set the pot on top of it. The car blocked the casual glances of passing motorists. "Cheryl!" I hissed, but she crouched down by the pot, not hearing me.

I opened my door just as a semi whooshed past. A gust of damp air sucked at me, and a horn blared aggressively. I staggered out in the wake, slamming the door behind me, and hurried around the car.

"What is going on?" I demanded, but I had a sick feeling I knew. Dougie was sliding the cat off the cardboard and into the pot. It didn't quite fit, so he bent it in half and tamped it down with the stick.

"Now we need the canteen of water," he announced, and they both looked up at me like I was supposed to bring it.

"This is sick," I told them. "And I'm leaving."

"Sheila!" Cheryl whiningly protested, even as Dougie asked her, "Well, what's the matter with her?"

I got back in the car and slammed the door. Cheryl opened the door and leaned in. "You can climb in and go with me," I told her. "Or you can pull your stuff out and stay here. But I'm leaving."

"Sheila, why? What's the matter with you?" She looked genuinely perplexed.

"Look. I'm not sticking around while you two barbecue a roadkill. It's disgusting."

"Oh, Sheila!" Cheryl started laughing. She reached over the seat and fished a canteen out of the old man's pack. "We aren't barbecuing anything, silly."

"Then what are you doing?"

"Just boiling it down," she said reasonably. "Dougie says we boil it down to the bones. Then there's this one certain bone, and you put it under your tongue and . . ."

"Oh, gross!"

"It confers perfect health and vitality upon you. Dougie says that's all he does anymore. He used to work for a living, go after that old paycheck, slave away for somebody, just to keep body and soul together. But no more. All he has to do now is hike along the road until he gets to a fifth squashed cat, boil it down, and put the bone under his tongue. Easy. And his life is his own."

Her cheeks were flushed with more than the wind that was blowing her hair across her face. Her blue eyes sparked through the net of her hair. *Oh, you True Believer, you!*

"That's stupid," I told her bluntly.

"Oh, Sheila, don't you ever try anything new? Look, it's only going to take a minute or two. Come on. Have an open mind."

I looked at her, unable to believe what I was hearing.

"In the interests of science," she added, as a finishing touch. She spun away from the car, leaving the door open. As I leaned across the seat to reach the handle, I saw her dumping water onto the cat in the pot. Yes. It had been a Persian with good tire tracks. Gotta give it to the man, he sure knew his roadkills. Dougie dug in his jacket pocket and came out with one of those camp knives that unfold a spoon at one end and a fork at the other. He prized the spoon out and began poking the cat down into the pot with it. That did it.

"Cheryl. I'm leaving. Either get in or get your stuff out of my car. You, too, Dougie."

They glanced over at me, then back at their cat. It was gently steaming now, and the smell of simmering cat blended with the smell of rainy freeway. Dougie spoke, but not to me. "For me, it's the fifth neck bone down from the head bone. Now, I don't know what one it's gonna be for you. Too bad you never had your aura done with a crystal, so's you'd know. But what we can do, Miss Cheryl, is just try the bones one at a time, keeping track of which one is which, until we get the right one. Okay?"

I slammed the door on it. Damn, I was mad. Furious. Because they knew, both of them, that my threats were empty. They weren't even worried. I am not the kind of person who can drive off and leave two people stranded on a freeway, even if they're sautéing a dead Persian. Because I'm a sucker. A wimp. I closed my eyes and worked on my anger. Remember the time I asked Cheryl to quit calling back orders for chicken tits? Remember how she smiled at the trucker and said that it was the girls with little tits who got offended about tit jokes, because they didn't have anything to laugh about? Remember the night her drunk boyfriend threw up all over the men's room and I had to clean it up because she had to drive him home and none of the guys would touch it and Ernie was coming in any second? Remember that I am almost sure she's the one who snitched all my tips out of the coffee mug I was keeping them in?

Remember that she's the one who has a cousin in New Mexico for me to stay with while I job-hunt?

So I heaved out a big sigh and lolled my head back on the headrest and looked at the ceiling. I have always been a spineless wimp. And I think I give off some signal that attracts people who prey on spineless wimps. I despised myself. And I despised those assholes out there boiling their cat. Cretins. But then, I thought, *Oh, well, what the hell,* and slid to the passenger seat and watched. It couldn't be any worse than what I was imagining.

It was raining in a misty, invisible way. Damp made a sheen on Dougie's wool jacket and jeweled Cheryl's hair. They were hunkered down beside the pot in cheerfully primeval companionship. The cat had softened and sunk into the pot. Maybe it had been dead longer than I thought. Dougie kept poking at it with his spoon and nodding approvingly. He noticed me watching them and waved the spoon at me and said something. Cheryl laughed. A few minutes later she got up and came back to the car. She opened the door, letting in rain and cat steam.

"Dougie says he's not offended or anything. Come on over and he'll figure out which cat bone is right for you."

Like Mommy tapping at your bedroom door and saying, "Okay, you can come down to dinner now if you promise to behave and not call your brother 'snotnose' anymore." Same answer to both.

"No. Thanks."

"Suit yourself, then." She turned and went back to her stewpot, leaving the door open. She whispered to Dougie and he shrugged elaborately. They ignored me assiduously.

She'd make someone a great mommy someday. *Now, Priscilla, don't sulk in your room. Come down to the family room and suck on your kitty bone like a good girl.* What a crock!

I slid out of the car to stretch my legs. The afternoon was fading. We could have been in California by now. Unremarkable stretch of freeway. Pavement, gravel shoulder, chain-link fence, nondescript woods beyond it. Cretins stewing a cat.

"There now! See how that's falling apart. I think she's ready. Now, you hold that cardboard steady."

I turned involuntarily as they fished out the cat. Soggy, steaming fur slipping off gray boiled meat that was sliding off bones. Dougie burned his fingers as he arranged it on the cardboard. It was falling apart, legs going different ways, the trailing guts swollen shiny.

"Usually I ain't so careful," Dougie exclaimed as he laid his patient out. "Usually I just count down from the head bone. But we gotta be careful until we find out what bone is right for you. And for your friend there." He tipped his head at me, but his eyes never left the stewed kitty. I folded my arms and watched from a distance.

"Hope you don't mind I go first, Missy Cheryl. I'm an old man, and it's been two days since my last fifth cat. My Vital Essences need recharging bad." The blade of his camp knife lifted the cat's neck and spine free of the clinging meat. I stepped closer to watch. He counted and coaxed free one tiny spinal bone. A gobbet of cord dangled from it when he picked it up in his thick fingers. He popped it into his mouth.

He closed his eyes, rocked back on his heels, and glowed. Glowed like a jack-o'-lantern with a candle inside it. The light outlined the bones of his skull, glowing redly through his nose and eye sockets, showing his teeth against his cheeks. Cheryl gazed at him raptly. I stumbled back until I felt the chain-link highway fence cold against my back.

The glow faded as slowly as embers being masked by ash. Dougie smiled and opened his eyes. He looked more like forty than seventy. My heart was hammering in my chest and the skin of my face went hot with blood. But I wasn't scared, or even awestruck. I was furious.

See, I'd never respected people who hung crystals from their rearview mirrors and suspended pyramids over their beds and read their horoscopes every day. I laughed at their ignorant hope that they could get through life that way. I respected people who knew the world was real and lumpy, and that you had to make your own way in it, not look for some mystical shortcut. Practical, realistic people who worked hard and bettered themselves with education and saved money for the future. People like me.

I was angry at the monstrous unfairness of it. It worked. It was real. But the whole thing was too damn easy. It wasn't fair for anything in life to be that easy, for anyone. I didn't want it to be real, and I was pissed off that it was. It's tough to find out you're wrong about something as basic as that.

Cheryl's eyes were wide. "What happened to the bone?"

"Gone," he told her, and opened his mouth wide to show her. She craned her head to peer into his mouth.

"So it is!" she exclaimed delightedly. "Okay. Now me. How do I start?"

"Well, let's just start with the tip of the tail and work forward from there. May take us a while, Missy Cheryl. These cats gotta lotta bones, specially when you get down to all their little toesie bones and such. Let's hope it ain't the head bone. Be awful hard to get that under your tongue."

They laughed together over their feline box social. The mesh fence was cold against my fingers. I let go of it, crept closer. Dougie was neatly laying the tail open, lifting the thread of bones out skillfully. He set it carefully on the grubby piece of cardboard. The tip of his knife blade freed the end one. "Here ya go," he said, picking it up. "Number one tailbone. Now we gotta keep track, unless you wanna try every bone in every number five cat you ever use. So pay attention. Just pop this under your tongue. If it takes, you'll know. If not, just pass it on to your friend there. Maybe it'll be the right one for her."

"Well, come on, Sheila, don't just stand there! This is gonna be fun!" Cheryl waved me over excitedly, then opened her mouth to receive the first bone from Dougie's grubby fingers.

I swallowed as I watched her take it like she was receiving communion. She shut her eyes and rocked back on her heels. After a few seconds she opened them. "Nothing," she said matter-of-factly, and reached fingers into her mouth to fish out the bone. "Here, Sheila." She held it out to me.

"No." I crossed my arms on my chest.

"Yes," she said simply. "You have to believe it. It works. You saw it. You'd be crazy not to try it."

"It's not that." My skepticism was hanging in tatters. No hiding behind that. "It's sick. The whole idea of spending your life that way. What are you going to do, Cheryl? Go hiking down freeways forever, sucking on the tailbones of every fifth squashed cat? Is that what life is going to be for you?"

"You're making it out a bit bare, missy," Dougie interceded. "It ain't all asphalt and exhaust, it ain't even all freeways. A lot of time it's backcountry roads, with the birches turning gold along the shoulders, or bare white stretches of snowy highway in Utah, or the hilly streets of San Francisco. I mean, squashed cats are everywhere. Crisscrossed this country ten or more times; seen a lot of Canada and Mexico, too. I've had blue-sky days and thunderstorm nights; I've waited out hailstorms under overpasses and slept in deep sweet-smelling hayfields under harvest moons. My time belongs to me. I get lonely, I hitch a little. Sure, I get a little cold, I get a little wet. But as long as I get my number five cat bone, I don't get old. Don't get tired, don't get sick. It may not be a fancy-dancy way to live. But it ain't a bad life, and you got no right to go scaring Missy Cheryl away from it."

Cheryl's chin had come up. She looked me straight in the eye and spoke with a dignity I'd never known she possessed. "No one's scaring me away from this. You and me, Sheila, we worked a few months together. You think you know all about me. But it's me who knows about you. I seen how you are. You're looking. You believe you're gonna end up doing something better. Being something better than I'll ever be. Well, maybe you will. But I won't. I know that. I've seen myself in every truck stop we passed. All those old waitresses, swollen ankles and big behinds. Still getting pinched by the truckers, still putting out cups of coffee for guys who don't tip. That's as good as it's ever going to get for me. And frankly, this looks better."

She set the rejected bone down on the dusty cardboard and took the next one from Dougie's fingers.

A curious embarrassment overtook me. I'd always known I was smarter than Cheryl. No. Smarter's not the right word for it. But the world's a different place for me. I've known hundreds of girls like her. Guys, too. High school was full of them, and all the seedy little jobs I'd taken since screwing up my college had put me right alongside them. The biggest dream the guys ever have is, like, rebuilding the '66 Thunderbird that's rusting behind Uncle Joe's shed. For the girls, it's always something to do with a guy. A handsomer guy, a richer guy, a sexier guy. The biggest change they ever make is going on a diet or dyeing their hair. I had plans and dreams they didn't understand. I'd always felt both pity and scorn for them. What I'd never realized was that Cheryl had known, all this time, that my future was brighter than hers, that the things that would work for me would crumble to pieces in her hands. She had always known it and lived with my secret scorn for her shopworn hopes and generic dreams.

What Cheryl was doing right now, placing the second bone under her tongue, took a sort of grubby courage. She was reaching for something a little better than she believed she was entitled to. And I, who had always believed that when my chance came, I would boldly seize it, I was hugging myself with cold hands, shivering in the gliding caress of the raindrops sliding down my arms.

Wimp out.

So I stepped into their magic circle and picked up the bone that Cheryl had discarded. It was warm from the pot and slick with her saliva, but I slipped it under my tongue and waited. Nothing. I set it aside and reached for the next one. Nothing. Now she was waiting for me, and I took the bone she fished out from under her tongue and put it under my own. Nothing. But there was an excitement building, an electrical current jumping and sparking from Dougie to Cheryl to me and yes, to the dead cat, and around again. A mystic togetherness that was warm and friendly. We three would soon be free of the world's bonds. Another bone. Nothing. We would walk with our heads bare under the bright blue skies of autumn, the scent of falling leaves blowing past us. Another bone. Spring would sprout about our feet. We'd see the Grand Canyon, hike across Death Valley. Nothing. Another bone. The snows of winter might chill us, but the ways of man, of jobs and money and petty rules, would no longer bind us. Nothing. True freedom to see the world with eyes uncluttered by schedules and obligations. Like the old gods, like fey folk. Another bone.

We were about halfway through the cat, going down the ribs, when Cheryl lit up. Twice as bright as Dougie, like a blast furnace. I felt the warmth radiate from her body before I even turned my head to see her transfigurement. She had a halo like a catechism saint. The brassy blondness burned out of her hair, and it went a rich mahogany. Her complexion cleared as if her body were casting off all impurities. I stared at her as the glow gradually faded. I crouched long moments in the rain, blinking the drops from my lashes, waiting for the last light to fade from her face before I realized it wasn't going to. That new light would stay, a vitality burning inside her, giving off the same aura of health and determination that had made me stop and pick Dougie up. She smiled, and it was like someone pulling up the blinds to let in a sunny day. I felt blessed.

"Well, go on," she told me, and it took an instant for me to realize what she was talking about.

"That there was the sixth rib on the left side, Missy Cheryl. You're going to want to remember that now."

Cheryl smiled her beatific smile and gestured toward me. Dougie passed me the next bone. We worked slowly through the rest of the ribs. I felt a shiver of excitement as we started down the left front leg. Soon. Only the leg bones left. Cheryl and I exchanged a smile as I started on the right front leg. Soon now. She was watching me closely, waiting for it. She reminded me of a lover I had who always tried to look at my face during orgasm. It seemed a very personal thing, but I wasn't bothered by it. Cheryl and Dougie and I would soon share a very unique bond. I didn't mind her witnessing my initiation.

The left hind leg. Dougie was handing me the bones more slowly now, and I held each under my tongue a few seconds longer, just to be sure. As I took the first bone of the right hind leg under my tongue, my heart began hammering against my ribs. I felt heat rise in my face. For a moment I thought this was it, but it was only my building excitement. "Come on, come on!" Cheryl was chanting as I continued down the leg bones, the fine thin bones of the leg, and then the smaller, knuckly bones of the foot and toes, and then . . .

There were no more bones.

I stared in disbelief as Dougie dropped the last remnant of boneless cat onto the heap of discarded fur, meat, and entrails. It still steamed faintly in the fading afternoon light.

"What happened?" I asked groggily. I felt as if I were just coming to after a faint. The blackened burner of the camp stove, the scorched pot, the slithered flat cat remnants, the mounded bones on the road, dusty cardboard. It was like a videocassette tape snapping, or sex suddenly interrupted. I couldn't grasp what had happened. Dougie looked like a man who had suddenly lost his erection just before his partner climaxed. "What happened?" I demanded again. "What went wrong?"

"Ain't gonna work for her," Dougie announced, and turned away.

"What do you mean?" I cried out, and Cheryl asked, "How come?"

Dougie jerked open the car door and started dragging his stuff out. "Look at her," he said gruffly. "She's not like us. I shoulda seen it. Bones don't work for someone like her."

I swung my gaze to Cheryl. I tried to meet her eyes, but her look roved over me, summing me up. "I see," she said slowly.

I looked back to Dougie. I felt like the family pet at the moment when the car door swings open on the country road and Bubby pushes you firmly out. Dumped. Cheryl stood up, took the kettle, and emptied out the liquor of cat.

"Wait a minute," I said as she handed Dougie the empty kettle. "I probably just missed a bone. Just missed it, that's all." I grabbed one at random, slipped it under my tongue. Nothing. Go on to the next one.

"Nope." Dougie's voice was final as he picked up the camp stove. "Don't work for people like you. And you knowed it all along."

"No!" I wailed around a mouthful of ribs. I spat them out,

grabbed another handful of tiny bones, and shoved them into my mouth. "Wait," I choked as I struggled to get my tongue over them. "Eweul see."

"What'd she say?" Cheryl asked Dougie.

"I don't know. Who cares? Now look, missy, you can't take all this stuff. You got like a pack or something?"

"I got a pillowcase," Cheryl said brightly. She dug through the back of the car, came up with her pillow. "And a sleeping bag."

"Well, good. Now that's real good. Dump out the pillow, 'cause you ain't gonna need that. Keep the sleeping bag. Now, in the pillowcase, you put a change of clothes, a comb, that sort of thing. Nothing much, 'cause you ain't gonna need much no more. No, forget makeup, you're prettier without it. Sure, take the Cheetos. Not that we'll be hungry, but snacking's fun as we walk along. Now let me tie it up for you."

The bones were wet with rain, and grit from the cardboard clung to them. I calmed myself, forced myself to do one bone at a time. They'd see. Any minute now, they'd see. As I watched them hike away, I thought how I'd jump and shout and they'd look back to see me glowing like a torch, brighter than either of them, burning like a bonfire. I'd show them. The rain pelted down faster. It grew harder to see them through the dusk and falling water. It didn't matter. I had the car, I'd catch up with them. I picked up the next bone.

I don't know how many times I went through the bones. I stopped when blue and white lights started flashing before my eyes, wondering if I'd hit it. A blaze of white light hit my face and blinded me, and a cop asked, "You okay, miss? I saw your dome light on and stopped. You sick or something?"

He took his flashlight beam off my face as I staggered upright and leaned against my car. I'd never closed the door, and the dome light inside was still burning. Cheryl's stuff was spilled half out of the car. I told him something about the stuff in my backseat falling over so I stopped to rearrange it. He couldn't have believed it, not with my clothes soaked to my body and my hair dripping down my back. He played his light over the deboned cat while I stuffed everything back into the car. Probably decided he didn't want to know what was going on. He stayed behind me while I got my car started again and watched me pull out onto the freeway before he spun off the gravel shoulder and passed me in a flicker of headlights.

I drove on, not going anywhere special now, just counting the cats. I never saw Dougie or Cheryl again, but I did once find another stewed cat by the side of the road. I gathered up what was left of it and took it to a motel that night. I tried every bone. Probably two or three times. Nothing.

I never got to New Mexico, either. I stopped off in San Rafael, to live between my car and the women's shelter there until I found a computer firm that would hire me.

They're paying me to go to night school now, and I know that things are getting better for me. If I study hard and pay attention to my job and get along with my coworkers, I'll get ahead. If I work at it.

There are still times when I think about it. Sometimes, when I'm lying in bed, semiawake after a restless night, waiting for my alarm clock to go off, I think of them, rising from a peaceful night in some dewy field, glowing with health, to start their daily trek down the highways and byways of America. No clocks to punch. No classes to study for. Nothing to do but hike down the road in the fresh morning air, looking for that fifth squashed cat. That's what works for them. And what works for me is getting up at five to leave the house at six so I can fight traffic and get to work by eight. Who's to say which way is better? Who's to say who has the better life? But sometimes, on those mornings when

I wonder, I step out of my door early, at five thirty, into the fresh morning air. I look at the wide blue sky, at the sun just opening the day. And I get into my car and drive slowly and carefully to work.

I wouldn't want to hit someone's cat by accident.

Strays

Theme anthologies are gold mines for some writers. Give them a topic, and they can write a story around it. Cat story, horse story, a story about a magician with a sword, a haunted house story, a story about a mermaid . . . And oh, how I envy those writers.

I just can't do it.

Lord knows I've tried. But it's sort of like the fable about the emperor who would give his fortune to the man who could look at a white horse and not think about its tail, but in reverse. The more someone gives me a theme, the more those stories elude me.

But once in a great while, I still manage to wriggle and wrangle a story into a theme anthology. "Strays" is a tale like that. I was approached by Elizabeth Ann Scarborough, a longtime friend and fellow writer. She was editing an anthology to be called Warrior Princesses. *Surely, as a fantasy writer, I could come up with a story that had such a character.*

Well. No. Or rather, yes and no. I was working on a story. And with a touch or two, perhaps I could convey a bit of royalty to my protagonist.

And once I did, I perceived that she'd actually been a princess all the time. For every female cat is a queen.

Lonnie Spencer looked like a boy. She sat on a rusty bike, one foot on the curb, the toe of her other ratty sneaker in the gutter. She had scabby knees, a smoking skull on her baggy sweatshirt, and a baseball hat backward over her chopped black hair. *What's wrong with that kid's face?* was my second thought when I saw her. My first had been to avoid him because he looked like he'd kick gutter water at you just to get it on your school clothes.

As I edged past, she spoke in a clear girl's voice, "Take a picture, it'll last longer."

I had been staring. I'd never seen anyone my own age with a big scar down her face. It ridged her Native American skin, pulling her cheek and her eye to one side. It was hard not to stare. So I looked down and saw the Barbie doll lashed to the front of her bike. It had a fur skirt and one boob. Her clumpy hair was tied back with gold thread. A tiny wooden bow was slung over her shoulder.

"Amazon," I said without thinking.

"Yeah!" Lonnie grinned and suddenly didn't look so scary. "She's an Amazon warrior. That's why I cut off her tit. So she can shoot a bow better. I read that they really did that."

"I know. I read about it too."

Our eyes met. Connection. We both read, and we read weird stuff, stuff about women who were warriors. It's so simple, when you're a kid.

In her next breath, Lonnie announced, "I'm a warrior too. I been teaching myself martial arts. Ninja stuff, swords and pikes, too. I want to learn to shoot a bow. Scars are okay, on a warrior. Hey. My name's Lonnie Spencer." She stuck out a grubby hand. She had a boy's way of doing things. "What's yours?"

Her hand was scratchy, scabs and dirt and dry skin. "Mandy Curtis."

"Mandy, huh. Bet you get teased a lot about that in school.

Handy Mandy. I hate school. All the teachers hate me and the kids tease me all the time. 'Cause of my scars, you know, and because I don't dress like they do. They think if you don't have the right kind of clothes, you're nothing. Lower than shit."

Her words spilled forth. I sensed she needed to talk but didn't find many listeners. I'm a listener, like my mom. She says it's our curse, to have total strangers tell us their darkest secrets. I glanced at Lonnie again. Not many of the girls I'd met at school would want to be seen talking to her. My clothes were a lot better than hers were and I was still having trouble making friends.

I kept walking. I was supposed to come straight home from school every day. We were new to this neighborhood and Mom was jumpy. Our building was okay, but two blocks away was a commercial strip, and the apartments that bordered it attracted what Mom called "a rougher element." Mom had never defined that but I looked at Lonnie and knew. She coasted her bike alongside in the gutter as I walked. "I didn't get my scars in a fight, though," she volunteered abruptly. "My mom threw me through a picture window when I was two. She was pretty drunk and I was fussy. That's what she says, anyway. Cut up my face and cut my leg muscles, too." She watched for my reaction. Her words challenged me. "That's why I limp when I walk. They had to put over a hundred and seven stitches in me. After that, they put me in a foster home, until my grandma came and got me. Now Mom has me."

Kids ask the questions that adults swallow. "Why do you want to live with someone who threw you through a window?"

Lonnie lifted one shoulder. "Well, you know, she's my mom. She went to counseling. And the court says it's okay, and Grandma is getting pretty old. So." Again the one-shoulder shrug.

So. That could sum up a lot of Lonnie Spencer. So.

The conversation lagged awkwardly. Mom wouldn't want me hanging around with Lonnie. I knew it. I think Lonnie knew it too. But I was as desperately lonely as she was. "You go to Mason School?" I asked her, just as she exclaimed, "Oh, no! Not Scruffy, oh, man . . ."

She hopped off her bike, letting it clatter into the gutter. Without a look at me she hurried to a sodden calico body at the edge of the street. I followed her, reluctant but curious. Lonnie crouched close over it; I stayed back. The cat's mouth was open, white teeth and a sprawling tongue. I wouldn't have touched that sunken body with a stick, but Lonnie stroked it, smoothing its soggy fur.

"I hope his next eight lives are better than this one was," she said quietly.

"You really believe a cat has nine lives?"

"Sure. Why not? One old lady, a foster mom, she told me if a cat really likes you, it can give you one of its lives. Wouldn't that be something? Get to live a cat's life?"

I looked at the dead cat. "Doesn't look like he enjoyed it much," I pointed out.

"I can think of worse lives than being a stray cat," she said darkly as she unslung her backpack. She pulled out a can of neon orange spray paint. The balls inside it rattled like dice as she shook it. Then she outlined the cat's body, meticulously tracing each leg and the tail, even the jab of an ear against the pavement. She surveyed her work, then capped the paint and put it away. Without squeamishness, she picked up the little body and moved it to the grassy strip between the sidewalk and the street. The orange outline of the body remained on the pavement, a grim reminder. I was speechless.

Lonnie wiped her hands self-consciously down her shirt. "I don't think people should just hit a cat and forget it," she said quietly. "This way, whoever hit that cat has to look at that outline every time they drive past. I put the bodies up off the street and some city guy comes and picks them up instead of the next fifty cars making him mush."

"Do you think we should try to find his owner?" I asked in a hushed voice. In a macabre way, I relished the idea of being the bearer of such sad tidings.

"Naw," Lonnie said dismissively. She looked down at the dead cat with bitterness. "Scruffy didn't belong to anyone except himself. A stray disappears, no one wonders about it." She shrugged into her backpack. As she picked her bike out of the gutter, she added, "I figure it's something I owe them, in a way. My loyal subjects should not be left dead in the street. I done all I can for him, now . . ."

"Your loyal subjects?" I asked skeptically. Being weird is okay unless it's fake-weird. A lot of kids pretend to be weird just to impress other people. I wondered about Lonnie. Maybe even her scar story was fake, maybe she'd just been in a bad car wreck.

She gave her shrug again. "I'm Queen of the Strays. Even my mom says so. Which reminds me, I'm supposed to be picking up some junk for my mom. See you around."

She was already pedaling down the street. When she hit puddles, muddy water rooster-tailed up her back, but she didn't avoid them. Fluorescent cats and a one-boobed Barbie. Genuinely weird, I decided. I liked her. "Yeah, see you," I called after her.

I got home just as the rain resumed. I called Mom's office and left a message on her voice mail that I was safely home. I dumped my books in my room and went to the kitchen. Not much in the fridge. There used to be little microwave pizzas or pudding cups when Mom and Dad were together. Not that we're starving now, just on a budget. I grabbed an apple and some cheese. Then I watched television and did homework until Mom got home. I forgot about Lonnie until late that night. I thought about rain soaking the cat's body and hoped someone had picked it up. Then I thought about all the live strays, shivering in the rain. Lonnie was Queen of the Strays. I wondered what she had meant and then I fell asleep.

Three weeks passed. I didn't see Lonnie. I watched for her, in the lunchroom at school or when I saw kids on bikes in the street, but I never saw her. Then one day, walking home from school, I found two outlines of dead cats in the street. The paint was bright and fresh.

I had reached the front of our apartment building and was fishing my key out of my shirt when Lonnie yelled to me from down the block. I waved back and she came in a lopsided run. She favored her right leg. As she came, I realized that her whole body twisted that direction. It hadn't been so obvious when she was on her bike.

"Hey, Mandy," she greeted me.

I was surprised at how glad I was to see her. "Hey, Lonnie! Long time, no see. Where's your bike?"

She shrugged. "Got stole. My mom left it out and someone took it while I was gone. She didn't even notice until I asked her where it went. So." She paused, then changed the subject. "Hey. Look what I made." She pulled a little drawstring bag out of her shirt. It was hanging around her neck on a string. "This is my new, uh, whatacallit, omelette."

"Amulet," I said reflexively.

She tugged the bag open. Inside was a little princess doll from a McDonald's Happy Meal. Like the Barbie, it was missing a boob. As it was dressed in a ball gown, it looked very peculiar. Lonnie shrugged at my frown. "It doesn't look as good as the other one."

I changed the subject. "So. Where were you, then?"

She shrugged again as she replaced her amulet. "CPS came and got me, 'cause I missed so much school. They stuck me in a foster home, but they couldn't make me go to school either. So now I got a deal with my social worker. She lets me live with my mom, I stay out of trouble and go to school."

"I didn't see you at school today," I pointed out. "If you live around here, you should go to Mason."

"Yeah, I *should,*" she conceded sarcastically. "But even when I'm there, you wouldn't see me. I'm in the special-ed classes at the end of the hall."

"But you're not retarded!" I protested.

"Special ed isn't all retarded. There's deaf kids. And ADD. Hyperactive. Emotionally disturbed. They got lots of names for us troublemakers. They just shove us together and forget about us."

"Oh," I said lamely.

"I don't care." She smiled and wagged her head to show how little it bothered her. "Mostly I just read all day. They don't bother me, I don't give them any grief."

"Well." I glanced up at the sky. "I've got to go in. I have to call my mom as soon as I get home from school."

"Oh, latchkey kid, huh?" She watched me stick my key in the security door. "Well, after that, do you want to hang out?"

I stopped. "I'm not supposed to have friends in when Mom isn't home," I said awkwardly. I hated saying it. I was sure she'd take it as an excuse to ditch her.

"So who's going to tell?" she demanded with a superior look. I quailed before it. Knowing I was going to regret this, knowing I'd have to tell my mom later, I unlocked the door and let her in ahead of me.

Our apartment was on the third floor. I was painfully conscious of Lonnie limping up the stairs. There was an elevator at the other end of the building but I'd never used it. I felt almost ashamed that my body was sound and whole and that the climb didn't bother me. As I unlocked my door, I automatically said, "Wipe your feet."

"Du-uh!" Lonnie retorted sarcastically. She walked in just like a stray cat, with that sort of wiggle that says they're doing you a favor to come in. She stopped in the middle of our living room. For an instant, the envy on her face was so intense it was almost hatred. Then she gave her shrug. "Nice place," she said neutrally. "Got anything to eat?"

"In the kitchen. I've got to phone Mom."

While I left my message, Lonnie went through the refrigerator. By the time I got off the phone, she had eaten an apple, drunk a big glass of milk and poured herself a second one, and taken out the bread and margarine. "Want a sandwich?" she asked as I turned around.

"I hate peanut butter and that's all there is," I said stiffly. I'd never seen anyone go through a refrigerator so fast. Especially someone else's refrigerator.

"There's sugar," she said, spreading margarine thickly on two slices of bread. "Ever had a sugar sandwich? Mom used to give them to me all the time."

"That's gross," I said as she picked up the sugar bowl and dumped sugar on the bread. She pushed it out in a thick layer, capped it with the other piece of buttered bread. When she lifted it, sugar dribbled out around the edges. Her teeth crunched in the thick layer of sugar. I winced. I imagined her teeth melting away inside her mouth.

"You ought to try it," she told me through a mouthful. She washed it down with half the glass of milk, sighed, and took another sandy bite.

As she drained off the milk, I suddenly knew that Lonnie had been really hungry. Not after-school snack hungry, but really hungry. I had seen the billboards about Americans going to bed hungry, but I never grasped it until I watched Lonnie eat. It scared me. I suddenly wanted her out of our house. It wasn't all the food she had eaten or the sugar mess on the floor. It suddenly seemed that by living near people like Lonnie and having her inside our house, Mom and I had gotten closer to some invisible edge. First there had been the real family and home, Mom and Dad and I in a house with a yard and Pop-Tarts and potato chips in the kitchen. Then there was Mom and I in an apartment, no yard, toast and jam instead of Pop-Tarts . . . We were safe right now, as long as Dad sent the support money, as long as Mom kept her job, but right down the street there were people who lived in cruddy apartments and their kids were in special ed and were hungry. That was scary. Mom and I weren't people like that. We'd never be people like that. Unless . . .

"Let's go hang out," I said to her. I didn't even put her glass in the dishwasher or sweep up the sugar. Instead, I took a pack of graham crackers out of the cupboard. I opened it as we walked to the door. She followed me, just like a hungry stray.

I felt safer as soon as I shut the door behind us. But now I was stuck outside with her on a cold and windy day. "Want to go to the library?" I offered. It was one of the few places Mom had approved for me to hang out on my own. Even then, I was supposed to say I was going there and phone again when I got back.

"Naw," Lonnie said. She took the package of graham crackers, shook out three, and handed the stack back to me. "I have to pick up some junk for my mom. But we can do my route before that. Come on."

I thought maybe she had a paper route. Instead it was her roadkill route. Lonnie patrolled for animal bodies. The only thing she found that day was a dead crow in the gutter. It had been there awhile, but she still painted around it and then moved the body reverently up onto the grassy strip. After that, we stopped at two Dumpsters, one behind Burger King and the other behind Kentucky Fried Chicken. They had concrete block enclosures and bushes around their Dumpsters. There was even a locked gate on Kentucky Fried Chicken's, but it didn't stop Lonnie. She made a big deal of waiting until no one was around before we crept up on them. "Warrior practice," she whispered. "We could get arrested for this. You keep watch."

So I stood guard while she went Dumpster diving. She emerged smelling like grease with bags full of chicken bones and half-eaten biscuits and a couple cartons of gravy. It amazed me how fast she filled up bags with stuff other people had thrown away. At Burger King, she got parts of hamburgers and fries. "What are you going to do with that stuff?" I asked Lonnie as we walked away. I was half afraid she'd say that she and her mom were going to eat it for dinner.

"Just wait. I'll show you," she promised. She grinned when she said it, like she was proud of what she carried.

"I've got to get home soon," I told her. "Mom sometimes calls me back and I didn't say I was going out. I'm supposed to be doing homework."

"Don't sweat it, sister. This won't take long, and I really want you to see it. Come on." She lurched along faster.

She lived on the other side of the main road and back two blocks off the strip. The sun goes down early in October. Lights were on inside the apartments. The building sign said Oakview Manor, but there were no oaks, no trees at all. Some boys were hanging out in the littered parking lot behind the building, smoking cigarettes and perching cool on top of a junk car. One called out as we walked by, "Hey, baby, wanna suck my weenie?" I was grossed out, but Lonnie acted like he didn't exist. The boys laughed behind us, and one said something about "Scarface." She kept walking, so I did too.

At the other end of the parking lot, three battered Dumpsters stank in a row. Beyond them was a vacant lot full of blackberry brambles and junk. Old tires and part of a chair stuck out of the brambles. The frame of a junk pickup truck was just visible through the sagging, wet vines. Lonnie sat down on the damp curb and tore open the bags. She spread the food out like it was a picnic, tearing the chicken and burgers to pieces with her fingers and then breaking up the biscuits on top of a bag and dumping the congealed gravy out on them. "For the little ones," she told me quietly. She looked around at the bushes expectantly, then frowned. "Stand back. They're shy of everyone but me."

I backed up. I had guessed it would be cats and I was right. What was shocking was how many. "Kitty, kitty," Lonnie called. Not loudly. But here came cats of every color and size and age, tattered veterans with ragged ears and sticky-eyed kittens trailing after their mothers. Blacks and calicoes, long-haired cats so matted they looked like dirty bath mats, and an elegant Siamese with only one ear emerged from that briar patch. An orange momma cat and her three black-and-white babies came singing. They converged on Lonnie and the food, crowding until they looked like a patchwork quilt of cat fur.

They were not delicate eaters. They made smacky noises and kitty *ummm* noises. They crunched bones and lapped gravy noisily. There were warning rumbles as felines jockeyed for position, but surprisingly little outright snarling or smacking. Instead, the overwhelming sound was purring.

Lonnie enthroned on the curb in the midst of her loyal subjects smiled down upon them. She judiciously moved round-bellied kittens to one side to let newcomers have a chance at the gravy and biscuits. As she reached down among the cats, the older felines offered her homage and fealty, pausing in their dining to rub their heads along her arms. Some even stood upright on their hind legs to embrace her. As the food diminished, I thought the cats would leave. Instead they simply turned more attention upon Lonnie. Her lap filled up with squirming kittens, while others clawed pleadingly at her legs. A huge orange tom suddenly leaped up to land as softly as a falling leaf on her shoulders. He draped himself there like a royal mantle, and his huge rusty purr vibrated the air. Lonnie preened. Pleasure and pride transformed her face. "See," she called to me. "Queen of the Strays. I told you." She opened her arms wide to indicate her swarm, and cats instantly reared up to bump their heads against her outstretched hands.

"Oh, yeah? Well, you're gonna be Queen of the Ass-Kicked if you don't get up here with my stuff!" The voice came from a third-floor window. To someone in the room behind him, the man said, "Stupid little cunt is down there fucking around with those cats again."

The light went out of Lonnie's face. She stared up at him. He glared back. He was a young man with dark, curly hair, his T-shirt tight on his muscular chest. A woman walked by behind him. I looked back at Lonnie. She had a sickly smile. With a pretense of brightness in her voice she called up, "Hey, Carl! Tell Mom to look out here, she should see all my cats!"

Carl's face darkened. "Your mom don't got time for that shit, and neither do you! Stupid fucking cats. No, don't you encourage . . ." He turned from the window, drawing back a fist at someone and speaking angrily. Lonnie's mom, I thought. He was threatening Lonnie's mom. We couldn't hear what he said. Lonnie stared up at the window, not with fear, but something darker. Carl leaned out again. "Get up here with my stuff!"

Lonnie stood up, the cats melting away around her, trickling away into the shadows. A lone cat stayed, a big striper, winding and bumping against her legs. She didn't seem to feel him. Shame burned in her eyes when her eyes grazed me. This was not how she wanted me to see her. She reached up to grip the little doll strung around her neck. Her eyes suddenly blazed. She squared herself. "I didn't go get your stuff." She put her fists on her hips defiantly. "I forgot," she said in a snotty voice.

Carl's scowl deepened. "You forgot? Yeah, right. Well, you forget dinner or coming in until you get it, Lonnie. And it better not be short, or I'll throw you outta *this* window. Get going, now!" He slammed the window shut. Across the parking lot, the boys laughed.

She stood a moment, then stuffed her hands in her pockets and walked away. The striper cat sat down with an unhappy meow. I hurried to catch up with her. It was getting really dark. Mom was going to kill me. "Lonnie?"

She didn't look back. "I got to go," she said in a thick voice.

I ran after her. "Lonnie! Lonnie, your cats are really something. You really are the Queen of the Strays."

"Yeah," she said flatly. She wouldn't look at me. "I got to go. See you around." She lengthened her stride, limping hastily away.

"Okay, I'll look for you at school tomorrow."

She didn't answer. Darkness swallowed her. Rain began to fall.

Before I got home, the headlights of the cars were reflecting off the puddles in the streets. I hurried upstairs, praying that Mom wouldn't be home yet. She wasn't. I hung up my dripping coat, kicked off my wet sneakers, and raced into the kitchen. The phone machine was flashing. Six messages. I was toast.

I was cleaning up sugar and listening to Mom's frantic, "Mandy? Are you there? Mandy, pick up!" when I heard her key in the front door. I was still standing in the kitchen looking guilty when she found me.

She looked me up and down. The lower half of my jeans and my socks were sopping. "Where have you been?"

I could have lied and said I was at the library, but Mom and I don't do that to each other. And I needed to tell someone about Lonnie. So I told her everything, from the one-boobed Barbie to the cat-carpet and Carl. Her face got tight, and I knew she didn't like what she was hearing. But she listened, while we fixed dinner. We didn't have to talk about dinner. Wednesday was spaghetti. I chopped mushrooms and peppers, she chopped the onions and smashed the garlic. She put the water to boil for the pasta, I sawed the frozen French bread open and spread it with margarine.

By the time everything was ready, she had heard all about Lonnie. Her first words were pretty hard on me. "I trust you to have good judgment, Mandy."

"I don't think I did anything wrong."

"I didn't say you did wrong. I said you used poor judgment. You let a stranger in while I was gone. You left without telling me where you were going or when you'd be back. If something bad had happened to you, I wouldn't even have known where to start looking."

"Why do you always assume something bad is going to happen? When am I supposed to have friends over? I can't have them in while you're gone, and I can't go out with them. What am I supposed to do, just come home and be alone all day?"

"You can have friends over," my mom objected. "But I need to know something about people before we let them into our home. Mandy, just because a person is your own age and a girl doesn't mean she can't hurt you. Or that she won't steal from us."

"MOM!" I exploded, but she kept on talking.

"Lonnie is probably a nice kid who's just had a hard time. But the people she knows may not be nice. If someone knew that I'm at work all day and you're at school, they could rip us off. I certainly couldn't afford to replace the stereo and the television and the microwave all at once. We'd just have to do without."

"You haven't even met Lonnie and you're judging her!"

"I'm not judging her. I'm trying to protect you." Mom paused. "Mandy. There's a lot of Lonnies in the world. As much as I'd like to, I can't save them all. Sometimes, I feel like I can't even protect you anymore. But I do my best. Even when it means . . ." She halted. Then she spoke gravely. "Mandy, if you hang out with Lonnie, people will treat you like Lonnie. Not that Lonnie deserves to be treated like she is; in fact, I'm sure she doesn't. But I can't protect Lonnie. All I can do is try to protect you."

She was so serious that my anger evaporated. We sat at the little table in the kitchen with our dinner getting cold between us. I tried to remember the big table in our old dining room with the hardwood floor and the wallpaper. I couldn't. "Mom?" I asked suddenly. "What is the difference between Lonnie and me?"

Mom was quiet for a long time. Then she said, "Maybe the difference is me. Someone who cares fiercely about you."

"Lonnie loves her mom, even if she did throw her out a window."

"Lonnie may love her mom, but it doesn't sound like her mom cares about her. It doesn't sound like anyone does."

"Only her cats," I conceded. "And half of them are deaders." *And me,* I thought. *I care about her.*

In the end, we made compromises. I could have Lonnie over if I told Mom she was there. Mom had to get Lonnie's phone number, address, and her mom's name. If we went out, it had to be somewhere like the library, not just to walk around. I had to call Mom before I went and when I got back. I had to stay out of Dumpsters. And I wasn't allowed to go to Lonnie's house.

"But why?" I ventured.

"Because," Mom said darkly, and that was the end of that.

I looked for Lonnie at school the next day. I even went to the special-ed rooms. No Lonnie. Three days later, I found one cat-body outline, but I couldn't tell if it was new or old because of all the rain. I was afraid to go to her building. Mom was right, it was a tough neighborhood. But on the fourth day, I screwed up my courage and took the long way home from school to walk through her neighborhood.

I saw her from half a block away. She was standing at the corner of a convenience store parking lot, her arms crossed on her chest. There were three boys facing her. Two were our age, one looked older. They had her bike.

It was so beat up I wouldn't have recognized it, except for the Amazon Barbie. One of the boys sat on the bike possessively while the other two stood between Lonnie and the bike.

"I don't care what he said," Lonnie told them. "It's my bike and I want it back." She tried to circle, to get close enough to get her hands on the bike, but the two boys blocked her lazily.

"Your dad said we could have it." The boy on the bike was cocky about it.

"Carl's not my dad!" Lonnie declared furiously. "Get off my bike!"

"So what? He said we could have it for picking up his junk for him. Gave us ten bucks, too." There was a sneer of laughter in the older boy's voice.

I froze, watching them. They moved by a set of unspoken rules. Lonnie could not physically touch the boys, and they knew it. All they had to do to keep her from the bike was to stand between her and it. She moved back and forth, trying to get past them. She looked stupid and helpless and she knew it. A man walked up to them and stopped. My hopes rose.

"It's a piece of shit bike anyway," one of the boys declared laughingly as they blocked her yet again.

"Yeah. We're gonna take it down to the lake and run it off the dock into the water."

The light changed. The man crossed the street. It was as if he had not even seen Lonnie and the boys and the bike. He didn't even look back.

"You better not!" Lonnie threatened helplessly. She darted once more at the bike. And collided with a boy.

"Hey!" he pushed her violently back. "Keep your hands off me, bitch!"

"Yeah, whore!"

Suddenly, in the physical contact, the rules of the game had changed. The boys pushed at her. Lonnie cowered back, and the one on the bike rode it up on her, pushing the wheel against her.

Now instead of trying to grab her bike back, she was trying to back away from it. The other boys touched her. Her face. "God, you're ugly!" Her chest. "She ain't got no tits, just like her dolly! Your momma cut them off, too?" Her crotch. "Whoo, whoo, you like that, ho?"

Across the street, a bus stopped and two people got off. They walked away into the darkness. Cars drove by in the gathering dusk of the overcast October evening. No one paid any attention to Lonnie's plight. Deep in my heart, I knew why. She was already broken, already damaged past repairing. If you can't fix something, then don't worry about hurting it even more. The boys knew that. She wasn't worth saving from them. It was like jumping on the couch that already had broken springs. She was just a thing to practice on.

"Stop it, stop it!" She flailed at them wildly, trying to slap away the hands that darted in to touch her insultingly, pushing, poking, slapping her face. She had forgotten she was a warrior. She was just a girl, and that was a boy's game. She couldn't win it. Leaves in the gutter rustled by. I was so cold I was shaking. So cold. I should get home; I was cold and it was getting dark and my mom would be mad at me. One of the boys pushed her hard as the other one rammed her with the bike. She fell down on the sidewalk and suddenly they ringed her, the bike discarded on the pavement as they sneered down at her.

Some tribal memory of what came next reared its savage face from my subconscious.

"No!" I suddenly screamed. My voice came out shrill and childish. I flew toward them, gripping my book bag by its strap. A stupid weapon, my only weapon. "Get away from her, get away from her!" I uttered the word I knew Lonnie could never say. "Help! Help me, someone, they're hurting her! Help! Get away from her!"

I waded into them, swinging my book bag, and they suddenly

fell back. Abruptly their ugly faces turned confused and surprised. Like magic, they were only boys again, just teasing boys who always push you as far as they can, especially if the playground teacher isn't around.

"Look out, it's Wonder Woman!" one yelled, and a man who had come to the door of the 7-Eleven across the parking lot laughed out loud. They grabbed the bike and ran away, shouting insults at one another—You pussy! You wimp! You sissy!—as they ran. No one came to help as I took Lonnie's hands and dragged her to her feet. The knee of her sweatpants was torn, and her backpack was muddy. There was mud on the side of her face, too.

"Are you hurt?" I asked her as she stood. I tried to hug her. She slapped my hands angrily away.

"They got my damn bike! Shit! Shit, shit, shit, why didn't you grab the bike while it was laying there!" Her eyes blazed as she turned on me. I fell back in surprise before her anger.

"I was worried about you! The bike wasn't that important!"

"That's easy for you to say. A bike isn't the only damn thing you've got!" She lifted her sleeve to wipe mud off her face. She might have wiped away tears as well. I stared at her, speechless. I thought I had been brave, almost heroic. She seemed to think I had been stupid. She glanced up from examining a bleeding scrape on her knee and knew she'd hurt me. She tried to explain. "Look, it's like this. If we had gotten the bike, we would have won. Now I got all bruised up and I lost, too. So they'll tease me with the bike again. I got to fight them all over again tomorrow."

"I think it's dumb to fight for that bike at all," I said quietly. "You could really get hurt. The bike isn't worth it."

"Yeah," she said sarcastically. "That's what they teach us girls. Don't get into fights over stuff. It's not worth getting hurt over. So guys keep taking stuff from us, knowing we won't fight. Those guys, if I don't fight them to get my bike back, then they'll take something else from me. And something more. They'll keep on taking stuff from me until I have to fight back. Only by then it'll be too late, because I'll never have learned to fight, so whatever it is that I finally fight for, they'll just take it from me anyway."

Her logic was torturous, and I shied away from her conclusion.

"Like Carl," she added bitterly. "I didn't fight him at first. He moved in. He eats our food and uses our phone and leaves the house a mess. He took my home. He took my mom. Shit. He even took my bike and gave it to those guys. Now he thinks he can take anything he wants and I won't fight. He's probably right, too."

"I know I probably can't beat those boys," she admitted a few minutes later as we walked slowly down the darkening street. "But I can make it cost them something to pick on me. They can hit me and knock me down, but they know I'm going to fight back, hit back. So maybe they'll go find an easier target. I know, everyone says that if you avoid a bully or ignore him, he'll go away. But that's bullshit. They don't. They just grow up and become your mom's boyfriend. Dead cat."

I don't know how she saw it in the dark. Black fur in a black gutter, but she saw it. She opened her pack and took out her spray can and inscribed his neon orange memorial on the pavement. She scooped up his body carefully and set it at the base of a No Parking sign. "Still warm," she said regretfully as she wiped her hands down her shirt. "Poor kitty." Crouched over the body, it was like she spoke to the cat. "Carl gave them my bike. That's like he gave them permission to pick on me, take stuff from me. Like I don't matter any more than a dead cat in the gutter. Run over me and just keep going." She smoothed the cat's rumpled fur a last time. "God, I hate Carl," she said quietly.

More conversationally, she added, "You know what really pisses me off? That Carl gave them my bike *and* some money for picking up his dope. He never gives me nothing for picking up his junk. I just have to do it. So that if someone gets caught with it, it's me. He told my mom, if I get caught, they won't do much, because I'm a kid."

"But doesn't your mom . . ." I began.

"Long as my mom gets her junk, she'll believe whatever he says," Lonnie said sadly. "Since Carl moved in, it's like I'm mostly invisible. She doesn't even yell at me anymore. The only time she talks to me is when I bring the junk home. She always thanks me. That's the only reason I do it." Her eyes swung to mine. "And *I* still talk to *her.* Carl's always telling me to shut up, but I don't. I tell her about my cats, I told her about you." In a quieter voice she added, "I tell her she shouldn't be tricking just to get money for junk. That's how I fight him. Maybe I won't win, but no one can say I didn't fight." She gave her one-shouldered shrug. "I won't stop, either. Long as I keep fighting, he can't say he won."

When I got in, Mom was waiting for me. Her face was white. "I damn near called the cops," she hissed at me. "You didn't call me; I came straight home, there's no sign of you . . ." Then she burst into tears.

I was stupid. I told her where I'd been and what had happened. When I was done, she just sat there on the couch with her face in her hands. She spoke through her fingers. "God, Mandy. You have no concept . . . look. Sweetie. You can't get involved in this. You just can't. Drugs and prostitution and abuse and . . . No. Mandy, you have to stay away from her. You must."

"I can't." I was telling the truth. "I can't just abandon her. Then she'd have no one! I have you, but she doesn't have anyone but a bunch of stray cats."

Mom got up and walked into her room without a word. That really shook me up. For a minute I thought that was it, that she was so mad she wasn't even going to talk to me anymore. Then she came back with a little red tube in her hand.

"This is not a toy," she told me severely, as if I had asked to play with it. "This is a serious weapon. Pepper spray. You point it like this, push this catch down, and then spray it. It will make anyone back off long enough for you to run away. Don't stick around and try to fight, just get away. And use it only if you are really in danger. Never for a joke, never as a threat. If you have to, use it. Other than that, don't even tell anyone you have it."

"There's two," I said out loud as I took them.

"Give the other one to Lonnie," she said. She walked to the window and peered out through the curtains. She talked to the night. "Show her how to use it. But after that, you are not allowed to see her anymore. Do you understand? This is as much as we can do for her. No more."

I couldn't argue with that voice, but I wondered if I would obey her. "Mom," I asked quietly, "if you had been there tonight, if you had been me . . . would you have used it on those boys?"

"No. Boys your age are just . . . Well, maybe, yes. Yes." She hesitated. "I don't know," she admitted. "Mandy, I don't know; I wasn't there, and you weren't the one being threatened . . . If Lonnie had just walked away, if she hadn't challenged them . . ." Her voice trailed away. She didn't know either. How could I know when to fight back if my own mom didn't know? In a quieter voice she added, "I have to get us into a better place. I have to."

I didn't see Lonnie for a while. I took a different route home from school, used a different door into my building. I pretended that if I didn't see her, I wasn't avoiding her. I liked her, but her problems were just too scary. I tried not to think about her, but my hand kept finding the extra vial of pepper spray in my coat pocket. Then one afternoon at four o'clock, I turned off the TV and put on my coat. I wrote Mom a note. I left the apartment.

It was dark but at least it wasn't raining. I walked fast, glad there were no boys hanging out around her building tonight. I wondered how I'd know which door was hers. I wondered if I'd have the guts to knock. But I didn't have to. Lonnie knelt on the ground by the Dumpster. The single parking lot light illuminated at least a dozen orange outlines of cats on the pavement. As I watched, another one slowly formed on the ground in front of Lonnie. I went to her.

The area around the Dumpster was littered with sprawled cat bodies. A terrible noise was coming from Lonnie as she painted around them. *Uh, huh, huh.* The noise people make when they can't cry. I was afraid to get too close to her. She crawled to the next cat and began outlining it.

"What happened?" I whispered into the darkness.

She looked up, startled. Even in the dimness, I could see she was broken. "I don't know," she choked out when she recognized me. "I don't know. They weren't hit by cars, they weren't killed by dogs. They're just dead. I just don't know." She sank down in defeat on the dirty pavement. "My strays. My loyal subjects." Her hand rested on one dead cat like a benediction. Behind her, a small kitten mewed questioningly in the bushes. "I got nothing left," she told me sadly. She shook her head. "I fought and I fought. But I still lost. In the end, it all got taken away." She seemed to get smaller.

"Lonnie!" Carl called from the window. He leaned out, craning to see her. "Lonnie, you down there? You got my stuff?"

It was the wrong time to ask her that. She came to her feet like a puppet hauled up on its strings. "No!" she screeched back. "No, I don't!" Then, in a plea for understanding, "Carl, my cats are dead! Something killed them." Her voice broke on the words.

"Oh, no, really?" His voice shook. "That's awful, Lonnie. That's just terrible." Then he laughed out loud, and I knew he'd been holding it back all along. "Well, maybe someone poisoned the fuckers so you'd quit wasting time on them. Quit sniveling and go get my stuff. Now!"

Her hands flew up to her face in horror. Speechless, she stared into the darkness beyond the Dumpsters. When she dropped her hands a moment later, her painty fingers had left fluorescent tabby-cat stripes on both her cheeks.

I couldn't believe what happened next. She didn't even look at me. She limped straight to the door of her building. She obediently went inside. Lonnie had stopped fighting.

The kitten found me. I felt her tiny claws in my sock. I picked her up. She was skinny and her little mouth opened hugely when she cried. "You've got the wrong person," I told her. I set her down and walked away.

Then I heard the sound. Not a shout. A roar, like the roar of a lioness, wordless in her fury. It came from the window above. Carl yelled back but it was a startled shout, full of dismay. I couldn't see much, but I saw her shadow crash into his, her fists pummeling at his face and chest. For an instant I thought that she could win. But it was still a boy's game. I heard his answering roar of anger. He seized her by the upper arms, lifted her off her feet, and threw her.

She hit the window. The glass shattered, flying out like a cloud of diamonds. Lonnie fell with it, twisting and yowling.

I did a stupid thing. Somehow I had the pepper spray in my hand and I pointed it up at the window. Lonnie seemed to be falling forever. I saw Carl look out as she fell; I even saw the shock on his face, heard someone else in the room behind him scream.

Then I squeezed the button and enveloped myself in a cloud of pepper gas. Carl was too far away. Even finally knowing when to fight, I thought to myself, was not enough. People like Carl still won. Blinded and choking, I fell to my knees as Lonnie struck the ground. Broken glass rang in a brittle rain with her.

Everything in the world stopped. I didn't kneel by her, I crumpled. I tried to touch her but I couldn't. I wasn't Lonnie, to touch death without fear. Then she lifted her head. She looked at me and her mouth opened. As if she moved a mountain, she turned her head. Her lips pulled back. With her last breath, she lifted her upper lip and snarled up at the window that framed Carl.

Summoned, the cats came. The queen's loyal subjects poured forth to her call. Without a rustle of leaves, without a patter of paws, they came. Orange shapes flickered in the night. They came in a wave that became a tide. From the bushes in back of the Dumpster, from under cars, from the distant streets, from everywhere, they came. They flooded the parking lot. A score, a hundred, five hundred fluorescent orange silhouettes lit the night as they answered her call. I saw Carl stagger back from the window. Like living flames, the cats licked up the side of the building, over the sill, and through the broken glass. The rumble of their snarls were like a big truck idling. The parking lot was darker when the last one disappeared inside. The hissing and spitting and caterwauling from up there almost drowned his screams.

Mom's headlights hit me just about the same time the cats poured out of the window again. Like molten gold or streaming honey, they flowed down the side of the building. They engulfed Lonnie and me. I felt the warmth of a hundred small bodies, the soft swipe of velvet paws as they rushed past and over me to get to her. I swear I saw them, and I swear I felt them.

They purred all over Lonnie, they marked her with their brows, they bumped her with their fluorescent noses. They nudged and they pleaded and they nagged, pushing at her body. They kneaded it with their paws demandingly, scores of little fluorescent paws pushing at her yielding flesh, making her smaller and more compact, re-creating her in a new and perfect image.

The Queen of the Strays sat up groggily. She blinked her great amber eyes. She lifted a velvet paw to swipe at her tabby face. She stood and she stretched, showing me four sets of razor claws and four powerful legs attached to a lithe and perfect body.

"Lonnie?" I asked incredulously.

The cat shrugged one shoulder.

In the next instant, Lonnie was gone. The tidal wave of fluorescent cats retreated, and she padded off in the midst of them. The great orange glow surged into the blackberry tangle. Their light dwindled as they faded into the thorny jungle of vines. Then it winked out. Lonnie was gone and my mom was there going, "Oh, my God, my God. Get in the car, Mandy. Right now. Get in the car."

I did. We were halfway home before I noticed the tiny black-and-white kitten that was stuck to my sock like a burr. When I put it in my lap, it curled up and began to purr.

I DON'T KNOW what Mom saw that night. She says I had pepper gas in my eyes and that I couldn't have seen anything. The papers said that a junkie whore got mad at her pimp and cut him to ribbons with a razor. The papers never even mentioned Lonnie.

No one ever wonders what happens to strays when they disappear.

I hope her next eight lives are better than this one was.

Finis

Sometimes it seems to me that the public appetite for certain types of stories comes and goes in waves. It's most visible, I think, on television. There is a decade of westerns, a decade of doctor shows, followed by a decade of forensic scientists or vampires or rich teenager tales.

Similar waves rise and fall in our genres. Steampunk gives way to urban fantasy. Psychic romance alternates with alternate history. Of course, our genre is probably the only place where we feel free to mix tropes and trends freely. I am sure that an urban steampunk fantasy that involved a psychic tracking down lost lovers in an alternate history setting could do quite well. One could even toss in a werewolf and an alien, and many readers would not find the mixture too heady.

For me, the most fun of working with an overworked topic is trying to burnish away the barnacles and rust to find the solid true core of story at the middle. When anything becomes a stereotype or a cliché, there is one sure truth about it: at the core of it, there is something vital, something that speaks so strongly to all of us that we return, over and over, to try to grasp completely the lesson it is trying to teach us.

This is my effort to knock some of the rust off a cliché and look at it from a slightly different perspective.

Josh was working with a hammer and chisel, cutting out just enough wood from the oak posts to make the gate hinges set flush when the rental sedan came inching slowly up the drive. Its tires crunched softly over the gravel; other than that, it was near silent, the driver letting the car almost idle up the lane. Arizona plates. Well, someone had driven a long ways to visit Mrs. Reid. Josh watched it for a moment, then went back to his work. Her guest was none of his beeswax; the visitor would be for the home owner, not him. He was just the handyman, finishing up the final work on her yard project, just as he was the handyman for a couple dozen other owners of rural cottages.

But of them all, Mrs. Reid was the oddest. Strange lady. The little cottage at the end of the winding lane looked almost exactly as it had when she'd bought it. Usually, when some rich lady bought up one of the cottages, the first thing they did was gingerbread it up. Fresh paint, a patio, a hot tub, and a privacy fence. Those were the standard changes he made for new clients. But not Mrs. Reid. He picked up a Yankee screwdriver, inserted a small bit, and jacked two pilot holes into the post. The only real changes she'd wanted him to make were out here in the yard. But that was none of his beeswax either. The customer got to say what she wanted done and how she wanted it done. No matter how strange the requests. He wiped sweat from his forehead with the back of his cuff and then tried the hinge in its place. Perfect. He'd have it done by dark.

He was reaching for the screws and screwdriver when the man spoke behind him, startling him. "I'm looking for a woman named

Doria. She goes by Doria Simmons. Does she live here?" He had a deep voice, and the softness of his words seemed intentional. The slight sibilance sounded like bad-fitting dentures.

Josh turned to look up at him. The short, stocky man standing over him had gotten out of his car quietly, not even shutting the door behind him. He was an old man, at least in his seventies and more likely in his eighties. The coarse curls of his hair had gone to gray, and there were deep furrows in his brow. A small silver cross on a silver chain rested snugly at the hollow of his throat. It looked odd on a man of his size and years. He lugged a heavy canvas satchel like a workman's tool bag, but he didn't have the physique of a man who worked with tools anymore. His shoulders were rounded, curling in toward his chest, and the veins and tendons stood out beneath the age spots on his hands. He just looked old, old and tired. But he also looked determined, in a mean old man sort of way that put Josh's hackles up without him even thinking about it.

Josh shook his head. "No sir. This is Mrs. Agatha Reid's cottage. She only moved in a couple months ago. Maybe someone named Simmons lived here before. I wouldn't know. People who buy these little cottages off the beaten track usually like to keep to themselves. It's not my place to ask a lot of questions, you know. I'm just the handyman."

The man's eyes had narrowed at the woman's name, a wince almost of pain. It deepened the lines around his mouth and the ones in his brow. "Reid? She's using the name Reid?"

"That's the lady that lives here, yes sir. I don't know about her 'using' that name. It's the only name I know her by." Josh positioned the hinge, licked the point of the screw, set the point of it into the pilot hole, and then pushed it in with the screwdriver. He leaned against it, pushing hard as the screw bit into the wood. Josh had expected the man to leave. Instead, he stepped closer.

"The woman I'm looking for used to be married to a man named Reid. Adam Reid. She might still be using his name."

"Well, she told me she was widowed. So Reid might have been her married name. She never told me her husband's name. I think it still makes her sad to talk about him." He positioned another screw and began working it in.

The man didn't reply directly to that. Instead, he leaned over Josh in a way that the handyman resented. He hated working under someone's scrutiny. That had been one pleasant thing about his job. Mrs. Reid slept days and worked nights. He'd only seen her when she'd given him the carefully written directions for what she wanted done, and the times when she'd given him money for his work and to buy materials. Nice working for a person who didn't ride him all the time. Even nicer working for someone who paid cash up front.

Now the old man spoke his opinion. "That's a pretty fancy gate you're putting up there. Lots of ornamental crosses in the ironwork. But what's that shiny stuff threaded all through the scrollwork?"

"Lady wanted it done that way. Mrs. Reid wanted all the iron pickets topped with crosses, and the gate to match." Josh answered reluctantly. It wasn't good business to talk about his customer's foibles. Folks who moved this far away from even a little town like McKenna usually valued their privacy. And he valued their business. There wasn't much else going in McKenna for a jack-of-all-trades.

"That wire looks like it's real silver." The old man leaned closer, peering at the wire without touching it. Then he turned his head slowly, following the gleam of the silver wire as it snaked the full length of the fence. It was real silver wire, ordered through the jeweler in town. Mrs. Reid had told Josh to run it in and out of the close-set pickets for the full perimeter of the fence. He'd thought it a terrible waste of her money and told her so. He'd warned her that someone might just see and decide to help themselves to it. She'd insisted, and the customer was always right. He'd done as she'd asked. He just hoped that it would make the young woman feel a bit safer. She was a pale, sickly sort to begin with, and her eyes were all full of sorrow, as if she were pining away.

"And is that garlic planted all along the fence?"

"Yes sir." Josh was feeling more than a bit irritated and less inclined to talk by the minute. He'd promised Mrs. Reid that the gate would be ready by tonight. She'd been looking forward to the completion of this project for weeks. A substantial bonus was riding on it, and this fellow was delaying him.

Now the man had stepped back to regard all of Josh's careful handiwork. As the old man's gaze traveled along the fence, his hand touched the silver cross at his throat. "Crosses worked into the ironwork of the gates, and each wooden picket is a cross at the top. And Saint-John's-wort and wolfsbane planted all along the outside of the fence."

"Yes sir. That's what the lady wanted done and so I did it. You and I might think it's a bit silly, but it's her fence and her yard, so she has the right to have it as she wants." Josh stood slowly, stretched the kink out of his back, and then stooped to pick up the heavy iron gate. Real wrought iron and heavy as all get-out. She could have had one that looked just like it for a fraction of the cost. She'd insisted on cold iron.

"And what's all that concrete there, that trough running through the yard."

It stung to hear his handiwork called a trough. Josh answered slowly. "It's a water feature. It's not turned on yet; the owner didn't want it started until all the rest of the work was done. She'll have a little stream that encircles the house. She calls it a moat. She hasn't decided yet if she wants stepping-stones or an ornamental dress. It was a simple shirtwaist dress, like something his mother might have worn in her youth, in a sensible dark fabric. Her hair framed her brow in two smooth dark wings that were pulled back into a loose bun at the back of her neck. Her makeup was perfect, but dated, as if she'd copied it from an old magazine. She looked at the both of them and did not speak.

"Evening, Mrs. Reid. I'm just finishing up here," he said, when the silence seemed to stretch a bit too long.

"And just when you said you would," she replied. Her voice was pleasant and husky and her words articulated. Her eyes moved from him to the stranger. Josh waited for the man to say something. When he didn't, he filled in.

"I try to make my estimates as exact as I can. And when you've been a handyman as long as I have, well, you get a fair idea of how long a job should take. Now, this cement is still wet, so try to use the gate latch as little as possible until it's set."

"I won't use it at all," she promised promptly. But she seemed to aim her words at the man next to him. The stranger spoke suddenly.

"I got a letter. All these years of trying to track you down, and suddenly a letter comes and tells me exactly where you are. I should have known it came from you."

She nodded slowly.

"So, all those years, did you know where I was?"

Her lips moved very slightly, stretching almost into a smile. "I did. Of course I did."

"You did." Josh heard the man swallow. "So. 'Keep your friends close and your enemies closer.' Was that it?"

"Something like that. And you've been both, haven't you, Raymond?"

"Many more years as the one than the other," he said, and his wariness came more harshly into his voice.

bridge for crossing it. She hasn't chosen the lilies for it either. I told her she might want to put koi in there. Be real pretty."

"Yes. It would. Moving water is always pretty. Here. Let me give you a hand with that gate," the old man offered, surprising Josh and making him feel a bit more kindly toward him. The visitor's canvas satchel clanked heavily when he set it down. The old fellow was stronger than he looked. He helped lift the gate and then held it steady while Josh aligned the two halves of the hinges. "She say why she wanted all this stuff done?" the man asked him, his voice tight with the effort of holding the gate steady.

Josh didn't want to answer him, but it seemed stingy to be rude while the fellow was still holding the gate in place for him. He took a breath and then spoke reluctantly. "She's afraid of vampires." The pin was being stubborn about dropping down into the hinge. He wriggled it hopefully, and it dropped a quarter inch. "All this stuff, the crosses and the silver, the garlic and wolfsbane, and all this stuff is supposed to keep vampires away. They can't cross it, she says. You and I might think that's silly, but she says her husband was killed by a vampire, and she's never gotten over it. Never been able to forget it, never been able to forgive it." The little holes for the pin were not lining up. Josh grunted as he tried to edge the pieces into a better alignment. "I think she's a little bit crazy, but she pays me on time."

"She told you all that?" The man gasped out the words. Evidently holding up the wrought-iron gate was a harder task for him than Josh had thought.

"Yeah. Lift a little more, I nearly got the hinges lined up. She said it happened a long time ago, but it couldn't have been that long. She doesn't look any older than my kid sister, and she's just twenty-two. That's one pin in, just let me get the second one. Mrs. Reid said she loved her husband more than life itself, more than she loved herself. Kind of funny. She's said that to me about six times now. That she wishes she'd realized sooner that she loved him more than life itself. That it would have changed everything."

The stranger lost his grip on the gate for a second, but it was all right. Josh had just slid the pin into place. "You can let go now," he told the man.

The old man did, and then he turned abruptly away. He coughed a couple of times and then pulled a handkerchief out of his pocket and blew his nose. When he spoke, his voice was hoarse. "She in there now, you think?"

"Oh, sure. She works at night, sleeps days. I think she's a writer or something. She told me that on the phone first time she called me. 'Hope you don't mind me calling so late, but I'm a night person,' she said. I suspect she doesn't sleep well at night. Too afraid of the vampires." He shook his head in sympathy for the woman. "Well. Just about done here. Only thing left to do is set the stop for the gate, and then start her water flowing. Should be done just about sunset. Then I'll get my pay and be gone."

The old man turned, wiped his face with his handkerchief, and then turned back to him. The lines on his face seemed deeper. He cleared his throat. "So she'll be coming out to pay you tonight?"

"Like clockwork. Every Thursday, right about sundown. Always pays cash, and last time, there were three old silver certificates mixed in with the regular bills. I showed them to her and told her that they were worth more than the others, that she should sell them to a coin collector or something. She just laughed and said money was just paper to her and that I could do whatever I wanted with them. She's a nice lady."

The old man cleared his throat again. "I might just stand here and wait with you for her to come out. That okay with you?"

"Sure. I don't mind. Long as you don't mind me finishing up my chore here." He was getting more and more uncomfortable with the man's questions. He decided to take a direct approach. "Look,

Mister, if you're a visitor, you can go knock on her door. I'm not the watchman or anything like that. I'm just the local handyman, doing odd jobs. She might already be awake."

"I think I'll just wait here with you, if it's all the same to you. It's a pleasure to watch a workman finish a task. Always good to see a job finished. Especially one that's been a long time in the works." A thin smile came to the old man's face.

Well, he was an odd duck. "Fine with me." Josh shrugged. There wasn't much left for him to do. He had a piece of iron pipe to pound into the ground, and then a sack of dry Redi-Mix and just enough water in a jerrican to finish up the job. Once the pipe was set in the ground, the catch for the gate would drop into it and hold it shut until someone lifted the latch. He'd already wrapped the latch handle in silver wire like she'd requested. He'd done that job on his workbench the night before, trying to lay the coils smooth and flat. He'd done a pretty good job, he thought. The silver looked nice against the black of the wrought iron.

The man was mostly quiet as he watched Josh work. Once he took out a pocket watch and consulted it, and then glanced up at the sky. "Going to be dark soon," he commented, and Josh nodded. He troweled the concrete flat and checked his work with a level. "That's done," he said, and with a grunt and a groan, he got to his feet. As he packed up his tools and tidied away the empty Redi-Mix bag, the lights in the cottage came on. "And just in time," he added.

The stranger didn't say a word. He just stood, staring toward the house, so silent he seemed to be holding his breath. His right hand stole into his coat pocket. He stared at the cottage door, and when the porch light came on, he gave a small gasp. A moment later, the door opened and Mrs. Reid stood framed in it. The porch light lit her as if it were a spotlight on a stage. She was dressed, as she always was, in what Josh had come to think of as her mourning

"That's true. Only a few years of being a friend. Back at the beginning." She said the words, and the man's confirming silence flowed up to drown the conversation.

Josh felt uncomfortable. He wasn't sure what he was witnessing, but knew he didn't want to know. He put the last of his tools into his toolbox, shut it, and latched it. Mrs. Reid had been a good customer, and he knew he couldn't just stand by if the stranger became rude or aggressive. He spoke into their silence, his voice too loud and his affability sounding false. "Well, if you're satisfied, Mrs. Reid, I'll call it a day and head for home. Got a cat to feed, you know." He glanced at the man and added, "Unless there's something else you need before I go. Anything else you want me to do?"

She looked at the man before she brought her gaze back to him. "No, Josh, I think you've done everything I need. I'm satisfied." She looked at the stranger again and added, "How about you, Raymond? Are you satisfied?"

The man was quiet for a moment and then said, "I think I am. But I don't understand why."

"You don't understand why you are satisfied? Come, Raymond. I thought this was what you longed for, all these years."

"It might be. But what I don't understand is why you are doing it? And why you sent me a letter. Unless you wanted to me to witness it?" The last words came slowly, even more reluctantly from him.

She lifted one slim shoulder in an elegant shrug. "Because it finishes it, I suppose. Because I thought it would give you pleasure. Give you, perhaps, a sense of something finished."

She stepped off the porch then and came down the path. The stranger made a small sound in his throat. But Josh carefully unlatched the gate and went to meet her. He'd recognized the fat envelope she carried. It would be the final payment for his work, in cash, just like before. As he took it from her, she smiled and then her mouth worked oddly, as if there were something she wanted to say. She swallowed hard and turned away from him abruptly. As she walked back toward her house, she spoke without looking back at him. She crossed the dry moat and stopped briefly on the other side. No bridge, she'd specified. Strange, but that was what the customer wanted, so that was how he'd built it. "Turn on the water for me, so the stream runs, before you leave. And shut the gate behind you when you go, will you?"

"Of course." He was a bit hurt by her abruptness but decided it probably had something to do with the stranger at the gate. The man hadn't even tried to come in, hadn't even greeted her, really. And she hadn't asked him in. Must be some very bad history between them, he decided, and resolved he'd see the stranger on his way before he left. He left the path and knelt in the dirt to find the spigot for the stream. He'd set it into the ground, along with the switch for the pump. It was only accessible from this side. She'd have to cross the running water if she wanted to turn it off. He'd pointed that out to her once, to be sure she understood. She'd just looked at him and then said quietly, "That's part of the plan. Build it that way, please."

And he had.

He opened the fiberglass hatch on the protective box and reached in to turn open the valve and then flick on the pump. Within minutes, the pipe hissed. He heard the gurgling as water filled the race. When the water reached the level, he heard the auto shutoff kick in, and then the quiet hum of the pump that would keep the water circulating. "Works perfectly," he said in satisfaction. He stood up and was surprised to see that Mrs. Reid was still standing on the porch, watching him. He could not read the emotion on her face. Regret? Resignation?

When he glanced at the gate, the stranger was still standing there. His face was a complete contrast to the widow's. The satisfaction was unmistakable. Josh felt a surge of revulsion for the fellow. What was the matter with the man? She was just a woman alone in the world, obviously consumed with her grief for her husband and beset with an irrational fear. The stranger stared at her as she stood alone, backlit by her porch light, as if his eyes could never drink enough of the sight. With both hands, he gripped the iron gate. The moment Josh stepped through it, he said, through gritted teeth, "Please, allow me." And he shut it with a clash of iron against iron that abruptly sounded to Josh like a weapon clashed against a shield. Behind him, he was startled to hear Mrs. Reid give a low moan.

When he turned to look at her, she was staring at them both, her face white and both her hands clasped over her mouth.

The stranger spoke, his voice gentle and his words harsh. "I hope it takes a long time, Doria."

She spoke through her muffling hands. "I loved him, Raymond. I loved your brother just as much as you did. I was clumsy. He was my first and it didn't end for him the way I'd planned it would. But I loved him. Loved him more than life itself." Her voice shook.

"And you call what you have now a life?" Raymond suddenly roared at her.

Her voice trembled as she replied. "No, Raymond. No, I don't. It's not life. And I don't want it anymore. Without Adam, it's not worth having. It took me years to realize that, and even longer to figure out what to do about it. But now I have. And I've given you the last thing that I have to give to anyone. Satisfaction."

"Damn right you have. Satisfaction." The man's voice was thick with it, cold with righteousness.

It was too much. He couldn't leave her standing there with this man threatening her from outside her gate. "Look, you, whoever you are, you're frightening her. I think you'd better leave."

"I'll be glad to. But I haven't frightened her. She's done that to herself. There's just one more thing I want to do for her before I go." With both his hands, he unfastened the silver chain and the tiny crucifix it bore from around his neck. He watched Mrs. Reid as he slowly wrapped it around the gate catch and then fastened it.

"That's not going to work," Josh pointed out quietly to him. "She'll have to undo it each time she wants to open the gate. I understand you think it might keep vampires out, but . . ."

"It will work just fine," Raymond Reid said as he picked up his canvas satchel. He looked older than he had a few moments before. As if he'd finished some task and no longer needed to force a vitality he didn't have. "Son, she won't be opening that gate. And she didn't have you build all this to keep vampires out."

Raymond gave a final glance to the lone figure standing so still on the porch. He bent to pick up the canvas satchel. The top had come open and a mallet had fallen out of it. Laboriously, he picked it up and put it back inside. He turned his back on both of them and walked toward his rental car. He didn't turn his head as he spoke. "It's to keep a vampire in."

Drum Machine

Sometimes that single sentence that heralds the approach of a story doesn't come at two in the morning or when I'm mowing a lawn. Sometimes, in the midst of a discussion with a friend, someone will say something so succinct and so true that the pieces of a story just start falling into place around it.

I think that many people assume that being a writer brings me into contact with all sorts of interesting people. And that's true. But wondrous to tell, the majority of fascinating people I've met have intersected with my life in other ways. Last summer, an extraordinary natural philosopher was part of the crew putting a new roof on my house. I spent several afternoons outside, listening to his random observations as he fastened roof tiles down on my house. Marty the junkman, who used to come by our old place to see if we had any scrap metal for him, was a fountain of stories from the Depression era. A random encounter that delivers a person like that to my life is like beachcombing and finding a little treasure chest.

One such friend is Jeff Lin of Harvey Danger. He came into my home years ago as my daughter's friend. In the course of sharing coffee, cats, and conversation, his thoughts on creativity in the music field, performing for an audience, and Who Owns the Work left a definite impression on me. I wrote "Drum Machine" as a direct result of one such conversation and indeed a single sentence from Jeff. It's languished in my files for a long time. In the course of looking over stories for this collection, I took it out, read it, and wondered if its time had finally come to see print.

The client leaned forward across the desk and all but hissed at me, "I have a right to the child of my choice."

I smiled at her warmly, reassuringly, and read my line from the prompter. "That's not precisely correct, Mrs. Daw. You have the right to a child. That's very clear." I tapped the notarized slip from her husband, ceding his population replacement right to her. "And you have the right to a choice. The Constitution guarantees you that."

She thrust her already prominent chin at me. "Then I want my choice. Another EagleScout12." She smiled exultantly. "Derek is almost six now, and he has been the perfect choice for my husband and me. When we decided we wanted another child, we decided, well, why take a chance? Get one we know we'll like."

I leaned back in my chair and blinked my eyes twice quickly to call up the next screen. I chose the conciliatory option. "I'm sure, on the face of it, that seemed logical to both of you. But consider the reality, Mrs. Daw. You would essentially be raising identical twins, born six years apart, into the same environment. Same nature, same nurture. Where's the variety in that? You'd be defeating our entire Genetic Variety Preservation program. Even if you can't choose an EagleScout12 again, that doesn't mean your next child won't be just as perfect for you as your first one was. That's the whole purpose of our counseling, Mrs. Daw. The embryo options that the program has chosen are selected to be compatible with you and Mr. Daw. And, I might add, with Derek."

Her eyes widened somewhat. “Could that be why we’re not offered another EagleScout12? Because he might not be compatible with Derek?”

I smiled and shrugged. “I suppose that could be so.” Actually, that particular embryo had been discontinued, but that was not something the client needed to know. They always asked why. Not even I had access to that information. “I’m just a Social Interface, ma’am, not a biologist. But I wonder if you haven’t hit on the very reason.” I eyed the timer in the bottom left quarter of my goggle-screen, but my smile never faltered.

She had taken up almost seventeen minutes of my time, over twice the normal allotment, trying to nag an approval out of me. When she had first sat down in my cubicle, I had popped her disk into my machine and tapped in the latest information. She hadn’t liked the choices we’d offered, but her request for another EagleScout12 had come up with a solid Denied. But you don’t flatly tell the applicant that. If that was all there was to my job, I wouldn’t have a job. The computer could do it. As a Social Interface, class 7, it’s up to me to select the right words and tones and mannerisms from the suggested dialogue on my screen. Mrs. Daw was a tough one, but in the next three minutes, I managed to send her on her way. She had even looked happy with her new selection, a female DutchDoll7. She strode away, clutching the appointment slip that would let her fetus be implanted tomorrow.

I was forty-five minutes from the end of my shift. Three, maybe four more people to counsel and I was through for the day. I was ready to go home. I rocked back in my chair in my cubicle and heard my spine crackle. Then I straightened up and pushed the “next client” button.

I work for the state in Reproductive Permits. My position is Social Interface. I’ve been there about seven years now, and I like to think that I’m good at what I do. It wasn’t a job I would have chosen for myself, but the state aptitude test rated me high for Social Interface duties. The woman in the Aptitude offices who told me about the job opportunities in the field was a Social Interface herself. There was something about her voice when she told me that she just knew I'd be right for the job. I couldn't help but believe her. And over the years, I've come to be like her. People come to me, and they listen to me, and they go away believing me. I make them contented with their choice. There's satisfaction in that. It's proof that I'm good at what I do. Everyone deserves to believe that he's good at what he does. I got little of that in my previous job.

Out in the waiting room, I saw my next applicant stand up. She clutched a slip of paper in her hand as she looked down the row of Social Interface cubicles. In her other hand, she carried a canvas shopping bag. She came straight for me. She wasn't looking at me; she was looking up at the number flashing green over my cubicle. But I saw her face, and despite her sunglasses and all the harsh years since I'd last seen her, I recognized her.

I should have red-lighted right then. There's no regulation that says we can't counsel people we know, but we all know it's frowned on. It's not like a Social Interface can change the computer's decision, but maybe that's why it's best for an applicant to hear it from a stranger. It's less personal that way. Many people don't want their friends to know they've been turned down for their first or second or even third choice. Everyone would like the neighbors to think that the child you gave birth to was your dream kid from the start.

I didn't red-light. Instead, I sat there, watching Cecily rush toward me like shrapnel from the past. The Blonde Banshee, Cliff had called her. That was when he wasn't calling her Cecily the Willing. How two people could love and hate each other so much, I still don't know. Being around them was like escorting a bomb. They could explode in any setting, in restaurants, on trains, even onstage. Public mayhem never bothered either of them. I'd seen Cecily overturn a table on the whole band for the sake of dumping an expensive dinner in Cliff's lap. But I'd also seen her beatific smile the time I nearly broke my neck falling over their coupled bodies in a hotel stairwell at two in the morning in Vancouver.

"No limits, Chesterton," Cliff had told me later. "No limits to what we can make each other feel. It's the magic. What good is a woman who can only make you love her? That's only half the passion, man. Only half."

He made it sound so logical that while he was talking, I believed it. Cliff was like that. He would have made a good Social Interface himself, if he'd lived long enough to hold down a real job. He killed himself when he was twenty-seven. He knew what people would say about that. He even left it as his death note. "All the real ones check out at twenty-seven," he wrote. And that was it.

By the time he reached that point, I didn't really know him anymore. The band had fallen apart three or four years before then. His death was something I read about in the newspaper, a scrap of news in a column full of celebrity notes. Cliff Wangle, former drummer for the Coolie Fish, Oberon's Jest, Hazardous Waste, and most recently with the Flat Plats, died of an overdose at twenty-seven. That was it. I read about it over my breakfast cereal and thought, *Well, that's it, it's really over now.* We had shared a year and a half of almost being famous. The Flat Plats had had one commercial CD release, with one Top Ten song and one in the high teens. We had barely tasted our success before the cup was dashed away from us. Cliff was the one who had done the smashing.

Even after his death, even after all the years, it was still hard to forgive him for that. Aloysius had gone on to doing sound-track arrangements, and I still could pick out Mikey's tenor in a lot of sampled backup stuff. I hadn't had the heart to go on with music after the disappointment. I'd gotten a day job, a wife, and eventually a kid, a KewpieDoll male the first year they'd come out. He was seven now, and still cuter than hell, with curly hair and big dark eyes. I'd made it, I told myself as I watched Cecily zoom in on me. I'd succeeded. I was good at what I did, and I knew it. What more than that could a man ask?

She sat down in front of my desk. Our Interface desks and chairs are elevated just slightly, only an inch or two. Even so, she didn't have to look up at me. But she didn't look at me at all. She merely handed me her disk. I popped it into my machine. I didn't have to open the confirmation port for her. She did that herself and expertly rolled her fingers across the glass. The reason for that flashed up immediately. She'd refused her reproductive choice nine times in the last four months. Of course, she would know the routine by now.

The computer immediately gave me a first option for terminating the interview.

The lines came up at the bottom of my screen specs. *"I'm sorry, Ms. Kelvey, but you are well aware of your reproductive status at this time." Firm tone recommended.* That was the weighted suggestion.

Alternative. If applicant appears agitated, press any key for Security now.

Alternative. If applicant is calm and Social Interface judges it prudent, proceed as for normal interview.

Cecily looked determined, not agitated. If she had looked overwrought, believe me, I would have called Security. I'd seen Cecily in a temper and knew what she was capable of doing. She wasn't angry, not yet. Both curiosity and nostalgia swayed me. From the way she looked at me, I didn't think she'd recognized me. I didn't think I had changed that much, but my screen spectacles are the bulky government-issue type, and I had them set at semiopaque. I double blinked to bring up the next screen. She saw it and waited silently.

The information surprised me. She'd completed a psychological evaluation followed by a personality reorganization class a year ago. Her obsessive/compulsive disorder was controlled with medication. Her preparenting scores were within the acceptable range. She had four preapproved fetus choices, all children selected from the "nondemanding" end of the spectrum. Her physical size had limited her to smaller infants for natural birth. Still. Four choices weren't bad. I'd interviewed prospective parents who were limited to one or two options and still managed to send them away happy. Mentally, I earmarked a Cherub2 male as being her best bet. I'd steer her that way.

1 smiled at her sunglasses and observed, "Well, Ms. Kelvey, does this visit mean you've reached a choice on your options?"

She took a breath. That brisk rise and fall of her small breasts that had always indicated she was going to take a stand with Cliff. Not a good sign. Her voice was as I remembered it, girlish and without depth. She'd wanted to do backup vocals for Flat Plats, had even bought an enhancer, but Cliff had refused her. "We're retro," he had reminded her harshly. "Real voices. Real instruments. Real people playing them." The flung enhancer had given him a black eye.

"Not exactly." Her voice jerked me back to the present. "This visit is so I can submit documentation as to why my request for a free conception should be granted." She bent down to the canvas tote at her feet and began taking out papers. Some were folded, some yellowed at the edges. Papers. The information hadn't even been scanned to disk. I accepted it from her hands the way you take wilted dandelions from a kid. It's the intention. A tap set my specs to scan as I looked over her "documentation."

None of it was biologically acceptable data. It was a weird spectrum of stuff, from old grade readouts from high school to IQ tests that documented Cliff's brilliance. There was even a newspaper clipping that called him a "rock Mozart." My heart sank as I realized what she was angling after. She didn't want an approved fetal implant. She was going for an egg/sperm conception. In some parts of the world, they were still common, but for the life of me, I couldn't figure out why anyone would choose to take such monumental risks.

I obediently finished blinking the material into her reproductive request file. The nature of the entries might set off a red flag. The behavior of compiling such a pile of nonrelevant information was a definite earmark of obsession. She might find her prescriptions adjusted the next time she got her monthly implant. Cecily's actions, I told myself, not mine. If it made trouble for her, she'd brought it on herself. I gave the sheaf of documents back to her. She held them and watched me hopefully.

"So." I glanced at my timer. Three more minutes before I went into overtime with her. "Apparently you wish to conceive a random fetus with eggs from yourself and sperm from Cliff Wangle. You have his permission to do this?"

Her shades were so dark, I couldn't tell if she met my gaze or not. "He's dead. But before his death, he made a sperm deposit at a private facility. They were a birthday gift to me. As my property, they are mine to use as I wish."

"That is true."

"But I can't schedule an insemination without a permit. That's all I'm here for today. A permit."

"One moment, please." I swiveled back to my keyboard. A blink or two brought up her genetic rating on my specs. I had to key in Cliff's SSN to do a search for his. Both were as I expected. *Unacceptable.* "I'm very sorry, Ms, Kelvey, but neither you nor your sperm donor is genetically qualified to reproduce. Fortunately, this does not mean that you cannot have a child. It is a woman's right to choose, of course, and we have four possible choices for you." I swiveled my monitor screen toward her and blinked to pull up a split screen of four adorable babies. One gurgled aloud and then sneezed endearingly. I damped the volume.

She took off her sunglasses and stared at me. The crow's-feet at the corners of her eyes reminded me of how many years had passed since I had last seen her. The flat anger in her blue eyes told me that my screen specs were no disguise at all.

"Cut the crap, Chesterton. I want a real baby, not a seed-catalog clone. I want Cliff's baby. I know you can do this for me. Push the button and hand me a slip. That's all you have to do."

The bottom dropped out of my stomach. I knew I was subject to random monitoring. Some Interfaces believe we are constantly monitored. My instructors had always counseled me to behave as if we were. That was how one stayed at maximum efficiency. It was also how to keep your job. "I can't do that, Cecily," I said quietly. "There is some latitude in my job, but not near that much. If your health allows it . . ." I punched some keys and got a tentative okay. " . . . by opting for a C-section delivery, one sometimes gains a few additional choices . . ." I punched a few more keys, then shook my head at the readouts on my specs. "But not in your case. Temperament can be more restrictive than physical biology." I winked and the Cherub2 male expanded to fill the screen. "But this little fellow is a perfect match for you. Look at that curly hair, and those big blue eyes."

"I don't want curly hair, or big blue eyes. I don't want perfect teeth and zero birth defects. I don't want any of the features and benefits I've been hearing about for nine months. I want Cliff's baby, Chesterton. And Cliff Wangle's baby deserves to be born just as much as any of these gen-engineered ones. More so. You guarantee any of those four will have average intelligence? Well, Cliff's baby would be a genius."

"Cecily, you know better than that. We all do. An exceptional donor doesn't guarantee an exceptional child." I was smooth. I didn't bother to challenge her assertion that Cliff was a genius. "I'm sure you've seen Cliff's genetic profile, and your own. Manic-depressives tend to assort. Left to themselves, they mate with other manic-depressives, increasing the child's chance of mental illness." I let her connect the dots.

She leaned forward to hiss at me. "That's stupid! How can something that is genetically determined be called an 'illness'? My moodiness should be seen as within the range of normal human development. If it wasn't, why the hell would there be so many of us? Society used to allow for us. Look at all the Byronic poets with 'melancholy temperaments.' Can you tell me it's right to silence an unborn poet simply because he may be a bit moody?"

I'd read the same article. It's part of my job as a Social Interface. I have to keep up with all the crackpot metaphysics of horoscopes, wonder diets, and "give birth under a crystal-hung pyramid" fads. The ones who argue for a random conception usually spout the old nonsense about a need to guarantee genetic diversity, as if new embryos weren't licensed every month. In the long run, it's about selfishness, not diversity. It was all about the belief that my genes were better than anyone else's, the same basic concept that is behind prejudice, racism, and even genocide. It's amazing what otherwise rational people will buy into when it comes to reproduction. In Cecily's case, she had found scripture to support her obsession. She'd cling to it no matter what. For old time's sake, I made one more effort.

"A bit moody is one thing. A history of suicide, social maladjustment, and public violence is another. Cecily, you can't have Cliff's baby. You can't expect society to support you in a bad choice. Choose another."

"I don't want another."

I winced. I was sure the monitor would record those words and store it in her files. Her words would register her as refusing her choices. That counted as an abdication of her right to reproduce. The next time she came in to bully someone in Reproduction, she would find her options changed to a flat Choices Relinquished.

Perhaps she saw something in my face. She pushed back her chair. "Forget it, Chesterton. I shouldn't even have bothered coming here. There are ways to get around this. I'll have Cliff's baby."

I wondered what she was imagining. Did she have some of his sperm in an ice tray in her home freezer? Would she inject herself with a turkey baster? According to the netbloids, that happened every day. There were still random births. No system was perfect. But ours was close to it, because it now excluded the imperfect. I kept my voice level as I reminded her. "Ms. Kelvey, I suppose that is theoretically possible. But if you should become pregnant without a permit, all support benefits from the state will instantly cease, including your Basic Individual Maintenance. Neither you nor your child will ever be eligible for a housing allowance or medical benefits. Your child would be ineligible for citizenship."

"That's not fair!" she cried. The eternal objection of the citizen who wants only her own way.

"It is ultimately fair. Why should your neighbor's taxes go to support a substandard child? Why should you be allowed to gamble genetically for the sake of your own ego? Suppose you give birth to an idiot, or someone with such a 'melancholy temperament' that he cannot become a productive member of society? Why should we have to extend health benefits to such a person, let alone continue to support him or her after you are dead? You are talking about a very selfish act, Cecily. I'm sure even you can see that."

"Selfish act!" She leaned forward and hissed the word at me. A centimeter closer and she would have triggered the automatic security alarm. A cool part of my mind wondered if she knew that, if she had stopped just short of making a legally threatening move.

She leaned back in her chair. She began stuffing her documents, willy-nilly, into her canvas tote. Furious words streamed from her as she thrust the papers in. "Selfish act, he says. Selfish act. From the king of the selfish acts."

She stood up. She snatched her dark glasses off and for the first time in years, I looked into her pale blue eyes. They were rimmed red and were a degree too shiny. Whatever she was using wasn't part of her monthly supplements. I had a duty to report that. But I just looked at her.

"You killed Cliff. When you destroyed the Flat Plats, you destroyed him. If you hadn't betrayed him, he'd be alive today. And rich, and famous, and everyone would know what a genius he was. Women would be lined up around the block to get a Cliff Wangle baby. It's all your fault, Chesterton. You were greedy and you were selfish. You had to go with the sure thing, didn't you? You couldn't take a chance, not on music, not on life. Well, look what it got you, just what the sure thing always gets you. A sure dose of nothing. Mediocrity."

She stood up so suddenly that her chair crashed over behind her. She didn't pause to right it. She shoved her sunglasses back onto her face and stormed out. As she went out the outer door, two security guards approached me. "Should we detain?" one asked me.

"I don't think it's necessary. I think she was able to vent her frustration at me. I don't think she's a danger to anyone at this time."

"You sure?" the other one asked.

I knew my response would be logged and filed under "legal culpability." If I were wrong, the security guards would be absolved of blame. I hedged my response.

"Reasonably sure," I replied. I longed to push my "break" button and get out of my cubicle for fifteen minutes. But that would be an extra break right at the end of my shift, and it might prompt someone to scrutinize the transaction immediately before. Any break in a pattern was a cause for concern. I gave security a small wave to dismiss them, and green-lighted. Out in the waiting room, a young man's face lit up with a smile and he hastened toward me.

The rest of the afternoon went well. I handled six more clients in record time, arranging good choices for all of them. After each happy customer, I offered myself a life choice affirmation. "I am good at my job. Because I am good at my job, I increase the satisfaction other people have in their lives." I knew it was true, and every one of my last six clients thanked me, but somehow the affirmations didn't work as well as they usually did.

My bus was late and filled up before I could get on, so I had to stand and wait for the next one. The early evening streets were filled with teens and twenties, some quietly studying palmscreens while they waited, others laughing and jostling and restless. I wondered who they would be ten years from now and wondered who they thought they were now. Sweet illusions of youth.

I thought back to my precareer days, when my whole life had been Basic Individual Maintenance, a Housing Allowance, and my music. I thought I had needed nothing more. I had been convinced that I was going to be rich and famous long before society mandated that I settle on a career choice. Mikey, Cliff, and I had lived together in an efficiency, using the extra HAs we saved to buy sound equipment. We had been at the crest of the retro-rock wave. We should have made it. Damn it, we had made it, until Cliff destroyed it. Cliff, not me. Cliff, who had to be wild and crazy for the sake of being wild and crazy. He always claimed it was for the music, but that was just crap. It was for the sake of Cliff Wangle. It had nothing to do with the sounds we made; he just wanted to be the star. He wanted to be worshipped as an old-fashioned rock bad boy.

We'd practice our set endlessly, but once we were onstage, there was no predicting what Cliff would do to us. A forty-five-second drum bridge might become a two-minute drum solo. It would throw the whole band into chaos. Mikey would improvise weird vocalizations to cover, and whatever guitar player we currently had would just about tear his fingers off trying to keep up. I'd usually get pissed and just stop playing until he was finished grandstanding and came back to the plan. Aloysius would use his bass as if it was a weapon, pointing it at Cliff and firing off chord after chord, always with this weird grin on his face. And the audience would go crazy, screaming and jumping, and Cliff would feed off it, drumming until the sweat flew from him. That was the title of our first commercial release: *Spattered Sweat.*

Blood Blisters, our second one, should have assured our careers. Instead, Cliff had axed it. He'd burned all the live masters, all our notes, everything he could get his hands on, in a fifty-gallon drum down on the beach one drunken evening after calling up our label and telling them that Flat Plats no longer existed. He said he'd sue the hell out of them if they tried to release *Blood Blisters.* And why? Simply because I had replaced one of his live wild man solos with a studio track we had done earlier. The label had loved it, our producer was wild about it, the decreased length made it a more commercially viable track, and the sound was cleaner—hell, even Mikey and Aloysius had grudgingly admitted it gave the rest of the band a chance to shine in their own right. The fans loved it; the prerelease teaser downloads from our site were incredible. Everyone who was anyone had agreed I'd made a wise choice for the band.

Everyone but Cliff.

He came back a month late from his "weekend" in Mexico with Cecily, listened to what was on the site, and exploded. I'd tried to reason with him, but we'd only gotten into the same old argument.

I couldn't understand why he couldn't play a piece live just the way we played it in the studio or at rehearsal. "Give the fans what they expect, what they paid for, not some unpredictable experimental . . ."

"Give them what they expect!" he'd roared. "Then it's theirs, not ours, you idiot! And there's no reason to play it again, if it comes out the same every damn time. Music isn't supposed to be 'right'; it's supposed to be music. Alive. Growing and changing. If it doesn't change, then how are you going to get from 'right' to 'better'?"

I'd made one final try. "Isn't it as likely to be 'worse' as 'better'?" I'd asked him.

"Chesterton. That's the chance you've got to take. That's how you know you're alive."

And they all just stared at me. I knew then that I'd lost. I'd lost the moment that Cliff Wangle walked back into the room. When Cliff was there, none of the others could ever do things any way but his. It was just how they were. And that had been the end of the Flat Plats and my musical career.

The bus came and I got on it.

THE APARTMENT WAS dark when I opened the door. The note on the table said she'd taken the boy to the movies with his friends. Dinner was in the fridge.

But I didn't eat. I went to the living room and took down my keyboard. I turned on the media wall and plugged it in. I set up for video, audio, body vibes, lights, the whole show. I pulled up *Blood Blisters,* the studio track that Cliff had despised. I helmeted in so the sound wouldn't disturb the neighbors, and I turned it on. Then I played along with it, keyboard in my lap, hammering every note at precisely the right moment, exactly as we'd played it that day in the studio, proving to myself that I still had it. Then I hit reset and played it again. I sounded just as great. By the time I finished the third run through, I was dripping sweat. I leaned back and cranked up the audience roar I'd spliced in at the end. I lifted my arms and held them wide until it died off into white noise.

I took off the helmet and shook my sweaty hair loose. So much for you, Cliff Wangle. You're dead and Chesterton is still as good as he ever was. So who's the real musician now? I headed for the shower, grinning, triumphant. There's nothing like knowing you can do it. I could have played it a hundred times, and each repetition would have been just as good as the first.

PART II

ROBIN HOBB

Homecoming

Robin Hobb. Short stories. The two seldom intersect, it seems to me. My style as Hobb loves to sprawl, to explore the incidental and to revel in details. None of those things play well in a short story setting, and I've seldom attempted short work as Hobb.

But in 2002, I was approached to contribute a story to the Legends II *anthology that Robert Silverberg was putting together. I was both dumbfounded and dazzled by the offer. Robert Silverberg wanted me to write a story for his anthology? Robert Silverberg!!!! Too good to resist!*

Now all I needed was a solid idea for a good story.

Days passed and my panic level rose as I considered and rejected story ideas. This one was great but demanded a novel to do it justice; I didn't know the ending to the next one; the third one made no sense when I considered what the characters were doing . . . but finally it came to me to take all the ingredients that I most enjoyed and stir them together and try to find a story in the mix. So I took some ancient buried cities and added some people pushed far outside their comfort zones by harsh necessity. Then I put in a foreign environment, elements of mystery, a protagonist with the potential for growth and put it all into the form of a journal.

I also really enjoyed the opportunity to return to the Rain Wild settings of the Liveship Trader books and spell out some of the history of the region for readers. I hope you'll enjoy reading it as much as I enjoyed writing it.

Day the 7th of the Fish Moon
Year the 14th of the Reign of the Most Noble and Magnificent Satrap Esclepius

Confiscated from me this day, without cause or justice, were five crates and three trunks. This occurred during the loading of the ship *Venture,* setting forth upon Satrap Esclepius's noble endeavor to colonize the Cursed Shores. Contents of the crates are as follows: one block fine white marble, of a size suitable for a bust; two blocks Aarthian jade, sizes suitable for busts; one large fine soapstone, as tall as a man and as wide as a man; seven large copper ingots, of excellent quality; three silver ingots, of acceptable quality; and three kegs of wax. One crate contained scales, tools for the working of metal and stone, and measuring equipment. Contents of trunks are as follows: two silk gowns, one blue, one pink, tailored by Seamstress Wista and bearing her mark; a dress length of mille-cloth, green; two shawls, one of white wool, one of blue linen. Several pairs of hose, in winter and summer weights; three pairs of slippers, one silk and worked with rosebuds; seven petticoats, three silk, one linen, and three wool; one bodice frame, of light bone and silk; three volumes of poetry, written in my own hand; a miniature by Soiji, of myself, Lady Carillion Carrock, née Waljin, commissioned by my mother, Lady Arston Waljin, on the occasion of my fourteenth birthday. Also included were clothing and bedding for a baby, a girl of four years, and two boys, of six and ten years, including both winter and summer garb for formal occasions.

I record this confiscation so that the thieves can be brought to justice upon my return to Jamaillia City. The theft was in this manner: as our ship was being loaded for departure, cargo belonging to various nobles aboard the vessels was detained upon the docks. Captain Triops informed us that our possessions would be held, indefinitely, in the Satrap's custody. I do not trust the man, for he shows neither my husband nor myself proper deference. So I make this record, and when I return this coming spring to Jamaillia City, my father, Lord Crion Waljin, will bring my complaint before the Satrap's Court of Justice, as my husband seems little inclined to do so.

This do I, Lady Carillion Waljin Carrock, swear.

Day the 10th of the Fish Moon

Year the 14th of the Reign of the Most Noble and Magnificent Satrap Esclepius

Conditions aboard the ship are intolerable. Once more, I take pen to my journal to record the hardship and injustice to preserve a record so that those responsible may be punished. Although I am nobly born, of the House of Waljin and although my lord husband is not only noble, but heir to the title of Lord Carrock, the quarters given us are no better than those allotted to the common emigrants and speculators; that is, a smelly space in the ship's hold. Only the common criminals, chained in the deepest holds, suffer more than we do.

The floor is a splintery wooden deck, the walls are the bare planks of the ship's hull. There is much evidence that rats were the last inhabitants of this compartment. We are treated no better than cattle. There are no separate quarters for my maid, so I must suffer her to bed almost alongside us! To preserve my children from the common brats of the emigrants, I have sacrificed three damask hangings to curtain off a space. Those people accord me no respect. I believe that they are surreptitiously plundering our stores of food. When they mock me, my husband bids me ignore them. This has had a dreadful effect on my servant's behavior. This morning, my maid, who also serves as a nanny in our reduced household, spoke almost harshly to young Petrus, bidding him be quiet and cease his questions. When I rebuked her for it, she dared to raise her brows at me.

My visit to the open deck was a waste of time. It is cluttered with ropes, canvas, and crude men, with no provisions for ladies and children to take the air. The sea was boring, the view only distant foggy islands. I found nothing there to cheer me as this detestable vessel bears me ever farther away from the lofty white spires of Blessed Jamaillia City, sacred to Sa.

I have no friends aboard the ship to amuse or comfort me in my heaviness. Lady Duparge has called on me once, and I was civil, but the differences in our station make conversation difficult. Lord Duparge is heir to little more than his title, two ships, and one estate that borders on Gerfen Swamp. Ladies Crifton and Anxory appear content with each other's company and have not called upon me at all. They are both too young to have any accomplishments to share, yet their mothers should have instructed them in their social responsibility to their betters. Both might have profited from my friendship upon our return to Jamaillia City. That they choose not to court my favor does not speak well of their intellect. Doubtless they would bore me.

I am miserable in these disgusting surroundings. Why my husband has chosen to invest his time and finances in this venture eludes me. Surely men of a more adventurous nature would better serve our Illustrious Satrap in this exploration. Nor can I understand why our children and myself must accompany him, especially in my condition. I do not think my husband gave any thought to the difficulties this voyage would pose for a woman gravid with child. As ever, he has not seen fit to discuss his decisions with me, no more than I would consult him on my artistic pursuits. Yet my ambitions must suffer to allow him to pursue his! My absence will substantially delay the completion of my *Suspended Chimes of Stone and Metal.* The Satrap's brother will be most disappointed, for the installation was to have honored his thirtieth birthday.

Day the 15th of the Fish Moon
Year the 14th of the Reign of the Most Noble and Magnificent Satrap Esclepius

I have been foolish. No. I have been deceived. It is not foolishness to trust where one has every right to expect trustworthiness. When my father entrusted my hand and my fate to Lord Jathan Carrock, he believed he was a man of wealth, substance, and reputation. My father blessed Sa's name that my artistic accomplishments had attracted a suitor of such lofty stature. When I bewailed the fate that wed me to a man so much my senior, my mother counseled me to accept it and to pursue my art and establish my reputation in the shelter of his influence. I honored their wisdom. For these last ten years, as my youth and beauty faded in his shadow, I have borne him three children and bear beneath my heart the burgeoning seed of yet another. I have been an ornament and a blessing to him, and yet he has deceived me. When I think of the hours spent in managing his household, hours I could have devoted to my art, my blood seethes with bitterness.

Today, I first entreated, and then, in the throes of my duty to provide for my children, demanded that he force the captain to give us better quarters. Sending our three children out onto the deck with their nanny, he confessed that we were not willing investors in the Satrap's colonization plan but exiles given a chance to flee our disgrace. All we left behind—estates, homes, precious possessions, horses, cattle—all are forfeit to the Satrap, as are the items seized from us as we embarked. My genteel respectable husband is a traitor to our gentle and beloved Satrap and a plotter against the Throne Blessed by Sa.

I won this admittance from him, bit by bit. He kept saying I should not bother about the politics, that it was solely his concern. He said a wife should trust her husband to manage her life. He said that by the time the ships resupply our settlement next spring, he would have redeemed our fortune and we would return to Jamaillian society. But I kept pressing my silly woman's questions. All your holdings seized? I asked him. All? And he said it was done to save the Carrock name, so that his parents and younger brother can live with dignity, untarnished by the scandal. A small estate remains for his brother to inherit. The Satrap's Court will believe that Jathan Carrock chose to invest his entire fortune in the Satrap's venture. Only those in the Satrap's innermost circle know it was a confiscation. To win this concession, Jathan begged many hours on his knees, humbling himself and pleading forgiveness.

He went on at great length about that, as if I should be impressed. But I cared nothing for his knees. "What of Thistlebend?" I asked. "What of the cottage by the ford there, and the monies from it?" This I brought to him as my marriage portion, and humble though it is, I thought to see it passed to Narissa when she wed.

"Gone," he said, "All gone."

"But why?" I demanded. "I have not plotted against the Satrap. Why am I punished?"

Angrily, he said I was his wife and of course I would share his fate. I did not see why, he could not explain it, and finally he told me that such a foolish woman could never understand and bid me hold my tongue, not flap it and show my ignorance. When I protested that I am not a fool, but a well-known artist, he told me that I am now a colonist's wife and to put my artistic pretenses out of my head.

I bit my tongue to keep from shrieking at him. But within me, my heart screams in fury against this injustice. Thistlebend, where my little sisters and I waded in the water and plucked lilies to pretend we were goddesses and those our white and gold scepters . . . Gone for Jathan Carrock's treacherous idiocy.

I had heard rumors of a discovered conspiracy against the Satrap. I paid no attention. I thought it had nothing to do with me. I would say that the punishment was just, if I and my innocent babes were not ensnared in the same net that has trapped the plotters. All the confiscated wealth has financed this expedition. The disgraced nobles were forced to join a company composed of speculators and explorers. Worse, the banished criminals in the hold, the thieves and whores and ruffians, will be released to join our company when we disembark. Such will be the society around my tender children.

Our Blessed Satrap has generously granted us a chance to redeem ourselves. Our Magnificent and Most Merciful Satrap has granted each man of the company two hundred leffers of land, to be claimed anywhere along the banks of the Rain Wild River that is our boundary with barbarous Chalced, or along the Cursed Shores. He directs us to establish our first settlement on the Rain Wild River. He chose this site for us because of the ancient legends of the Elder Kings and their Harlot Queens. Long ago, it is said, their wondrous cities lined the river. They dusted their skin with gold and wore jewels above their eyes. So the tales say. Jathan said that an ancient scroll, showing their settlements, has recently been translated. I am skeptical.

In return for this chance to carve out new fortunes for ourselves and redeem our reputations, Our Glorious Satrap Esclepius asks only that we cede to him half of all that we find or produce there. In return, the Satrap will shelter us under his protective hand, prayers will be offered for our well-being, and twice yearly his revenue ships will visit our settlement to be sure we prosper. A charter for our company, signed by the Satrap's own hand, promises this.

Lords Anxory, Crifton, and Duparge share in our disgrace, though as lesser lords, they had less far to fall. There are other nobles aboard the other two ships of our fleet, but no one I know well. I rejoice that my dear friends do not share my fate, yet I mourn that I enter exile alone. I will not count upon my husband for comfort in the disaster he has brought upon us. Few secrets are kept long at court. Is that why none of my friends came to the docks to bid me farewell?

My own mother and sister had little time to devote to my packing and farewells. They wept as they bade me farewell from my father's home, not even accompanying me to the filthy docks where this ship of banishment awaited me. Why, oh Sa, did they not tell me the truth of my fate?

At that thought, a hysteria fell upon me, so that I could not continue my writing. I trembled and wept, with occasional shrieks bursting from me whether I would or no. Even now, my hands tremble so violently that this desperate scrawl wanders the page. All is lost to me, home, loving parents, and most crushing, the art that gave me joy in life. The half-finished works I left behind will never be completed, and that pains me as much as a child stillborn. I live only for the day that I can return to gracious Jamaillia by the sea. At this moment, forgive me Sa, I long to do so as a widow. Never will I forgive Jathan Carrock. Bile rises in my throat at the thought that my children must wear this traitor's name.

Day the 24th of the Fish Moon
Year the 14th of the Reign of the Most Noble and Magnificent Satrap Esclepius

Darkness fills my soul; this voyage to exile has lasted an eternity. The man I must call husband orders me to better manage our household, but I scarcely have the spirit to take up my pen. The children weep, quarrel, and complain endlessly, and my maid makes no effort to amuse them. Daily her contempt grows. I would slap her disrespectful scowl from her face if I had the strength. Despite my pregnancy, she lets the children tug at me and demand my attention. All know a woman in my condition should experience a serene existence. Yesterday afternoon, when I tried to rest, she left the children napping beside me while she went out to dally with a common sailor. I awoke to Narissa crying and had to arise and sing to her until she calmed. She complains of a painful belly and a sore throat. No sooner was she settled than both Petrus and Carlmin awoke and started some boyish tussling that completely frayed my spirit. I was exhausted and at the edge of hysteria before she returned. When I chided her for neglecting her duties, she saucily replied that her own mother reared nine children with no servants to aid her. As if such common drudgery were something I should aspire to! Were there anyone else to fulfill her duties, I would send her packing.

And where is Lord Carrock through all of this? Why, out on deck, consulting with the very nobles who led him into disgrace.

The food grows ever worse and the water tastes foul, but our cowardly captain will not put into shore to seek better. My maid says that her sailor has told her that the Cursed Shore is well named, and that evil befalls those who land there as surely as it befell those who once lived there. Can even Captain Triops believe such superstitious nonsense?

Day the 27th of the Fish Moon
Year the 14th of the Reign of the Most Noble and Magnificent Satrap Esclepius

We are battered by storm. The ship reeks of the vomit of the miserable inhabitants of its bowels. The constant lurching stirs the foul waters of the bilge, so that we must breathe their stench. The captain will not allow us out on the deck at all. The air down here is damp and thick, and the beams drip water on us. Surely, I have died and entered some heathen afterlife of punishment.

Yet in all this wet, there is scarcely enough water for drinking, and none for washing. Clothing and bedding soiled with sickness must be rinsed out in seawater that leaves it stiff and stained with salt. Little Narissa has been most miserable of the children. She has ceased vomiting but has scarcely stirred from her pallet today, poor little creature. Please, Sa, let this horrid rocking and sloshing end soon.

Day the 29th of the Fish Moon
Year the 14th of the Reign of the Most Noble and Magnificent Satrap Esclepius

My child is dead. Narissa, my only daughter, is gone. Sa, have mercy upon me, and visit your justice upon treacherous Lord Jathan Carrock, for his evil has been the cause of all my woe! They wrapped my little girl in canvas and sent her and two others into the waters, and the sailors scarce paused in their labors to notice their passing. I think I went a little mad then. Lord Carrock seized me in his arms when I tried to follow her into the sea. I fought him, but he was too strong for me. I remain trapped in this life his treachery has condemned me to endure.

Day the 7th of the Plough Moon
Year the 14th of the Reign of the Most Noble and Magnificent Satrap Esclepius

My child is still dead. Ah, such a foolish thought to write, and yet still it seems impossible to me. Narissa, Narissa, you cannot be gone forever. Surely this is some monstrous dream from which I will awake!

Today, because I sat weeping, my husband pushed this book at me and said "Write a poem to comfort yourself. Hide in your art until you feel better. Do anything, but stop weeping!" As if he offered a squalling baby a sugar teat. As if art took you away from life rather than plunging you headlong into it! Jathan reproached me for my grief, saying that my reckless mourning frightens our sons and threatens the babe in my womb. As if he truly cared! Had he cared for us as a husband and a father, never would he have betrayed our dear Satrap and condemned us to this fate.

But, to stop his scowl, I will sit here and write for a time, like a good wife.

A full dozen of the passengers and two crewmen have died of the flux. Of one hundred sixteen who began this voyage, ninety-two now remain. The weather has calmed but the warm sunlight on the deck only mocks my sorrow. A haze hangs over the sea, and to the west the distant mountains smoke.

Day the 18th of the Plough Moon
Year the 14th of the Reign of the Most Noble and Magnificent Satrap Esclepius

I have no spirit to write, yet there is nothing else to occupy my weary mind. I, who once composed the wittiest prose and most soaring poetry, now plod word by word down a page.

Some days ago we reached the river mouth; I did not note the date, such has been my gloom. All the men cheered when we sighted it. Some spoke of gold, others of legendary cities to plunder, and still others of virgin timber and farmland awaiting us. I thought it marked an end to our voyage, but still it drags on.

At first the rising tide aided our upriver progress. Now the crew must labor at their oars for every ship-length we gain. The prisoners have been taken from their chains and utilized as rowers in tiny boats. They row upriver and set anchors and drag us against the current. By night, we anchor and listen to the rush of the water and the shrieks of unseen creatures from the jungle on the shore. Daily the scenery grows both more fantastic and threatening. The trees on the banks stand twice as tall as our mast, and the ones behind them are taller still. When the river narrows, they cast deep shadows over us. Our view is a near impenetrable wall of greenery. Our search for a kindly shore seems folly. I see no sign that any people have ever lived here. The only creatures are bright birds, large lizards that sun themselves on the tree roots at the water's edge, and something that whoops and scuttles in the treetops. There are no gentle meadows or firm shores, only marshy banks and rank vegetation. Immense trees root stiltlike in the water, and dangling vines festoon them, trailing in the chalky water. Some have flowers that gleam white even in the night. They hang, fleshy and thick, and the wind carries their sweet, carnal breath. Stinging insects torment us, and the oarsmen are subject to painful rashes. The river water is not potable; worse, it eats at both flesh and wood, softening oars and ulcerating flesh. If left to stand in vessels, the top layer of the water becomes drinkable, but the residue swiftly eats into leaks in the bucket. Those who drink it complain of headaches and wild dreams. One criminal raved of "lovely serpents" and then threw himself overboard. Two crewmen have been confined in chains because of their wild talk.

I see no end to this horrid journeying. We have lost sight of our two companion vessels. Captain Triops is supposed to put us off at a safe landing that offers opportunity for a settlement and farming. The company's hope of open sunny meadows and gentle hills fades with every passing day. The captain says that this fresh water is bad for his ship's hull. He wishes to put us ashore in the swamp, saying that the trees on the shore may be concealing higher land and open forest. Our men argue against this, and often unroll the charter the Satrap has given us and point out what was promised to us. He counters by showing the orders the Satrap gave him. It speaks of landmarks that don't exist, navigable channels that are shallow and rocky, and cities where only jungle crawls. Sa's priests made this translation and they cannot lie. But something is very wrong.

The entire ship broods. Quarrels are frequent, and the crew mutters against the captain. A terrible nervousness afflicts me, so that tears are never far away. Petrus suffers from nightmares and Carlmin, always a reclusive child, has become near mute.

Oh, Fair Jamaillia, city of my birth, will I ever again see your rolling hills and graceful spires? Mother, Father, do you mourn me as lost to you forever?

And this great splotch is Petrus jostling me as he climbs upon my lap, saying he is bored. My maid is next to useless. She does little to earn all the food she devours, and then she is off, to slink about the ship like a cat in heat. Yesterday, I told her that if she got with child from her immoral passions, I would immediately turn her out. She dared to say she did not care, for her days in my service were numbered. Does the foolish slat forget that she is indentured to us for another five years?

Day the 22nd of the Plough Moon
Year the 14th of the Reign of the Most Noble and Magnificent Satrap Esclepius

It has happened as I feared. I crouch on a great knee of root, my writing desk a chest of my meager possessions. The tree at my back is as big around as a tower. Strands and tangle of roots, some as big around as barrels, anchor it in the swampy ground. I perch on one to save my skirts from the damp and tussocky earth. At least on the ship, in the middle of the river, we were blessed with sunlight from above. Here, the foliage overshadows us, an eternal twilight.

Captain Triops has marooned us here in the swamp. He claimed that his ship was taking on water, and his only choice was to lighten his load and flee this corrosive river. When we refused to disembark, there was violence as the crew forced us from the ship. After one of our men was thrown overboard and swept away, our will to resist vanished. The stock that was to sustain us they kept. One of our men frantically seized the cage of messenger birds and fought for it. In the tussle, the cage broke, and all our birds rose in a flock to disappear. The crew threw off the crates of tools, seed, and provisions that were supposed to aid us in establishing our colony. They did it to lighten the ship, not to help us. Many fell in deep water, out of reach. The men have salvaged what they could of those that fell on the soft riverside. The muck has sucked the rest down. Now we are seventy-two souls in this forsaken place, of which forty are able-bodied men.

Great trees tower over us. The land trembles under our feet like a crust on a pudding, and where the men marched over it to gather our possessions, water now seeps, filling their footprints.

The current swept the ship and our faithless captain swiftly from our sight. Some say we must stay where we are, beside the river, and watch for the other two ships. Surely, they say, they will help us. I think we must move deeper into the forest, seeking firmer land and relief from the biting insects. But I am a woman, with no say in this.

The men hold council now, to decide leadership of our company. Jathan Carrock put himself forward, as being of the noblest birth, but he was shouted down by others, former prisoners, tradesmen, and speculators who said that his father's name had no value here. They mocked him, for all seem to know the "secret" that we are disgraced in Jamaillia. I walked away from watching them, feeling bitter.

My own situation is a desperate one. My feckless maid did not leave the ship with us, but stayed aboard, a sailor's whore. I wish her all she deserves! And now Petrus and Carlmin cling to me, complaining that the water has soaked their shoes and their feet sting from the damp. When I shall have a moment to myself again, I do not know. I curse the artist in me, for as I look up at the slanting beam of sunlight slicing through the intervening layers of branch and leaf, I see a wild and dangerous beauty to this place. Did I give in to it, I fear it could be as seductive as the raw glance of a rough man.

I do not know where such thoughts come from. I simply want to go home.

Somewhere on the leaves above us, it is raining.

Day the 24th of the Plough Moon

Year the 14th of the Reign of the Most Noble and Magnificent Satrap Esclepius

I was jolted from sleep before dawn, thrown out of a vivid dream of a foreign street festival. It was as if the earth leaped sideways beneath us. Then, when the sun was fairly up in the unseen sky, we again felt the land tremble. The earthquake passed through the Rain Wild about us like a wave. I have experienced earthquakes before, but in this gelid region, the tremor seemed stronger and more threatening. It is easy to imagine this marshy ground gulping us down like a yellow carp swallowing a breadcrumb.

Despite our inland trek, the land remains swampy and treacherous beneath our feet. Today, I came face-to-face with a snake hanging down from a tangle of green. My heart was seized both by his beauty and my terror. How effortlessly he lifted himself from his perusal of me to continue his journey along the intertwining branches overhead. Would that I could cross this land as effortlessly!

Day the 27th of the Plough Moon

Year the 14th of the Reign of the Most Noble and Magnificent Satrap Esclepius

I write while perched in a tree like one of the bright parrots that share the branch with me. I feel both ridiculous and exhilarated, despite hunger, thirst, and great weariness. Perhaps my headiness is a side effect of starvation.

For five days, we have trekked ponderously through soft ground and thick brush, away from the river, seeking dryer ground. Some of our party protest this, saying that when our promised ship comes in spring, it will not be able to find us. I hold my tongue, but I doubt that any ship will come up this river again.

Moving inland did not improve our lot. The ground remains tremulous and boggy. By the time our entire party has passed over it, we leave a track of mud and standing water behind us. The damp inflames our feet and rots the fabric of my skirt. All the women go draggle hemmed now.

We have abandoned whatever we could not carry. Every one of us—man, woman, and child—carries as much as possible. The little ones grow weary. I feel the child inside me grow heavier with each sucking step.

The men have formed a council to rule us. Each man is to have one vote in it. I regard this ignoring of the natural order as perilous, yet there is no way for the outcast nobles to assert their right to rule. Jathan told me privately that we do best to let this happen, for soon enough the company will see that common farmers, pickpockets, and adventurers are not suited to rule. For now, we heed their rules. The council has gathered the dwindling food supplies into a common hoard. We are parceled out a pittance each day. The council says that all men will share the work equally. Thus Jathan must stand a night watch with his fellows as if he were a common soldier. The men stand watch in pairs, for a sole watchman is more prone to the strange madness that lurks in this place. We speak little of it, but all have had strange dreams, and some of our company seem to be wandering in their minds. The men blame the water. There is talk of sending out exploring parties to find a good dry site for our settlement.

I have no faith in their brave plans. This wild place does not care for our rules or council.

We have found little here to sustain us. The vegetation is strange, and the only animal life we have seen moves in the higher reaches of the trees. Yet amid this wild and tangled sprawl, there is still beauty, if one has an eye for it. The sunlight that reaches us through the canopy of the trees is gentle and dappled, illuminating the feathery mosses that drape from the vines. One moment I curse it as we struggle through its clinging nets, and in the next, I see it as dusky green lace. Yesterday, despite my weariness and Jathan's impatience, I paused to enjoy the beauty of a flowering vine. In examining it, I noticed that each trumpetlike flower cupped a small quantity of rainwater, sweetened by the flower's nectar. Sa forgive me that I and my children drank well from many of the blossoms before I told the others of my find. We have also found mushrooms that grow like shelves on the tree trunks, and a vine that has red berries. It is not enough.

It is to my credit that we sleep dry tonight. I dreaded another night of sleeping on the damp ground, awakening wet and itching, or huddled atop our possessions as they slowly sink into the marshy ground. This evening, as the shadows began to deepen, I noticed bird nests dangling like swinging purses from some of the tree limbs. Well do I know how cleverly Petrus can climb furniture and even curtains. Selecting a tree with several stout branches almost at a level, I challenged my son to see if he could reach them. He clung to the vines that draped the tree while his little feet found purchase on the rough bark. Soon he sat high above us on a very thick limb, swinging his feet and laughing to see us stare.

I bade Jathan follow his son and take with him the damask drapes that I have carried so far. Others soon saw my plan. Slings of all kinds now hang like bright fruit in these dense trees. Some sleep on the wider branches or in the crotches of the trees, others in hammocks. It is precarious rest, but dry.

All praised me. "My wife has always been clever," Jathan declared, as if to take the credit from me, and so I reminded him, "I have a name of my own. I was Carillion Waljin long before I was Lady Carrock! Some of my best-known pieces as an artist, *Suspended Basins* and *Floating Lanterns,* required just such a knowledge of balance and support! The difference is one of scale, not property." At this, several of the women in our party gasped, deeming me a braggart, but Lady Duparge exclaimed, "She is right! I have always admired Lady Carrock's work."

Then one rough fellow was so bold as to add, "She will be just as clever as Trader Carrock's wife, for we will have no lords and ladies here."

It was a sobering thought to me, and yet I fear he has the right of it. Birth and breeding count for little here. Already they have given a vote to common men, less educated than Lady Duparge or I. A farmer has more say in our plans than I do.

And what did my husband mutter to me? "You shamed me by calling attention to yourself. Such vanity to boast of your 'artistic accomplishments.' Occupy yourself with your children's needs, not bragging of yourself." And so he put me in my place.

What is to become of us? What good to sleep dry if our bellies are empty and our throats dry? I so pity the child inside me. All the men cried "Caution!" to one another as they used a hoist and sling to lift me to this perch. Yet all the caution in the world cannot save this babe from the wilderness being his birthplace. I miss my Narissa still, and yet I think her end was kinder than what this strange forest may visit upon us.

Day the 29th of the Plough Moon

Year the 14th of the Reign of the Most Noble and Magnificent Satrap Esclepius

I ate another lizard tonight. It shames me to admit it. The first time, I did it with no more thought than a cat pouncing on a bird. During a rest time, I noticed the tiny creature on a fern frond. It was green as a jewel and so still. Only the glitter of its bright eye and the tiny pulse of life at its throat betrayed it to me. Swift as a snake, I struck. I caught it in my hand, and in an instant I cupped its soft belly against my mouth. I bit into it, and it was bitter, rank and sweet all at once. I crunched it down, bones and all, as if it were a steamed lark from the Satrap's banquet table. Afterward, I could not believe I had done it. I expected to feel ill, but I did not. Nevertheless, I felt too shamed to tell anyone what I had done. Such food seems unfit for a civilized human, let alone the manner in which I devoured it. I told myself it was the demands of the child growing in me, a momentary aberration brought on by gnawing hunger. I resolved never to do it again, and I put it out of my mind.

But tonight, I did. He was a slender gray fellow, the color of the tree. He saw my darting hand and hid in a crack of the bark, but I dragged him out by his tail. I held him pinched between my finger and thumb. He struggled wildly and then grew still, knowing it was useless. I looked at him closely, thinking that if I did so, then I could let him go. He was beautiful, his gleaming eyes, his tiny claws and lashing tail. His back was gray and rough as the tree bark, but his soft little belly was the color of cream. There was a blush of blue on the soft curve of his throat and a pale stripe of it down his belly. The scales of his belly were tiny and smooth when I pressed my tongue against them. I felt the pattering of his tiny heart and smelled the stench of his fear as his little claws scrabbled against my chapped lips. It was all so familiar somehow. Then I closed my eyes and bit into him, holding both my hands over my mouth to be sure no morsel escaped. There was a tiny smear of blood on my palm afterward. I licked it off. No one saw.

Sa, sweet Lord of all, what am I becoming? What prompts me to behave this way? The privation of hunger or the contagious wildness of this place? I hardly know myself. The dreams that plague my sleep are not those of a Jamaillian lady. The waters of the earth scald my hands and sear my feet, until they heal rough as cobs. I fear what my face and hair must look like.

Day the 2nd of the Greening Moon

Year the 14th of the Reign of the Most Noble and Magnificent Satrap Esclepius

A boy died last night. We were all shocked. He simply did not wake up this morning. He was a healthy lad of about twelve. Durgan was his name, and though he was only a tradesman's son, I share his parents' grief quite strongly. Petrus had followed him about and seems very shaken by his death. He whispered to me that he dreamed last night that the land remembered him. When I asked what he meant by that, he could not explain, but said that perhaps Durgan had died because this place didn't want him. He made no sense to me, but he repeated himself insistently until I nodded and said perhaps he was right. Sweet Sa, do not let the madness be taking my boy. It frightens me so. Perhaps it is good that my boy will no longer seek the companionship of such a common lad, yet Durgan had a wide smile and a ready laugh that we will miss.

As fast as the men dug a grave, it welled full of murky water. At last his mother had to be taken away while his father condemned his son's body to the water and muck. As we asked Sa's peace on him, the child inside me kicked angrily. It frightened me.

Day the 8th of the Greening Moon

(I think. Marthi Duparge says it is the 9th.)

Year the 14th of the Reign of the Most Noble and Magnificent Satrap Esclepius

We have found a patch of drier ground and most of us will rest here for a few days while a chosen party of men scouts for a better place. Our refuge is little more than a firmer island amid the swamp. We have learned that a certain type of needled bush indicates firmer ground, and here it is quite dense. It is resinous enough to burn even when green. It produces a dense and choking smoke, but it keeps the biting insects at bay.

Jathan is one of our scouts. With our child soon to be born, I thought he should stay here to help me care for our boys. He said he must go, to establish himself as a leader among the company. Lord Duparge is also to go as a scout. As Lady Marthi Duparge is also with child, Jathan said we could help each other. Such a young wife as she cannot be of much use at a birthing, and yet her company will be preferable to none at all. All of us women have drawn closer as privation has forced us to share our paltry resources for the good of our children.

Another of the women, a weaver's wife, has devised a way to make mats from the abundant vines. I have begun to learn this, for there is little else I can do, so heavy have I become. The mats can be used as bed pallets and also laced together into screens for shelter. All the nearby trees are smooth barked, with the branches beginning very high, so we must contrive what shelter we can on the ground. Several women joined us, and it was pleasant and almost homey to sit together and talk and work with our hands. The men laughed at us as we raised our woven walls, asking what such frail barriers can keep out. I felt foolish, yet as dark fell, we took comfort in our flimsy cottage. Sewet the weaver has a fine singing voice and brought tears to my eyes as she sang her youngest to sleep with the old song of "Praise to Sa in Tribulation." It seems a lifetime since last I heard music. How long must my children live with no culture and no tutors save the merciless judgment of this wild place?

As much as I disdain Jathan Carrock for bringing about our exile, I miss him this evening.

Day the 12th or 13th of the Greening Moon

Year the 14th of the Reign of the Most Noble and Magnificent Satrap Esclepius

A madness came upon our camp last night. It began with a woman starting up in the darkness, shouting, "Hark! Hark! Does no one else hear their singing?" Her husband tried to quiet her, but then a young boy exclaimed that he had heard the singing for several nights now. Then he plunged off into the darkness as if he knew where he was going. His mother ran after him. Then the woman broke free of her husband and raced off into the swamp. Three others went after her, not to bring her back but crying, "Wait, wait, we will go with you!"

I rose and held on to both my sons, lest the madness take them. A peculiar undark suffuses this jungle by night. The fireflies are familiar, but not an odd spider that leaves a glob of glowing spittle in the middle of its web. Tiny insects fly right into it, just as moths will seek a lantern's fire. There is also a dangling moss that gleams pale and cold. I dare not let my lads know how gruesome I find it. I told them I shivered because of the chill, and in concern for those poor benighted wretches lost in the swamp. Yet it chilled me even more to hear little Carlmin speak of how lovely the jungle was by night, and how sweet the scent of the night blooming flowers. He said he remembered when I used to make cakes flavored with those flowers. We never had such flowers in Jamaillia City, yet as he said it, I almost recalled little brown cakes, soft in the middle and crispy brown at the edges. Even as I write the words, I almost recall how I shaped them into blossoms before I cooked them in hot bubbling fat.

Never have I done such cooking, I swear.

As of midday, there is no sign of those the night madness took. Searchers went after them, but the search party returned wet and insect-bitten and disconsolate. The jungle has swallowed them. The woman left behind a small boy who has been wailing for her most of the day.

I have told no one of the music that haunts my dreams.

Day the 14th or 15th of the Plough Moon
Year the 14th of the Reign of the Most Noble and Magnificent Satrap Esclepius

Our scouts still have not returned. By day, we put a fine face on it for the children, but by night Marthi Duparge and I share our fears while my boys sleep. Surely our men should have returned by now, if only to say that they found no better place than this boggy island.

Last night Marthi wept and said that the Satrap deliberately sent us to our deaths. I was shocked. Sa's priests translated the ancient scrolls that told of cities on this river. Men dedicated to Sa cannot lie. But perhaps they erred, and grievously enough to cost our lives.

There is no plenty here, only strangeness that lurks by day and prowls among our huts by night. Almost every night, one or two folk awake shrieking from nightmares they cannot recall. A young woman of easy virtue has gone missing for two days now. She was a whore for coin in Jamaillia's streets and continued her trade here, asking food from the men who used her. We do not know if she wandered off or was killed by one of our own party. We do not know if we harbor a murderer in our midst, or if this terrible land has claimed another victim.

We mothers suffer the most, for our children beg us for more than the meager rations allotted us. The supplies from the ship are gone. I forage daily, my sons at my side. I found a heaped mound of loosened earth a few days ago and, poking through it, discovered eggs with brown speckled shells. There were almost fifty of them, and though some of the men refused them, saying they would not eat snake or lizard eggs, none of the mothers did. One lilylike plant is difficult to pull from the shallows, for inevitably I am splashed with stinging water and the roots are long and fibrous. There are nodules on the roots, no bigger than large pearls, and these have a pleasantly peppery flavor. Sewet has been working with the roots themselves, making baskets and recently a coarse cloth. That will be welcome. Our skirts are in tatters up to our calves, and our shoes grow thin as paper. All were surprised when I found the lily pearls. Several people asked how I knew they were edible.

I had no answer to that. The flowers looked familiar somehow. I cannot say what made me pull up the roots nor what prompted me to pick the pearly nodules and put them in my mouth.

The men who stayed here constantly complain of standing watches by night and keeping our fires alight, but in truth I think we women work as hard. It is taxing to keep our youngsters safe and fed and clean in these circumstances. I confess I have learned much of managing my boys from Chellia. She was a laundress in Jamaillia, and yet here she has become my friend, and we share a little hut we have built for the five children and ourselves. Her man, one Ethe, is also among the explorers. Yet she keeps a cheerful face and insists that her three youngsters help with the daily tasks. Our older boys we send out together to gather dry dead wood for the fire. We caution them never to go beyond the sounds of the camp, but both Petrus and Olpey complain that no dry wood remains nearby. Her daughters, Piet and Likea, watch Carlmin while Chellia and I harvest the water from the trumpet flowers and scavenge whatever mushrooms we can find. We have found a bark that makes a spicy tea; it helps to stave off hunger as well.

I am grateful for her company; both Marthi and I will welcome her help when birth comes upon us. Yet her boy, Olpey, is older than my Petrus and leading him into bold and reckless ways. Yesterday the two were gone until dusk, and then returned with only an armful of firewood each. They told of hearing distant music and following it. I am sure they ventured deeper into this swampy forest than is wise. I scolded them both, and Petrus was daunted; but Olpey snidely asked his mother what else should he do, stay here in the mud and grow roots? I was shocked to hear him speak so to his mother. I am sure that he is the influence behind Petrus's nightmares, for Olpey loves telling wild tales full of parasitic specters that float as night fogs and lizards that suck blood. I do not want Petrus influenced by such superstitious nonsense and yet, what can I do? The boys must fetch wood for us, and I cannot send him alone. All of the older boys of our company are given such chores. It grieves me to see Petrus, the descendant of two illustrious bloodlines, put to such work alongside common boys. I fear he will be ruined long before we return to Jamaillia.

And why has Jathan not returned to us? What has become of our men?

Day the 19th or 20th of the Greening Moon
Year the 14th of the Reign of the Most Noble and Magnificent Satrap Esclepius

Today three muddy men and a woman walked into our campsite. When I heard the hubbub, my heart leaped in excitement, for I thought our men had returned. Instead, I was shocked to discover that this party was from one of the other ships.

Captain, crew, and passengers were flung into the river one evening when the ship simply came apart. They had little opportunity to salvage supplies from the foundering ship. They lost more than half the souls aboard it. Of those who made it to shore, many took the madness and in the days following the shipwreck ended their own lives or vanished into the wilds.

Many of them died in the first few nights, for they could find no solid ground at all. I covered my ears when they spoke of people falling and literally drowning in the mud. Some woke witless and raving after experiencing strange dreams. Some recovered, but others wandered off into the swamp, never to be seen again. These three were the vanguard of those who remained alive. Minutes later, others began to arrive. They came in threes and fours, bedraggled and bug-bitten and horribly scalded from prolonged contact with the river water. There are sixty-two of them. A few are disgraced nobles, and others are commoners who thought to find a new life. The speculators who invested wealth in this expedition in the hope of making fortunes seem the most bitter.

The captain did not survive the first night. Those sailors who did are distressed and bewildered by their sudden plunge into exile. Some of them hold themselves apart from the "colonists" as they call us. Others seem to understand they must claim a place among us or perish.

Some of our party drew apart and muttered that we had little enough shelter and victuals for ourselves, but most of us shared readily. I had never thought to see people more desperate than we were. I feel that all profited from it, and Marthi and I perhaps most of all. Ser, an experienced midwife, was of their party. They also had a thatcher, their ship's carpenter, and men with hunting skills. The sailors are fit and hearty creatures and may adapt enough to be useful.

Still no sign of our own men.

Day the 26th of the Greening Moon
Year the 14th of the Reign of the Most Noble and Magnificent Satrap Esclepius

My time came. The child was born. I did not even see her before the midwife took her away. Marthi and Chellia and Ser the midwife all say she was born dead, yet I am sure I heard her wail once. I was weary and close to fainting, but surely I recall what I heard. My babe cried out for me before she died.

Chellia says it is not so, that the babe was born blue and still. I have asked why I could not have held her once before they gave her to the earth? The midwife said I would grieve less that way. But her face goes pale whenever I ask about it. Marthi does not speak of it. Does she fear her own time, or do they keep something from me? Why, Sa, have you taken both my daughters from me so cruelly?

Jathan will hear of it when he returns. Perhaps if he had been here, to help me in my last heavy days, I would not have had to toil so hard. Perhaps my little girl could have lived. But he was not with me then and he is not with me now. And who will watch my boys, find food for them, and make sure they return safe each night while I must lie here and bleed for a babe that did not live?

Day the 1st of the Grain Moon

Year the 14th of the Reign of the Most Noble and Magnificent Satrap Esclepius

I have risen from my lying-in. I feel that my heart is buried with my child. Did I carry her so far and through such hardship for nothing?

Our camp is now so crowded with newcomers that one can scarce thread a path through the makeshift shelters. Little Carlmin, separated from me for my lying-in, now follows me like a thin little shadow. Petrus has made fast his friendship with Olpey and pays no mind to my words at all. When I bid him stay close to camp, he defies me to venture ever deeper into the swamps. Chellia tells me, let him go. The boys are the darlings of the camp for discovering dangling bunches of sour little berries. The tiny fruits are bright yellow and sour as bile, but even such foul food is welcome to folk as hungry as we are. Still, it infuriates me that all encourage my son to disobey me. Do not they listen to the wild tales the boys tell, of strange music, distantly heard? The boys brag they will find the source of it, and my mother's heart knows it is nothing natural and good that lures them ever deeper into this pestilential jungle.

The camp grows worse every day. Paths are churned to muck, and they grow wider and more muddy. Too many people do nothing to better our lot. They live as best they can today, making no provision for tomorrow, relying on the rest of us for food. Some sit and stare, some pray and weep. Do they expect Sa himself to swoop down and save them? Last night a family was found dead, all five of them, huddled around the base of a tree under a pitiful drape of mats. There is no sign of what killed them. No one speaks of what we all fear: there is an insidious madness in the water, or perhaps it comes up from the ground itself, creeping into our dreams as unearthly music. I awaken from dreams of a strange city, thinking I am someone else, somewhere else. And when I open my eyes to mud and insects and hunger, sometimes I long to close them again and simply go back to my dream. Is that what befell that hapless family? All their eyes were wide open and staring when we discovered them. We let their bodies go into the river. The council took what little goods they had and divided them, but many grumble that the council only distributed the salvage to their own friends and not to those most in need. Discontent grows with this council of few who impose rule on all of us.

Our doubtful refuge is starting to fail us. Even the paltry weight of our woven huts turns the fragile sod to mud. I used to speak disdainfully of those who lived in squalor, saying, "they live like animals." But in truth, the beasts of this jungle live more graciously than we do. I envy the spiders their webs suspended in the shafts of sunlight overhead. I envy the birds whose woven nests dangle over our heads, out of reach of mud and snakes. I envy even the splay-footed marsh rabbits, as our hunters call the little game animals that scamper so elusively over the matted reeds and floating leaves of the shallows. By day, the earth sucks at my feet with every step I take. By night, our sleeping pallets sink into the earth, and we wake wet. A solution must be found, but all the others say, "Wait. Our explorers will return and lead us to a better place."

I think the only better place they have found is the bosom of Sa. So may we all go. Will I ever see balmy Jamaillia again, ever walk in a garden of kindly plants, ever again be free to eat to satiation and drink without regard for the morrow? I understand the temptation to evade my life by dozing away the hours in dreams of a better place. Only my sons keep me anchored in this world.

Day the 16th of the Grain Moon

Year the 14th of the Reign of the Most Noble and Magnificent Satrap Esclepius

What the waking mind does not perceive, the heart already knows. In a dream, I moved like the wind through these Rain Wilds, skimming over the soft ground and then sweeping through the swaying branches of the trees. Unhindered by muck and caustic water, I could suddenly see the many-layered beauty of our surroundings. I balanced, teetering like a bird, on a frond of fern. Some spirit of the Rain Wilds whispered to me, "Try to master it and it will engulf you. Become a part of it, and live."

I do not know that my waking mind believes any of that. My heart cries out for the white spires of Jamaillia, for the gentle blue waters of her harbor, for her shady walks and sunny squares. I hunger for music and art, for wine and poetry, for food that I did not scavenge from the crawl and tangle of this forbidding jungle. I hunger for beauty in place of squalor.

I did not gather food or water today. Instead, I sacrificed two pages of this journal to sketch dwellings suitable for this unforgiving place. I also designed floating walkways to link our homes. It will require some cutting of trees and shaping of lumber. When I showed them, some people mocked me, saying the work is too great for such a small group of people. Some pointed out that our tools have rapidly corroded here. I retorted that we must use our tools now to create shelters that will not fail us when our tools are gone.

Some willingly looked at my sketches, but then shrugged, saying what sense to work so hard when our scouts may return any day to lead us to a better location? We cannot, they said, live in this swamp forever. I retorted they were right, that if we did not bestir ourselves, we would die here. I did not, for fear of provoking fate, utter my darkest fear: that there is nothing but swamp for leagues under these trees, and that our explorers will never return.

Most people stalked away from my scorn, but two men stood and berated me, asking me what decent Jamaillian woman would raise her voice in anger before men. They were only commoners, as were the wives who stood and nodded behind them. Still, I could not restrain my tears, nor how my voice shook as I demanded what sort of men were they, to send my boys into the jungle to forage food for them while they sat on their heels and waited for someone else to solve their problems? They lifted their hands and made the sign for a shamed woman at me, as if I were a street girl. Then all walked away from me.

I do not care. I will prove them wrong.

Day the 24th of the Grain Moon
Year the 14th of the Reign of the Most Noble and Magnificent Satrap Esclepius

I am torn between elation and grief. My baby is dead, Jathan is still missing, and yet today I feel more triumph than I did at any blessing of my artwork. Chellia, Marthi, and little Carlmin have toiled alongside me. Sewet the weaver woman has offered refinements to my experiments. Piet and Likea have gathered food in my stead. Carlmin's small hands have amazed me with their agility and warmed my heart with his determination to help. In this effort, Carlmin has shown himself the son of my soul.

We have floored a large hut with a crosshatching of mats atop a bed of reeds and thin branches. This spreads the weight, so that we float atop the spongy ground as gently as the matted reeds float upon the neighboring waters. While other shelters sink daily and must be moved, ours has gone four days without settling. Today, satisfied that our home will last, we began further improvements. Without tools, we have broken down small saplings and torn their branches from them. Pieces of their trunks, woven with lily root into a horizontal ladder, form the basis for the walkways around our hut. Layers of woven matting to be added tomorrow will further strengthen our flimsy walkways. The trick, I am convinced, is to spread the weight of the traffic out over the greatest possible area, much as the marsh rabbits do with their splayed feet. Over the wettest section, behind our hut, we have suspended the walkway, anchoring it like a spiderweb from one tree to its neighbors as best we can. It is difficult, for the girth of the trees is great and the bark smooth. Twice it gave way as we struggled to secure it, and some of those watching jeered, but on our third effort, it held. Not only did we cross over it several times in safety, we were able to stand upon our swaying bridge and look out over the rest of the settlement. It was no lofty view, for we were no more than waist high above the ground, but even so, it gave me a perspective on our misery. Space is wasted with wandering paths and haphazard placement of huts. One of the sailors came over to inspect out effort, with much rocking on his heels and chewing on a twig. Then he had the effrontery to change half our knots. "That'll hold, madam," he told me. "But not for long and not under heavy use. We need better rigging to fasten to. Look up. That's where we need to be, rigging onto all those branches up there."

I looked up to the dizzying heights where the branches begin and told him that, without wings, none of us could reach those heights. He grinned and said, "I know a man, might could do it. If anyone thought it worth his trying." Then he made one of those ridiculous sailor bows and wandered off.

We must soon take action, for this shivering island diminishes daily. The ground is overtrodden and water stands in our paths. I must be mad to try; I am an artist, not an engineer or a builder. And yet if no one else steps forward, I am driven to the attempt. If I fail, I will fail having tried.

Day the 5th or 6th of the Prayer Moon

Year the 14th of the Reign of the Most Noble and Magnificent Satrap Esclepius

Today one of my bridges fell. Three men were plunged into the swamp, and one broke a leg. He blamed his mishap upon me and declared that this is what happens when women try their knitting skills as construction. His wife joined in his accusations. But I did not shrink before them. I told them that I did not demand that he use my walkways, and that any who had not contributed to them and yet dared to walk upon them deserved whatever fate Sa sent them for laziness and ingratitude.

Someone shouted "Blasphemy!" but someone else shouted "Truth is Sa's sword!" I felt vindicated. My workforce has grown enough to be split into two parties. I shall put Sewet in charge of the second one, and woe betide any man who derides my choice. Her weaving skills have proven themselves.

Tomorrow we hope to start raising the first supports for my Great Platforms into the trees. I could fail most spectacularly. The logs are heavier, and we have no true rope for the hoisting, but only lines of braided root. The sailor has devised several crude block-and-tackles for us. He and my Petrus were the ones who scaled the smooth trunk of a tree to where the immense limbs branch overhead. They tapped in pegs as they went, but even so, my heart shook to see them venture so high. Retyo the sailor says that his tackles will make our strength sufficient for any task. I wait to see that. I fear they will only lead to our woven lines fraying all the more. I should be sleeping and yet I lie here, wondering if we have sufficient line to hoist our beams. Will our rope ladders stand up to the daily use of workers? What have I undertaken? If any fall from such a height, they will surely die. Yet summer must end, and when winter rains come, we must have a dry retreat.

Day the 12th or 13th of the Prayer Moon
Year the 14th of Satrap Esclepius

Failure upon failure upon failure. I scarce have the spirit to write of it. Retyo the sailor says we must count as a success that no one has been injured. When our first platform fell, it sank itself into the soft earth rather than breaking into pieces. He cheerfully said that proved the platform's strength. He is a resourceful young man, intelligent despite his lack of education. I asked him today if he felt bitter that fate had trapped him into building a colony in the Rain Wilds instead of sailing. He shrugged and grinned. He has been a tinker and a share-farmer before he was a sailor, so he says he has no idea what fate is rightfully his. He feels entitled to take any of them and turn it to his advantage. I wish I had his spirit.

Idlers in our company gawk and mock us. Their skepticism corrodes my strength like the chalky water sears the skin. Those who complain most about our situation do the least to better it. "Wait," they say. "Wait for our explorers to return and lead us to a better place." Yet daily our situation worsens. We go almost in rags now, though Sewet experiments daily with what fibers she can pull from the vines or rub from the pith of reeds. We find barely enough food to sustain us daily and have no reserves for the winter. The idlers eat as much as those who work daily. My boys toil alongside us each day and yet receive the same ration as those who lie about and bemoan our fate. Petrus has a spreading rash at the base of his neck. I am sure it is due to poor diet and the constant damp.

Chellia must feel the same. Her little daughters, Piet and Likea, are no more than bones, for unlike our boys who eat as they gather, they must be content with what is handed to them at the end of the day. Olpey has become a strange boy of late, so much so that he frightens even Petrus. Petrus still sets out with him each day, but often comes home long before Olpey. Last night, I awoke to hear Olpey softly singing in his sleep. It was a tune and a tongue that I swear I have never heard, and yet it was haunting in its familiarity.

Heavy rains today. Our huts shed the most of it. I pity those who have not made any effort to provide shelter for themselves, even as I wonder at their lack of intelligence. Two women came to our hut with three little children. Marthi and Chellia and I did not want to let them crowd in with us, yet we could not abide the pitiful shivering of the babes. So we let them in, but warned them sternly that they must help with the construction tomorrow. If they do, we will help them build a hut of their own. If not, out they must go. Perhaps we must force folk to act for their own benefit.

Day the 17th or 18th of the Prayer Moon
Year the 14th of Satrap Esclepius

We have raised and secured the first Great Platform. Sewet and Retyo have woven net ladders that dangle to the ground. It was a moment of great triumph for me to stand below and look up at the platform solidly fixed among the tree limbs. The intervening branches almost cloaked it from sight. *This is my doing,* I thought to myself. Retyo, Crorin, Finsk, and Tremartin are the men who have done most of the hoisting and tying, but the design of the platform, how it balances lightly on the branches, putting weight only where it can be borne, and the selection of the location was my doing. I felt so proud.

It did not last long, however. Ascending a ladder made of vines that gives to each step and sways more the higher one goes is not for the faint of heart nor for a woman's meager strength. Halfway up, my strength gave out. I clung, half swooning, and Retyo was forced to come to my rescue. It shames me that I, a married woman, wrapped my arms about his neck as if I were a little child. To my dismay, he did not take me down, but insisted on climbing up with me, so that I could see the new vista from our platform.

It was both exhilarating and disappointing. We stood far above the swampy land that has sucked at our feet for so long, yet still below the umbrella of leaves that screens out all but the strongest sunlight. I looked down on a deceptively solid-appearing floor of leaves, branches, and vines. Although other immense trunks and branches impeded our view, I could suddenly see a distance into the forest in some directions. It appears to go on forever. And yet, seeing the branches of adjacent trees nearly touching ours filled me with ambition. Our next platform will be based in three adjacent trees. A catwalk will stretch from Platform One to Platform Two. Chellia and Sewet are already weaving the safety nets that will prevent our younger children from tumbling off Platform One. When they are finished with that, I will put them to work stringing our catwalks and the netting that will wall them.

The older children are swiftest to ascend and the quickest to adapt to our tree dwelling. Already, they are horribly careless as they walk out from the platform along the huge branches that support it. After I had warned them often to be careful, Retyo gently rebuked me. "This is their world," he said. "They cannot fear it. They will become as sure-footed as sailors running rigging. The branches are wider than the walkways of some towns I've visited. The only thing that prevents you from walking out along that branch is your knowledge of how far you may fall. Think instead of the wood beneath your feet."

Under his tutelage, and gripping his arm, I did walk out along one of the branches. When we had gone some way and it began to sway under our weight, I lost my courage and fled back to the platform. Looking down, I could only glimpse the huts of our muddy little settlement below. We had ascended to a different world. The light is greater here, though still diffuse, and we are closer to both fruit and flowers. Bright-colored birds squawk at us, as if disputing our right to be there. Their nests dangle like baskets hung in the trees. I look at their suspended homes and wonder if I cannot adapt that example to make a safe "nest" for myself. Already I feel this new territory is mine by right of ambition and art, as if I inhabit one of my suspended sculptures. Can

I imagine a town composed of hanging cottages? Even this platform, bare as it is right now, has balance and grace.

Tomorrow I shall sit down with Retyo the sailor and Sewet the weaver. I recall the cargo nets that lifted heavy loads from the dock onto the deck of the ship. Could not a platform be placed inside such a net, the net thatched for privacy, and the whole hung from a sturdy branch, to become a lofty and private chamber here? How, then, would we provide access to the Great Platforms from such dwellings? I smile as I write this, knowing that I do not wonder if it can be done, but only how.

Both Olpey and Petrus have a rash on their scalps and down their necks. They scratch and complain, and the skin is rough as scales to the touch. I can find no way to ease it for either of them, and fear that it is spreading to others. I've seen a number of the children scratching miserably.

Day the 6th or 7th of the Gold Moon
Year the 14th of Satrap Esclepius

Two events of great significance. Yet I am so weary and heartsick I scarce can write of either of them. Last night, as I fell asleep in this swinging birdcage of a home, I felt safe and almost serene. Tonight, all that is taken from me.

The first: Last night Petrus woke me. Trembling, he crept under my mats beside me as if he were my little boy again. He whispered to me that Olpey was frightening him, singing songs from the city, and that he must tell me even though he had promised he would not.

Petrus and Olpey, in their ranging for food, discovered an unnaturally square mound in the forest. Petrus felt uneasy and did not wish to approach it. He could not tell me why. Olpey was drawn to it. Day after day, he insisted that they return to it. On the days when Petrus returned alone, it was because he had left Olpey exploring the mound. At some point in his poking and digging, he found a way into it. The boys have entered it several times now. Petrus describes it as a buried tower, though that made no sense to me. He said the walls are cracked and damp seeps in, but it is mostly solid. There are tapestries and old furniture, some sound, some rotted, and other signs that once people lived in it. Yet Petrus trembled as he spoke, saying that he did not think they were people like us. He says the music comes from it.

Petrus had only descended one level into it, but Olpey told him it went much deeper. Petrus was afraid to go down into the dark, but then by some magic, Olpey caused the tower to blossom with light. Olpey mocked Petrus for being fearful and told tales of immense riches and strange objects in the depths of the tower. He claimed that ghosts spoke to him and told him its secrets, including where to find treasure. Then Olpey began to say that he had once lived in the tower, a long time ago when he was an old man.

I did not wait for morning. I woke Chellia, and after hearing my tale she woke Olpey. The boy was furious, hissing that he would never trust Petrus again and that the tower was his secret and the treasures all his, and he did not have to share it. While the night was still dark, Olpey fled, running off along one of the tree branches that have become footpaths for the children, and thence we knew not where.

When morning finally sifted through the sheltering branches, Chellia and I followed Petrus through the forest to his tower-mound. Retyo and Tremartin went with us, and little Carlmin refused to stay behind with Chellia's girls. When I saw the squared mound thrusting up from the swamp, my courage quailed inside me. Yet I did not wish Retyo to see me as a coward and so I forced myself on.

The top of the tower was heavily mossed and draped with vinery, yet it was too regular a shape to blend with the jungle. On one side, the boys had pulled away vines and moss to bare a window in a stone wall. Retyo kindled the torch he had brought, and then, one after another, we cautiously clambered inside. Vegetation had penetrated the room as tendrils and roots. On the grimy floor were the muddy tracks of the boys' feet. I suspect they have both been exploring that place for far longer than Petrus admits. A bed frame festooned with rags of fabric sat in one corner of the room. Insects and mice had reduced the draperies to dangling rags.

Despite the dimness and decay, there were echoes of loveliness in the room. I seized a handful of rotted curtain and scrubbed a swath across a frieze, raising a cloud of dust. Amazement stilled my coughing. My artist's soul soared at the finely shaped and painted tiles and the delicate colors I had uncovered. But my mother's heart stood still at what was revealed. The figures were tall and thin, humans rendered as stick insects. Yet I did not think it was a conceit of the artist. Some held what might have been musical instruments or weaponry. We could not decide. In the background workers tended a reed bed by a river like farmers harvesting a field. A woman in a great chair of gold overlooked all and seemed pleased with it. Her face was stern and yet kind; I felt I had seen her before. I would have stared longer, but Chellia demanded we search for her son.

With a sternness I did not feel, I bade Petrus show us where they had been playing. He blanched to see that I had guessed the truth, but he led us on. We left the bedchamber by a short flight of downward stairs. On the landing, there was heavy glass in two windows, but when Retyo held our torch close to one, it illuminated long white worms working in the wet soil pressed against it. How the glass has withstood the force of earth, I do not know. We entered a wide hall. Rugs crumbled into damp thread under our tread. We passed doorways, some closed, others open archways gaping with dark maws, but Petrus led us on. We came at last to the top of a stair, much grander than the first. As we descended this open staircase into a pool of darkness, I was grateful to have Retyo at my side. His calmness fostered my poor courage. The ancient cold of the stone penetrated my worn shoes and crept up my legs to my spine as if it reached for my heart. Our torch illuminated little more than our frightened faces, and our whispers faded, waking ghostly echoes. We passed one landing, and then a second, but Petrus neither spoke nor faltered as he led us down. I felt as if I had walked into the throat of some great beast and was descending to its belly.

When at last we reached the bottom, our single torch could not penetrate the blackness around us. The flame fluttered in the moving air of a much larger chamber. Even in the dimness, I knew this room would have dwarfed the great ballroom of the Satrap's palace. I slowly groped my way forward, but Carlmin suddenly strode fearlessly beyond the reach of both my hand and the torchlight. I called after him, but the sound of his pattering footsteps as he hurried away was my only answer. "Oh, follow him!" I beseeched Retyo, but as he started to, the room suddenly lit around us as if a horde of spirits had unhooded their lanterns. I gave one shriek of terror and then was struck dumb.

In the center of the room, a great green dragon was up-reared on its hind legs. Its hind claws were sunk deep in the stone and its lashing tail stretched halfway across the room. Its emerald wings were unfurled wide and supported the ceiling high overhead. Atop its sinuous neck was a head the size of an oxcart. Intelligence glittered in its shining silver eyes. Its smaller forelimbs clutched the handle of a large basket. The basket itself was elaborately beribboned with bows of jade and streamers of ivory. And within the basket, reclining serenely, was a woman of preternatural authority. She was not beautiful; the power expressed in her made beauty irrelevant. Nor was she young and desirable. She was a woman past her middle years; yet the lines the sculptor had graved in her face seemed wisdom furrows on her brow, and thought lines at the corners of her eyes. Jewels had been set above her brow lines and along the tops of her cheeks to mimic the scaling of the dragon. This was no expressionless representation of Sa's female aspect. I knew, without doubt, that this statue had been fashioned to honor a real woman, and it shocked me to my bones. The dragon's supple neck was carved so that he twisted to regard her, and even his reptilian countenance showed respect for her that he carried.

I had never seen such a representation of a woman. I had heard foreign tales of Harlot Queens and woman rulers, but always they had seemed fabrications of some barbarous and backward country, seductive women of evil intent. She made such legends lies. For a time, she was all I could see. Then my mind came back to me, and with it my duty.

Little Carlmin, all his teeth showing in a wide smile, stood some distance from us, his hand pressed against a panel attached to a column. His flesh looked like ice in the unnatural light. His smallness put the huge chamber into perspective, and I suddenly saw all that the dragon and woman had obscured.

The light flowed in pale stars and flying dragons across the ceiling. It crawled in vines across the walls, framing four distant doorways to darkened corridors. Dry fountains and statuary broke up the huge expanse of dusty floor. This was a great indoor plaza, a place for people to gather and talk or idly stroll among the fountains and statuary. Lesser columns supported twining vines with leaves of jade and carnelian blossoms. A sculpture of a leaping fish denied the dry fountain basin below it. Moldering heaps of ruin scattered throughout the chamber indicated the remains of wooden structures, booths or stages. Yet neither dust nor decay could choke the chilling beauty of the place. The scale and the grace of the room left me breathless and woke a wary awe in me. Folk who created such a chamber would not perish easily. What fate had overtaken a people whose magic could still light a room years after their passing? Did the danger that destroyed them threaten us? What had it been? Where had they gone?

Were they truly gone?

As in the chamber above, it felt as if the people had simply departed, leaving all their goods behind. Again, the boys' muddy tracks on the floor betrayed that they had been here before. Most led toward a single door.

"I did not realize this place was so big." Petrus's small voice seemed shrill in the vastness as he stared up at the lady and her dragon. He turned round in a slow circle, staring at the ceiling. "We had to use torches here. How did you light it, Carlmin?" Petrus sounded uneasy at his small brother's knowledge.

But Carlmin didn't answer. My little one was trotting eagerly across the vast chamber, as if called to some amusement. "Carlmin!" I cried, and my voice woke a hundred echoing ghosts. As I gawked, he vanished through one of the archways. It lit in a murky, uncertain way. I ran after him, and the others followed. I was breathless by the time I had crossed the plaza. I chased him down a dusty corridor.

As I followed him into a dim chamber, light flickered around me. My son sat at the head of a long table of guests in exotic dress. There was laughter and music. Then I blinked and empty chairs lined both sides of the table. The feast had dwindled to crusty stains in the crystal goblets and plates, but the music played on, choked and strained. I knew it from my dreams.

Carlmin spoke hollowly as he lofted a goblet in a toast, "To my lady!" He smiled fondly as his childish gaze met unseen eyes. As he started to put it to his lips, I reached him, seized his wrist, and shook the glass from his grasp. It fell to shatter in the dust.

He stared at me with eyes that did not know me. Despite how he has grown of late, I snatched him up and held him to me. His head sagged onto my shoulder, and he closed his eyes, trembling. The music sagged into silence. Retyo took him from me, saying sternly, "We should not have allowed the boy to come. The sooner we leave this place and its dying magic, the better." He glanced about uneasily. "Thoughts not mine tug at me, and I hear voices. I feel I have been here before, when I know I have not. We should leave this city to the spirits that haunt it." He seemed shamed to admit his fear, but I was relieved to hear one of us speak it aloud.

Then Chellia cried that we could not leave Olpey here, to fall under whatever enchantment had seized Carlmin. Sa forgive me, all I wanted to do was seize my own children and flee. But Retyo, carrying both our torch and my son, led us on. His friend Tremartin smashed a chair against the stone floor and took up one of the legs for a club. No one asked him what use a club could be against the spiderwebs of alien memory that snagged at us. Petrus moved up to take the lead. When I glanced back, the lights in the chamber had winked out.

Through a hall and then down another flight of stairs that wound down to a smaller hall we went. Statues in niches lined the walls, with the dwindled remnants of dust-grimed candle stubs before them. Many of the statues were representations of women, crowned and glorified like kings. Their sculpted robes glittered with tiny inset jewels, and pearls roped their hair.

The unnatural light was blue and uncertain, flickering with the threat of utter darkness. It made me oddly sleepy. I thought I heard whispering, and once, as I brushed through a doorway, I heard two women singing in the distance. I shuddered with fear, and Retyo glanced back as if he, too, had heard them. Neither of us spoke. We went on. Some passages blossomed into light around us as we entered. Others remained stubbornly dark and made our failing torch seem a lie. I do not know which was more daunting to me.

We found Olpey at last. He was sitting in a little room on an opulently carved chair before a gentleman's dressing table. The gilt had fallen from the wood to scatter in flakes all round it. He looked into a mirror clouded with age; black spots had blossomed in it. Shell combs and the handle of a brush littered the table before him. A small chest was open on his lap, and looped around his neck were many pendants. His head drooped to one side, but his eyes were open and staring. He was muttering to himself. As we drew near, he reached for a scent bottle and mimed dabbing himself with its long dried perfume as he turned his face from side to side before his hazy reflection. His motions were the preening of a lordly and conceited man.

"Stop it!" his mother hissed in horror. He did not startle, and almost I felt that we were the ghosts there. She seized him and shook him. At that he woke, but he woke in a terror. He cried out as he recognized her, glanced wildly about himself, and then fell into a faint. "Oh, help me get him out of here," poor Chellia begged.

Tremartin put Olpey's arm across his shoulders and mostly dragged the lad as we fled. The lights quenched as we left each area, as if pursuing darkness were only a step behind us. Once music swelled loudly around us, subsiding as we fled. When we finally clambered out of the window into open air, the swamp seemed a healthful place of light and freshness. I was shocked to see that most of the day had passed while we were below.

Carlmin recovered quickly in the fresh air. Tremartin spoke sharply to Olpey and shook him, at which he angrily came back to his senses. He jerked free of Tremartin and would not speak sensibly to us. By turns sullen or defiant, he refused to explain why he had fled to the city or what he had been doing. He denied fainting. He was coldly furious with Petrus and extremely possessive of the jeweled necklaces he wore. They glittered with bright gemstones of every color, and yet I would no more put one around my neck than I would submit to a snake's embrace. "They are mine," he kept exclaiming. "My lover gave them to me, a long time ago. No one will take them from me now!"

It took all of Chellia's patience and motherly wiles to convince Olpey to return with us. Even so, he dawdled grudgingly along. By the time we reached the outskirts of camp, the dwindling light was nearly gone and insects feasted on us.

The platforms high above were humming with excited voices like a disturbed beehive. We climbed the ladders, and I was so exhausted I thought only of my own shelter and bed. But the moment we reached the Platform, cries of excitement greeted us. The explorers had returned. At the sight of my husband, thin, bearded and ragged, but alive, my heart leaped. Little Carlmin stood gawking as if at a stranger, but Petrus rushed to greet him. And Retyo gravely bid me farewell and vanished from my side into the crowd.

Jathan did not recognize his son at first. When he did, he lifted his eyes and looked over the crowd. When his eyes had passed me twice, I stepped forward, leading Carlmin by the hand. I think he knew me by the look on my face rather than by my appearance. He came to me slowly, saying, "Sa's mercy, Carillion, is that you? Have pity on us all." By which I judged that my appearance did not please him. And why that should hurt so much is something I do not know, nor why I felt shamed that he took my hand but did not embrace me. Little Carlmin stood beside me, staring blankly at his father.

And now I shall leave this wallowing in self-pity and sum up their report. They found only more swamp. The Rain Wild River is the main drainage of a vast network of water that straggles in threads through a wide valley on its way to the sea. The water runs under the land as much as over it. They found no sound ground, only bogs, marshes, and sloughs. They never had clear sight of a horizon since they had left us. Of the twelve men who set out, seven returned. One drowned in quicksand, one vanished during the night, and the other three were overtaken by a fever. Ethe, Chellia's husband, did not return.

They could not tell how far inland they had traveled. The tree cover hampered their efforts to follow the stars and eventually they must have made a great circle, for they found themselves standing at the riverside again.

On their journey back to us, they encountered the remnants of those who had been on the third ship. They were marooned downriver from where we were abandoned. Their captain gave up on his mission when he saw wreckage from a ship float past them. Their captain was more merciful than ours, for he saw that all their cargo was landed with them, and even left them one of the ship's boats. Still, their lives were hard and many wished to go home. The jewel of good news was that they still had four messenger birds. One had been dispatched when they were first put ashore. Another was sent back with news of their hardship after the first month.

Our explorers dashed all their hopes. They decided to abandon their effort at a settlement. Seven of their young men came back with our explorers to help us evacuate as well. When we join them, they will send a message bird to Jamaillia, begging for a rescue ship. Then we will journey down the river and to the coast, in hopes of rescue.

When Chellia, Retyo, and I returned, our company was sourly predicting that no ship would be sent. Nonetheless, all were packing to leave. Then Chellia arrived with her jewel-draped son. As she tried to tell her story to a crowd of folks too large to hear it, a riot near broke out. Some men wanted to go immediately to the buried tower, despite the growing dark. Others demanded a chance to handle the jewels, and as young Olpey refused to let anyone touch them, this set off a scuffle. The boy broke free, and leaping from the edge of the Platform, he sprang from one branch to another like a monkey until his shape was lost in the darkness. I pray he is safe tonight, but I fear the madness has taken him.

A different sort of madness has taken our folk. I huddle in my shelter with my two sons. Outside, on the platforms, the night is full of shouting. I hear women pleading to leave, and men saying, yes, yes, we will, but first we will see what treasure the city will offer us. A messenger bird with a jewel attached to its leg would bring a ship swiftly, they laugh. Their eyes are bright, their voices loud.

My husband is not with me. Despite our long separation, he is in the thick of these arguments rather than with his wife and sons. Did he even notice that my pregnancy had passed, yet my arms were empty? I doubt it.

I do not know where Chellia and her daughters have gone. When she discovered that Ethe had not returned, it broke her. Her husband is dead and Olpey may be lost, or worse. I fear for her and mourn with her. I thought the return of the explorers would fill me with joy. Now I do not know what I feel. But I know it is not joy or even relief.

Day the 7th or 8th of the Gold Moon
Year the 14th of Satrap Esclepius

He came to me in the dark of the night, and despite the soreness of my heart and our two sons sleeping nearby, I let him have what he sought. Part of me hungered only for a gentle touch; part of me mocked myself for that, for he came to me only when his more pressing business was done. He spoke little and took his satisfaction in darkness. Can I blame him? I know I have gone to skin and bones, my complexion rough and my hair dry as straw. The rash that has afflicted the children now crawls like a snake up my spine. I dreaded that he would touch it, mostly because it would remind me that it was there, but he did not. He wasted no caresses. I stared past his shoulder into the darkness and thought not of my husband, but of Retyo, and he a common sailor who speaks with the accents of the waterfront.

What have I become here?

Afternoon

And so I am Lord Jathan Carrock's wife again, and my life is his to command. He has settled our fate. As Olpey has vanished, and neither Retyo nor Tremartin can be found, Jathan has declared that his son's discovery of the hidden city gives him prime claim to all treasure in it. Petrus will lead him and the other men back to the buried tower. They will search it systematically for treasure that will buy our way back into the Satrap's graces. He is quite proud to claim that Petrus discovered the tower and thus the Carrocks merit a larger share of the treasure. It does not disturb him that Olpey is still missing, and that Chellia and her daughters are distraught with worry. He talks only of how the treasure will secure our glorious return to society. He seems to forget the leagues of swamp and sea between Jamaillia City and us.

I told him that the city was a dangerous place and he should not venture into it thinking only of spoils. I warned him of its unhealthy magic, of lights that brighten and fade, of voices and music heard in the distance, but he disdains it as a "woman's overwrought fancy." He tells me to stay out of danger here in my "little monkey nest" until he returns. Then I spoke bluntly. The Company does not have reserves of food or the strength to make a trek to the coast. Unless we better prepare, we will die along the way, treasure or not. I think we should remain here until we are more organized, or until a ship comes here for us. We need not admit defeat. We might prosper if we put all our men to gathering food and found a way to trap rainwater for our needs. Our tree city could be a thing of grace and beauty. He shook his head as if I were a child prating of pixies in flowery bowers. "Ever immersed in your art," he said. "Even in rags and starving, you cannot see what is real." Then he said he admired how I had occupied myself in his absence, but that he had returned now and would take charge of his family.

I wanted to spit at him.

Petrus did not wish to lead the men. He believes the tower took Olpey and we shall never see him again. He speaks of the underground with deep dread. Carlmin told his father he had never been to a buried city, and then sat and sucked his thumb, as he has not since he was two.

When Petrus tried to warn Jathan, he laughed and said, "I'm a different man than the soft noble who left Jamaillia. Your silly mama's goblins don't worry me." When I told him sharply that I, too, was a different woman than the one he had left alone to cope in the wilds, he stiffly replied that he saw that too clearly and only hoped that a return to civilization would restore me to propriety. Then he forced Petrus to lead them to the ruins.

No amount of treasure could persuade me to return there, not if there were diamonds scattered on the floor and strands of pearls dangling from the ceiling. I did not imagine the danger, and I hate Jathan for dragging Petrus back to it.

I shall spend the day with Marthi. Her husband returned safely, only to leave her again to hunt treasure. Unlike me, she is overjoyed with his plans and says that he will return them to society and wealth again. It is hard for me to listen to such nonsense. "My baby will grow up in Sa's blessed city," she says. The woman is thin as a string, with her belly like a knot tied in it.

Day the 8th or 9th of the Gold Moon
Year the 14th of Satrap Esclepius

A ridiculous date for us. Here there will be no golden harvest moon, nor does the Satrap mean anything to me anymore.

Yesterday Petrus showed them to the tower window, but he ran away when the men entered, leaving his father shouting angrily after him. He came back to me, pale and shaking. He says the singing from the tower has become so loud that he cannot think his own thoughts when he is near it. Sometimes, in the corridors of black stone, he has glimpsed strange people. They come and go in flashes, he says, like their flickering light.

I hushed him, for his words were upsetting Marthi. Despite Jathan's plans, I spent yesterday preparing for winter. I put a second thatch on both our hanging huts, using broad leaves laced down with vines. I think our shelters, especially the smaller hanging cottages and the little footbridges that connect them to the Great Platforms will require reinforcement against winter winds and rain. Marthi was little help to me. Her pregnancy has made her ungainly and listless, but the real problem was that she believes we will soon go home to Jamaillia. Most of the women are now only waiting to leave.

Some of treasure hunters returned last night, with reports of a vast buried city. It is very different from Jamaillia, all interconnected like a maze. Perhaps some parts of it were always underground, for there are no windows or doors in the lowest chambers. The upper reaches of the buildings were homes and private areas, and the lower seemed to have been shops and warehouses and markets. Toward the river, a portion of the city has collapsed. In some chambers, the walls are damp and rot is well at work on the furnishings, but others have withstood time, preserving rugs and tapestries and garments. Those who returned brought back dishes and chairs, rugs and jewelry, statues and tools. One man wore a cloak that shimmered like running water, soft and supple. They had discovered amphorae of wine, still sealed and intact in one warehouse. The wine is golden and so potent that the men were almost instantly drunk. They returned laughing and spirit breathed, bidding us all come to the city and celebrate with wine the wealth that had come to us. There was a wild glitter in their eyes that I did not like.

Others returned haunted and cringing, not wishing to speak of what they had experienced. Those ones began immediately to plan to leave tomorrow at dawn, to travel downriver and join the other folk there.

Jathan did not return at all.

Those obsessed with plunder talk loudly, drunk with old wine and mad dreams. Already they gather hoards. Two men came back bruised, having come to blows over a vase. Where will greed take us? I feel alone in my dismal imaginings.

That city is not a conquered territory to be sacked, but more like a deserted temple, to be treated with the respect one should accord any unknown god. Are not all gods but facets of Sa's presence? But these words come to me too late to utter. I would not be heeded. I feel a terrible premonition, that there will be a consequence to this orgy of plundering.

My tree settlement was almost deserted earlier today. Most of our folk had been infected with a treasure fever and gone underground. Only the infirm and the women with the smallest children remain in our village. I look around me and I am suffused with sorrow, for I am seeing the death of my dreams. Shall I wax more eloquent, more dramatic, more poetic as I once would have thought it? No. I shall simply say I am engulfed in disappointment. And shocked to feel it.

It is hard for me to confront what I mourn. I hesitate to commit it to paper, for the words will remain here, to accuse me later. Yet art, above all, is honesty, and I am an artist before I am a wife, a mother, or even a woman. So I will write. It is not that there is now a man that I would prefer over my husband. I admit that freely. I care not that Retyo is a common sailor, seven years my junior, without education or bloodlines to recommend him. It is not what he is but who he is that turns my heart and eyes to him. I would take him into my bed tonight, if I could do so without risking my sons' future. That I will write in a clear hand. Can there be shame in saying I would value his regard above my husband's, when my husband has so clearly shown that he values the regard of the other men in this company over his wife's love?

No. What turns my heart to rust this day is that my husband's return, and the discovery of treasure in the buried city and the talk of returning to Jamaillia, dismantles the life I have built here. That grieves me. It is a hard thing to contemplate. When did I change so completely? This life is harsh and hard. This country's beauty is the beauty of the sunning snake. It threatens as it beckons. I fancy that I can master it by giving it my earnest respect. Without realizing it, I had begun to take pride in my ability to survive and to tame some small part of its savagery. And I have shown others how to do that. I did things here, and they were significant.

Now that will be lost to me. I become again Lord Jathan Carrock's wife. My caution will be discarded as a woman's foolish fear, and my ambitions for a beautiful abode built among the trees will be dismissed as a woman's silly fancy.

Perhaps he would be right. Nay, I know he is right. But somehow, I no longer care for what is right and wise. I have left behind the life where I created art for people to admire. Now my art is how I live and it daily sustains me.

I do not think I can set that aside. To be told I must abandon all that I have begun here is more than I can bear. And for what? To return to his world, where I am of no more consequence than an amusing songbird in a filigreed cage.

Marthi was with me today when Chellia came to ask Petrus to help her look for Olpey. Petrus would not look at her. Chellia began to plead, and Petrus covered his ears. She nagged him until he began to weep, frightening Carlmin. Chellia shrieked as if mad, accusing Petrus of not caring anything for his friend, but only for the riches of the city. She lifted a hand as if to strike my boy, and I rushed in and pushed her. She fell, and her girls dragged her to her feet and then pulled her away, begging her simply to "come home, Mother, come home." When I turned around, Marthi had fled.

I sit by myself on the limb above my cottage while my boys sleep within tonight. I am ashamed. But my sons are all I have. Is it wrong for me to keep them safe? What good would it do to sacrifice my sons to save hers? We might only lose them all.

Day the 5th of the City
Year the 1st of the Rain Wilds

I fear we have come through many trials and tribulations, only to perish from our own greed. Last night, three men died in the city. No one will say how; they brought the unmarked bodies back. Some say it was the madness; others speak of evil magic. In the wake of the gruesome development, seventeen people banded together and bid the rest of us farewell. We gave them ropes and woven mats and whatever else we could spare and wished them well as they left. I hope they reach the other settlement safely, and that someday, someone in Jamaillia may hear the tale of what befell us here. Marthi pleaded with them to tell the other folk to wait a day or two longer before they depart for the coast, that soon her husband will be bringing her to join them.

I have not seen Retyo since my husband returned. I did not think he would go to hunt treasure in the city, but it must be so. I had grown accustomed to being without Jathan. I have no claim to Retyo, and yet I miss him the more keenly of the two.

I visited Marthi again. She has grown paler and is now afflicted with the rash. Her skin is as dry as a lizard's. She is miserable with her heaviness. She speaks wildly of her husband finding immense wealth and how she will flaunt it to those who banished us. She fantasizes that as soon as the message bird reaches Jamaillia, the Satrap will send a swift ship to fetch us all back to Jamaillia, where her child will be born into plenty and safety. Her husband returned briefly from the city, to bring her a little casket of jewelry. Her dull hair is netted with chained jewels, and gleaming bracelets dangle from her thin wrists. I avoid her lest I tell her that she is a fool. She is not, truly, save that she hopes beyond hope. I hate this wealth that we can neither eat nor drink, for all have focused upon it, and willingly starve while they seek to gather ever more.

Our remaining company is divided into factions now. Men have formed alliances and divided the city into claimed territories. It began with quarrels over the heaps and hoards, with men accusing each other of pilfering. Soon it fostered partnerships, some to guard the hoard while the others strip the city of wealth. Now it extends to men arming themselves with clubs and knives and setting sentries to guard the corridors they have claimed. But the city is a maze, and there are many routes through it. The men fight one another for plunder.

My sons and I remain with the infirm, the elderly, the very young, and the pregnant here at the Platform. We form alliances of our own, for while the men are engrossed in stealing from one another, the gathering of food goes undone. The archers who hunted meat for us now hunt treasure. The men who had set snares for marsh rabbits now set traps for one another. Jathan came back to the hut, ate all that remained of our supplies, and then left again. He laughed at my anger, telling me that I worry about roots and seeds while there are gems and coins to be gathered. I was glad when he went back to the city. May he be devoured by it! Any food I find now, I immediately give to the boys or eat myself. If I can think of a secret place to cache it, I'll begin to do so.

Petrus, forbidden the city, has resumed his gathering duties, to good end. This day he returned with reeds like the ones we saw peasants cultivating in that mosaic in the city. He told me that the city people would not have grown them if they did not have some use, and that we should discover what it was. It was more disturbing to me when he told me that he remembered that this was the season for harvesting them. When I told him that he could not possibly remember any such thing, he shook his head at me and muttered something about his "city memories."

I hope that the influence of that strange place will fade with time.

The rash has worsened on Carlmin, spreading onto his cheeks and brows. I slathered a poultice on it in the hopes of easing it. My younger son has scarcely spoken a word to me this day, and I fear what occupies his mind.

My life has become only waiting. At any time, my husband may return from the city and announce that it is time for us to begin our trek down the river. Nothing I build now can be of any consequence, when I know that soon we will abandon it.

Olpey has not been found. Petrus blames himself. Chellia is near mad with grief. I watch her from a distance, for she no longer speaks to me. She confronts any man returning from the city, demanding word of her son. Most of them shrug her off; some become angry. I know what she fears, for I fear it, too. I think Olpey returned to the city. He felt entitled to his treasures, but fatherless as he is and of common birth, who would respect his claim? Would they kill the boy? I would give much not to feel so guilty about Olpey. What can I do? Nothing. Why, then, do I feel so bad? What would it benefit any of us to risk Petrus in another visit to the city? Is not one vanished boy tragedy enough?

Day the 8th of the City
Year the 1st of the Rain Wilds

Jathan returned at noon today. He was laden with a basket of treasure, jewelry and odd ornaments, small tools of a strange metal, and a purse woven of metal links and full of oddly minted gold coins. His face was badly bruised. He abruptly said that this was enough, there was no sense to the greed in the city. He announced that we would catch up with the others who had already left. He declared that the city holds no good for us and that we are wiser to flee with what he has than to strive for more and die there.

He had not eaten since he last left us. I made him spice bark tea and lily-root mush and encouraged him to speak of what is happening underground. At first he spoke only of our own company there and what they did. Bitterly he accused them of treachery and betrayal. Men have come to bloodshed over the treasure. I suspect Jathan was driven off with what he could carry. But there is worse news. Parts of the city are collapsing. Closed doors have been forced open, with disastrous results. Some were not locked but were held shut by the force of earth behind them. Now slow muck oozes forth from them, gradually flooding the corridors. Some are already nearly impassable, but men ignore the danger as they try to salvage wealth before it is buried forever. The flowing muck seems to weaken the city's ancient magic. Many chambers are subsiding into darkness. Lights flash brightly, then dim. Music blares forth and then fades to a whisper.

When I asked him if that had frightened him, he angrily told me to be quiet and recall my respect for him. He scoffed at my notion that he would flee. He said it was obvious that the ancient city would soon collapse under the weight of the swamp, and he had no wish to die there. I do not believe that was all of it, but I suppose I am glad he was intelligent enough to leave. He bade me get the children ready to travel and gather whatever food we had.

Reluctantly, I began to obey him. Petrus, looking relieved, sprang to the meager packing. Carlmin sat silently scratching the poultice off his rash. I hastily covered it afresh. I did not want Jathan to see the coppery scaling on his son's skin. Earlier I had tried picking the scab loose, but when I scrape it off, he cries and the flesh beneath is bloody. It looks as if he is growing fish scales. I try not to think of the rash down my spine. I make this entry hastily, and then I will wrap this small book well and add it to my carry basket. There is precious little else to put in it.

I hate to leave what I have built, but I cannot ignore the relief in Petrus's eyes when his father said we would go. I wish we had never ventured into the city. But for that haunted place, perhaps we could have stayed here and made it a home. I dread our journey, but there is no help for it. Perhaps if we take Carlmin away from here, he will begin to speak again.

Later

I will write in haste and then take this book with me into the city. If ever my body is found, perhaps some kind soul will carry this volume back to Jamaillia and let my parents know what became of Carillion Waljin and where she ended her days. Likely it and I will be buried forever in the muck inside the hidden city.

I had finished our packing when Chellia came to me with Tremartin. The man was gaunt and his clothing caked with mud. He has finally found Olpey, but the lad is out of his wits. He has barricaded a door against them and will not come out. Retyo and Tremartin had been searching the city for Olpey all this time. Retyo has remained outside the door, striving to keep it clear of the relentlessly creeping muck filling the passageway. Tremartin does not know how long he can keep up with it. Retyo thinks that Petrus could convince Olpey to open the door. Together, Tremartin and Chellia came to us to beg this favor.

I could no longer ignore the desperation in my friend's eyes and felt shamed that I had for so long. I appealed to Jathan, saying that we could go directly to where the boy is, persuade him to come out, and then we could all leave together. I even tried to be persuasive, saying that such a larger party would do better in facing the Rain Wilds than if we and our sons went alone.

He did not even call me apart or lower his voice as he demanded why he should risk his son and his heir for the sake of a laundress's boy, one we would not even employ as a servant were we still in Jamaillia. He berated me for letting Petrus become attached to such a common lad and then, in a clear voice, said I was very much mistaken if I thought him such a fool that he did not know about Retyo. Many a foul thing he said then, of what a harlot I was to take a common man into a bed by right a lord's, and treacherously support a low sailor as he made his bid to claim leadership of the company.

I will not record any more of his shameful accusations. In truth, I do not know why he still has the power to make me weep. In the end, I defied him. When he said I must follow him now or not at all, I told him, "Not at all. I will stay and aid my friend, for I care not what work she used to do; here she is my friend."

My decision was not without cost to me. Jathan took Petrus with him. I saw that my elder son was torn, and yet he wished to flee with his father. I do not blame him. Jathan left Carlmin behind, saying that my poor judgment had turned his son into a moron and a freak. Carlmin had scratched the poultice from his face, baring the scales that now outline his brows and upper cheeks. My little boy did not even wince at his father's words. He showed no reaction at all. I kissed Petrus good-bye and promised him that I would follow as soon as I could. I hope I can keep that promise. Jathan and Petrus took with them as much as they could carry of our goods. When Carlmin and I follow, we will not have much for supplies until we catch up to them.

And now I shall wrap this little book and slip it, and my pen and inkpot, into the little carry basket they left to me, along with materials for torches and fire starting. Who knows when I shall write in it again? If you read this, my parents, know that I loved you until I died.

Day the 9th of the City, I think
Year the 1st of the Rain Wilds

How foolish and melodramatic my last entry now looks to me.

I pen this hastily before the light fails. My friends wait for me patiently, though Chellia finds it foolish that I insist on writing before we go on.

Less than ten days have passed since I first saw this city, but it has aged years. The passage of many muddy feet was evident when we entered, and everywhere I saw the depredations of the treasure seekers. Like angry boys, they had destroyed what they could not take, prying tiles out of mosaics, breaking limbs off statues too big to carry, and using fine old furniture for firewood. As much as the city frightens me, still I grieve to see it plundered and ravaged. It has prevailed against the swamp for years, only to fall prey to our greed in days.

Its magic is failing. Only portions of the chamber were lit. The dragons on the ceiling had dimmed. The great woman-and-dragon statue bears marks from errant hammers. The jade and ivory of the woman's basket remain out of the reach of the treasure hunters. The rest of the pavilion had not fared so well. The fish fountain was being used as a great dish to hold someone's hoard. A man stood atop the heap of plunder, knife in one hand and club in the other and shouted at us that he would kill any thieves who came near. His appearance was so wild, we believed him. I felt shamed for him and looked aside as we hurried past. Fires burn in the room, with treasure and a guard by each one. In the distance we could hear voices, and sometimes challenging shouts and hammering. I caught a glimpse of four men ascending the steps with heavy sacks of loot.

Tremartin kindled one of our torches at an abandoned fire. We left that chamber by the same passage we had used before. Carlmin, mute since morning, began to hum a strange and wandering tune that stood up the hair on the back of my neck. I led him on, while Chellia's two girls wept silently in the dimness as they followed us, holding hands.

We passed the shattered door of a chamber. Thick mud-water oozed from the room. I glanced inside the chamber; a wide crack in its back wall had allowed mud to half fill the room. Still, someone had entered and sought treasure. Moldy paintings had been pulled loose from the walls and discarded in the rising muck. We hastened on.

At an intersection of corridors, we saw a slowly advancing flow of mud and heard a deep groaning in the distance, as of timbers slowly giving way. Nonetheless, a guard stood at that juncture, warning us that all behind him belonged to him and his friends. His eyes gleamed like a wild animal's. We assured him that we were only seeking a lost boy and hurried on. Behind him, we heard hammers begin and surmised that his friends were breaking down another door.

"We should hurry," Tremartin said. "Who knows what will be behind the next door they break? They won't leave off until they've let in the river. I left Retyo outside Olpey's door. We both feared others might come and think he guarded treasure."

"I just want my boy. Then I shall gladly leave this place," Chellia said. So we still hope to do.

I can write little of what else we saw, for the light flickers. We saw men dragging treasure they could never carry through the swamp. We were briefly attacked by a wild-eyed woman shrieking, "Thieves, thieves!" I pushed her down, and we fled. As we ran, there was first damp, then water, then oozing mud on the floor. The mud sucked at our feet as we passed the little dressing chamber where we had found Olpey the first time. It is wrecked now, the fine dressing table hacked to pieces. Tremartin took us down a side corridor I would not have noticed, and down a narrow flight of stairs. I smelled stagnant water. I tried not to think of the sodden earth ever pressing in, as we descended another, shorter flight of steps and turned down a wide hall. The doors we passed now were metal. A few showed hammer marks, but they had withstood the siege of the treasure seekers.

As we passed an intersection, we heard a distant crack like lightning, and then men shouting in terror. The unnatural veins of light on the walls flickered and then went out. An instant later, men rushed past us, fleeing back the way we had come. A gush of water that damped us to the ankles followed them, spending itself as it spread. Then came a deep and ominous rumbling. "Come on!" Tremartin ordered us, and we followed, though I think we all knew we were running deeper into danger, not away from it.

We turned two more corners. The stone of the walls suddenly changed from immense gray blocks to a smooth black stone with occasional veins of silver in it. We went down a long flight of shallow steps, and abruptly the corridor was wider and the ceiling higher, as if we had left behind the servants' area and entered the territory of the privileged. The wall niches had been plundered of their statues. I slipped in the damp on the floor. As I put my hand on a wall to catch myself, I suddenly glimpsed people swarming all around us. Their garb and demeanor were strange. It was a market day, rich with light and noise of conversation and the rich smells of baking. The life of a city swirled around me. In the next moment, Tremartin seized my arm and jerked me away from the wall. "Do not touch the black stone," he warned us. "It puts you in the ghosts' world. Come on. Follow me." In the distance, we saw the brighter flare of a fire gleaming, shaming the uneasily flickering light.

The fire was Retyo's torch. He was grimed from head to foot. Even when he saw us, he continued to scoop mud away from a door with a crude wooden paddle. The watery ooze was a constant flow down the hall; not even a dozen men could hope to keep up with it. If Olpey did not open the door soon, he would be trapped inside as the mud filled the corridor.

I stepped down into the shallow pit Retyo had been keeping clear. Heedless of the mud on him, heedless that my son and my friend watched me, I embraced him. If I had had the time, I would have become what my husband had accused me of being. Perhaps, in spirit, I am already a faithless wife. I care little for that now. I have kept faith with my friends.

Our embrace was brief. We had little time. We called to Olpey through the doors, but he kept silent until he heard his little sisters weeping. Then he angrily bade us to go away. His mother begged him to come out, saying that the city was giving way and that the flowing mud would soon trap him. He retorted that he belonged here, that he had always lived here and here he would die. And all the while that we shouted and begged, Retyo grimly worked, scraping the advancing muck away from the doorsill. When our pleas did not work, Retyo and Tremartin attacked the door, but the stout wood would not give to boots or fists, and we had no tools. In a dull whisper, Tremartin said we must leave him. He wept as he spoke. The mud was flowing faster than both men could contain, and we had three other children to think of.

Chellia's voice rose in a shriek of denial but was drowned by an echoing rumble behind us. Something big gave way. The flow of the muck doubled, for now it came from both directions. Tremartin lifted his torch. In both directions, the corridor ended in blackness. "Open the door, Olpey!" I begged him. "Or we all perish here, drowned in muck. Let us in, in Sa's name!"

I do not think he heeded my words. Rather it was Carlmin's voice, raised in a command in a language I've never heard that finally won a reaction. We heard latches being worked, and then the door grated grudgingly outward through the muck. The lit chamber dazzled our eyes as we tumbled into it. Water and flowing muck tried to follow us onto the richly tiled floor, but Tremartin and Retyo dragged the door shut, though Retyo had to drop to his knees and push mud out of the way to do so. Mud-tinged water crept determinedly under the closed door.

The chamber was the best preserved that I had seen. We were all dazzled by the richness of the chambers and the brief illusion of safety amid the strangeness. Shelves of gleaming wood supported exquisite vases and small stone statues, intricate carvings and silver ornaments gone black with time. A little winding staircase led up and out of sight. Each step of it was lined with light. The contents of the room could have ransomed our entire company back into the Satrap's goodwill, for the objects were both fine and strange. Olpey stooped down protectively to roll back a carpet in danger of being overtaken by the ooze. It was supple in his hands, and as he disturbed the dust, bright colors peeped out. For a few moments, none of us spoke. As Olpey came to his feet and stood before us, I gasped. He wore a robe that rippled with colors when he moved. About his forehead he had bound a band of linked metal disks, and they seemed to glow with their own light. Chellia dared not embrace him. He blinked owlishly, and Chellia hesitantly asked her son if he knew her.

His reply came slowly. "I dreamed you once." Then, looking about the room he said worriedly, "Or perhaps I have stepped into a dream. It is so hard to tell."

"He's been touching that black wall too much," Tremartin growled. "It wakes the ghosts and steals your mind. I saw a man two days ago. He was sitting with his back to the wall, his head leaned against it, smiling and gesturing and talking to people who weren't there."

Retyo nodded grimly. "Even without touching them, it takes a man's full will to keep the ghosts at bay after a time down here in the dark." Then, reluctantly, he added, "It may be too late to bring Olpey all the way back to us. But we can try. And we must all guard our minds as best we can, by talking to one another. And get the little ones out of here as quickly as we can."

I saw what he meant. Olpey had gone to a small table in a corner. A silver pot awaited beside a tiny silver cup. As we watched in silence, he poured nothing from the pot to the cup, and then quickly quaffed it. He wiped his mouth on the back of his hand and made a face, as if he had just drunk liquor too strong for him.

"If we're going to go, we must go now," Retyo added. He did not need to say, "Before it's too late." We were all thinking it.

But it was already too late. There was a steady seepage of water under the door, and when the men tried to open it, they could not budge it. Even when all the adults put our shoulders to it, it would not move. And then the lights began to flicker dismally.

Now the press of muck against the door grows heavier, so that the wood groans with it. I must be short. The staircase leads up into absolute darkness, and the torches we have contrived from the articles in the room will not last long. Olpey has gone into a daze, and Carlmin is not much better. He barely responds to us with a mutter. The men will carry the boys, and Chellia will lead her two girls. I will carry our supply of torches. We will go as far as we can, hoping to discover a different way back to the dragon-woman chamber.

Day . . . I do not know
Year the 1st of the Rain Wilds

So I head this account, for we have no concept of how much time has passed. For me, it seems years. I quiver, but I am not certain if it is from cold, or from striving to remain who I am. Who I was. My mind swims with the differences, and I could drown in them, if I let go. Yet if this account is to be of any use to others, I must find my discipline and put my thoughts into order.

As we ascended the stairs, the last breath of light in the chamber sighed out. Tremartin lifted our torch bravely, but it barely illuminated his head and shoulders in the engulfing blackness. Never have I experienced darkness so absolute. Tremartin gripped Olpey's wrist and compelled the boy to follow him. Behind him went Retyo, carrying Carlmin, then Chellia leading her trembling daughters. I came last, burdened with the crude torches created from the furniture and hangings in the chamber. This last act had infuriated Olpey. He attacked Retyo and would not stop until Retyo struck him a hard openhanded blow to the face. It dazed the boy and horrified his mother and sisters, but he became compliant, if not cooperative.

The stair led to a servants' room. Doubtless the privileged noble in the comfortable chamber below would ring a bell, and his servants would spring to satisfy the master's wish. I saw wooden tubs, perhaps for washing, and glimpsed a worktable before Tremartin hurried us on. There was only one exit. Once outside, the corridor offered blackness in both directions.

The noise of the burning torch seemed almost loud; the only other sound was the dripping of water. I feared that silence. Music and ghostly voices lingered at the edge of it.

"The flame burns steadily," Chellia observed. "No drafts."

I had not thought of that, but she was right. "All that means is that there is a door between us and the outside." Even I doubted my words. "One we must find and open."

"Which way shall we go?" Tremartin asked all of us. I had long ago lost my bearings, so I kept silent.

"That way," Chellia answered. "I think it goes back the direction we came. Perhaps we will see something we recognize, or perhaps the light will come back."

I had no better suggestion to offer. They led and I followed. Each of them had someone to hold tight, to keep the ghosts of the city at bay. I had only the bundled torches in my arms. My friends became shadows between me and the unsteady torchlight. If I looked up, the torch blinded me. Looking down, I saw a goblin's dance of shadows around my feet. Our hoarse breathing, the scuff of our feet on the damp stone, and the crackling of the torch were the only sounds I perceived at first. Then I began to hear other things, or to think that I did: the uneven drip of water and once a sliding sound as something in the distance gave way.

And music. It was music thin as watered ink, music muffled by thick stone and time, but it reached out to me. I was determined to take the men's advice and ignore it. To keep my thoughts my own, I began to hum an old Jamaillian lullaby. It was only when Chellia hissed, "Carillion!" at me that I realized my humming had become the haunting song from the stone. I stopped, biting my lip.

"Pass me another torch. We'd best light a fresh one before this one dies completely." When Tremartin spoke the words, I realized he'd spoken to me twice before. Dumbly I stepped forward, presenting my armload of makeshift torches. The first two he chose were scarves wrapped around table legs. They would not kindle at all. Whatever the scarves were woven from, they would not take the flame. The third was a cushion tied crudely to a chair leg. It burned smokily and with a terrible stench. Still, we could not be fussy, and holding aloft the burning cushion and the dwindling torch, we moved slowly on. When the torch had burned so close to Tremartin's fingers that he had to let it fall, we had only the smoldering glow of the cushion to light our way. The darkness pressed closer than ever, and the foul smell of the thing gave me a headache. I trudged along, remembering the annoying way the long coarse hair tangled on my rough-skinned fingers when I bundled the coiled hair in among the pith to make the cushion more springy and longer lasting.

Retyo shook me, hard, and then Carlmin came into my arms, sniffling. "Perhaps you should carry your son for a while," the sailor told me, without rebuke, as he stooped to gather the spare torches that I had dropped. Ahead of us in the dark, the rest of our party was shadows in shadow, with a red smear for our torch. I had just stopped in my tracks. If Retyo had not noted my absence, I wonder what would have happened to me. Even after we spoke, I felt as if I were two people.

"Thank you," I told him ashamedly.

"It's all right. Just stay close," he told me.

We went on. The punishing weight of Carlmin in my arms kept me focused. After a time, I set him down and made him walk beside me, but I think that was better for him. Having once been snared by the ghosts, I resolved to be more wary. Even so, odd bits of dreams, fancies, and voices talking in the distance drifted through my mind as I walked, eyes open, through the dark. We trudged on endlessly. Hunger and thirst made themselves known to us. The seeping runnels of water tasted bitter, but we drank sparingly from them anyway.

"I hate this city," I said to Carlmin. His little hand in mine was becoming chill as the buried city stole our body warmth from us. "It's full of traps and snares. Rooms full of mud waiting to crush us, and ghosts trying to steal our minds."

I had been speaking as much to myself as him. I didn't expect a response. But then he said slowly, "It wasn't built to be dark and empty."

"Perhaps not, but that is how it is now. And the ghosts of those who built it try to steal our minds from us."

I heard more than saw his scowl. "Ghosts? Not ghosts. Not thieves."

"What are they, then?" I asked him, mostly to keep him talking.

He was silent for a time. I listened to our footsteps and breathing. Then he said, "It's not anyone. It's their art."

Art seemed a far and useless thing to me now. Once I had used it to justify my existence. Now it seemed an idleness and a ploy, something I did to conceal the insignificance of my daily life. The word almost shamed me.

"Art," he repeated. He did not sound like a little boy as he went on, "Art is how we define and explain ourselves to ourselves. In this city, we decided that the daily life of the people was the art of the city. From year to year, the shaking of the earth increased, and the storms of dust and ash. We hid from it, closing our cities in and burrowing under the earth. And yet we knew that a time would come when we could not prevail against the earth itself. Some wished to leave, and we let them. No one was forced to stay. Our cities that had burgeoned with life faded to a trickle of souls. For a time, the earth calmed, with only a shiver now and then to remind us that our lives were daily granted to us and could be taken in a moment. But many of us decided that this was where we had lived, for generations. So this would be where we perished. Our individual lives, long as they were, would end here. But not our cities. No. Our cities would live on and recall us. Recall us—would call us home again, whenever anyone woke the echoes of us that we stored here. We're all here, all our richness and complexity, all our joys and sorrows . . ." His voice drifted away in contemplation once more.

I felt chilled. "A magic that calls the ghosts back."

"Not magic. Art." He sounded annoyed.

Suddenly Retyo said unsteadily, "I keep hearing voices. Someone, talk to me."

I put my hand on his arm. "I hear them, too. But they sound Jamaillian."

With pounding hearts our little party hastened toward them. At the next juncture of corridors, we turned right and the voices came clearer. We shouted, and they shouted a reply. Through the dark, we heard their hurrying feet. They blessed our smoky red torch; theirs had burned out. Four young men and two women from our company hastened toward our light. Frightened as they were, they still clutched armloads of plunder. We were overjoyed to find them, until they dashed our relief into despair. The tale they told us was a grim one. The passage to the outside world was blocked. They had been in the dragon-and-woman chamber when they heard heavy pounding from the rooms above. A great crash was followed by the slow groan of timbers giving way. As a grinding noise grew in volume, the lights in the big chamber flickered and watery mud began to trickle down the grand staircase. They had immediately tried to escape, only to find the stairway blocked by collapsed masonry oozing mud.

Perhaps fifty other scavengers had gathered in the dragon-and-woman chamber, drawn back there by the ominous sound. As the lights dimmed and then went out, all had fled, some going one way and some another, seeking for escape. Even facing the danger of being trapped below the earth, their suspicion of one another as thieves had prevented them from joining forces. Their tale filled me with despair. Lost in the dark, and still these six clutched treasure and greed to their hearts. I was disgusted with them and said as much. To my surprise, they sheepishly agreed. Then, for a time, we stood uselessly in the dark, listening to our torch burn away and wondering what to do.

When no one else spoke, I asked, “Do you know the way back to the dragon chamber?” I fought to speak steadily.

One man said he did.

“Then we must go back there. And gather all the people we can, and pool what we know of this maze. It is our only hope of finding a way out before our torches are gone. Otherwise, we may wander until we die.”

Grim silence was their assent. The young man led us back the way they had come. As we passed plundered rooms, we gathered anything that might burn. Soon the six who had joined us must abandon their plunder to carry more wood. I thought they would part from us before surrendering their treasure, but they decided to leave it in one of the rooms. They marked their claim upon the door, with chalked threats against any thieves. I thought this foolishness, for I would have traded every jewel in the city simply to see honest daylight again. Then we went on.

We reached at last the dragon-woman chamber. We knew it more by its echoes than by the view that our failing torch offered. A weight of earth had collapsed on the grand staircase. A small fire still smoldered in the center of the room near the dragon's feet, with a few hapless folk gathered around it. We added fuel to wake it to flames. It drew others to join us, and we then raised a shout to summon any who might hear us. Soon our little bonfire lit a circle of some thirty muddy and weary people. The flames showed me frightened white faces like masks. Many of them still clutched bundles of plunder and eyed one another suspiciously. That was almost more frightening than the slow creep of thick mud spreading down from the staircase. Heavy and thick, it trickled inexorably down, and I knew that our gathering place would not long be a refuge from it.

We were a pitiful company. Some of these folk had been lords and ladies, and others pickpockets and whores, but in that place, we finally became equals and recognized one another for what we were: desperate people, dependent on each other. We had convened at the foot of the dragon statue. Now Retyo stepped up onto the dragon's tail and commanded us, "Hush! Listen!"

Voices ebbed away. We heard the crackling of our fire, and then the distant groans of wood and stone, and the drip and trickle of watery muck. They were terrifying sounds, and I wondered why he had made us listen to them. When he spoke, his human voice was welcome as it drowned out the threats of the straining walls.

"We have no time to waste in worrying about treasure or theft. Our lives are the only things we can hope to carry out of here, and only if we pool what we know, so we don't waste time exploring corridors that lead nowhere. Are we together on that?"

A silence followed his words. Then a grimy, bearded man spoke. "My partners and I claimed the corridors from the west arch. We've been exploring them for days now. There are no stairs going up, and the main corridor ends in collapse."

It was dismal news, but Retyo didn't let us dwell on it.

"Well. Any others?"

There was some restless shifting.

Retyo's voice was stern. "You're still thinking of plunder and secrets. Let them go, or stay here with them. All I want is a way out. Now. We're only interested in stairways leading up. Anyone know of any?"

Finally, a man spoke up reluctantly. "There were two from the east arch. But . . . well, a wall gave way when we opened a door. We can't get to them anymore."

A deeper silence fell on us, and the light from the fire seemed to dwindle.

When Retyo spoke again, his voice was impassive. "Well, that makes it simpler for us. There's less to search. We'll need two large search parties, one that can divide at each intersection. As each group goes, you'll mark your path. On your way, enter every open chamber, and seek always for stairs leading up, for doubtless that is our only way out. Mark every path that you go by, so that you may return to us." He cleared his throat. "I don't need to warn you. If a door won't open, leave it alone.

"This is a pact we must make: that whoever finds a way out will risk their lives again to return and guide the rest of us out. To those who go out, the pact we make is that we who stay here will try to keep this fire burning, so that if you do not find a way out, you can return here, to light and another attempt." He looked around carefully at all the upturned faces. "To that end, every one of us will leave here whatever treasure we have found. To encourage any who find a way out to come back, for gain if not to keep faith with us."

I would not have dared to test them that way. I saw what he did. The mounded hoard would give hope to those who must stay here and tend the fire, as well as encourage any who found an escape to return for the rest of us. To those who insisted they would take their treasure with them, Retyo simply said, "Do it. But remember well what you choose. No one who stays here will owe you any help. Should you return and find the fire out and the rest of us gone, do not hope that we will return for you."

Three men, heavily burdened, went aside to heatedly argue among themselves. Other people had begun to trickle back to the dragon pavilion, and we quickly informed them of the pact. These folk, having already tried to find a way out, easily agreed to the terms. Someone said that perhaps the rest of our company might dig down to free us. A general silence greeted that thought as we all considered the many steps we had descended to reach this place, and all the mud and earth that stood between us and outside air. Then no one spoke of it again. When finally all agreed to abide by Retyo's plan, we counted ourselves and found that we numbered fifty-two bedraggled and weary men, women, and children.

Two parties set out. Most of our firewood went with them, converted to torches. Before they left, we prayed together, but I doubted Sa could hear us, so deep beneath the ground and so far from sacred Jamaillia. I remained with my son, tending the fire. We took turns making short trips to nearby rooms, to drag back whatever might burn. Treasure seekers had already burned most of the close fuel, but still we found items ranging from massive tables it took eight of us to lift to broken bits of rotted chairs and tatters of curtain.

Most of the children had remained by the fire. In addition to my son and Chellia's children, there were four other youngsters. We took turns telling stories or singing songs to them, trying to keep their minds free of the ghosts that clustered closer as our small fire burned lower. We begrudged every stick of wood we fed to it.

Despite our efforts, the children fell silent one by one and slipped into the dreams of the buried city. I shook Carlmin and pinched him, but could not find the will to be cruel enough to rouse him. In truth, the ghosts plucked at my mind as well, until the distant conversations in an unknown language seemed more intelligible than the desperate mutterings of the other women. I dozed off, then snapped awake as the needs of the dying fire recalled me to my duty.

"Perhaps it's kinder to let them dream themselves to death," one of the women said as she helped me push one end of a heavy table into the fire. She took a deeper breath and added, "Perhaps we should all just go to the black wall and lean against it."

The idea was more tempting than I liked to admit. Chellia returned from a wood-foraging effort. "I think we burn more in torch than we bring back as fuel," she pointed out. "I'll sit with the children for a while. See what you can find to burn."

So I took her stub of torch and went off seeking firewood. By the time I returned with my pitiful scraps, a splinter group of one of the search parties had returned. They had swiftly exhausted their possibilities and their torches and returned hoping that others had had better luck.

When a second party returned shortly afterward, I felt more

discouragement. They brought with them a group of seventeen others whom they had discovered wandering in the labyrinth. The seventeen were the "owners" of that section of the city and said that days ago they had early discovered that the upper stories in that section were collapsed. In all the days they had explored it, always the paths had led outward and downward. Any further explorations in that direction would demand more torches than we presently had.

Our supply of wood for the bonfire was already dwindling, and we weren't finding much in the pillaged rooms that we could use for torches. Hunger and thirst were already pressing many of us. Too soon we would have to confront an even more daunting shortage. Once our fire failed, we would be plunged into total darkness. If I dared to think of it, my heart thundered and I felt faint. It was hard enough to hold myself aloof from the city's lingering "art." Immersed in blackness, I knew I would give way to it.

I was not the only one who realized this. Tacitly, we let the fire die down and maintained it at a smaller size. The flow of mud down the grand stair brought damp that chilled the air. People huddled together for warmth as much as companionship. I dreaded the first touch of water against my feet. I wondered which would overtake me first, total darkness or rising mud.

I don't know how much time passed before the third party returned to us. They had found three staircases that led up. All were blocked before they reached the surface. Their corridor had become increasingly ruined the farther they had gone. Soon they had been splashing through shallow puddles, and the smell of earth had grown strong. When their torches were nearly exhausted and the water growing deeper and colder about their knees, they had returned. Retyo and Tremartin had been members of that party. I was selfishly glad to have him at my side again, even though it meant that our hope was now whittled to a single search party.

Retyo wished to shake Carlmin out of his daze, but I asked him, "To what end? That he might stare into the darkness and know despair? Let him dream, Retyo. He does not seem to be having bad dreams. If I can carry him out of here into daylight once more, then I will wake him and try to call him back to me. Until then, I will leave him in peace." I sat, Retyo's arm around me, and thought silently of Petrus and my erstwhile husband, Jathan. Well, he had made one wise decision. I felt oddly grateful to him that he had not allowed me to squander both our sons' lives. I hoped he and Petrus reached the coast safely and eventually returned to Jamaillia. At least one of my children might grow to adulthood.

And so we waited, our hopes dwindling as swiftly as our firewood. Our men had to venture farther and farther into the darkness in search of fuel. Finally Retyo lifted his voice. "Either they are still exploring, in hope of finding a way out, or they have found a way out and are too fearful to return for us. In either way, we gain nothing more by sitting here. Let us go where they went, following their marks, while we still have light to see them. Either we will find the same escape route they did, or die together."

We took every splinter of firewood. The more foolish among us gathered treasure to carry out. No one remonstrated with them, though many laughed bitterly at their hopeful greed. Retyo picked up Carlmin without a word; it moved me that my son was treasure to him. In truth, weakened as I was by hunger, I do not know if I could have carried my son. I do know that I would not have left him there. Tremartin took Olpey slung across his shoulders. The boy was limp as a drowned thing. *Drowned in art,* I thought to myself. Drowned in memories of the city.

Of Chellia's two daughters, Piet still clung to wakefulness. She stumbled piteously along beside her mother. A young man named Sterren offered to carry Likea for Chellia. She was so grateful, she wept.

And so we trudged off. We had one torch to lead us, and one at the tail of our procession, so that no one would fall victim to the city's allure and be left behind. I walked in the middle of the company, and the darkness seemed to pluck and snag at my senses. There is little to say of that endless walk. We took no rest, for our fire ate our torches at an alarming rate. There was dark, and wet, the mutter of hungry and thirsty and weary folk all around me, and more darkness. I could not really see the halls we walked through, only the smudge of light that we followed. Bit by bit, I gave up my burden of wood to our light bearers. The last time I moved forward to offer a new torch, I saw that the walls were of shining black stone veined with silver. They were elaborately decorated with silhouettes of people, done in some shining metal. Curious, I reached out a hand to touch one. I had not even realized that Retyo was at my side. He caught my wrist before I could touch the silhouette. "Don't," he warned me. "I brushed against one once. They leap into your mind if you touch them. Don't."

We followed the marks of the missing search party. They had marked off the dead ends and drawn arrows as they progressed, and so we trudged on, hoping. Then, to our horror, we caught up with them.

They were huddled in the middle of the corridor. Torches exhausted, they had halted there, paralyzed by the complete blackness, unable to either go on or to come back to us. Some were insensible. Others whimpered with joy at the sight of us and clustered around our torch as if light were life itself flowing back into them.

"Did you find a way out?" they asked us, as if they had forgotten that they were the searchers. When they finally understood that they had been our last hope, the life seemed to go out of them. "The corridor goes on and on," they said. "But we have not yet found one place where it leads upward. The chambers we have been able to enter are windowless. We think this part of the city has always been underground."

Grim words. Useless to dwell on them.

And so, we moved on together. We encountered few intersections, and when we did, we made our choice almost randomly. We no longer had torches to explore every possibility. At each intersection, the men in the lead debated and then chose. And we followed, but at each one we had to wonder if we had made a fatal error. Were we walking away from the passage that would have led to light and air? We gave up having a torch at the end of our procession, instead having folk hold hands and come behind us. Even so, too swiftly we had but three torches, and then two. A woman keened as the final torch was kindled. It did not burn well, or perhaps the dread of the dark was so strong in us that no light would have seemed sufficient. I know we crowded closer around our torchbearer. The corridor had widened and the ceiling retreated. Every now and then, the torchlight would catch a silver silhouette or a vein of silvery mineral in the polished black wall and it would blink beckoningly at me. Still we marched hopelessly on, hungry, thirsty, and ever more weary. We did not travel fast, but then, we did not know if we had any destination save death.

The lost spirits of the city plucked at me. Ever stronger grew the temptation to simply let go of my puny life and immerse myself in the beckoning remembrance of the city. Snatches of their music, conversation heard in a distant mutter, even, it seemed to me, whiffs of strange fragrances assailed me and tempted me. Well, was not that what Jathan had always warned me? That if I did not take a firmer grip on my life, my art would immerse and then devour me? But it was so hard to resist; it tugged at me like a hook in a fish's lip. It knew that it had me; it but waited for darkness to pull me in.

The torch burned lower with every step we took. Every step we took might be one more step in the wrong direction. The passage had widened around us into a hall; I could no longer see the gleaming black walls, but I could feel them commanding my attention. We passed a still fountain flanked by stone benches. We watched in vain for anything that might fuel our fire. Here, these elder folk had built for eternity, from stone and metal and fired clay. I knew that these rooms now were the repository of all they had been. They had believed they would always live here, that the waters of the fountains and the swirling beams of light would always dance at their touch. I knew that as clearly as I knew my own name. Like me, they had foolishly thought to live forever through their art. Now it was the only part of them that lingered still.

And in that moment, I knew my decision. It came to me so clearly that I am not sure it was solely my own. Did some long dead artist reach out and tug at my sleeve, begging to be heard and seen one last time before we tumbled into the dark and silence that had consumed her city?

I put my hand on Retyo's arm. "I'm going to the wall now," I said simply. To his credit, he immediately knew what I meant.

"You would leave us?" he asked me piteously. "Not just me, but little Carlmin? You would drown yourself in dreams and leave me to face death alone?"

I stood on tiptoe to kiss his whiskery cheek and to press my lips briefly against my son's downy head. "I won't drown," I promised him. It suddenly seemed so simple. "I know how to swim in those waters. I have swum in them since my birth, and like a fish, I will follow them upstream to their source. And you will follow me. All of you."

"Carillion, I don't understand. Are you mad?"

"No. But I cannot explain. Only follow me, and trust, as I followed you when I walked out on the tree limb. I will feel the path surely; I won't let you fall."

Then I did the most scandalous thing I've ever done in my life. I took hold of my weary skirts, long tattered halfway up my calf, and tore them free of my stained waistband, leaving only my pantaloons. I bundled them up and pushed them into his shocked hands. Around us, others had halted in their shadowy trudging to watch my strange performance. "Feed these to the torch, a bit at a time, to keep it alive. And follow me."

"You will walk near naked before all of us?" he asked me in horror, as if it were of great concern.

I had to smile. "While my skirts burn, no one will notice the nakedness of her who stripped to give them light. And after they have burned, we will all be hidden in the darkness. Much like the art of these people."

Then I walked away from him, into the engulfing darkness that framed us. I heard him shout to our torchbearer to halt, and I heard others say that I had gone mad. But I felt as if I had finally plunged myself into the river that all my life had tantalized my thirst. I went to the city's wall willingly, opening my mind and heart to their art as I approached it, so that by the time I touched the cold stone, I was already walking among them, hearing their gossip and corner musicians and haggling.

It was a market square. As I touched the stone, it roared to life around me. Suddenly my mind perceived light where my closed eyes did not, and I smelled the cooking river fish on the smoky little braziers and saw the skewers of dripping honeyed-fruit on the tray of a street hawker. Glazed lizards smoked on a low brazier.

Children chased one another past me. People paraded the streets, dressed in gleaming fabrics that rippled color at their every step. And such people, people that befitted such a grand city! Some might have been Jamaillian, but among them moved others, tall and narrow, scaled like fish or with skin as bronzed as polished metal. Their eyes gleamed too, silver and copper and gold. The ordinary folk made way for these exalted ones with joy rather than cold respect. Merchants stepped out from their stalls to offer them their best, and gawking children peeped from around their mothers' trousered legs to glimpse their royalty passing. For such I was sure they were.

With an effort, I turned my eyes and my thoughts from this rich pageantry. I groped to recall whom and where I truly was. I dragged Carlmin and Retyo back into my awareness. Then, I deliberately looked around myself. Up and sky, I told myself. Up and sky, into the air. Blue sky. Trees.

Fingers lightly touching the wall, I moved forward.

Art is immersion, and good art is total immersion. Retyo was right. It sought to drown me. But Carlmin was right, too. There was no malice in the drowning, only the engulfing that art seeks. And I was an artist, and as a practitioner of that magic, I was accustomed to keeping my head even when the current ran strongest and swiftest.

Even so, it was all I could do to cling to my two words. Up and sky. I could not tell if my companions followed me or if they had abandoned me to my madness. Surely, Retyo would not. Surely, he would come behind me, bringing my son with him. Then, a moment later, the struggle to remember their names became too great. Such names and such people had never existed in this city, and I was a citizen of the city now.

I strode through its busy market time. Around me people bought and sold exotic and fascinating merchandise. The colors, the sounds, even the smells tempted me to linger, but Up and Sky were what I clung to.

They were not a folk who cherished the outside world. Here they had built a hive, much of it underground, lit and warm, clean and immune to wind and storm and rain. They had brought inside it such creatures as appealed to them, flowering trees and caged songbirds and little glittering lizards tethered to potted bushes. Fish leaped and flashed in the fountains, but no dogs ran and barked, no birds flew overhead. Nothing was allowed that might make a mess. All was orderly and controlled, save for the flamboyant people who shouted and laughed and whistled in their precisely arranged streets.

Up and Sky, I told them. They did not hear me, of course. Their conversations buzzed uselessly around me, and even once I began to understand them, the things they spoke of did not concern me. What could I care about the politics of a queen a thousand years gone, for society weddings and clandestine affairs noisily gossiped about? Up and Sky I breathed to myself, and slowly, slowly, the memories I sought began to flow to me. For there were others in this city for whom art was Up and Sky. There was a tower, an observatory. It rose above the river mists on foggy nights, and there learned men and women could study the stars and predict what effect they might have on mortals. I focused my mind on it, and soon "remembered" where it was. Sa blessed us all, in that it was not far from their marketplace.

I was halted once, for though my eyes told me that the way ahead of me was well lit and smoothly paved, my groping hands found a cold tumble of fallen stone and earth seeping water. A man shouted by my ear and restrained my hands. Dimly I recalled my other life. How strange to open my eyes to blackness and Retyo gripping my hands in his. Around me in the darkness, I heard people weeping or muttering despairingly that they followed a dreamer to their deaths. I could see nothing at all. The darkness was absolute. I had no idea how much time had passed, but I was suddenly aware of thirst that near choked me. Retyo's hand still clutched at mine, and I knew then of the long chain of people, hands clasped, that trustingly followed me.

I croaked at them. "Don't give up. I know the way. I do. Follow me."

Later, Retyo would tell me that the words I uttered were in no tongue he had ever known, but my emphatic shout swayed him. I closed my eyes, and once more the city surged to life around me. Another way, there had to be another way to the observatory. I turned back to the populous corridors, but now as I passed the leaping fountains, they taunted me with their remembered water. The tantalizing memories of food smells lingered in the air, and I felt my belly clench on itself in longing. But Up and Sky were my words, and I walked on, even as I became aware that moving my body was becoming more and more taxing to me. In another place, my tongue was leather in my mouth, my belly a cramped ball of pain. But here, I moved with the city, immersed in it. I understood now the words that flowed past me, I smelled familiar foods, even knew all the words to the songs the corner minstrels were singing. I was home, and as the city as art flowed through me; I was home in a deeper way than ever Jamaillia had been home to me.

I found the other stairs that led to the observatory, the back stairs for the servants and cleaners. Up these stairs, humble folk carried couches and trays of wineglasses for nobles who wished to recline and gaze up at the stars. It was a humble wooden door. It swung open at my push. I heard a murmured gasp behind me, and then words of shouted praise that opened my eyes.

Daylight, thin and feeble, crept down to us. The winding stair was wooden, and rickety, but I decided we would trust it. "Up and Sky," I told my company as I set my foot to the first creaking step. It was a struggle to recall my precious words and speak them aloud. "Up and Sky." And they followed me.

As we ascended, the light came stronger, and we blinked like moles in that sweet dimness. When at last I reached the stone-floored upper chamber, I smiled so that my dry lips split.

The thick glass panels of the observatory windows had given way to cracks, followed by questing vines that faded to pale writhing things as they left the daylight behind. The light through the windows was greenish and thick, but it was light. The vines became our ladder to freedom. Many of us were weeping dry tears as we made that last painful climb. Unconscious children and dazed people were passed up and out to us. I took a limp Carlmin in my arms and held him in the light and fresh air.

There were rain flowers awaiting us, as if Sa wished us to know it was her will we survive here, enough rain flowers for each of us to wet our mouths and gather our senses. The wind seemed chill, and we laughed joyfully to shiver in it. We stood on top of what had been the observatory, and I looked out with love over a land I had once known. My beautiful wide river valley was swamp now, but it was still mine. The tower that had stood so high above all was only a mound now, but around us were the hunched and mossy remains of other structures, making the land firm and dry beneath our feet. There was not much dry land, less than a leffer, and yet after our months in the swamp, it seemed a grand estate. From atop it, we could look out over the slowly moving river where slanting sunlight fell on the chalky waters. My home had changed, but it was still mine.

Every one of us who left the dragon chamber emerged alive and intact. The city had swallowed us, taken us down and made us hers, and then released us, changed, in this kindlier place. Here, by virtue of the city buried beneath us, the ground is firmer.

There are great, strong branched trees nearby, in which we can build a new platform. There is even food here, a plenitude by Rain Wild standards. A sort of climbing vine festoons the trunks of the trees and is heavy with pulpy fruit. I recall the same fruit sold in the vendor stalls of my city. It will sustain us. For now, we have all we need to survive this night. Tomorrow will be soon enough to think on the rest of it.

Day the 7th of Light and Air
Year the 1st of the Rain Wilds

It took us a full six days to hike downriver to our original settlement. Time in the light and air have restored most of us to our ordinary senses, though all of the children have a more detached air than they used to have. Nor do I think I am alone in my vivid dreams of life in the city. I welcome them now. The land here has changed vastly since the days of the city; once all was solid ground, and the river a silver shining thread. The land was restless in those days, too, and sometimes the river ran milky and acid. Now the trees have taken back the meadows and croplands, but still, I recognize some features of the land. I recognize, too, which trees are good for timber, which leaves make a pleasantly stimulating tea, which reeds can yield both paper and fabric when beaten to thread and pulp, and oh, so many other things. We will survive here. It will not be lush or easy living, but if we accept what the land offers us, it may be enough.

And that is well. I found my tree city mostly deserted. After the disaster that sealed us in the city, most of the folk here gave up all for lost and fled. Of the treasure they collected and mounded on the platform, they took only a pittance. Only a few people remained. Marthi and her husband and her son are among them. Marthi wept with joy at my return.

When I expressed my anger that the others could go on without her, she told me, quite seriously, that they had promised to send back help, and she was quite sure that they would keep their word, as their treasure is still here.

As for me, I found my own treasure. Petrus had remained here, after all. Jathan, stonyhearted man that he is, went on without the boy when Petrus had a last-moment change of heart and declared that he would wait here for his mother to return. I am glad that he did not wait for me in vain.

I was shocked that Marthi and her husband had remained, until she put in my arms her reason. Her child was born, and for his sake, they will dwell here. He is a lithe and lively little thing, but he is as scaled as a snake. In Jamaillia, he would be a freak. The Rain Wilds are where he belongs.

As we all do, now.

I think I was as shocked at the changes in Marthi as she was in the change in me. Around her neck and wrists where she had worn the jewelry from the city, tiny growths have erupted. When she stared at me, I thought it was because she could see how much the city memories had changed my soul. In reality, it was the beginning of feathery scales on my eyelids and round my lips that caught her eye. I have no looking glass, so I cannot say how pronounced they are. And I have only Retyo's word that the line of scarlet scaling down my spine is more attractive than repellent.

I see the scaling that has begun to show on the children, and in truth, I do not find it abhorrent. Almost all of us who went down into the city bear some sign of it, either a look behind the eyes, or a delicate tracing of scales, or perhaps a line of pebbled flesh along the jaw. The Rain Wilds have marked us as their own, and welcome us home.

The Inheritance

My parents both lived through the Great Depression and World War II. My father met my mother when he was stationed near Norwich with the Eighth Air Force. She married him and followed him to the United States. Both of them had known affluence in their lives, and also knew how quickly wealth and easy lives could disappear.

As I grew up, they let me know that education and experiences were to be valued high above material things. These things were the riches that one could not easily be stripped of. And when they died, first my mother and then my father, there was very little in the way of physical goods for any of us to claim. Some photo albums, some books. A rocking chair, a wooden salad bowl, a chiming clock my uncle had made for them. That was my inheritance.

And on the surface, such an inheritance can seem trivial, even pathetic. Unless one recalls that an inheritance isn't about material wealth, but about the experiences that came with it.

It was in my grandmother's jewel box. I found it after she died. Perhaps jewel box is too fine a name to give to the plain wooden cask that held so little. There was a silver ring with the stone long prized from the setting, sold to pay family debts no doubt. I wondered why she had not sold it whole. There were two necklaces, one of garnets and another of polished jasper. In the bottom, wrapped in layer upon layer of linen, was the pendant.

It was a lovely carving of a woman's face. She looked both aristocratic and yet merry, and I recognized in her features some of my own. I wondered which of my female ancestors she was, and why someone had taken such care to make so delicate a carving from such an ugly piece of wood. It was gray and checked with age and weighed unnaturally heavy in my hand as I examined it. The chain it was fixed to was fine silver, however. I thought it might be worn alone if the pendant could be removed. I heard a footstep in the hall outside her bedroom and hastily slipped the chain about my neck. The cameo hung heavy between my breasts, concealed by my blouse. My cousin Tetlia stood suddenly in the doorway. "What do you have there?" she demanded.

"Nothing," I told her and hastily set the box back on grandmother's chest.

She quickly came into the room and snatched it up. She opened it and dumped the necklaces into her hand. "Nice," she said, holding up the jasper one. My heart sank, for I had liked it best of the three. "I'm eldest of the granddaughters," she pointed out smugly and slipped it over her head. She weighed the garnets in her hand. "And my sister, Coreth, comes next. This for her." Her lips twisted in a smile as she tossed me the robbed ring. "For you, Cerise. Not much of an inheritance, but she did feed and clothe you for the last two years and kept you in a house that long ago should have come to my father. That is more than she ever did for my sister and me."

"I lived here with her. I looked after her. When her hands twisted so that she couldn't use them anymore, I bathed her and dressed her and fed her . . ." My hidden anger pushed the words stiffly out.

Tetlia waved my words away contemptuously. "And we all warned you that you'd get nothing for it. She burned through her own family fortune when she was a girl, Cerise. Everyone knows that if my grandfather had not married her, she'd have starved in the streets. And my father has been good enough to let her live out her life in a house that should have come to him when his father died. Now she's gone, and the house and land revert to my father. That's life." She tossed the plundered casket onto my grandmother's stripped bed and left the room.

"I loved her," I said quietly into the stillness. Rage burned bright in me for an instant. It was an old family dispute. Tetlia's father was the son of Grandfather's first wife, and the rightful heir to all, as they so constantly reminded me. It counted for nothing with them that my grandmother had raised their father as if he were her own child. It scalded me that Tetlia would claim my grandmother as kin for the sake of being entitled to her jewelry, but deny that I had any right to share the family wealth. For a second I clutched that anger to me. Then, as if I could feel my grandmother's gentle hand on my shoulder, I let the strength of my just wrath leak away from me. "Useless to argue," I told myself. In my grandmother's looking glass I saw the same defeated resignation I had so often seen in her eyes. "It's not worth fighting for," she had told me so often. "Scandal and strife serve no purpose. Let it go, Cerise. Let it go." I looked at the gaping ring in my hand, and then slipped it onto my finger. It fit as if made for me. Somehow, it seemed an appropriate inheritance.

I left the room and went to my own chamber to pack. It did not take long. I had one set of clothes besides my own, and Grandmother's old Trader robe of soft saffron. I hesitated before I put it in my rucksack. I had never seen her wear it. Once I had asked her about that only unused garment in her chest. She had shaken her head. "I don't know why I kept it. It has nothing to do with my life anymore. In Bingtown, Trader families wear them when they go to the Traders' Council to vote on Trader matters. Saffron was my family's color, the Lantis family. But I gave all that up years ago."

I fingered the soft wool. It was cut in an archaic style, but the wool would be warm, I told myself. Besides, I had no intention of leaving it for my cousins. Now that my grandmother was dead, her little house on the sea cliffs and the sheep pastures behind it would go to my uncle, son of my grandfather's first wife. And I, the sole daughter of her daughter, would have to make my own way in the world. My uncle had scowled at me when I had told him last night that I had no place to go and asked his leave to stay on a week.

He replied heavily, "The old woman was dying for two years, Cerise. If, in two years, you couldn't make a plan for your future, you won't do it in a week. We need this house, and it's fairly mine. I'm sorry, but you'll have to go."

So I went, but not far. Hetta, the shepherd's wife, took me in for the night. They were as angry with my uncle as I was, for he had already announced to them that he was raising their rent. In all the years that they had been my grandmother's tenants, she had never raised their rent. Hetta was older than I, but that had never kept us from being good friends. She had two small children and was big with her third. She was glad to offer me a bed by the fire and a hot supper in exchange for help with her chores, "for as long as you want." I tidied the house as we talked; she was relieved to sit down and put her feet up while she put the last stitches into a quilt. I showed her both my ring and my pendant and chain. She exclaimed at the sight of the pendant and pushed it away from her.

"The chain will bring you some coin, and maybe the empty ring. But that pendant is an evil thing. I'd get rid of it if I were you. Throw it in the sea. It's wizardwood, the stuff a liveship is made from. I wouldn't wear it next to my skin for the world."

I picked up the pendant and looked at it more closely. In the candlelight, I could see faint colors on it, as if it had once been painted but had faded. The grain of the wood seemed finer, the features of the face more distinct than I recalled. "Why is it evil?" I demanded of Hetta. "Liveships aren't evil. Their figureheads come to life and talk and guide the boat on its way. They're magic, but I've never heard them called evil."

Hetta shook her head stubbornly. "It's Rain Wild magic, and all know no good ever came down the Rain Wild River. A lot of folk say that that's where the Blood Plague came from. Leave magic like that to those Trader folk who are born to it. It's not for you and me. It's bound to bring you bad luck, Cerise, same as it brought your grandmother. Get rid of it."

"She came from Trader stock," I reply stoutly. "Maybe that's how it came to Grandma. Maybe she inherited from the days when we were Traders."

Hetta pursed her mouth in disapproval as I put the chain back around my neck. I heard Hetta's husband at the door and hastily slipped the pendant inside my shirt again. I'd always liked Hetta, but her husband made me edgy.

Tonight was no exception. He grinned to see me there and grinned broader when Hetta said she'd invited me to stay the night. "You're always welcome here, Cerise, for as long as you want to stay. There's many a wifely chore that Hetta hasn't been able to do for a time. You could take them on for room and board here."

I smiled stiffly as I shook my head. "Thank you all the same, but I think I need to find a future for myself. I think I'll go to Bingtown and see what work I can find there."

"Bingtown!" Hetta was horrified. "That den of vice? Stay in the country, girl, where folks have hearts. No one will treat you well in the city."

"Stay," her husband urged me. His eyes decided me as he declared, "Live here, and I'll treat you just like one of my own."

And that night, he was as good as his word. As I slept on the hearth, I heard the scuff of his big bare feet as he came into the room. His children slept in the loft, and Hetta in their small bedchamber. In the past, he had done no more than stroke my buttock as I passed him, or casually brush my breast with the back of his hand as he reached past me, as if it were an accident. But I had never slept the night in his cottage. I smelled his sweat as he hunkered down beside me. "Cerise?" he whispered in the darkness. I kept my eyes shut and pretended to be asleep. My heart was hammering as I felt him lift the corner of the blanket Hetta had given me. His big hand came to rest on the angle of my neck. I gritted my teeth but could do no more than that. Useless to resist. Hetta and the children might wake, and then what would I say? I tried to be as stoic as my long-enduring grandmother. Let him touch me. If I refused to wake, surely he would leave me alone.

"Cerise, honey," he whispered again, inching his fingers along my flesh.

"Faithless man!" a whisper answered him. Every muscle in my body tightened, for it seemed to come from my own throat. "Touch me, and I rake your face with scratches that Hetta won't ignore."

He jerked his hand back from me as if scalded, so startled that he sat down hard on the floor behind me. I lay still, frozen in silent terror.

"And that's how you'd pay back my hospitality, is it? Go to Bingtown, then, you little baggage. There the men will take what they want of you, and not offer you a roof nor a bed in exchange for it."

I said nothing, fearing his words were true. I heard him get to his feet and then shuffle back to his marriage bed. I lay still and sleepless the rest of the night, trying to pretend that I had said those words. The pendant lay against my skin like a cold toad; I feared to touch it to remove it.

I left the next morning, though Hetta near wept as she urged me to stay. All my possessions still made a light load. Bingtown was only two days away by foot, but even so, I'd only been there twice in my life. Both times, I had gone with my parents. My father had carried me sometimes on his shoulder, and my mother had cooked food for us at night. But they were both long gone. Now I walked the road alone, and my heart pounded fearfully at the sight of every passing traveler. Even when I was alone, fear rode with me, dangling from the necklace about my neck.

That night I left the road, to unroll my blanket in the lee of some rocks. There were no trees for shelter, no friendly nearby stream, only a hillside of lichen-sided boulders and scrubby brush. Hetta had given me a little sack of meal cakes to last me on my way. I was too frightened of thieves to build a fire that might draw them, so as the westering sun stole the colors from the day, I huddled in my blanket and nibbled on one of my meal cakes.

"A fine beginning to my new life," I muttered when the last dry crumbs of the cake were gone.

"No worse than what other women of your line have faced," whispered a voice. It came from my shirtfront. In an instant, I had snatched off chain and pendant and flung it from me. It caught on a bush and hung there, silver chain glinting in the last of the sunset. The dangling pendant came to rest facing me. Even in the fading light, I could see that it had taken on lifelike colors. It raised tiny eyebrows at me in disdain. "It's a foolish choice you're making, girl," it warned me. "Throw me away, and you throw away your inheritance. Just as your grandmother did."

Frightened as I was, the small voice was so like my grandmother's that I could not ignore it. "What are you?" I demanded.

"Oh, come," the pendant exclaimed in disdain. "I am exactly what you see and know me to be. Let us not waste time in foolishness."

"You were gray and still when I took you from Grandmother's jewelry box."

"She had not worn me for many a year. She put me aside, just as she put aside the rest of her life. But you have revived me. You are young and your anma rushes strong as your blood through your veins."

The pendant had a tiny voice, and despite my fear, I drew closer to hear her words. The eyes that met mine held kindly amusement. A smile bent the mouth. "What are you afraid of?" she demanded. "For generations I have been in your family, passed down from mother to daughter. With me comes all the wisdom of your line. You were wise enough to steal me. Are you so foolish that you will fear your fortune now that it is in your hands?"

"You're magic," I said. "You're alive."

"I am. And so are you, if you would bother to find it in yourself. It's part of your inheritance, and if you are wise, it will be the first part you reclaim."

"My inheritance?" I asked quietly.

The little eyes narrowed. "What goes with the empty ring that you wear. That is your inheritance. As you have donned both it and me, I suggest that you reclaim all that went with it. All that your Grandmother Aubretia possessed before she chose to set us aside and live quietly."

It was growing darker. Strange as may be, the little carved face seemed like a companion in the night. I took up the pendant and held the carved face closer to my own so I could see her. "Tell me," I begged. "For all the years that I lived with my grandmother and cared for her, I know little of her past."

"Well." The small dark eyes, so like my own, cast about consideringly. "Where shall I begin? Tell me what you do know of her."

I cast my mind back. "She told me little. Mostly I have guessed. I think that when she was very small, her family was wealthy. She often warned me against trusting handsome young men. While I lived with her, she would not permit anyone to court me. So I think that—"

"You think that her heart was broken when she was young. And you are correct. Aubretia did grow up in a family that had substance if not real wealth. Her father died when she was young. The Lantis family had little wealth save their name, but her mother was wise and set aside an inheritance for her youngest daughter. It was her intention that her child need never marry for wealth, only for love. I told them I did not see why the two could not go hand in hand, but they both dismissed it as a jest. When your great-grandmother was on her deathbed, she passed me to her daughter. And she left this world in peace, knowing she had passed on both worldly wealth and a secret counselor to Aubretia."

I tugged my blanket closer around my shoulders and leaned back against the largest rock. It still held some small heat from the day. I drew my knees up and set the pendant atop them to listen to her tale. Night crept closer around us.

"For a time, she lived wisely and well. Then she met a young man, a lovely young man. He was new to Bingtown, come to the great trading city to make his fortune. Howarth was a younger son, with no fortune to his name but rich in ambition. Aubretia would have married him a day after she met him, but he would not take her so. 'When I have made a fortune of my own, then I will claim you as a bride. I will not have folk say I wed you for your money.' And so Howarth courted her with bouquets of simple wayside flowers and sat in her house before her fire and told her daily of how hard he struggled to wrest out a living as a clerk in a mercantile. He often scoffed at the fellow who owned the store where he worked, for he said the man had no imagination in his dealings, and that he might easily be twice as successful if he had but a bit of daring and imagination. Howarth planned that as soon as he had money enough to finance it, he would go on a trading journey to far Jamaillia, and bring back fine goods such as all Bingtown would clamor to buy. On his dreams were your grandmother's dreams founded.

"But her dreams and his were a long time in coming true. Your grandmother's lover saved his coins, true, but Howarth no sooner had one to stack upon two than he had to spend it for new boots or a winter cloak. Your grandmother despaired that he would ever wed her. She begged him to marry her, saying she did not care if he was penniless, that with his job her inheritance would be sufficient for them both. But again he refused, saying he would not wed until he had built a fortune of his own."

The pendant fell silent for a time, the small face gone pensive. I waited.

The small face pursed her lips in disapproval. "Then Aubretia had an idea. I warned her against it. In vain, I tried to persuade her to let this young man go his own way, but she would not listen. She went to Howarth and offered him money. He could take her money off to Jamaillia to buy the trade goods that would make them both wealthy. Half of whatever profits they made would be his, and then they could be married. He quickly agreed. Far too quickly for my liking.

"Howarth took her money and sailed away. Months passed,

and Aubretia pined, but I was relieved, knowing that even though her money was gone, he was gone with it. She still had enough left to get on with, and now perhaps was wiser. But just when she began to put memories of him aside, he returned. He wore fine clothes and brought gifts with him, perfumes and silk, but little else. Most of the coin, he told her, had been spent to court trading partners in that distant city. All was in readiness, now, and as soon as he had worked hard and saved a bit of money, he could go south and make their fortune."

My heart sank in me. I thought of my gentle grandmother and the unspoken sorrows that had seemed to live behind her eyes. "She believed him?" I murmured.

"Of course. And she persuaded him to take more of her money and set out again immediately. Aubretia kept back only the tidy little house she lived in, some family jewels, and enough to support herself until he returned. When over a year passed with no word from him, she admitted to me she had been a fool. More, she admitted it to her friends and they aided her, not only with money but with introductions to suitable young men. But she swore her love would not be easily won again. She lived quietly and simply and alone."

"Until she met my grandfather?" I guessed.

The charm scowled at me. "Your grandfather was a hard-handed, flinty-hearted man. He married your grandmother solely to have someone to tend to his squalling son and keep his house in order after his first wife died of his ill treatment. She married him solely to have a place to rest her head at night. But he does not come into this story. Not yet."

Ignoring my shocked silence, the pendant spoke on. "One cold wet evening, who should come and knock at her door but her wayward suitor. I thought surely Aubretia would drive him away, but she welcomed him in and unquestioningly embraced him. Howarth wept, telling her that all had gone awry for him, and that he had been too ashamed to come home and face her, but finally his heart could stand to be parted from her no longer. He had come back, to beg her forgiveness." The little face gave a disdainful snort. "And she believed him."

"But you did not?"

"I believed he had spent all her money, that it was not his heart that had brought him back, but his greed. She told him it mattered nothing to her, that all would be well if he would but marry her. Side by side they could toil and still make a good, if simple life for themselves. She still had her house and some family jewelry and somehow they would manage."

I closed my eyes, pitying my grandmother that she could love so much and so blindly.

"I warned her. Her friends warned her, too, saying that if she listened to that rogue again, they would disown her. But Aubretia cared nothing for anyone but him. And he, speaking so nobly, said he would not let her family think her a fool. Howarth would not marry her while he was penniless. A fortune was still within his grasp. If only he had enough money, he could recoup his losses and go on."

"How could that be?" I demanded.

"An excellent question. One that your grandmother never asked, or at least not directly. He implied all sorts of things. That a bribe to a tariff official would free up a seized shipment, that if he were seen to be successful, others would lend him the money to complete some transaction. He spoke so skillfully and knowingly of how one must have money and spend money in order to make money."

A terrible sadness welled up in me. How often had I heard my mother lament our poor circumstances and wish for better days, only to have Grandmother say, "But it is hopeless, my dear. One must have money in order to make money."

"She went to her grave believing that was so."

The pendant was silent for a moment. Then she gave a tiny sigh. "I feared as much. For of course you have guessed the rest of the story. Aubretia sold all she had and gave him the money to redeem his fortune. When she dared to ask to go with him, he said that her passage south would cost too much, and the hardships would be too much for her to endure. That ring you wear once held an emerald, flawless and deep green. Even that he took. Howarth pried the stone out of the setting himself, saying he would sell the stone in Jamaillia only if he had to, but that he hoped to bring it back and restore it to her hand. He promised her that, no matter how he fared, he would come back within a year. She watched him sail from the Bingtown docks. Then she went to her oldest friend and confessed her situation. She threw herself on her mercy. Well, they had been friends since girlhood. Despite her threats, she took your grandmother in, and gave her a bed to sleep in and a place at the table. Aubretia was, after all, still a Lantis and a Trader. It was expected that she would find a way to make her way in the world, and eventually make a suitable match. There is a saying in Bingtown. 'Money does not make a Trader, it is the Trader that makes the money.' Her friends hoped she had learned her lesson.

"Yet it was hard for them to be patient with her, for she did little except moon after her absent lover. A year went by and then another. All of us told her both man and fortune were gone, and she should make a fresh start for herself. Aubretia insisted she would wait, that Howarth would come back for her." The carved face pursed her lips in ancient disappointment. "She waited. And that was all she did."

"Did Howarth ever come back?" I asked in a whisper.

The pendant's small face twisted in disgust. "Oh, yes. He returned. Some three years later, he came back to Bingtown, but it was months before your grandmother knew of it. She recognized him one day as he strolled through the market with his fine foreign wife at his side. A servant walked behind them, carrying a parasol to shade them. A nurse carried their little son. And his pale, plump Jamaillian wife wore the Lantis emerald at her throat."

"What did she do?" I whispered.

The pendant's small voice grew heavy with an old weariness. I sensed it was a memory often pondered but still painfully fresh. "She stood and stared. She could not believe her eyes. And then a cry of purest disbelief broke out of her. At the sound, he turned. Howarth recognized her, and yet he turned aside from her. She shrieked his name, demanding to know why he had abandoned her. In the streets of Bingtown, before Traders and common merchants, she wailed like a madwoman and tore out her hair. She fell to her knees and begged him to come back to her, crying that she could not live without him. But Howarth only took his wife's arm and hurried her way, whispering something to her about 'that poor mad woman.' " The pendant fell silent.

"Then what happened?" I demanded. My heart was beating strangely fast. "Did she go to him and confront him and his wife, denounce how he had taken her fortune, demand the return of her emerald?"

In a trembling whisper, the pendant confided, "No."

"Why?" Pain hushed my voice. I recalled my grandmother's resigned eyes and feared I already knew the answer.

"I do not know. I will never understand it. Her friends urged her to confront him, to bring a complaint against them. When she spoke with them, she was strong. But whenever she was alone and set pen to paper, she lost her resolve. Weeping, she would confess to me that she loved him still. She would spin tales that he had been drugged or was bewitched by the woman. Her hands would shake and she would wonder aloud what she herself lacked, what was wrong with her that the Jamaillian woman could steal Howarth from her. Never, ever did she see him for the scoundrel and the cheat that he was. I could not make her see that the man she loved had never existed, that she persisted in loving an idealized image of Howarth, that the real man was worthy only of her contempt. She would sit down, pen in hand, to denounce him. But always, her accusing letters somehow changed into pleas to him to come back to her. The worst was the night that she went by darkness to his door. She sought entry there, like a beggar, pleading with a servant to let her in so she might speak privately with the master of the house. The servant turned her aside with disdain, and she, Aubretia Lantis of the Bingtown Traders, crept away weeping and shamed. I think that night broke her. The next evening she packed the few possessions that remained her own, and we left Bingtown, walking away in the dimness while her friends were at dinner. She did not even bid them good-bye. She felt she had lost all standing with them and could never be seen as anything but a fool."

I felt ill, dizzied with the dirty little story. It twisted my memories of the gentle old woman I had tended for the last two years. I had believed her contained and stoic. I had deemed it strength, that she had endured my grandfather's harsh ways and tolerated the disrespect of her stepson. Now it seemed something else. The implacable little voice went on.

"She left Bingtown. Just walked away. She said she did not care what became of her, just so long as she could escape everyone telling her she should confront Howarth. She came to the countryside and floundered through work as an inn-maid until she married a man she did not love, to tend his son and bear him a daughter. Shortly after your mother was born, she set me aside, for I was the final reminder of the life she had abandoned." The tiny face pressed her lips together in a flat line. "I begged her to listen to me, even as she wrapped me in linen. I could not stand to see her raise her daughter in submission to her brutish father and that loutish boy of his. She should have her birthright, I said. I told her it was not too late to go back and reclaim her inheritance. But she muffled my voice and shut me away."

I thought of all the years the pendant had waited in the box. "Why did you tell me this?" I asked the pendant in a low voice.

For the first time, a question seemed to give her pause. She lifted her brows as if amazed I did not know. "Because she lives on in me, as do all the women of your line who have worn me. And I would see things set right. I would see you regain what is rightfully yours."

Rightfully mine. The concept seemed almost foreign. It frightened me. "But how? I have no proof, I do not know him, if Howarth still lives and—"

"Hush. I will guide you. You have the empty ring on your hand and me at your throat. You need no more than this."

My head so whirled with stories, I do not know how I slept that night. But I woke, still clutching the wizardwood pendant in my hand. Stiff in every joint, I rose, and donned the silver necklace and made my way to Bingtown.

In the next few weeks, the pendant became my guide. My ears swiftly became attuned to its soft whisper. The advice it gave me was difficult to follow, and yet when I listened to it, I found that my life progressed. In Bingtown, I sought and found a position caring for an elderly Trader woman. The food at Trader Redof's table was better than any I had ever eaten before, and the cast-off garments of her granddaughters were the finest clothing I had ever worn. My years of caring for my grandmother served me in good stead. I became a willing ear for any gossip Trader Redof wished to share, and despite all the difficulties of escorting such an old woman in Bingtown, I saw to it that she visited her friends often.

Tending to her, I soon came to know well the bustling trade city. Supporting her elbow and carrying her foot cushion, I moved invisibly among Bingtown society. I saw the power of the Bingtown Traders, power based not solely on wealth, but on heritage. I marveled at all my grandmother had abandoned, all that might have been my mother's life. From marveling at it, I grew to hunger for it. I changed my country manners to mimic Trader Redof's and flattened the twang of my speech. Schooled by my pendant in the evening, I changed how I carried myself in public and how I dressed my hair. I took on the mannerisms of a Bingtown woman, where women who were Traders for their families held as much power as their male counterparts. Seeing all that my grandmother had surrendered made my hatred of Howarth grow. I longed to seek him out and confront him. Yet month after month passed, and still the pendant bid me bide my time in patience.

My yearnings for vengeance surprised me. My grandmother and my mother had both schooled me in self-effacing resignation. I had thought it the lot of all women. Only in Bingtown did I come to see that a woman might live alone and manage her own life. I looked back on how Tetlia had robbed me of my grandmother's necklaces and could not recall why I had not challenged her. I recalled the liberties Hetta's husband had attempted on me and wondered why I had not vigorously resisted him. My old self in the countryside faded to a young woman whose docility was as incomprehensible to me as my grandmother's fatalistic surrender of her life.

I listened to my pendant. I never spoke Howarth's name aloud or asked after him and his family. I was a devoted servant, well nigh invisible. Twice, other families tried to hire me away but I kept my place. And finally, one day as I hovered near my mistress's chair at a tea, I heard his name mentioned, in connection with some other tattle about a Jamaillian family that had moved to Bingtown and was putting on airs. "A page from Howarth's book," someone said with a sniff, and I knew then that he still lived and that my grandmother's scandal was still recalled by these old women. I listened as they chewed through that old tale, and I gained tidings not only that Howarth still lived but that knowing Traders in Bingtown still regarded him with disdain.

That night, in my small chamber off my mistress's room, I consulted with my pendant. "Are we ready now to take revenge? To confront Howarth and demand that he return all he stole from my grandmother?"

The small lips pursed as if tasting wine that had gone to vinegar. She gave a tiny sigh. "I suppose it is time you saw the man. In some ways, that could be the culmination of your education." The little eyes narrowed and glittered speculatively. "When we go, you will take the empty ring. Let me pick the day, however. And on that day, you must do and say exactly what I tell you to. In this, you must trust me, or all will be for naught."

Twice every forty days, my mistress granted me a half day to myself. My pendant chose a day for me. It was one my mistress was loath to grant me, for it was a day of celebration in Bingtown, but I persuaded her to allow it, promising her that I would return early to help her with her evening preparations. It was the anniversary of the Traders arriving at Bingtown Bay. In the evening, there would be parties and dinners hosted by the wealthier Traders. But earlier in the day, the whole city would celebrate. There would be speeches and dancing in the center of the Great Market, food and drink would flow free to all, and the streets would be thronged with folk of all persuasions. Although the evening festivities were reserved for Traders and their families only, all the folk of Bingtown would join in the municipal celebration. From all the gossip I had heard, I knew it was a day when more recent arrivals to Bingtown courted the Old Trader families. Those who did not share Trader blood would seek to make more secure their social alliances with the powerful Traders. Howarth and his family would certainly be there.

That morning, I brought my mistress her breakfast tray. I laid out her clothing and left her dressing maid to attend her. In my tiny chamber, I bathed and dressed as carefully as if it were my wedding day. At my pendant's bidding, the hoarded coins I had earned had gone for enameled pins and a choker of lace. I swept my hair high and secured it. When I slipped into my mistress's room to steal a glance in her mirror, I stared at my reflection. My mistress, setting down her teacup, opened her eyes wider at sight of me. "You remind me of someone," she said sleepily. She sat up in her bed, regarding me more closely. As if I were her daughter, she commanded me to turn before her, and then to turn my face to the light. "Paint your lips with my carmine," she instructed me suddenly. "And touch your eyes with black." When I had done so, she inspected me critically. "You'll do," she observed. "There's Bingtown in your bloodline, my little country wren," she added with satisfaction. "So I've been telling those old biddies I call my friends. Off you go, to whomever you've chosen to captivate. He won't stand a chance before those eyes."

Her words heartened me as much as the approving murmur from my pendant. I returned to my room, to don my final layer of courage. The saffron wool of my grandmother's Trader robe was soft against my skin. It fit as if made for me. My determination swelled as I set out through the morning streets of the city I had made mine. The bustle of commerce no longer daunted me, nor did I look aside from the approving glance a Trader's son sent my way. Like me, he wore his Trader robe today. The garment proclaimed me his equal, and by his glance, I could tell me accepted me as that. I held my head higher. I made my way confidently into the heart of the city.

Occasionally, an older Trader would regard me with a puzzled stare. I knew it had been years since anyone had worn the saffron Trader robes of the Lantis family. I smiled at their puzzlement and strode on. The festive crowds grew denser, yet it seemed they parted for me. The music drew me, as did the savory aromas that floated on the morning air.

I reached the great circle of the Market. Today, the center had been cleared. Music was playing, and sailors and shopgirls were already dancing in the morning sun. On the edges of the circle, pavilions had been raised, and people of social note welcomed their friends and business associates. The grandest pavilions belonged to Bingtown Trader families and bore their colors, but the tents of the wealthy merchants of lesser bloodlines competed to draw the eye. The sides of the pavilions had been roped open to reveal carpets and expensive furniture. Trader families welcomed one another with tables of dainty foods in these temporary dwellings, competing in opulence and comfort. No expense had been spared for this single day of celebration. I walked a slow circuit of these, listening to the murmur of my pendant as it peeked through the lacy choker that concealed it.

"Those are the Hardesty colors; well, they seem to have prospered in the last generation. And that tasseled one would be the Beckerts; they were always given to show. Wait. Stop here."

I halted, and I swear I felt a vibration of tension from the pendant. The pavilion before us was pitched almost in line with those of the Bingtown Traders' tents, as if to claim near equal status. Whereas the Trader pavilions bore the simple colors of each of the old Bingtown families, the newcomers' tents were striped or parti-colored. The pavilion before me was white and green. The family was arrayed within as if for a portrait; parents and grown children sat about a table heavy with a rich morning repast. Two young men in the robes of Bingtown Traders were guests there. From a separate, higher table, on tall chairs almost like thrones, an elderly couple looked down benevolently on their family. The matriarch was a small plump woman. Her thinning white hair was carefully coifed, and rings adorned her pale little hands. The emerald at her throat seemed to burn with a green fire. Beside her sat a handsome old man, as elegantly dressed and groomed. As I looked at him, I felt the pendant share my glance. From it, I felt a sudden wave of hatred greater than any I had ever known. Mingled with it was fury, and outrage that he and the wife he had bought with Aubretia's money had both outlived her in luxury and grace. Hardship and privation, I now saw, had cut short my grandmother's life. Not just wealth and respect, but life itself he had stolen from her.

"But for your betrayal, Howarth, Aubretia Lantis would still be alive!"

The words rang out from my throat. I scarce recognized my own voice. All about me, the festivities faltered. Conversation in the adjoining pavilions ceased. All eyes were turned toward the scene I had abruptly created. My heart near stopped in my chest, but I found myself going on without it, stepping forward without conscious volition, shouting words whose source was not myself. "I bring you word of her death. Poverty and privation shortened her life, but it was your betrayal of her heart that killed her, Howarth. Aubretia Lantis was my grandmother. I give to you now the last bit of wealth that you were unable to strip from her: this ring, as empty as your promise. Keep it, along with all else you swindled from her." I pulled the silver circle from my hand and threw the empty setting with a skill not my own. It sparkled as it flew through the air, and it landed squarely in Howarth's empty glass, setting it ringing in the silence that followed my words. The old man's eyes stood out from his face, and a vein pulsed wildly on his brow. I suspected he felt he saw a ghost, come back to waken old scandal just when his reputation most needed to be sound. I looked aside from him to his wife. She was scarlet with humiliation. "Study it well, Howarth's wife," I bade her disdainfully. "Would not the Lantis emerald you wear about your neck fit well in its setting? Believe what you have denied to yourself all these years; a dead woman's wealth bought you. Know that you married a liar and an upstart, know that your whole family is founded on his betrayal of a Bingtown Trader." I rounded disdainfully on the two young Trader men who sat at his table. The young women beside them, obviously Howarth's granddaughters, stared at me in white-faced horror. "Consider well what you join your names to, Traders' sons," I told them. "It is the Lantis wealth you are marrying, stripped of the Lantis name."

Howarth had found his tongue. The dapper old man now looked drawn and pale. He pointed a shaking finger at me but spoke to his wife in the pitched voice of the near deaf. "She can prove nothing! Nothing! The money Aubretia gave me, she gave me for love of me. She cannot legally force me to return it."

His wife's jaw dropped. I thought she would faint from mortification. I let the silence gather, then floated my words upon it. "And with those words, you admit a guilt and a shame greater than anything I could wish to prove. Keep the wealth, Howarth. Choke on it. You have dirtied it, and I have no need of anything you have touched."

I turned on my heel then and walked away. A stunned silence hung behind me like a curtain, one that was suddenly rent by the wind of a thousand tongues flapping. Like a stirred beehive, all of the Great Market circle hummed and buzzed. The scandal that Howarth thought he had left behind him would now mark his declining years.

"Nor will his granddaughters wed Traders' sons. His wife would do best to sweep them back to Jamaillia and marry them off where she can, for after this, they will never mount into Bingtown society." My pendant whispered to me in savage joy. "You have done it, my dear. You have done us all proud with your success."

I made no reply, but cut my way through the crowds, ignoring the comments and stares that followed me. My steady walk slowly cooled the angry flush from my cheeks and calmed the thundering of my heart. I had found my way down to the Bingtown docks where the cool wind off the water swept the heat from my face. I pondered the words I had said and what I had done. At the time it had seemed so perfectly fulfilling. Now I wondered at it.

"But what did I accomplish?" I lifted the pendant from my neck and looked at the tiny face. "I thought I was doing all this to regain my inheritance. I thought I would force him to give up the wealth he had stolen from my grandmother. Instead, I walked away with nothing. Not even an empty ring remains to me. Only you."

"Only me," the pendant agreed. "And your name. Taken back out of the dust and raised to pride once more. It is what your grandmother abandoned, and what I wished you to reclaim. Not money or jewels, but the rightful self-worth of a Lantis. You are a Bingtown Trader now, by resolution as well as by right. Perhaps you will work as a servant by day, but what you earn will be your own. And when the Bingtown Council meets, you will wield your rightful vote." The little face smiled up at me. The warmth in the small voice was a family's love. "And that, girl, is your inheritance."

Cat's Meat

How is it, I sometimes wonder, that a dog person like myself writes so many stories that feature cats?

I really don't have an answer to that. While dogs have dominated my life as companions, I've had a fair number of cat companions as well. The first that was mine, really all mine, was Loki, a long-haired black tom when I was a young teenager. He was fearless and as much dog as cat it sometimes seemed. Sometimes I'd find him outside in the dead of a Fairbanks winter, curled up snug between a couple of huskies.

When I was newly married in Kodiak, we enjoyed the company of my husband's childhood cat, Chlorophyll. As an unspayed female, she contributed quite a bit to the gene pool of cats on Kodiak Island and was fondly known as "Cat Factory" by the neighbors.

Today, I am owned by Pi, a black-and-white tuxedo cat who is currently nineteen years old. She has been the most faithful of writing cats, sitting on my lap for long hours while I typed over and around her. Sam, a junior cat at only eighteen years old, is the table-walking, snack-stealing bane of my husband's existence. And despite my resolution not to acquire any more cats, in December of 2009 both Princess and Fatty were added to our household. Grown littermates, they've proven remarkably adaptable to our dogs, kids, and senior cats.

Fatty is orange. With blue eyes. And full of tales to tell.

"I made a mistake and I'm still paying for it." Rosemary tried to sound stronger than she felt. Less forlorn and more matter-of-fact.

"You've already paid enough for that mistake," Hilia responded stoutly. Her best friend since childhood, Hilia always took her part. She might be tactless sometimes, but she was loyal. Loyalty had come to mean a great deal to her.

Rosemary picked up little Gillam and bounced him gently. The toddler had been clutching at her knees and wailing since she set him down. The moment she picked him up, he stopped.

"You're spoiling him," Hilia pointed out.

"No, I'm just holding him," Rosemary replied. "Besides, I don't think he's the mistake. If anything, he's the only good thing I got out of my mistake."

"Oh, I don't mean *him*!" Hilia responded instantly. Her own baby, only a month old, was at her breast, eyes shut, all but asleep as she nursed. Gillam arranged himself in Rosemary's lap and then leaned over to look down curiously at the baby. He reached a hand toward her.

"Let her sleep, Gillam. Don't poke her."

"You paid enough for your mistake," Hilia went on, as if there'd been no interruption. "You've suffered for close to three years. It's not fair he should come back and try to start it all up again."

"It's his house," Rosemary pointed out. "Left him by his grandfather. His bit of land. And Gillam is his son, as he bragged yesterday at the tavern. He has rights to all of them."

"This is *not* his house! Don't you dare say that! Don't you dare defend that wretch! His grandfather said it was for Gillam when he deeded it over. Not Pell. His own grandfather knew he couldn't trust Pell to do the right thing by you and his child! And you are Gillam's mother, so you have just as much right to be here as Pell does. More, because you're the one who did all the work on it. What was this place when he left you here, with your belly out to there while he went traipsing off with that Morrany girl? A shack! A leaky-roofed shack, with the chimney half fallen down, and the yard full of thistles and milkweed. Now look at it!" Hilia's angry words rattled like hail on frozen ground as she gestured around the tiny but tidy room. It was a simple cottage, with a flagged floor and stone walls and a single door and one window. On the sill of that window, an orange cat slept, slack as melted honey in the spring sun.

"Look at those curtains and the coverlet on the bed! Look at that hearth, neat as a pin. Look up! That roof's tight! Well, it needs a new thatch, but where you patched it, it held! Look out the window! Rows of vegetables sprouting in the garden, half a dozen chickens scratching, and a cow with a calf in her belly! Who did that, who did all that? You, that's who! Not that lazy, good-for-nothing Pell! That stupid little slut winked an eye and wriggled her rump at him, and off he went, to live off her and her parents. And now that she's done with him, now that her father sees what a bent coin he is and has turned him out, what makes him think he can come back here and just take over everything you've built? What right does he have to it?"

"As much right as I do, Hilia. Legally, we are both Gillam's parents. We both have the right to manage his inheritance for him until he's a man. As Gillam's mother, I can claim that right, but I can't deny it to Pell, too. And that is how it is." She spoke sadly, but a smile had come to her face to hear her friend defend her so stoutly.

"Legally." Hilia all but spat the word. "I'm talking about what is right and real, not what is legal! Has that wretch actually dared to come here?"

Rosemary bit down on her rising fear and hoped none of it showed on her face. "No. Not yet. But I heard yesterday that he'd come back to town and was talking in the tavern, saying it was time he went home and took up his duties as a father and landowner. I think he's working up the courage to confront me. I heard he was staying up at his father's house. I don't think his mother has any more use for Pell than I do. Her life is hard enough, with the way Pell's father knocks her around, without having another man to wait on. So I don't know how long she'll tolerate him under her roof. They'll both lean on him to leave, and I suspect his father will push him in this direction. He's always resented me living here. He's always said that the cottage and land should have come to him first, not gone directly to Pell."

"Didn't his grandfather offer it to Pell when he got you pregnant?"

From anyone else, such a blunt reminder might have stung. But this was Hilia, her oldest, truest friend. Rosemary sighed. "Yes. He actually brought us both out here, with a minstrel to witness the vows. He told Pell it was time he stood up and acted like a man and took care of the child that he'd caused and the woman he'd ruined." It was still hard to say the phrase aloud. She sighed and looked at the wall. "Pell refused then. He said we were both too young, that one mistake shouldn't cause another. And a month or two later, he proved he was right on that. He left me. But at least I'm not married to him. He gave me that much freedom."

"Freedom!" scoffed Hilia. "No woman with a babe on her hip is free of anything. What did his grandfather say when Pell said no?"

Rosemary forced her mind back to her tale. "Soader was a good man. He tried to help Pell do what he thought was right.

When Pell said he wouldn't wed me, Soader said he wouldn't waste the minstrel's fee. He willed the cottage and land to my unborn child, boy or girl, right then. It made Pell angry but he dared say nothing. He was already out of favor with the rest of his family. Our baby owning a cottage at least gave us a place to live. It made Pell's father furious, I heard later. He felt that the cottage should have gone to Soader's daughter, his wife, so that he could have the good of the land. Not that there was much good to it when we got it.

"But Soader meant well. He said that a couple that works together takes the true measure of each other." Rosemary sighed again. "Well, I guess that when I was here alone, I got Pell's true measure. I was sad when Soader died last year. He was Pell's mother's father, and the only one of Pell's family who came to see Gillam at all after Pell left. Right up until he took the lung cough, he came every month."

"He gave you money, then?"

Rosemary shook her head. "No. But he brought food sometimes, and other things. He gave me a rhubarb start, and walking onion bulbs that spread. Things I could use to better my life, if I were willing to work with them. He was a good man."

"Good man or not, letting Pell refuse to marry you was not the 'right' thing for him to do."

"Actually, it was. Hearing him refuse to speak the marriage oath before a minstrel was important. Up until then, I was sure he would marry me, right after the baby was born. Not that he'd ever asked me or I'd ever asked him. I guess I was afraid to ask. Soader wasn't. I didn't want to hear what he made Pell say, but it was a good thing for me to know sooner rather than later."

Rosemary sipped at her cooling tea. It loosened her throat that had closed tight as she recalled that humiliation. Kendra the minstrel had looked aside from her shame, but Soader had met her gaze steadily and quietly observed, "So that is how it will be."

"Of course, later, when we were alone, Pell had all sorts of reasons why I shouldn't be angry at him." Rosemary forced the words out, trying to keep her tone light. "And I believed them. I believed that he was 'married to me in his heart' and that there would 'never be another woman.' I was so foolish."

For the past three years, she'd been pushing herself to take responsibility for the mess she'd made of her life. Sometimes it helped. Sometimes she looked around and thought, *If I can make that big a mistake, I can make just as big of a correction.* And she'd thought she'd done so. She'd worked hard. The repairs to the cottage had been done by her own hand or paid for by barter. She'd turned the old garden over, one shovelful of earth at a time. She'd barrowed in manure dropped on the roadside by passing horses and worked it into the soil herself. She'd traded labor for seed and starts, and she and Gillam lived cheap and stingy to save up the coins for a spindly, worm-plagued yearling cow. That cow, healthy now, was soon to drop her first calf. The chickens had been eggs, kept warm near the hearth and turned daily, a dozen eggs to hatch a mere two pullets and a cockerel. But they had multiplied to a decent flock now. Her daily gathering kept a stack of wood by the side of the house and a neat pile of split and ready kindling beside it. She could do things, make things, and cause change to happen.

She looked away from the window to find Hilia staring at her, eyes full of tears and sympathy. "You deserved better, Rosemary."

But, "I can't run away from what I did, Hilia. I made a bad choice when I let that man into my bed. My mother warned me about him. I didn't listen. Let's admit the truth. There were two of us in that bed. And I'm going to have to deal with him the rest of my life. Pell will never be my husband, but he will always be Gillam's father."

"You were scarcely more than a girl and your father had just died. Pell took advantage of you."

Rosemary shook her head at her friend. "Don't. It took me six months to come out of wallowing in self-pity. I won't go back to that."

Hilia sighed. "Well. I won't argue that you're a lot more pleasant to be around now that you're not constantly weeping. You're tougher than you think, girl. When that man shows up here, I think you ought to bar the door and pick up the poker. Don't you let him under this roof!"

Rosemary looked down at Gillam in her lap. His lids were heavy; the fuss had only been because he was tired. "The boy has a right to know his father," she said. She wondered if that were true.

Hilia snorted. "The boy has the right to grow up in a peaceful home. And if Pell is here, you won't have that." She stood with a sigh, closing her blouse and shifting her dozing baby to her shoulder. "I have to go home. There's butter to churn and the house to tidy. Two of our cows are with calf and will drop any day now. I need to stay home for the next week or so. But you listen to me. If Pell is drunk or even unpleasant when he gets here, you just take Gillam and walk away. You know the way to my house."

Rosemary managed a smile. "Weren't you telling me to stand my ground just a few minutes ago?"

Hilia pushed a straggling black curl back from her face. "I suppose I was. In truth, Rosie, I don't know what to advise you to do, so maybe I'd better shut my mouth. Except to say that I'm always your friend. There isn't anything I wouldn't do for you."

"I know that," Rosemary assured her.

Hilia stood up to leave. She paused by the window and stroked the sleeping cat. He lifted his head and regarded her with cobalt eyes. "Now is not the time to be lazy, Marmalade. I'm counting on you to look after Rosemary and Gillam," she cautioned the cat aloud.

The cat sat up slowly and yawned, curling a pink tongue at her. She scratched him under the chin and he closed his eyes in pleasure. "I mean it, now! You'd have gone right into the river in a sack if I hadn't saved you! You owe me, cat. I saved your life." He returned Hilia's gaze with narrowed eyes.

Cats do not enjoy being reminded of debts. Cats do not incur debts. You did what you wanted to do. My being alive as a result of it is something you caused, not something I owe you.

Rosemary stood up from her chair. She deposited her sleeping boy on the bed and came to join her friend by the window. She put out a hand toward Marmalade, and the tom butted his head against it. "Don't say mean things to Marmalade, Hilia. He is the best thing that anyone ever gave me. In those days before Gillam was born, when I felt I was all alone, little Marmy was always with me." She moved her fingers to tickle the white triangle at his throat. A grudging purr ground its way out of the big tom.

Hilia narrowed her eyes and spoke to him. "Well, even if you don't owe me, cat, you owe Rosemary. You'd better take care of her."

The orange tom closed his eyes and curled his front paws toward his chest. *I have no idea what you think I can do against a human male.*

Hilia cocked her head at him. *You're a cat. You'll think of something. Or you'll help Rosemary think of something.*

She doesn't have the Wit to listen to me. He tucked his head to his chest and apparently sank into sleep.

I'm not stupid, cat. No one needs the Wit magic to hear a cat. Cats talk to whomever they please.

Obviously true. But I didn't say she couldn't hear me. I said she doesn't listen to what I tell her.

Hilia reached over to tug at one of his orange ears, demanding his attention. *Then you'd better make her. Pell is not kind to beasts of any kind. If you're used to being fed and sleeping inside, you'll find a way to help her. Or your life will be just as miserable as hers will be.* "Rotten cat," she added aloud. "I should have let Pell's father drown you."

"Pell's father was the man with the sack of kittens? You never told me that!" Rosemary was horrified.

"Not a pretty thing to tell at any time, and right then you didn't need any cause to add any more people to your hate list." Hilia leaned over to kiss Rosemary on the cheek. "You take care of yourself and Gillam, now. And at the first sign of any trouble, you come running to my house."

"Oh, I don't think there will be any trouble I need to run from."

"Um. Well, I'm not sure I agree with you about that. But just remember that my door is open."

"I will."

ROSEMARY WATCHED HER friend climb the little hill in front of her cottage and disappear over the rim of it. There was a cliff-top path that followed the line of the bay, but Hilia would probably take the steeper path down to the beach itself. When the tide was out and the rocky beach was bare, the quickest route back to the village was to cut across the exposed tide flat. Idly, Rosemary wished they lived closer to each other. The dell that sheltered her home from the worst of the winter storms off the water also shaded it for much of the day. The holding for Gillam's cottage was small, a crescent strip of sloping but arable land between the sea cliffs and the salt marsh that reached around the back of it. An odd bit of land, too small to be a real farm, but enough, perhaps, for a woman and a child. "It could have been enough for all three of us, Pell. If you'd wanted us."

The shadows of evening were already reaching toward her

home. She gave a small shiver and glanced over at her sleeping child. "Well. I don't think your father will be coming to see you tonight. And I have chores to do." She took up her shawl before she left the house. The day had been warm, a promise of summer, but now the cool winds were sweeping in from the coast. She brought in her cow and shut her up in her rough byre. It was a rude structure, scarcely more than four poles holding up a slanted thatched roof. Perhaps this summer she'd have the time and resources to close in the sides of it. Come winter, the cow would welcome at least a break from the wet winds.

The chickens were aware of the westering sun and were already coming home to roost. She counted her precious flock and found all nine were there. Soon, as the days lengthened, they'd resume laying. Picky the rooster had been energetic about mating with his harem. She looked forward to fresh eggs again, and to the possibility of letting one hen set a batch for chicks. She'd be willing to forgo eggs for a time if it meant she could put roast chicken on the table later. She wished she had a coop for the chickens. Right now, they roosted on the wall of the cow's byre. A coop would keep them safer from foxes and hawks and owls.

There was always more to do, always something more to build. That was good, really. What would her life have been without something more to do each day?

As was her ritual, her next stop was the garden. The rhubarb had thrust up tightly curled leaves, and the early peas had sprouted. Most of the other furrows were bare brown earth. Or were they? She crouched down low and then smiled. Tiny seedlings were breaking from the earth in two other rows. Cabbages. She didn't much like cabbage, but it grew well for her, and the tight-leaved heads kept well in the small root cellar she had dug. She sighed and hoped that next winter would not be another endless round of cabbage and potato soups. Well, if it was, perhaps a few of them would have a little bit of chicken in them.

She was coming to her feet when she heard his voice behind her. Startled, she stumbled away from him, trampling her own seedlings. "Damn!" she cried, and then spun to face him.

"All I said was hello." Pell smiled at her. The expression was uneasy on his face, as if it clung to his mouth despite his eyes. He was as tall as she remembered him, and as handsome. He'd grown a beard, and it was as curly as his dark hair. His shirt was blue with embroidery on the sleeves, and his shining knee boots were black. His belt was heavy black leather, and he wore an ivory-handled knife in a fine sheath at his hip. Dressed like a merchant's son, and as always, aware of just how good he looked. Handsome, handsome Pell, the dandy of the village. She stared at him, and his smile grew broader. He had once been hers. How amazed she had been at that, when he chose her. How grateful and how accommodating she had been, in her astonishment. She should have known she couldn't hold him. Not even with his baby in her belly. He had left her, just as her mother had warned her he would.

And now he had come back. She found herself gripping her old anger, telling herself that she felt no attraction to him at all. She reminded herself of all the nights of weeping over how he had left her, heavy with child, to chase after lovely Meddalee Morrany and her father's wealth. All those nights of anguish and longing for his presence in her bed, for a man to protect her and help her. She recalled all the doubts that had plagued her; she'd been too homely to hold him, too fat with her pregnancy, too undesirable. And now she looked at him, her long-strayed lover, and felt not one jot of desire for him. Beautiful Pell meant only sorrow to her. She would not be a fool for him again.

"Aren't you going to say anything to me?" he asked her. He tilted his head, his soft brown hair dancing in the evening wind and aimed his smile at her. Once that smile had been deadly to her willpower. Had it changed, or was it weakened by the brown beard that masked it? Had she changed that much?

"Can't think of anything to say." She stooped and carefully plucked at a cabbage seedling to coax it upright again. She gently patted earth back around it. When she looked up, he was still smiling down on her. Fondly. She gritted her teeth. "What do you want?"

"I'm home," he said simply, as if that explained everything, excused everything. "I've come back to you, Rosemary." He sighed and softened the smile a bit. "I know what you're thinking, girl. But it was a boy who ran away and left you. It's a man who has come back to you, and a wiser man, now. I've been out in the world and seen how things are." His voice seemed to firm. "I know what I've got to do now to set my life right. I'm ready to do it, no matter how hard."

That was all he offered, she noticed. That he was wiser. That coming back to her and her son was hard. No apology for what he'd done to her, how he'd humiliated her before the whole village. No thought for what she'd been through, how she'd managed the birth of his child and the raising of the boy since then. No questions on how she had survived while he was "out in the world." Nothing like that. Only that he was wiser for the experience.

"I think I'm wiser, too," she said. She dusted her hands on her skirts as she rose. Dirt clung to the rough skin of her palm and had packed under her nails. Why did she notice that now? Was it only because he was back? She circled wide of him and then was annoyed that she had to wait for him to leave the garden patch before she could shut the gate behind him. If she didn't gate it shut, the chickens would be up at dawn to scratch and peck every seed and seedling from the earth. Even with the fence, she had to keep an eye on them. Often it was only Marmalade sleeping on the warm dry earth of the garden that kept the birds out.

"We were too young, Rosemary. We made a lot of mistakes, and those mistakes trapped me. I got scared. I should have been stronger. I wasn't. But I don't think they should shape the rest of my life. I'm going to face up to my tasks and make things right. I'm ready to build the life I was meant to live." He looked so earnest. He never looked away from her. Once she would have fallen into that dark gaze. Once she had believed she could read his heart in that gaze. She shook her head and looked away from it.

"I've built my life, Pell. And there's no room in it for you. Gillam fills it up completely."

He stiffened at that. "Gillam?" He sounded puzzled.

It took her a moment to realize the cause. "Your son," she replied crisply. "I named him Gillam."

"Gillam? But I said we'd name him Will, if the baby was a boy. After my friend, Will the tailor. Remember?"

"I remember." She dragged the stubborn gate into place. "I changed my mind when he was born. I changed my mind about a lot of things in those days." She looped the tie around the gate. "Gillam is a name from my family line. My mother's father was named Gillam. I decided I'd give Gillam my family's heritage."

She stood still, staring at him. The day was growing cooler. She gathered her shawl around her. She wanted to go back to the cottage, to poke up the banked embers and warm the soup and toast some bread for supper. Gillam would wake soon. He was a good little fellow, but she didn't like to leave him alone when he was awake. Yet as much as she wanted to do those things, she didn't move. If she went back to the cottage, she was certain he would follow her. And she didn't want to see him go inside, didn't want to see him look at her son. She didn't want his praise for all she'd done, or his disdain that it was, still, a little run-down cottage on the farthest outskirts of the village. He'd never liked the place, not since the first day his grandfather had given it to him. He'd never wanted to live in it, with its smoky chimney and leaky roof. Yet now she feared that he would want it, if he saw it tidy and cozy.

Worse, she feared he would want his son. And Gillam was all she had. He belonged to her, every bit of him. It was why she had named him to anchor him to her lineage, not Pell's. There would be no sharing of Gillam. Pell had missed his chance for that.

"Let's go inside and talk," he said quietly. "You have to listen to what I have to say to you."

"I have nothing to say to you," she replied.

"Well, perhaps I have things to say to you. And it's getting cold. I'm going inside. Follow me."

And he turned and walked away from her, toward the cottage, knowing that she must follow him. It galled her. It reminded her too sharply of the last time she'd had to obey him.

It had been winter, with the rain coming down in sheets as it always did along the Buck coast. They'd gone to town, to spend most of the few coins they had on a sack of potatoes and three pieces of salt cod. She'd been carrying the cod, wrapped in a piece of greased paper, and he'd had the sack of potatoes on his shoulder. A sudden rain squall had caught them just at the edge of town. Her head had been bent to the wind, and the rain had been running down into her eyes. When he spoke sharply to her, she knew that he must have said her name before. "Rosemary! Take the potatoes, I said!"

She turned back to him, wondering why he wanted her to carry them. They were not a large load, but her belly was big with the baby, and the mud sucking at her old shoes made her so tired she already wanted to cry. "Why?" she asked, blinking rain away as he put the mesh bag into her arms.

"Can't you see I've got to help her? She's trapped, poor thing!"

She had not had a hand free to wipe her eyes. She blinked her lashes quickly and saw that a child in a yellow dress was standing under a tree at the side of the road. Her arms were wrapped around her, her shoulders hunched to the rain. Her flimsy cloak of lace was no protection against the sudden storm.

Rosemary had blinked again as Pell broke into a run toward the girl. No, it wasn't a child. It was a young woman, as slender as a child, with rippling waves of black hair blowing in the wind with the edges of her silly little cloak. Her garments made her look younger than she probably was. And more foolish. Who would go out dressed so lightly on a day at the end of autumn? Rosemary shook rain from her eyelashes and recognized her. Meddalee Morrany. The sea trader's daughter. She lived across the bay, but sometimes came to visit her cousins. Always well dressed was she; even as a child, she had flaunted embroidery on her skirts and ribbons in her hair. Well, she wasn't a child anymore, but her father's wealth still wrapped her.

"She just needs to stay there until the squall passes," she called after him. She hefted the sack in her arms. Damp had penetrated her shoes, and her toes were icy.

He'd already greeted the shivering girl. They were speaking, the girl smiling, but the rising wind swept their words away from her. He turned to call to her, "I'm going to help her get to town. You take the potatoes home. I'll be along in a bit."

She'd stood in the rain in shocked disbelief as he opened his black cloak as if it were a raven's wing, smiling and gesturing to Meddalee to take shelter under it. And the girl laughed and did.

"What about her?" Meddalee Morrany's question had blown to her on the wind. She was smiling as she pointed at Rosemary.

"Oh, she'll be fine. She can deal with the rain. I'll see you later, Rosie!"

She'd had no choice then. She'd been cold and wet, weighted with the potatoes and fish and her unborn child and the hurt he'd loaded onto her. He hadn't offered to put his cloak around her when the storm had blown up. No. He'd saved that for a stranger. For a pretty girl in a pretty dress, with a slender waist and rings on her fingers. Not for the girl who was pregnant with his bastard. She'd watched them walk away from her and could not think what to do. Then the wind blew stronger, pushing her toward home, and she'd gone.

She'd staggered home, arrived soaked to the bone and made their supper and waited for him. And waited. Waited for all that night, and the next day and night, and through the weeks and then months that followed. She'd wept and hoped and waited past the birth of the boy, waited for him to come back to his senses and come home to his new family, waited for the girl's family to see how worthless he was and drive him off, waited even after his grandfather had come, shamefaced, to see his great-grandson.

By then, the gossip was known to all. Pell had followed Meddalee that day, right onto the boat that was to take her back across the bay to her father's big house in Dorytown. The gossips of the village had taken great pains to see that she knew all the details. Her father had taken a liking to Pell. Everyone always took a liking to Pell, with his handsome face, his wide smile, and his easy ways. He'd given Pell a job in one of his warehouses. For a short time, she tried to believe he had done it for both of them. She pretended that he'd gone off to make a fortune for them. Soon he'd come home, his pockets full of his wages, to make things right for them. Perhaps he'd carry her and Gillam off to a cozy little house in Dorytown. Perhaps he'd stride into the cottage one night, his arms laden with toys and warm clothing for his son. Then wouldn't the villagers have to swallow their mocking words! Then wouldn't they see that he had loved her all along.

But Pell never came. The days passed, she struggled on, and her boy grew, day by hard day. Her foolish dreams had turned to bitterness. She'd mourned and wept and cursed her fate. She'd hated him and longed for revenge. She'd blamed Pell, and then Meddalee, and then herself and Meddalee and finally Pell again. She had, as Hilia told her bluntly, been a bit mad. Impossible to reason with. And then, sometime in the last year or so, she'd stopped feeling anything about Pell, except to hope that he'd never come back and disturb the peace that she'd finally found.

"I'll see you later," he'd said all those years ago. She bit back the impulse to ask him if this was "later." She watched him as he walked toward her door. His hair was as glossy and well kept as ever, his boots were new, and the coat he wore must have been tailored to display his broad shoulders so well. Had Meddalee chosen it for him? She glanced down at her mended skirt, soiled where she had knelt to inspect her plants. Her shoes were worn and stuffed inside with dry grass, not stockings. She brushed her rough hands against her skirt again and felt grubby and angry. She'd been a pretty girl once, if a poor one. Now she was only a poor woman in worn clothing with a growing child.

That was another thing he'd taken from her. There would never be a suitor knocking at her door, never be a man courting her. There would never be a partner for her, only her son sharing her life.

He didn't even hesitate as he opened her door. Did he notice that she'd repaired the leather hinges, that it no longer scraped against the ground or gapped at the top and let the wind in? If he did, he made no comment. He paused only an instant on the threshold, and then stepped inside. She found herself hurrying after him. She didn't want him to wake Gillam, didn't want the boy's first sight of his father to be as a frightening stranger looming over him.

She found Pell gazing around the room and felt a hot pulse of satisfaction at how surprised he looked. It wasn't the cobwebby hovel that his grandfather had first given them, nor the shoddy cottage it had been during the few months they'd lived here together. Her gaze followed his and she found herself almost as surprised as he must have been. Not at the changes she'd made; she'd become accustomed to the blue curtains at the window, the moss and clay chinking in the walls and the neatly swept hearth and kindling box and Gillam's little three-legged stool beside it. No, what surprised her was to realize that when Pell had lived there, she had accepted the hovel as it had been, thinking that surely if it could be made better, he would know how and would do it. It was only after he had left her, only after she had roused herself from the torpor of despair and become angry that she had decided that whatever she could fix, she would. She'd decided then that whatever she did to the place didn't have to be perfect, only better than it had been. And it was.

"He's big!"

Pell's words brought her back to the present with a jolt. He was looking at Gillam in shock. Emotions struggled on his face—pride, guilt, and something else perhaps. Dismay?

"He's nearly three," she pointed out briskly. "He's not a baby anymore."

"Three," he breathed, as if the number were astonishing. He continued to stare.

"You were gone three years," she enumerated for him. "Children grow."

"He's a little boy. It didn't seem that long," he said, and then, as if he realized that perhaps that was a tactless thing to say, "I never meant for it to happen that way, Rosie. It was just, well, you were pregnant, and we were huddled in this place with next to nothing and my parents were furious with me. I felt so trapped.

I was a young man and there was no fun left in my life. The idea of having a wife and a baby both, and I hadn't intended to have either, not for a long time. I couldn't stand it."

"And she was pretty and her family was wealthy and for whatever reason, they let you move in on them like a tick on a hound. And then she threw you off and here you are, back here because you can't think of any other place to go."

She spoke flatly, in a low voice, but without anger. It surprised her. She didn't feel angry, just impatient for him to leave. Let him look around and see how humbly they lived and then be gone. She had to wake Gillam soon and give him some supper, or he'd not want to go to sleep until late. And she had planned to work on a quilt tonight, fine meticulous work after Gillam had gone to sleep. The last quilt she'd made carefully, she'd traded for a ham. This one, if she were fortunate, might get her a piglet. She wanted to sit by the fire tonight, hunched over her work, sewing carefully, and think about how she would build a pen for the pig and feed him garden waste and take him to the beach to scavenge. She wanted Pell to be gone. Once he'd been a future full of golden dreams and promises. Now he was a past that stung whenever she thought of him. She didn't want to look at him and wonder how it might have gone if he'd truly been the man she'd thought he was. She wanted to be alone and dreaming about her own plans, the plans that she could make real.

"All I wanted was a chance to do what I wanted to do, to do things I enjoyed doing. To make a try for the life I should have had before it was all ruined. Is that so much to ask?" He stopped talking abruptly, taking a sharp breath. Then he said, as if promising something to himself, "Things are going to be different." He clipped his words off as if she were the one who had hurt him. He added firmly, "And now, we're done talking about it."

His words struck her dumb. He spoke as if he had authority

over her. A wave of dread rose up in her, followed by a pitiful hope that sickened her. She suddenly knew that he intended to stay. Right now. From now on.

Why?

Gillam stirred on the bed and opened his eyes. For a moment, his big dark eyes, so like his father's, were full of dreams still. Then he blinked and focused his gaze on the stranger. "Mama?" he asked with some trepidation.

"It's all right, Gillam. I'm right here."

He crawled quickly across the bed to her, and she scooped him up in her arms. He hugged her tight around her neck, tucking his face into her shoulder.

"And I'm here, too, boy." Pell spoke with a heartiness that did not ring true to her. "Your papa. Come here and let me look at you."

In response, the boy tightened his grip on her neck. He didn't look up at Pell. The man's face darkened. "Give him time. He's never seen you before. He doesn't know you," she pointed out.

"I said we were done talking about that," he replied abruptly. He came toward her. "Let me see the boy."

She didn't think about it but backed away toward the door. "Give him some time to get used to your being here," she countered. It wasn't a direct refusal. Once she had adored Pell's assertiveness and how he made decisions for them. It had seemed manly and sheltering. Now she found herself remembering how quickly he'd move to anger when his will was thwarted. Hilia's advice to her suddenly came to mind. *Run. Run to Hilia's house.* She shook her head to the stray thought. Gillam was heavy. If she tried to run, she'd be out of breath before she got to the top of the hill. And she didn't want to give Pell any reason to run after her. She feared where that sort of confrontation might lead.

"Let me see him." He insisted as he advanced on her. His voice became contemptuous. "You've made him into a timid little mouse. When I was his age, I wasn't afraid to stand and face a man and offer my hand. What sort of sniveling whelp are you raising under my name? What sort of a mama's little titmouse is he?"

She recognized the mockery in his voice as he aimed his words at Gillam. If he hoped to rouse the boy to defy him, he failed. Gillam only clutched more tightly at her neck. She held her ground until Pell was almost an arm's length away and then, despite her resolve, backed up. "Let me calm him. You don't want his first memory of you to be that you frightened him."

"First memory, last memory, what does it matter? Let's see this boy that bears my name. Can he stand up to something that frightens him? Is there anything of me in him at all? Will. Look at me. Come to me. Right now."

She had not seen the cat underfoot. He must have been right behind her. She didn't feel her foot tread on him, but she must have, for suddenly, with a furious yowl and a spattering of hisses, the tomcat exploded from the floor. He leaped into the air between them and then clawed his way up Pell, literally running up his face and then leaping from his head into the low rafters. There he crouched, yowling and growling low as he lashed his abused tail back and forth.

Pell held his scratched face with both hands and cursed shrilly through his fingers Obtusely, Gillam had popped up his head at the cat explosion and now giggled wildly at the big man squeaking through his peekaboo fingers. Rosemary's breath caught and she choked back a fear-strangled giggle of her own. Pell dropped his hands from his face. "It's not funny!" he roared at them both.

Gillam turned astonished eyes on his mother. Rosemary managed to keep her expression calm. "See," she told the child. "You don't need to be afraid of Pell."

In response to her remark, the boy gazed at his father, staring intently at the long stripe of red that crossed the top of his cheek above his beard. Fear had left him to be replaced by fascination.

"Where'd that damned beast come from?" Pell demanded. He dabbed at his face with his fingers, scowled at the blood, and then peered up into the dim space above the rafters. Marmalade had already vanished into the shadows. He was probably outside by now, having left via the eaves.

"Hilia gave him to me. He keeps rats out of the cottage and away from the chicken yard." She tried to keep her voice calm for Gillam's sake. The boy was now peering at his father with curiosity. There was tension in his little body, and she knew from experience that he would either dissolve into wails or decide to explore the situation, depending on what happened in the next few moments. She desperately wanted him to stay calm.

"Hilia? Hilia Borse? Everyone knows her family is Wit tainted. They do the beast magic in their home. They talk to animals. You let her put an animal into this house? Are you mad?"

She bounced Gillam a time or two, then set him down on the taller stool at the table. There were only two places to sit; she wondered if Pell had noticed that. As if Pell were any other inconvenient visitor, she decided she would simply go on with her routine. She pulled the simmering pot of soup back from the fire and crouched down to ladle a portion into Gillam's shallow bowl. "You know who Hilia is," she said, trying not to sound confrontational. "She has been my best friend since we were girls."

"Yes, I know who she is! And I know what she is! Everyone in the village knows her family has the Wit. Her mother talks to sheep!"

She sighed, blew on Gillam's soup to cool it a bit, and then set it on the table. Gillam grinned happily. The stranger in the house was eclipsed by the prospect of hot food. The boy was always hungry. His constant hunger both pleased her and frightened her.

He would eat and grow strong, as long as she had food to feed him. From the mantel shelf, she took down half a loaf of bread wrapped in a clean cloth. She broke off a piece for him and set it beside his bowl with a spoon. "Eat nicely," she warned the boy.

She marked how Pell was eyeing the food. She clenched her jaw. She wasn't going to offer him any. Let him ask, if he had the nerve. She ignored his interest in the food as she filled her own bowl. "No one knows for certain the family is Witted," she pointed out. "And if they are, well, no ill has ever come of them having that magic that I know. The wool from their flock is the best in Buck Duchy. They are respected in town. Hilia and her husband have always been kind to me. And Marmalade is my cat."

"And for all you know, he could be her Wit beast, spying on you from dawn to dusk. I wouldn't allow a Wit beast in my house. Don't you care about your own child? Don't you fear he'll be tainted with that magic?'

She took her bowl, a spoon, and another piece of the bread to the table. She sat down with her back to him and stirred the soup thoughtfully. Potato and cabbage and onion. Sometimes she dreamed of meat. Rich brown broth with hunks of beef in it. Greasy pork cooked on skewers. Don't think about what you don't have. She spoke over her shoulder. "The Wit is not contagious. You are born with it or you don't have it. I think if you could just go get that magic for yourself, a lot of people who look down on Witted ones would have gone out and done it by now. I think half the hatred of the Witted is jealousy, pure and simple." She took a spoonful of her soup and a bite of her bread.

Pell made a sound between derision and disbelief. "That's what they'd have you believe," he said in a thick voice. "But if you'd seen half of what I've seen, you'd know better."

She had to turn to look back at him. That was when she discovered that he had taken the remaining chunk of the loaf and was dipping it into the soup pot and eating it. She knew a flash of anger. She put her eyes back on her food and forced herself to eat. Gillam had been watching his father and now he dipped his bread in his soup and took an exploratory bite of it. She looked back at Pell and managed to say calmly, "What you're eating? That was to be Gillam's breakfast tomorrow."

"This?" He was incredulous. "You should be feeding him meat by now. Meat and eggs and hot porridge for breakfast. Not soup. No wonder he's so timid."

"I feed him what I have," she retorted. The implied criticism stung. She had worried, often enough, that Gillam was not as well fed as other children. She had compared his size and his alertness to other boys of his age and told herself that he did not suffer in that comparison. But there had been times when he had asked for "more" and there was no more to give him. "Soon enough, the chickens will start to lay, and then he can have eggs. And after Tessie drops her calf, I hope there will be milk for him as well." She finished her food; it had not taken her long to eat it. If not for Pell, she might have allowed herself and Gillam another break of the bread.

But Pell was wiping out her pot with the last crust of her bread. She would have to make Gillam hearth cakes in the morning if he was to have anything to eat. When Pell set the pot down, she asked him directly. "What do you want? Why are you here?"

He looked surprised. "I told you. I've come home. My grandfather left me this house."

She stared at him silently. She wouldn't ask him if he meant to stay, because then he might think she wanted him to. Instead, she said bluntly, "No, Pell. Your grandfather left his house to Gillam, not you. It's our home, not yours. There's no room in my life for you, Pell. You shamed me and you abandoned your son. I don't love you and I don't want you here."

She'd expected at least one flicker of hurt at her words. She didn't want to admit to herself how much satisfaction that would have given her. Instead, he just set his jaw. After a moment he said, "Well, none of that has anything to do with the fact that you're living in my son's house. I've as much a right to be here as you do. I'm back, and that's that." He thudded the empty pot back onto the table. "I thought you might be smart enough to make the best of it. I thought I should give you another chance to do that. To be fair."

Fair? She tried to shape her thoughts about Pell around that word. He waited for her to say something. No words came to her and despite how tight her throat went, she refused to cry. She would not weep over this. Weeping, she knew, solved nothing. She looked at Gillam. He was regarding his father with a small scowl. He thrust his jaw out, and Pell suddenly laughed. She looked back at him incredulously.

"Look at him. He looks just like my little brother when he got angry." He sobered suddenly. "I never expected him to look so much like my family."

"Everyone says he looks more like you than he does me," she admitted stiffly. Then she asked, "Why wouldn't you expect your son to look like you?"

"Well," he said and shrugged one shoulder. "There was talk, you know. Back then. That perhaps he wasn't mine."

She stared at him, cold rushing through her. "Talk? There was never any talk. Everyone knew he was yours." She dragged in an outraged breath. "Who ever said he wasn't? Because that person was a liar!"

"Don't shout! It was a long time ago, and it scarcely matters now. He looks like me, so that's done with, eh?"

"You just said that because perhaps you hoped it was true. But there was never any talk, Pell. You were my first and if you must know, my only. I've never been with another man than you, before or since. He's yours. There was never any talk otherwise."

"Have it your way, if it matters to you so much. Yes. He's mine."

And when he claimed the boy, she could have bitten the tongue out of her own mouth. Why had she said that, why had she herself admitted what she wished were not true? Pell was watching her face, smiling slightly, knowing well he'd won. She looked away from him.

"I'm tired," he said. The bed was only three steps away in the little house. He sat down on the edge of it and bent over to tug off his fine boots. He set them side by side and followed them with his thick wool socks. Next he dragged off his shirt and dropped it on the floor. His trousers followed it. He stood, almost inviting her to look at him. He'd always been proud of his body. He was lean and muscled still, but no longer boyish. She hadn't wanted to see him; his mean little smile showed that he knew she had looked at him. Naked, he rucked his way into her clean bed and drew the covers up nearly over his head. "Brr. Blankets are chilly." He laughed a small laugh. "I could use some company under here to warm me."

"You won't get any."

"As you will, Rosie. And you will when you will, and it will be soon enough for me."

"I won't."

"We'll see," he said and yawned as if bored. Then he was still.

She stared at him. There was only one bed. Since Gillam had been born, they had shared it. "He go my bed," Gillam exclaimed between wonder and dismay.

"Yes he did," she confirmed for him. She pulled her gaze away from the sight. "Finish your food, Gillam."

She doubted that Pell was really asleep. Could he have been that relaxed about all of this? She doubted it. If she had been alone, she would have hit him with the pan and told him to get out of her house. No, she realized. If she were alone, she would have left here long ago. The only reason she had stayed was that her child needed a roof over his head and regular meals on the table. He still did. And that, she told herself, was the only reason she wasn't confronting Pell now. She didn't wish to frighten Gillam.

Or provoke Pell.

She did *not* want him to stay. She was clear with herself on that. It was too late for the old dreams that had once sustained her. He'd hurt her too badly, humiliated her too deeply. She could never feel about him as she once had. Never.

She tried to go about her evening tasks as if Pell did not exist. She tidied away the dishes and brushed off the table. She gave Gillam a tin cup, three broken buttons, an empty spool, and a spoon to play with and set out her sewing on the table. She faced a real challenge with this quilt. She had no rags of her own to quilt from, but her friends saved her the pieces of cloth that they judged too small or oddly colored to work into their own piecework. She worked painstakingly with scissors and pins. She did not have many pins, and sometimes had to resort to a quick loop of thread to hold a bit in place. And she dared not sew any of it permanently until she had enough bits to make an entire quilt top, for who knew what colors and textures might come her way the next time she went begging for fabric scraps? She was glad to lose herself in the detailed work, glad to push her present problem out of her mind.

Gillam was content at her feet, and she was so engrossed in her work that she didn't notice when he disappeared. When her eyes grew weary with squinting through the dimness, she rolled up her work and looked about for her son. She caught her breath at what she saw. With the pragmatism of small children, he had put himself to bed, on his side of the bed where he always slept. He was a smaller lump under the covers next to Pell.

That forced her to confront her next decision. Did she sleep on the hard flagged floor, as a message to Pell that she'd rather be cold than sleep beside him? If she claimed a spot in the bed, would he understand she wasn't surrendering territory, or would it make him think she would willingly come back to his bed? She did her nightly chores as she pondered it. Was she a coward? Should she have flown at him, kicking and scratching and screaming the moment he showed up? She felt her pulse quicken with enthusiasm at the idea, and as quickly she refused it. He would have been delighted. They had quarreled once, violently, before she was pregnant with Gillam. He had slapped her, hard, to "bring her to her senses" as he put it then. And then apologized so abjectly and made love to her so earnestly that she'd accepted his behavior. Stupid girl. What if she'd run away from him then? What if he'd never got her with child, never lived with her, never left her, never returned? What life would she have now? Would she be like Hilia, with a husband and a home and a legitimate baby in her arms? Would she be in safe harbor? Useless to wonder.

She built up the fire for the night after she put her sewing away. As she went to pull in the latchstring to secure the cottage for the night, she wondered what she feared out there. Her worst fear was already inside the door and in her bed. She blew out her candle and undressed under her worn flannel nightgown. Then she crept in beside Gillam, balancing almost on the edge of the bed. The blanket didn't quite cover her. She tugged a bit more of it free, and then lost it when Marmalade thudded into place between her and Gillam. He settled in, surrounded by warmth, and began his loud purr. She stroked him. "Go to sleep now," she told him, and he gently bit her hand to say that she had petted him enough.

She awoke, as she always did, to Picky the rooster's crowing. She slipped out of the bed and took Gillam with her, taking him to the back house before he could wet the bedding. They hurried back, shivering, through the dew wet grasses and dressed hastily in the dimness of the cabin. Pell slept on. She let out the chickens and picketed the cow in a fresh spot. With her hatchet, she split kindling to wake the flames. She brought in firewood and built up the fire. The chickens had produced two eggs, and Gillam was terribly excited about that. He had wanted to carry the warm, brown eggs, but she feared to trust him with the precious bounty. He sat at the table and stared at them as she began to stir together ground oats and water.

"We'll put the eggs in the hearth cakes and they'll taste wonderful," she told him, and he wriggled with excitement. Marmalade came and perched on her chair to watch the process. His whiskers were pricked forward with interest. "You can have a corner of mine," she promised the cat. "Even if you didn't give me any of the mouse you caught this morning!"

"Mama eat mouse!" Gillam exclaimed and dissolved into giggles. For that moment, they were as happy as they had ever been.

Then Pell spoke from the dim corner where the bed was. "What's for breakfast?"

Her stirring slowed. She admitted to herself that she'd hoped to feed both of them and be out the door and doing chores before Pell awoke. "I'm making meal cakes for Gillam," she told him.

For a time, there was only the sound of her spoon against the bowl. She tried not to feel Pell watching her from the bed. Then he spoke again. His voice was softer, considering. "You'd look younger if you let your hair down, like you used to wear it. I remember it well. All loose around your face and bare shoulders."

"I'm not younger. I'm older," she said brusquely.

He laughed.

She formed two hearth cakes in the pan and set it by the fire to cook. Gillam pulled his little stool over and sat down on it, watching intently. It was just a slice of log with three legs pegged into it, but he had helped make it and was inordinately proud of it. When he had settled himself, she tried to follow the pattern she'd established for herself, telling them both the shape of their day. "After we eat and wash up, we'll take a basket and go looking for spring greens, shall we? Maybe we'll find some mushrooms, too. And we need to visit the beach and find more firewood and bring it home. Then we'll go to Serran's house and do washing for her, and maybe we'll bring a fish home for dinner."

"Fish!" Gillam exclaimed happily and clapped his hands. She had noticed that when words were related to food, he learned them very quickly. She hoped that Serran's husband had made a good catch that week and that Serran would feel generous in barter. Today was wash day at Serran's house. Next week, she'd help Widow Lees plant her garden. And sheep shearing time was not far away. The widow had said she might help with that, and that she'd pay her in hard coin for her work. She could barter for most of her needs, but hard coin was needed for some things. She turned the cakes in the pan, and Gillam sighed in happy anticipation. "Soon," she told him.

"Damn!" Pell roared. "Damn him! I'll kill him!"

He kicked his clothes across the floor at her, and Gillam shrieked in terror at the explosion of violence as Pell lunged wildly at Marmalade. But the cat had been in motion at the man's first exclamation. He leaped from chair to table to shelf and up to the rafters in a motion as smooth as water flowing. He vanished.

Pell cursed loudly, kicked over the chair, and stood glowering. Gillam had pressed up against her so suddenly as she crouched by the hearth that Rosemary had sat down hard on the floor. Now the boy clambered into her arms, and she held him protectively as he whimpered in fear. Her own heart was racing as he stared at Pell. The muscles were knotted under his bared skin, and his eyes were wild.

"That damn cat pissed all over my good clothes! They're soaked with piss!"

She didn't laugh. Something inside her rejoiced at his misfortune and took pleasure in his anger, but a wiser part of her held still. She could have told him that the tom saw him as an intruder and that he should have hung up his clothes. A mousy part of her wanted to stammer apologies and offer to launder his clothes for him. Instead she looked away from his naked body. She'd been alone for a long time, but not so long that she'd want him again.

"What are you crying about?" Pell barked at Gillam, which turned his whimper into a wail. Pell turned his anger on her. "Shut him up! And do something about my clothes! That damn animal has to go. He's infected with Wit, that's what he is."

Don't answer. Don't defend. She managed to get to her feet with the wailing Gillam on one hip. She didn't look at Pell as she stooped down and took the pan off the fire. It was hard to get the door open with her arms full, but she managed, and she carried her boy and their breakfast outside.

"Rosemary? Rosemary!"

Pell bellowed her name after her, but she ignored him. She carried Gillam over to the garden and they sat down together on the firewood pile in the brisk morning air. "Let's eat here near our garden. Eat your cake quickly, while it's hot and nice."

The cakes were not quite done in the middle, and too hot to eat easily. She scooped them both out of the pan and set them down on the clean cut side of a piece of wood. She blew on them hastily.

"ROSEMARY!"

She looked up to see Pell naked in the door. He had draped her blanket across his shoulders. In another moment, he'd come out.

She wolfed down half a hearth cake without enjoyment of the

precious food. She breathed in air through her mouth to cool it as she chewed and swallowed quickly. "You stay here, Gillam, and eat the rest of that. It's good. Okay?"

He was still crying, but the permission to eat diverted his attention from the angry man in the door of his home. He sniffed and nodded once and then poked a finger at the cake. "Ow!"

"It will cool fast out here. Break it up in pieces. And don't let the chickens steal it from you!" For the curious flock already had come running to see what the boy had.

"Mine!" he said decisively, and she almost smiled. She rose, pan in hand, and turned back to the door as Pell bellowed her name again.

"What do you want?" she asked him calmly. She stood at a safe distance.

"That damn cat pissed all over my clothes!" He tried to gather the blanket closer. He was shivering.

His fine clothes, cut and sewn to fit him, soaked with cat piss. She didn't let herself smile. "So you've told us. Why are you yelling *my* name?"

"What are you going to do about it?"

She gripped the pan in her hand and found herself marching up to the door. "Nothing," she said, and she actually shouldered past him. "It's your problem, not mine."

He stared as she hung the empty pan on its hook. "Where's my breakfast?"

"I really don't know." She rounded on him with a quizzical stare. "Did you bring something for your breakfast? If so, I haven't seen it. If you brought any food into this house in the last three years, I haven't seen it." She caught up her basket and shawl and managed to get out the door before he could decide how to react to that.

As she started down the path, he shouted after her, "What did you do with my other clothes?"

Did he mean the ones he'd left behind when he abandoned them? "I used them for rags and quilting," she said. She didn't lift her voice. He'd either hear her or not.

"If I see that damn cat again, I'll kill him."

She knew Marmalade and had no fear for him. But, "Kill Marm? Kill my Marmy?" Gillam came toward her at a trot, his face full of childish concern.

She stooped down to speak quietly to him. "No, Gillam. Marmalade is too smart for him. Don't worry. I tell you what. Let's go to Serran's house and do washing first and hang it up in the nice wind to dry. Then we'll look for greens on the way home."

"With fish?" he asked her hopefully.

"Maybe with fish. Let's see how far the tide is out. Perhaps we can cut across the beach."

"Beach!" he exclaimed, and she smiled. Gillam loved the beach, and exploring it would add time to their journey, not reduce it. Usually she didn't take him down the steep rocky path, but today she wished to get as far away from Pell as fast as she could, and stay away as long as she could.

"You had no right!" Pell bellowed after her when he realized she was leaving. "Those clothes belonged to me!"

She didn't look back.

"You can't take a man's rightful possessions! What is mine is mine, and I will take it back!"

Cold clutched at her heart. He meant Gillam. His son. Her son. Her most precious of all things precious. That was why he had come back, she suddenly knew. Not for her or the cottage. To take Gillam.

"Let's run!" she suggested, as she seized her boy's hand and set off at a trot with Gillam jogging beside her.

FROM THE RAFTERS, the tom watched the man below him. The intruder kicked his wet clothes again, cursed some more, and then began to rummage through the sparse contents of the shelves. The cat watched him; there was no meat there, but he found a turnip and ate it. While he chewed, he took the lids off several other containers, grumbling all the while, and then abandoned his search for easy food. The cat could have told him there was nothing in the cupboard worth eating. All it was good for was attracting meaty little mice, which the cat had no intention of sharing.

Hilia was right. The big male human was going to be a problem. He took up too much of the bed, he smelled as if he might try to claim the territory, and he'd caused the cat to miss out on a nice eggy bit of cake this morning. And he'd made the boy wail, and the cat detested that awful sound. And he'd driven the woman away before she had built up the fire for the day. The cottage was rapidly cooling.

He glared down at the man. *You need to leave. This is my territory and you are not welcome.*

The man paused in his turnip chewing and looked up into the rafters. He had that stubborn look that people got when they knew that a cat was thinking about them but they didn't want to accept it. "Cat? You up there? I'm going to kill you, you little bastard!"

I doubt it. You're clumsy and heavy and slow. Everything that I'm not. The cat dug his claws into the beam and noisily sharpened them. When the man turned to peer up at him, he deliberately strolled across the rafter over the man's head. He leaped up at the cat, batting futilely at him while roaring angrily. The cat sat down and wrapped his tail neatly around his feet. The man threw things, a vegetable, then a cup that shattered when it hit the wall, and then his boot, which landed in the fire. None of the objects hit the cat. The man was throwing them too hastily.

When he dragged a stool over and began to climb up on it,

the cat stood, stretched, and then strolled along the beam until he reached the eaves. From there it was easy to push his way out through the storm-worn thatch. With a quick twist of his body he was up on the roof. He climbed quickly to the peak and sat down. He caught a glimpse of Rosemary and Gillam just as they turned and took the path that would take them down to the beach. He wondered if they would come back. The big human male was making an obvious claim to the territory. The female might be wise to take her kit and move on. He knew the ways of rogue males. He might very well kill the kit in the hopes of taking her as his mate again.

He didn't like that idea. The female brought home food and shared it. She kept the shelter warm, and she was comfortable to sleep with. He doubted that the male human would provide any of that for him. So. How to be rid of him? He settled on the roof, folding his paws neatly under his chest and tucking his tail around him. He stared out to the horizon and pondered. How did one kill game that size?

ROSEMARY HAD TO take the long way home. The tide was in, and that meant she had to follow the meandering path on top of the sea cliffs rather than cut across the bared beach. She paused for a moment to stare across the wide blue bay. On the opposite tooth of the land, she could just see the hazy buildings of Dorytown. Meddalee's home. She wished Pell would just go back there. Let him chase his pretty girl with the fancy clothes and rich father. Just let him go away.

The wind blew harshly, pushing against her. She pulled her shawl tighter around her shoulders. "Come on, Gillam. Let's get home and get warm."

"Too tired. Too cold." He sat down on the beaten earth of the path. His nose and cheeks were bright red, as were the tips of his ears. What had become of spring? And would she have warmer clothes for him before winter returned? He was growing so fast. She refused to think that far ahead. With a sigh she stooped down, hoisted him to her hip, and fashioned her shawl into a sling to take some of his weight. He'd already eaten more than half the smoked fish that Serran had given them for doing the wash. Rosemary had eaten some of it and concealed the rest in her bag for later. Damned if she would share it with Pell! But she might give the cat a bite or two.

Something in her had hardened. She was weary and Gillam was heavy, but heavier still were the words that Serran and Tarsha Wells had loaded onto her. "You should run, girl," Serran had said bluntly after Rosemary had admitted that Pell had come back to the house and spent the night there. "Run while you can. Today. Don't wait until he gets another child on you. Everyone knows what a charmer that man is. He'll talk you into his bed, plant a baby in your belly, and then be off again. Don't let him. Don't even go back there."

"But everything I own is there, and not much of it is portable! And the cottage rightfully belongs to Gillam, not him."

"The cottage will still be there when he is a man grown and he can come back to claim it then." Tarsha was emphatic. "Run, girl."

"I can't. I won't! Should I run off and leave the cow? The chickens? Everything I've worked so hard to build up in the last three years? Just take Gillam and set off into the world without a coin to my name?"

Tarsha had been visiting Serran when Rosemary arrived. They'd all been washing together, for Serran had decided her house needed a spring cleaning that included laundering all the bedding. It had been a companionable time, with Gillam playing with little Marsh and the women all chatting together. It would have been fun if the topic hadn't been her personal danger.

"Better a live beggar than . . . well, than anything else you might become." Serran's words were ominous.

"What are you saying?" Rosemary demanded.

"I know why Pell has come back here," Tarsha had said suddenly.

Both women had turned to stare at her. Serran shook her head as if to warn her against indiscretion. Tarsha had looked down at her hands and spoken anyway. "I heard it from my cousin. It started a couple of months ago, with little things. A push in the market, calling her a bitch after a squabble in a tavern. But about a month ago, Pell put hands on Meddalee and not in a kind way. He'd pushed her before and once he knocked her down right in the market. But this was his hands on her throat. Her father saw the marks and he threatened to kill Pell. But he came, all tears and apologies, and knelt outside her father's house and begged pardon. So she took him back. But then he actually hit her, a week ago. Loosened a tooth, and that was it. Her father's servants put Pell out of the house and told him never to come back, that he no longer worked for her father or had permission to see Meddalee. Said Pell had no prospects and no right to touch his daughter. I heard Pell lingered for a time, hoping he could make it up, but when he couldn't and he ran out of coin, he came home." Tarsha looked up from her washing and said bluntly, "You should leave him, Rosemary. Take Gillam and go. If he hit one woman, he'll hit another."

Shame flushed her face. She'd never admitted to anyone that Pell had struck her. She wouldn't admit it now. "I've got nowhere to go," she said bluntly. Both women looked away from her. Times were hard. No one could afford to take in a woman and her child, while risking the displeasure of Pell and his family. It wasn't fair of her to ask it, and so she didn't. "The cottage belongs to Gillam. He has a right to live there. And I can take care of myself." She said it, but no one really believed it. And when Tarsha hugged her good-bye, she slipped a coin into her hand, a small silver one.

"Just go!" she whispered. "Run. Don't you have cousins in Forge? Go there."

Rosemary had nodded grimly and then started the long walk home. Home. Was it really her home anymore? Could she run off to Forge? Her father's sister had settled there; she barely remembered the woman. She had cousins there, yes, cousins she'd never met. No. There was no easy sanctuary. But it was her problem, not her friends'. It was up to her to solve it for herself.

She saw the smoke from her chimney long before she could see her house. And when she stood looking down on it, her heart nearly broke. She'd put so much into it, and Gillam was so heavy as he slept in the sling. She tried to imagine running away, taking him off down the long road to somewhere. Buckkeep Town? She could probably find some kind of work in a big city like that. But the journey would be hard. Sleeping by the road with little more than her shawl to cover them, eating what they could find. There were dangerous men on the road; there always were and always had been. They might do worse to her and her son than Pell would even imagine. Bad as Pell was, there was worse out there. And Gillam was his only son. He wouldn't hurt him. She'd face him and see what came next.

Her washing tub was in the front yard, full of dirty water. The scatter of feathers in the front yard was a grim warning. With a sinking heart, she saw the long, shining feathers of a rooster's tail among them. "Picky-pick," she whispered to herself. Her hatchet was sunk deep into the stump where she split kindling. Feathers were trapped around the embedded blade. As she opened the door, the smell of scorched meat greeted her. The carcass of a bird was on the spit over the fire with Pell crouching nearby. Feathers were everywhere.

"What have you done?" she demanded in a stricken voice, but she knew. He'd killed the rooster and with him, every generation of birds to come. He hadn't even salvaged the feathers.

Pell turned round to smile up at her with his disarming grin. "What does it look like I'm doing? I'm cooking dinner for us. Thought I'd show you that I'm a useful sort to have around the house."

"You idiot!"

His eyes narrowed, the smile gone. "I'd think you'd show a little gratitude, after you left me here with no breakfast and dirty clothes. I had to wash them out myself. And put them on when they were still wet."

She'd already seen that. His fine shirt was wrinkled, and the damp still showed in every seam of his trousers. She didn't care.

"You killed Picky-pick. Without asking me. Without thinking about it at all."

"Rosemary. Is that what's troubling you?" A wealth of disbelief in his uttering of her name, and then he smiled indulgently as he explained it to her. "It wasn't a hen, but a rooster. Doesn't lay eggs, Rosie. I have no idea why you were wasting feed on him."

"So he could father a batch of chicks! So we could raise extra chickens this summer for meat next winter, you idiot!"

The bed was a rumpled mess. She twitched a blanket flat and set Gillam down on it. He stirred and sat up. He looked around sleepily, and then took in the scorched carcass. "Cook meat?" he asked hopefully.

Pell had been glaring at her. He turned to the boy when he spoke. "There. You see. The boy needs meat. I told you so. A father has to take care of his son, and that's all I'm trying to do. If it's so important to you, I can get another rooster for you. Later. But tonight, little Will gets to eat his fill of nice roast chicken. Right, son?"

He smiled at her boy. It seemed a false smile to her, but the boy was taken in. Gillam nodded eagerly and bounced on the bed.

She stared at her smiling son, suddenly so like his father. Some terrible being inside her wanted to tell Gillam that it was Picky-pick on the fire, the rooster he'd seen raised from a chick and named himself, wanted to make her son dissolve in howls of sorrow. Perhaps that would chase the smug smile from Pell's face. Perhaps that would keep her son's heart as hers alone. But a stronger part of her could not do that to her boy. Soon enough, when there was no crowing in the morning, the boy would realize the bird was gone. Then was soon enough for him to mourn. And dead, the bird might as well be eaten as not.

She gritted her teeth and silently cleaned the feathers from the room, trying to gather what she could of them. She'd thought that if Picky sired enough chicks, there might have been not just meat for the winter, but feathers for stuffing a small comforter. All gone in an idiot's impulse. And he'd expected her to thank him for destroying a year's work! The idiot. She watched him crouched by the fire, turning the spit this way and that. Gillam had come to crouch beside him, studying the man as much as the cooking bird. She couldn't stand it. She took herself outside.

There was worse to discover. In his pursuit of the rooster, Pell had trampled two rows of her garden. The wilted seedlings with their wisps of roots were drying on the disturbed rows. Without much hope, she hoed the earth back into place, pushed the plants back into the soil and gave them a sprinkle of water. The green things lay flat and limp on the wet soil. They would not rise again. And that was another food source gone. The cold wind whipped her hair across her face.

Gillam had stayed in the house watching his father. She hadn't liked that but could think of no way to lure him away. And it had been easier to tidy up his father's mess without the toddler at her heels, asking a dozen questions and sometimes undoing half her work as she did it. As she hung up her tools and wiped her hands on her apron, she allowed herself to wonder what her life would have been like if she'd had a husband for the last three years. What if there had been someone who had brought home food, helped to dig the garden, and sometimes watched the child? Would the garden be twice the size it was now? Would the worn thatch of the roof have been completely replaced last year instead of patched? Perhaps, she thought to herself, and then shook her head. Perhaps, but not if Pell were the man involved.

Inside the house, she found them at the table, eating meat that was scorched on the outside and bloody within. "Chimney doesn't draw right," Pell excused it. "And the firewood is too small. You need good chunks for coals to cook meat over, not a bunch of little sticks."

"You used up all my kindling," she replied. "The pile of larger wood is over in the shelter of the spruce tree, to keep it dry." Both of her bowls and chairs were in use. It didn't matter. She didn't think she could have faced eating Picky anyway. She wondered if she would still wake in the dawn tomorrow without his raucous crowing. Set it aside. Too late to fix it. She just had to go on. His gleaming knife lay on the table beside the butchered bird. He picked it up and sawed on the butchered bird. To her surprise the knife slid through the tough bird as if it were butter. It was only when he put the meat in his mouth that he had to chew and chew. She tried not to take satisfaction in how tough the meat was.

"That must be a sharp knife, to shear through that meat so easily," she observed, and he started as if she had jabbed him with it. He hastily returned it to his sheath, uncleaned.

"It was a gift," he said, and then, as if he couldn't resist the urge to brag, "Chalcedean steel. The best money can buy."

She made no answer to that. He hadn't heard the hidden mockery in her comment. The fool hadn't even known that a grown rooster was not fit for roasting but only the stew pot. How had he managed to live in the village all his life and not know such simple things? How had he kept himself above and apart from the simple work that could have put food on the table? She forced herself to think back through the years. Rory, the carter's boy, had fancied her once. He'd been a hard worker, but his plain face and callused hands had not charmed her. No. She had fallen to the boy with the soft hair and fine clothes. He was never dirty, she told herself, because he never worked. Did she think he was an idiot for not knowing how to work? What did that make her? How could she have taken up with a man who did no more than smile and be handsome and sing tavern songs well?

She barely stopped him in time when he gathered what was left and began to throw it on the fire. "That will stink if you burn bones in the house. Besides, I can make a soup of the bones and what's left on them. I have a couple of turnips and an onion . . ." and she glanced at her cupboard to see that was a lie. The turnips were gone.

"You can't just eat everything you see around here!" she exclaimed angrily. "I have to plan what we use and be sparing of it."

"Well, if you think I'm going to go hungry while there are chickens running around in the yard, think again. I'm not that helpless. Or foolish."

A thousand responses came to her mind. But only one clear thought formed. That handsome fool would destroy everything she had built up in the last three years before he was finished here. He would not listen to her. He would do as he pleased with her things. She was speechless. She gathered the rags she had used to clean up his butchering mess and went outside.

She dumped the dirty water from her washtub, rinsed it, and filled it again. She was washing out her cleaning rags when he came out of the house. He was walking softly but she heard him. He came up behind her. "You work so hard," he said gently. "Rosie, I never meant for you to live like this."

Simple words in a kind voice. They stabbed her. Three years ago, even two years ago and they would have won her heart.

"It's work and it has to be done," she said and hated how her voice was choked with tears.

She started when his hands settled on her shoulders. She twitched but he did not lift them. They were so warm, and he gently squeezed just where her shoulders ached most.

"Don't," she said sharply and twisted away from his touch. He let her go.

"I'm going to stay, Rosie," he said. "I know you don't believe it. I know you don't want to give me another chance. You're still angry at me, and who could blame you? I've thought about it. For me, it seems like something I did a long time ago, three years ago. I left you, and for me, that was the end of it. But you stayed here, and I suppose that every single day you've missed me. Every single night, you've been alone, and I suppose that's why the hurt is so fresh for you.

"But I'm back now. You can stop being angry, and there's nothing to be hurt about any more. I'm here, ready to be husband to you and father to your child."

"You're not my husband. You never married me. You wouldn't. Not even when your grandfather asked you to."

"I told you, Rosie. A scared boy ran away from you and the baby. But a man has come back. Give me a chance."

"No."

She heard him take a deep breath through his nose. "You will," he said confidently. Then, as if he were changing the subject to indulge her, he asked her, "What are you doing?"

"Washing out bloody rags," she told him savagely.

He was silent for a time and she thought he'd finally read her mood. But then he asked in a voice between dismay and disgust, "It's your blood time?"

"Yes." She heard herself lie promptly, and he abruptly stepped back from her. She wondered what instinct had made her protect herself.

He'd always expressed a disdain for touching her or even being around her during her menses. And now he retreated from her in a way that did not reassure her. Retreated because . . . why? Because he had been preparing to advance on her in some way? Tonight, after the boy was asleep? A cold dread rose in her, but something else twisted inside her along with it. She had the same hungers that any woman had, hungers that had nothing to do with food. Hungers that paid no attention to sensible thoughts, hungers that wanted his warm hands on her aching shoulders, hungers that recalled well how once they had warmed a bed together.

But what if? Her thoughts wriggled out of her control and ran off on a sunlit path. What if Pell were sincere in his return? He'd said, more than once, now, that he wished to make his life what it should have been, to be a father to the boy and a husband to her. What if he meant it and was groping his way toward that path? Could he change? Could they find the love they'd once felt for each other and build something with it? What if she gave ground to him and tried to awaken that in him again? Would it be so terrible a thing? Could that old dream be called to life again?

Unbidden, she recalled the passion she had once felt for Pell, the physical arousal his touch had created and their joyous unions. For one moment, heat surged through her. Then it faded. Her memories of their joinings were eroded, like a wooden carving that had weathered away, leaving only lumps where it had once had a face. She'd been wild about him, uncontrollably drawn to him. But now she could not think of him without recalling how he had humiliated and abandoned her. Those memories abraded any joy she had felt in him to expose the foolishness beneath it. No. No girlish silliness. She would force herself to see Pell only as he was, not as she had once dreamed him to be.

He was still standing behind her. It made the skin of her back and neck prickle, and she was torn between hoping he'd touch her again so she could reject him and praying he wouldn't touch her again because she might turn into his embrace. Her heart was beating too fast. She risked a glance over her shoulder, but he wasn't even looking at her anymore. Instead he was staring intently at the top of the hill.

"Is someone coming?" she asked him and followed his gaze just in time to see a lantern vanish from sight.

"No. Just someone passing by," he said. Then he announced abruptly, "I might go into town tonight." He turned and went back into the cottage. She welcomed his absence, but his hasty withdrawal surprised her. Obviously, he found her that disgusting. Odd, that his rejection could still sting. No. Not odd. Stupid that she could even care about him to that extent. He'd left her and their child for three years. How could she let herself crave his company, even if she only craved it for the chance to hurt him? She'd thought she'd gotten wiser than that.

She wrung out her cleaning rags and hung them to dry. The evening was closing in. Would he go to town or stay at the cottage? With that question, she realized that she dreaded another night confined with Pell. She could only tolerate it if she believed it would be the last one. Her mixed feelings, her emotional anger, and her physical need for a male were shredding her. She'd be better off to sleep with a wandering minstrel than to take a known traitor into her bed. Remember who he was, not what his body was like, she counseled herself. Protect herself and her child.

Slowly she went back into his house. The dishes were on the table as he had left them, and the hearth was spattered with grease and ash. Everywhere she looked in the cottage, she could see his marks, as if he were a cat who had to spray and scratch to claim his territory. He reclined on the bed, his boots on and a gleaming smudge of grease at one corner of his mouth from the meal. Gillam was on the bed beside him, playing with a handful of the rooster's tail feathers. The rumpled bed, the dirty dishes, the ransacked cupboard . . . slowly she recalled that after Pell had left, there was actually less work for her to do. Less clothing to wash and less careless mess to tidy. She didn't want this life back. With or without Pell's touch on her at night, she didn't want to live with him, clean up after him, and take his orders. She cleared her throat and tried to speak casually as she tidied the room.

"The cow will drop her calf soon. I'd best take her to Ben's tomorrow."

He turned his head and squinted at her. "Take the cow to Ben's? Why?"

"When I bought her, he warned me that sometimes a cow's first drop is difficult. He knows how to turn a calf if it needs doing. He said he'd help me when the time came, if I brought the cow to him." More lies. He'd never said any such thing. She wouldn't take the cow to Ben's. She'd take the cow to Hilia. She and her husband were not wealthy, but they were solid. They'd give her what they could for the cow and the calf inside her.

"Best do it, then." There was no suspicion in his voice. Plainly he cared nothing for the cow or the calf to come. "But leave the boy here with me. It's time Will got to know his papa. Time I taught him a thing or two about being a man." He poked the boy and Gillam giggled.

No. Never. She had been right. It was her son he was after; that was why he'd come back. Her beautiful, clever Gillam; that was what Pell would take and twist him into someone she didn't know. Her fledgling plan sprouted wings. "I'll go very early so I can be back in time to do my regular chores," she said. And she'd take Gillam with her when she went. Pell had always been a heavy sleeper. Tomorrow, before dawn, she'd slip away. She'd have to go the long way; the tide would be in, and the heavy cow couldn't go down the cliff-side path. By the time Pell woke and then eventually wondered where they were, she and Gillam would have left Hilia's and be on their way. If he thought to look for them, he'd go to Ben's first. She doubted that he'd make much real effort to find them and bring them back. He'd wait here and expect her to come cowering home. She wouldn't. She'd leave it all behind and run.

She tried not to care about what would happen next. He'd kill her chickens, of course, one at a time and eat them. That couldn't be helped. The garden, she knew, would go to weeds and vanish. There was only one other creature to worry about . . . Anxiety clutched at her heart as she realized that Marmalade hadn't come to greet her when she returned. She hadn't seen the cat at all.

"Odd. I haven't seen the cat," she said. Her heart was thudding sickly against her stomach.

Pell gave her a sideways glance. "Neither have I. But when I do, I'll kill him."

"Kill him," Gillam repeated with no concept of the meaning. He jogged the end of the rooster feather against his own chin and giggled.

"That's right, Willy," his father said and leaned across the bed to tickle him. Gillam wriggled and shrieked with delight. It was all Rosemary could do to keep from leaping across the room, seizing her child, and fleeing with him. For a fleeting instant, the two of them looked so alike, the man grinning hard and the child flinging himself about and shrieking with laughter as he sought to escape his father's touch. For a heart-stopping instant, she couldn't love her son, not when he looked so like Pell. She turned away from both of them unable to abide that.

Tomorrow, she would run. Before things could become any worse.

Some things, you can't run from. You have to deal with them and be done with them.

She wasn't sure where the thought came from, but something not a sound made her glance up into the dimness under the rafters. A cat's eyes glowed at her from the shadows. *Don't come down!* she mentally begged him. She made a pretense of gathering garbage from around the cottage, added a handful of bones from around the chicken carcass, and carried them outside. She walked to the edge of the farmyard near the trash heap and set them down. In a heartbeat, Marmalade was there. He wound twice around her ankles, purring like a storm and then settled down to crunching the bones. She crouched down beside the cat in the gathering darkness. "I have to go away, Marmy. So do you. I wish I could tell you to run to Hilia's house and live there. She'd take you in."

He stopped his crunching and looked up at her, his eyes boring into hers. *I live here,* his gaze seemed to say.

"So did I," she said, and sudden tears choked her. "But I can't stay here any longer. He's going to change too many things. He's going to kill my chickens. And make Gillam into someone named Will, someone like him. And make me into . . . something." She didn't have a word for what she would become. Something he ordered about, something that cleaned up after him and gave her body over for his use, and never spoke about the things that had used to belong to her, never spoke of the ways he had hurt her and wronged her. "I can't become that. So I can't stay here."

Marmalade rumbled a growl.

"I can't defend my territory like you do. Not without risking that he'd hurt me. And if he hurt me badly enough, or killed me, then who would protect Gillam from him? Even if I stay here and battle him every day, he will change Gillam in ways I don't want him to change. I have no choice, cat. I have to run."

"Rosie! Rosie, where are you?" Pell sounded more annoyed than concerned at her absence. She hissed at the cat, startling him so that he dashed off into the darkness. She wiped her face on her apron and walked around the end of the byre.

"I was checking the cow," she lied. "Truly, I'd best take her to Ben's tomorrow."

"Yes, I know, you told me." He was impatient. "Come back to the house. I can't find the money."

Her heart lurched. The money? What did he mean by that? Then she knew. Her money. When he'd left, they'd already spent the last of his on the fish and potatoes. Every copper pence in the small cloth bag behind the kindling box was hers, earned by hard work, a shard at a time. Not that there was much. But he'd take it all. She knew it. She thought of the silver bit she'd earned today. That at least was still tied in her apron pocket. He had no way to know about it. She walked slowly back to the cottage, debating with herself. He would know she had at least some money. And once she'd shown him any of it, he'd take it all. Which was worth more, the silver in her pocket or the coppers in the pot?

"Rosemary!" His shout was angry, and she suddenly heard Gillam wail.

"No, no, no! You bweak it!" She broke into a run and burst through the door.

"What? What is it?"

Gillam sprawled in the corner, sobbing. He clutched the broken pieces of his three-legged stool to his chest. The bedding was in a heap on the floor. An angry Pell spun to face her. "Where have you hidden the money? It's not in the pot on the rafter."

"What did you do to him?" she demanded. Gillam was gasping as if he could not get his breath.

He gave his son a disdainful glance. "Nothing. I tried to use the stool to look for the money and it collapsed under me. Then he burst into tears about it." He shook his head. "The boy wants toughening."

"No." Gillam wailed indignantly. "No, you bweak it and you push me down! You pushed me down! Pushing is wude! You bweak my stool."

"It was badly built. It's not my fault. And you are too big to cry about every little thing. None of this would have happened if the money pot were where it is supposed to be. Rosemary, what did you do with the money?"

She was shocked at how swiftly he descended to the level of a two-year-old, trying to shift blame for his idiocy onto someone else. A cold deadly calm suddenly flowed through her, as chilling as if her blood had turned to seawater as she realized what he had been about. The pot on the rafter. He'd stood on Gillam's little stool to reach for the rafter.

"That's where *you* used to keep the money. Out of my reach. Remember? So I couldn't be 'foolish' with it." She crossed the room and picked up Gillam. He clung to her tightly, bundling the pieces of his beloved stool between them, and she found herself returning that grip. "Don't you cry, son. We'll build another stool."

Gillam took a shuddering breath and emboldened by his mother's embrace, he peered around her neck and cried out, "I don't wike you! You bweak my stool!"

"Oh, shut up. Rosie. I'm asking you something important. Ignore that brat for a moment. Where did you move the money? I need to go to town, and I can't go without a penny to my name."

A sudden vivid memory flooded her. She'd stood here and with a long stick had poked the money pot out of the rafters. Heavy with pregnancy, she'd not trusted the chair she'd stacked on the table to take her weight. And when the small pot fell and shattered, it had confirmed what she'd already known. Not even a copper shard was left in it. He'd left her penniless. She'd been hungry that night.

Gillam still in her arms, she strode across the room and snatched up the small bag from behind the kindling box. She opened the neck of it and dashed the contents to the floor. The scatter of small coins rang and rolled against the stones. She tossed the emptied bag onto the bedding. "Take it," she said. "Take every penny that you never earned. Take every bit of it. And go away and never come back."

"Stupid bitch," he said with great feeling. "I *am* taking it." Without shame, he dropped to his knees and went grubbing after the coins. He grunted as he crawled under the table and spoke as if short of breath. "I'm going to town. I have to meet someone there, to talk business. And I may have a beer or two with old friends. But I *will* be back. Because this is *my* house. My grandfather may have willed it to the boy, but everyone in town knows it should have come to me. That's how it should be. And that's how it's going to be. Accept that, and things might be easier for you. Or get out. I don't care which."

With a louder grunt, he heaved himself to his feet. His face was red, and his fine shirt was so wrinkled it looked crumpled. He pulled his own empty purse from his belt and funneled her small collection of coins into it. His telling her to get out suddenly changed everything. "This is Gillam's house and land, given him by his grandfather when you would do nothing for your son. I won't let you take them from him."

"Don't talk to me like that!" he warned her. He tied the purse at his belt and glared at her. She stood where she was, her foot firmly planted to cover two of the errant coins that had rolled toward her. She needed them, and so she stood her ground as he advanced on her. She met his gaze. She wasn't quite brave enough to say anything more to the angry man, but her need to keep the money made her stand defiantly before his sudden charge.

As he lifted his hand, disbelief froze her. She turned her body, shifting Gillam away from the blow. *He wouldn't!* her mind shrieked.

He will. He'll kill you if he dares. It's in his mind right now.

He can't! Her argument with herself took less than a second. His hand was in motion and she still hadn't moved, still covered the bits of money she hoped to keep for herself. Faster than his falling hand, the cat leaped down from the rafters. Claws out, he lit on Pell's head and shoulder, raking his face and yowling. The blow Pell dealt Rosemary was a glancing one as he spun to confront the snarling, spitting cat. It still sent her to one knee as she sought to keep Gillam from hitting the floor. Pain shot through her leg, but she didn't drop her child.

Pell seized Marmalade in both hands, and the cat sank his fangs into the soft meat between Pell's thumb and fingers. Pell shouted wordlessly and flung the hapless cat. He struck the wall, fell to the floor, and then impossibly swift, shot out of the open door.

"MARMY!" Gillam shrieked.

Pell clutched his scored face with his bleeding hands and glared at them. "No howling," he warned the boy. He pointed a shaking finger at Rosemary. "You clean this mess up before I get back." A nasty smile showed his teeth as he glared at the white-faced child. "Kitty likes to fly," he said and laughed.

Rosemary struggled to her feet, her child still in her arms. "No. My cat, my Marmy!" Gillam's little body, she realized, was tight with anger, not fear. "You bad! Bad, bad, bad!"

"Mind your mouth, boy!" Anger flushed Pell's face, and the

cords on either side of his neck stood out. He advanced toward them, blood streaming down his clawed cheeks and fury in his eyes. "Mind your mouth or I'll shut it for you, you little bastard!"

She stumbled back from him, and then turned and dashed out into the night, carrying Gillam with her. "Bad, bad!" the child shouted defiantly over her shoulder as she fled.

"Shush!" she warned him and covered the child's roar with her hand. A panicky Gillam clutched and clawed at her stifling hand, but she ignored that as she ran and stumbled and ran again. Her knee wanted to fold under her. She couldn't let it. She fled to the deep meadow grasses beyond the chicken yard and then dove to the earth and lay still. "Be quiet!" she hissed in the boy's ear. "Be quiet. We're hiding. We don't want him to find us."

She lifted her hand and a terrified Gillam hiccuped once and then clung to her silently. His breathing was harsh and loud; she feared Pell would find them. Her knee throbbed so badly that she thought she would not be able to stand again, let alone run. Pell appeared in the lamplit doorway, looking all around. He couldn't see them.

"Rosemary!" he shouted.

She held her breath and Gillam huddled tight against her.

"Rosemary! Get in here, you stupid bitch. Clean up this damn mess. I want it all cleaned up before I come back!" He waited. She cowered silently. "Don't think I'm going to forget this. I won't. If you don't come now, it will just be worse for you later!" He waited again. "You can't stay out there forever."

She watched him through a screen of grass stalks. He pulled his cloak up tight against the rising wind and threatened rain. He scowled helplessly at the vacant landscape around him. He wanted so badly to win this encounter. She feared he would stand there all night. But suddenly Pell strode away from the cottage, headed for the cliff-side road that went to town. She watched him as a darker figure against the evening twilight as he marched up the pathway. She suddenly felt another small warm body pressed against hers. She put her hand down and found Marmalade crouched in the grass beside her. She flinched with him when she set a hand on his ribs, and he cowered away from her touch with a rebuking growl.

"He nearly killed you, cat. I'm so sorry." She barely breathed the words as she watched Pell hiking up the hill. She touched the cat and he rumbled again.

A thought slowly dawned on her. The cat had taken the blow to save her. "He was trying to hit me. He could have thrown me against the wall. Or Gillam." She shook her head, trying to deny the thought. How had Gillam got into that sprawl in the corner? Had he already struck his own son? She heard again the word he'd flung, the one she sheltered Gillam from every day. Bastard. From his own father's mouth. Their cottage was no longer a refuge, but a prison. Her defiance blew away with the wind.

"I have to run." Rainy roads and no shelter. Unknown dangers for her and her boy. Hunger. What future could she possibly find? What would she have to do to feed them?

Marmalade stood and butted his head against her. Pell was nearly out of sight. She spoke slowly, scarcely daring to utter the thought aloud. "If I don't run, I have to fight for my territory. Maybe to the death." She shook her head at herself. Where had such an idea come from. "What am I thinking? I don't know how to fight. He's too big for me. I can't win against him."

The cat bumped his head against her hand and then slipped away. The grasses parted and swayed in his wake. He was headed up the hill, off on his night hunting. Pell had vanished.

She spoke aloud the thought that hung in the air. "Everything knows how to fight. Anyone with young knows how to protect them."

Slowly she got to her feet. She reached down to touch her knee and felt the warmth. It was swelling. She picked up Gillam. He was still shaking and uncharacteristically silent. "Don't worry. He's gone. Let's go back to our house."

She tried to set him down to walk with her, but he just let his legs fold under him. He lay on his side, just as Marmalade had sprawled for that instant at the bottom of the wall. Her mind suddenly showed her a vision of her boy, flung against the wall and broken at the bottom of it. "No," she said in a low voice. She wouldn't wait for that to happen. She gathered him up, thinking how heavy he had grown, and tried not to think of taking him to the roads and how far she would have to carry him each day after he wearied. She didn't try to bend her knee as she lurched along.

The cottage was a mess. Furniture and stores were the victims of Pell's hasty search. She set Gillam down in a heap on the unswept hearth. He immediately began to wail. "Just a minute, son," she told him as she put the bedding back on the roped bed frame. Already it stank of Pell. The whole house smelled of him, she thought to herself. She picked up her small money poke. She'd gripped the bottom of it when she shaken money out on the floor, and then tossed it onto the bed where the chink of the concealed coins would not be heard. She glanced inside. Five coppers. Not much but better than nothing.

Once the bed was back together and the blankets smooth on it, she scooped up Gillam and set him on it. He hadn't stopped wailing, but his cries were becoming feebler. Terror and fury had exhausted him.

"I can't tend you right now, son. Mama has to put some things together for us."

She had the smoked fish she'd hidden from Pell, and the silver coin. She built up the fire and searched the floor with the lamp, righting the chairs and putting the cloth back on the table as she did so. Pell had missed the two coins that she'd had her foot on, and she found another copper stuck in a crack. Scarcely a fortune, but she slid it back into the poke. She put the poke in the bottom of a canvas sack, save for two coppers that she slid into her pocket. Never show all your money when you travel.

She looked into her cupboards, but Pell had eaten whatever could be immediately eaten. Habit made her tidy as she went, putting the house back in order even though she intended to leave it forever tomorrow. When she thought of that, she was tempted to wreck the place, but only for an instant. No. She had come to love the little cottage. Putting it to rights now was her apology to it for what Pell would make it: a dingy, run-down hovel with garbage strewn around it.

Gillam had stopped wailing. He was sound asleep. She left him in his clothes. She packed all their extra clothing into the bag. It didn't even fill it. She used her quilting rags to create two straps on the canvas bag, and then packed her needles, threads, and scraps. One pan for cooking. Flint and steel. A few other odds and ends. There would just be room for the blanket from the bed. She slipped quietly from the house lest she wake Gillam and went out to the cow's byre. She hid the bag there; if Pell came back early, she didn't want him catching a glimpse of it and asking any questions. She patted the wakeful cow and went back to the cottage.

Her decision to run made, she could find no peace. She longed to leave immediately and knew that would be stupid. In the dark, carrying Gillam and leading the gravid cow? No. She would go at dawn. Pell would come in drunk if he came in at all, and he'd sleep late. She'd be up by dawn and gone, with her boy rested and light to see by. It was the sensible thing to do, and she was a sensible woman. If he came back tonight, she'd pretend deference to him, no matter what he demanded of her. She was strong. She'd make her preparations.

That, she told herself, was why she sat down in her battered old chair, the one that was even more battered now that Pell had tossed it aside in his search for her money, and did her crying then. She wept for how stupid she had been, and then for how much work and love she had put into the ugly little hovel between the fens and the cliffs to make it her own little cottage. And when she was finished, she found she was done with tears. The foolish connection she had felt to a place that had never truly belonged to her was gone. It would be Pell's. Let him have it. He could have the cabin; she'd never let him have the boy.

MARMALADE TROTTED EARNESTLY through the dark. His ribs ached, and his ears still rang from hitting the wall. He let a small rumble of anger emerge from his throat, then silenced himself sternly. Was he a kitten to betray himself to his prey with a yowl or a lashing tail? Of course not.

The female had a point. The man was large and very strong. And quicker than the cat had allowed for. He'd thought he could slip right though his hands, but he'd gotten a good grip on him. If he'd had the sense to break the cat in his hands instead of throwing him, he'd be dead now.

Which meant that if he didn't get rid of the man, he'd be dead very soon. Marmalade understood territory. It could not be surrendered. His fight with the man was to the death.

But how did one kill so large a beast?

The man did not know the cliff-side path. Perhaps, once, it had been familiar territory for him, but no longer. The night was dark, with clouds taunting the moon. The man stumbled more than once, swore loudly, and went on. The cliffs were bare of trees; only brush and tall grasses carpeted them. There was no shelter from the wind. And little, the cat thought to himself, between the man and the land's end. The shore below the cliffs was broken shale. When the tide came in, it came right to the cliff's edge.

But the man stayed to the path, hurrying and sometimes tripping in his haste to reach town. Marmalade matched his pace but stayed well back. The man bumbled along in the near dark, keeping to the path along the winding cliff tops. The spring wind blew, warm and full of rain to come. The night was alive and it would have been good hunting for the cat, if only he hadn't needed to kill this big fool first. He was invisible in the grasses as he slunk after the man. The wind on the tall dry stalks of last year's grass and the whisper and hush of the waves against the rocky beach below covered the slight sounds the cat made as he stalked after him. It wasn't hard to keep up. Light that was plenty for a cat was black night for the man. He was not walking fast. He muttered and cursed as he trudged along. He halted a moment to look back and down into the dell; in the distance, light shone still from the cottage window and through the battered thatch of the roof. The man spat out a vicious word and lurched on.

Marmalade watched him for a time, noting how high he lifted his feet and gauging his pace. Then, with a dart no mouse could have avoided, he dashed across the man's path, yowling as he came. The man leaped in surprise, tangled his own feet, and came down hard on his hands and knees. Marmalade had already vanished himself. *I want to kill you,* he told the intruder.

The man got to his feet, wiping his skinned hands on his trousers. "Just a cat," he said, and then, "Just *that* damned cat." He considered for a moment, then shouted, "You can't hurt me, cat! And if I get my hands on you, I'm going to kill you."

He stood for a time, staring all around himself in the dimness. Marmalade had no fear. When the man set off again, he ghosted along behind him. When the man ceased glancing back over his shoulder, he waited a dozen steps more. Then, silent as the spring wind, he raced up behind him and shot up his back. He scratched the man's face in passing, not as deeply as he would have liked, for he wouldn't chance the man grabbing him again. The man shrieked and cursed and clutched at his face. Marmalade ran to the side of the path and crouched in the grasses.

"You damn Witted beast! Damn you! I'm going to kill you."

Try. Marmalade invited him. *Just try.* He lashed his tail. He saw the man stoop and grope for stones. He wouldn't find any on the grassy path. Marmalade growled in his throat. It was amusing to watch the intruder straighten up. It was even more amusing to watch him pretend he wasn't sneaking up on the cat as he ventured closer.

When the man sprang, Marmalade leaped back, but only a dozen paces. He crouched again, growling and lashing his tail in unmistakable challenge. *Go ahead. Catch me. Kill me.*

The man was in a fury now. He sprang and fell on the place where the cat had been. Marmalade yowled victoriously and dashed away. The man scrabbled to his feet and followed, shouting threats.

Shout all you want! Words can't hurt me!

"I'll give you more than words when I catch you, you demon beast!"

Twice more the cat taunted him and twice more the man sprang. The third time, Marmalade darted into deep tussocks of grass and crouched. But he was not hidden. He saw the man spot him, and he tensed every muscle in a desperate need to be ready. The man sprang and Marmalade darted back to where Pell had been as the undercut edge of the grassy cliff gave way. The man roared and as the earth collapsed beneath him, he clutched desperately at the tussocks. They tore free and went down with him, falling toward the rocky beach and clutching waves below. He shouted as he fell.

Marmalade, heart thudding, ventured closer to the cliff and peered over. At first, not even his cat's eyes could penetrate the deepening night. He could make out the white lace as the waves met the rocks.

"I'll kill you, cat!" the man shouted from below. "I'll hunt you down and kill you."

It hadn't worked. The man hadn't fallen far enough, and the earth collapsing with him had cushioned his fall. The intruder clung to the cliff face, glaring up. The cat was reasonably certain the man couldn't see him. He poked his head out a bit farther to look directly into his face.

Perhaps you'll kill me. But not tonight.

Then Marmalade turned and retreated into the deep grasses. He hunkered down to wait. He listened to the noises the man made as he climbed, slipped, and climbed again. The night was getting away from him; he'd have no time to hunt tonight. It was very irritating. He shouldn't have to be doing this. The female should be defending her own territory. What was wrong with her?

It was some time before the man slithered up onto the top of the cliff. He lay there for a long time, just breathing, before he pulled himself to his hands and knees and then staggered to his feet. He brushed uselessly at the wet mud that streaked the front of his fine clothes. Then he gave it up. "Damn you, cat!" he shouted to the open night. Marmalade remained still, and the man resumed his journey to town. The cat followed.

The cat had been to town before. Sometimes he followed the woman when she went to do errands or work for others. She would turn and shake her apron at him and tell him to go home, but he simply hid and then followed her. Town was an interesting place. There were fat rats beneath the fishmonger's shop. There were female cats, too, some sleek and some ragged, and all howling for him to come join in battle and then in mating with them.

He'd made his share of kits for the village. And thus he knew that there were dogs, too. During the day, they roamed the streets, but at night, they stayed closer to their doorsteps, guarding their masters' homes. As the man entered the village and the cat followed him, he became less than a shadow as he wound his way along the fronts of porches and through weedy alleys. Some of the homes and businesses of the village had wooden boardwalks in front of them, and they provided excellent shelter for a small animal seeking to remain unseen. The streets were mostly dark. Lamplight fingered its way between shutters to lie as bars across the street. But there were carts with empty traces and deep shadows under them, left in front of their owners' homes. A drapery of fishing nets hanging and waiting to be mended offered him a long stretch of dappled shadow.

He was crossing a street to follow the human male when a yellow hound spotted him. With a snarl of delight, it sprang after him. Marmalade fled. A wooden porch beckoned. Another very large dog slept curled in front of the door it served. There was no help for it; it was the only shelter close enough and he darted under it, only to discover that it concealed an older, collapsed walkway that blocked his retreat. A moment later, the hound's front shoulders collided with the porch step as he thrust his snapping jaws and head under the planks. Marmalade flattened himself against the collapsed structure and found himself just out of reach of the dog's jaws. He leaned in with a slash of razor claws, scoring blood on the dog's sensitive nose. The hound gave a loud yelp and withdrew.

An instant later, however, it was back and starting to dig. The stupid hound would not have to move much earth to be able to cram himself under the boardwalk and reach the cat. He was a large enough dog that Marmalade had no hope of winning against him in a fight. Yet fight he would. He stood his fur up proudly, fluffed his tail, and growl-yowled his defiance. He hated this, hated going into a fight he would lose, one that might even cost his life. Yet there was no help for it, just like his uneven combat against the intruding male. If one must die, one died fighting.

He danced forward to deal the dog a slash across his face. But before his claws could connect, the dog vanished with a startled yelp. A moment later, the sounds of a full-fledged dogfight greeted his ears. The cat wasted no time. He poked his head out of his hiding place and then streaked away at top speed. In passing, he observed that the watchdog from the porch had seized the hound by his hind leg and jerked him out. *Mine, mine, mine* was his sole brutish canine thought. The porch was his, whatever was under it was his, and he would kill the intruder before surrendering it. He was a huge dog with massive jaws; the hound had no more chance against him than the cat had had against the hound. Let him see how he liked such a fight!

He found a quiet spot in an alley and groomed all his fur straight again before he went on. The damn hound had put him off the man's trail. Well, the night did not have to be entirely wasted. There were always the fat rats under the fishmonger's shop to consider. He shuddered his coat all over, gave his shoulder one more lick to make one orange stripe match the next, and then trotted purposefully on.

There were rats aplenty creeping about under the fishmonger's, and even more nudging through the trash heap of the tavern next to it. He had just killed his third one and was eating the tender belly out of it when he heard a voice he knew, raised in an anger that was also tediously familiar. Gripping what was left of the rat in his jaws, he padded through the darkness to the front of the tavern.

The intruder male was there, with a noisy woman at his side. "You have no right," she was shrieking, but not at Pell. "I'm a woman grown and I can do as I please. You can't make me go with you." She was not the cat's woman who fed and sheltered him, so he had little interest in her. Yet he dropped the rat and, under cover of the tall grasses along the side of the tavern, crept closer. He flattened his ears and paid no attention to the woman's yammering. She was not what interested him; what fascinated him were the three men who stood in a half circle, almost ringing Pell and the shrieking woman. One was an older man, big but looking both tired and sad. He would fight, thought the cat, but without much heart. The men who flanked him, however, were hard muscled and narrow eyed. Their shoulders were up as if they were wild dogs putting up their hackles, and their feet were set wide. And they were glaring at Pell.

The cat sat down. He curled his tail neatly around his feet. *Hello, bigger dogs,* Marmalade greeted them. He watched.

There was shouting, but the woman remained defiant. It reminded him very much of a queen in season. There was the yowling female and the circle of males who wanted to claim her. But a true queen would have been slapping and slashing at them, daring them to prove themselves worthy of possessing her. This woman merely shrieked and shouted and stood defiantly behind her very poor choice of a male. The cat rumbled low and waited for the bigger dogs to attack.

The oldest male seemed to be the leader of the three. They would not charge Pell and pull him down unless he gave the signal. Pell was clearly overmatched, and yet the old man did not take action. He appeared to be listening to what the female was yowling rather than merely subduing her with his strength. Foolishness.

Don't let her defy you. He tried the thought carefully against the man's mental boundaries. In the dim light of the tavern lanterns, he saw the man scowl. He narrowed his eyes as if he'd just remembered something.

She is yours, the cat reminded him. *Not his. Don't let him take her away with him. He has no right to her!*

The old man suddenly stepped forward and grabbed the woman by the upper arm. She turned on him, claws raised to scratch, but the man blocked her with the ease of experience. "Come with me, Meddalee. For your own good. You're drunk right now. I'm taking you back to the boat so you can sleep it off. And tomorrow, when the tide changes, we'll be going home. And by the time we get there, maybe you will have decided which you want more: this ass who has no future other than making more bastards, or an inheritance from your father. Because I promise you this, girly. You can't have both. Ever."

His words took something out of the girl. Her fight faded and she pushed the hair back from her face, to stare at her father in blurry disbelief. "You wouldn't," she slurred out, but she did not sound certain.

"I would," her father asserted. He lifted his stare to the intruder. Pell was standing with his fists lifted, as if he only waited a reason to attack. But with his seizure of the female, the moment had come and gone and Pell had not acted. "I assure you, Pell. You may lead my Meddalee away from me and down a garden path, but my money won't follow her. Not now, not ever. You've abandoned one woman and one child. And that for me is your measure, forever. I'm done with you. And if my daughter has even a fraction of her mother's good sense, she's done with you, too. Come along, Meddalee."

And that was it. The cat hissed low to himself in dismay. They hadn't attacked the intruder male, hadn't killed him or even struck him. He lashed his tail in frustration, then stilled. Provocation. That might be the key.

She thinks you're a coward. They all think you are a coward. They're walking away and you're doing nothing. Nothing. They're right. You are a coward. You've always been a coward.

"Meddalee!" Pell suddenly bellowed and stumbled forward in a drunkard's charge. Her father kept his grip on her arm and pushed her to keep walking. She looked over her shoulder and cried dramatically, "Pell, oh, Pell!" But by then her father's men had closed on the hapless man. They pushed him down easily. Marmalade watched them from the shadows, big blue eyes wide. But they toyed with him as if he were a mouse. When he stood, they pushed him down, talking and laughing as they did so. But there was less good play in him than there had been in the rats Marmalade had caught earlier. The fifth time he was shoved into the dirt, he still muttered oaths but crawled off into the darkness on his hands and knees. At the edge of the tavern porch, he collapsed and rolled himself into a ball. The two men looked at each other.

"No," one said. "He's done, Bell. Let him go. He ain't worth killing."

The cat did not share their assessment. He remained where he was for a time, pondering his own chances against the man now. But he remembered that the man had been faster than he had first thought. He recalled too well the savage clutch of the man's hands around his body. No. There had to be a better way.

He moved out of the sheltering shadows. The men were vanishing up the street. He went to where Pell was curled and sat down just out of reach. He yowled loudly until the man uncovered his head and stared at him.

Coward.

The man just stared at him, eyes wide.

Get up. Go after her. Fight them.

"Go away. Damn Wit beast!"

The cat stared at him for a moment longer. Then he sprang at him with a sharp hiss and was pleased to see Pell cover his face with his arms. *No,* he thought as he trotted away. That one was too cowardly to start what needed to be started. He'd have to find another way.

The woman was drunk and walking unsteadily. She was also weeping noisily. It was easy for the cat to catch up to them. Night was deeper, even the dogs were sleeping more soundly, and Marmalade trotted unseen down the very center of the road. He followed them as they walked down to the boat harbor. He did not like walking out on the wooden dock; the boards were spaced for a man's stride, not a cat's. But he was sure-footed and silent as a shadow. They came to a boat, one that smelled more of wheat than fish. One of the men lifted the woman and set her feet on the boat. She sank down bonelessly, bowing her head and sniveling miserably. A watchman came out of the dark to greet them.

"It's just us. Bringing Meddalee back."

There was some conferring, and someone was sent to wake someone else. Another female, stumbling with sleep, came out on the deck. The cat wondered if the males knew how annoyed she was to be given charge of the drunken girl. But she accepted the burden, dragging her to her feet and walking her into the boat's house and down a short walkway. Unnoticed, the cat followed her.

She took the woman into a small room and sat her down on a narrow bed. She pulled the shoes from her feet, then pushed her back on the bed and spread a blanket over her. "Sleep it off," she muttered to her, and then leaned across her to open a porthole. "Fresh air do you good," she added, and then left, shutting the door behind her. For a time, there were other noises, the sounds of men's boots, the mumble of conversation.

When all was still on the boat, the cat jumped lightly to the bunk. He poked the sleeping woman's face. She did not stir. He leaned closer and bit her lightly on the cheek, as if he were rousing Rosemary to be fed. She muttered and turned her face away from him. Her graceful neck shone white in the lantern light that filtered in from the small window.

There would be no sport to this.

ROSEMARY LAY DOWN next to her boy but did not dare to sleep. Exhaustion buzzed her head, and she traversed the night in that state that is neither rest nor wakefulness. She arose before dawn, refusing to think about the crowing that did not happen. She had let the fire go out, and it felt very strange to rise and perceive her usual chores as useless things. Marmalade had not come back. Her heart smote her when she realized that; she hoped he had not gone off somewhere to die, and then she thought that perhaps that was for the best if he had. He had no home now, any more than she did, and no one to offer him kindness or shelter. "Eda take him into your heart," she prayed to the goddess and did not think that she wasted a prayer on a mere cat.

She decided to ready the cow for travel before she woke Gillam. When she limped out to the cow's byre, she could only stand and shake her head at the terrible trick fate had played on her. Two gleaming new calves, red and white as their mother, lay curled together in the straw beside the cow. She had dropped them both in the night without even a bellow. The cow looked at Rosemary with placid, trusting eyes. "Good cow," Rosemary whispered, and then walked away, leaving the door of the byre open. Pell would not, she was sure, put the cow in and out and bring her buckets of fresh water or stake her on the best grass. All she could do for her was to leave the door open so she could come and go as she would. Her thoughts were bitter as she walked back to the cottage. Had Pell never come back into her life, she would have been shouting and dancing for joy at this multiplication of her wealth. Now she was just giving her good fortune to a man she despised, a man who would not treasure it, and losing whatever coin she might have gained from Hilia.

In the cottage, she rolled up one coverlet and stuffed it into her carry bag. She slung it from her shoulder and wished her goods were heavier even as she wondered how long she could carry them and Gillam. Her knee was swollen and thick. It didn't matter. She didn't try to wake the boy, but picked him up, settled him on her shoulder, and limped out. She left the door hanging open behind her. Clouds hung low, threatening rain. Not a good day to begin a journey, but her only choice.

Pell hadn't come home. Was he sleeping it off in the tavern? Had he gone to his parents' house? How long would it be before he came home and discovered she was gone, stealing his son? When would he see the cow and her calves and realize that she hadn't taken the animal anywhere, that she had simply left? She contemplated the climb up the steep trail to the cliff-top path reluctantly, comforting herself that once she was there, the trail leveled out and the walking would be easier.

"Good-bye, cottage," she said.

Gillam lifted his head. "Look. Marmy!"

It was the cat. He was coming down the path from the cliff's edge at a dogged trot. He was wetter and more bedraggled than she'd ever seen him; he must have been out on the hills all night. Probably too afraid to come home after what Pell had done to him. Gillam suddenly struggled in her arms.

"Marmy! Marmy hurt!" He twisted out of her grasp, hit the ground, and darted up the path to the cat.

"Oh, Gillam," she cried, and limped after him.

As soon as they reached the cat, Marmalade sat down and licked his shoulder. He purred when Gillam hugged him, then wriggled gently from his grip. She could tell his ribs were sore, but he hadn't scratched the boy. The cat stood up on his hind legs against her, and she took him up, cradling him gently in her arms. He was wet and smelled musky and was uncharacteristically dirty. He'd been into something sticky, and it had clotted dirt onto his chest. "What am I going to do, Marmalade? I can't leave you here, and I can't take you with me."

She set the cat down gently. He rumbled as if displeased and went to Gillam. The youngster sat down and the cat clambered into his lap. Purring, he rubbed his face against the boy's. She watched them for a long moment, wishing this was the start of an ordinary day, and that she could leave them as they were and go about her chores. Then she glanced at the path up to the cliffs. At any moment now, Pell might return. The tide would be all the way out. Should she follow the cliff path or cut across the beach? Which way would Pell come home?

"Gillam, we have to leave now. We can't stay here any longer."

"Don't weave. Stay here."

The words came from Gillam. His child's voice was at odds with the adult diction. He sat looking up at her, his dark eyes wide and confident. The cat sat beside him, his blue eyes echoing the boy's stare. "No," she said softly. She knew whose thoughts he was uttering. Her mind reeled with the idea that her child was Witted, blessed or cursed with that forbidden magic. It couldn't be. Pell was not Witted, and there was no history of the blood magic in her family. She stared at him.

He isn't. He's no more Witted than you are. Cats talk to whomever they please, Witted or not. He can hear me because he has the sense to listen to me. Unlike you. You hear me, you know I'm telling the truth, but you keep trying to ignore me. You can't run from him. You'll have to stand and fight him. I did my best, but I fear it wasn't enough.

The thoughts took shape in her mind, unwelcome and unavoidable.

"I can't, cat. I can't fight him. He's too big and strong. He'll hurt me, or kill me. I can't fight him. I won't."

Gillam spoke again, a babyish inflection of adult words. "You have no choice. Here he comes."

If you don't fight him, he will hurt you or kill you. If you do fight him, he may hurt you or kill you. But at least you'll have the satisfaction of hurting him first. It won't be free for him. I saw him in the streets in town. I ran ahead of him, but he's coming. Coming soon.

She turned to follow the cat's stare. There, indeed, was Pell trudging down the path toward them. He looked much the worse for wear. She wondered what had befallen him; he looked much more bedraggled than an ordinary night at the tavern should have left him. He limped as he came down the hill toward them, and mud had smeared all the fineness from his clothes, just as anger had chased all the handsomeness from his face.

She gathered Gillam into her arms and stood up. If she could have, she would have fled, but it was too late now. There was nowhere she could run, no place to hide from him. The cat sat by her feet. He curled his tail neatly around his paws.

"He comes to kill," Gillam said softly. The words chilled her. She knew the thought belonged to Marmalade, but to hear her son verbalize it made the truth ring louder. Today, he would kill the cat. Tomorrow, it might be her. Even if he did not take their lives, he would kill the life she had built here and with it the future she had imagined for herself and her boy. It wouldn't matter if she were dead or alive; he would steal the boy from her and change him into someone she could not love.

"Go inside," she instructed them both. "Gillam. After you shut the door, pull in the latchstring. You know how; you've seen me do it. And then go up in the loft and stay there."

She didn't wait to see if he would obey her. It was a stupid, useless precaution. The cottage was not so well made that Pell could not get into it, even with the latchstring drawn. There was no place inside that a boy or a cat could hide from him. But the orders might, she thought, at least keep the boy from seeing what was to come. As she heard the door thud shut, she went to the chopping block and wrenched her hatchet free of the stump. She turned to watch Pell come down the hill to her. Something bumped her ankle. She looked down to see Marmalade sitting calmly beside her. *Wait until he's closer,* the cat cautioned her, and she was rattled by how clearly his thoughts reached her mind.

We think as one on this topic, the cat wryly agreed.

She hefted the hatchet in her hand, then clutched it to her chest, gripping it with both hands. Her heart was pounding. She had no chance. She could imagine how it would unfold; she would swing her weapon at him, he could catch her arm and twist it, disarming her. And then he would either beat her or kill her. Probably both.

And then Gillam would be alone with him. Brutalized into submission. Or worse. Raised to be just like his father. With no one to intervene, no one to suggest a different way to him.

"I can't do this," she said aloud. Sanity seemed to flow back through her veins. "He didn't really hurt me, cat. He just pushed me aside. He left Gillam and me, but he didn't try to kill us . . ."

No. He thought he didn't have to. You had no leash on him, no proof the boy was his. Perhaps he hoped you would die in childbirth and free him from the burden of both of you. Perhaps he thought you'd both starve or catch your death of cold in this cottage. I wish I could say that he hadn't tried to kill me. He nearly succeeded.

"But . . ."

I have to admit I don't understand your strategy. You're going to wait until he really hurts you or Gillam before you fight back? Doesn't seem to put the odds in your favor. The cat's thoughts were so calm in her mind. So dry of mirth and brittle with sarcasm. He sat beside her, calm as a king, his tail curled neatly around his front feet.

Pell was getting closer. He was limping; his clothes were

muddy, wet, and torn; and his face was set in a rictus of fury.

Not a strategy I think he *plans to use. I think he's going to kill me and give you a severe beating first. Before he even talks to us.*

She huffed out her breath and held the hatchet up in her shaking hand. There was no strength in her arms. Her ears were ringing and she wondered if she would collapse from terror. "Go away, Pell!" She tried to shout the words. Her heart was beating so fast that she had no strength to put into them. "You don't live here anymore. I won't let you come in. I won't let you touch me or be around Gillam. Go away!"

In response to her words, the man broke into a lurching downhill run. "Bitch!" he shouted. "You and your Wit cat. You tried to kill me last night! You both deserve death. You trapped me! You ruined my life!" The cat vanished suddenly, streaking off behind her. She couldn't blame him. She wished she could run away. But she was the only thing that stood between Pell and Gillam.

She brandished the hatchet. "I mean it!" she shouted, but her voice squeaked and then broke on the words. Did she? Did she mean it? Wasn't this a huge mistake, one that would get her killed?

"You stole everything from me! My inheritance, the future I was meant to have, my grandfather's regard for me. Everything! It was all your fault, Rosemary. You made me do this! You remember that! You made me do this!" Pell's gaze met hers as he drew his knife from his sheath.

She gasped in disbelief. The cat was right. Flee!

At the last possible minute, she turned and ran. Where, where? Her frantic mind demanded of her, but she didn't know. There was no place she could go to escape him. But she ran, over the fence and through her own garden, spurning her seedlings under her flying feet, then over the fence she had built, tearing her skirts and half knocking it down, and then through the tall dead weeds behind the cow's byre.

"You stupid slut!" Pell shouted, only steps behind her. "I won't let you ruin my life!"

And stupidly she spun and swung the hatchet, knowing he was still out of reach, knowing that she couldn't win. In horror, she felt it slip from her sweaty grip, saw her only weapon fly away from her.

It struck him on the brow. Pell advanced two more staggering steps and then fell like a chopped tree. His outstretched hand struck her ankle and she shrieked, jumping backward as the knife tumbled from his grip. She spun, ran toward the house, and then, hooting and panting with fear, forced herself to turn back and dash for the dropped hatchet. She snatched it up and rounded on him, expecting him to come up from the earth and after her. But he didn't move.

She paced around him anxiously, fearing it was a trick, fearing she had killed him, dreading that she had not. He sprawled unmoving in the crushed vegetation. Was he pretending, hoping to lure her closer? She lifted the hatchet threateningly and stood perfectly still. Was she breathing too loud? She closed her lips and breathed through her nose, feeling as if she were smothering herself. His face was turned away from her. How long would he lie there, hoping she'd come close enough that he could rise up and drag her down? She gritted her teeth, willing her body to be content with less air. She was still shaking all over. Was he breathing? She stared at him, saw the slow rise and fall of his back. He was alive. Stunned or faking.

She tightened her grip on the hatchet. This was her best chance to finish him off. One good hard smashing blow to the back of his head and he'd be all done. She lifted her weapon and willed herself to bring it down. Could not. Her fingers were made of grass, of yarn.

"Mama!" It was a long drawn cry of pure terror. *Gillam!* Cowardice prevailed. She turned and ran, hatchet in hand, leaving Pell facedown in the tall grass.

Gillam was standing in front of the cottage, and by the time she reached him, he was screaming uncontrollably. He held his arms out from his body, and his hands were shaking wildly. She flew to him and gathered him into her arms. His body was stiff, and he continued to scream as if not even her reappearance could comfort him. "Mama, mama, you were gone. Gone!"

The cat appeared suddenly, winding himself comfortingly around her ankles, and she sank down, the last of her strength spent. "We have to get out of here," she whispered to them both. "Hush. Hush. We have to go now, right now. You, too, cat. Come on."

"Where? Where we go, Mama?" Gillam barely choked out the words.

"We're going to go visit. We're going visiting, we're going to see . . . On a visit. You'll see, you'll see." Where could she go? Was there anywhere she could flee that Pell wouldn't find her? She carried Gillam despite her throbbing knee. Odd. While she had been fleeing from Pell, she hadn't even felt it. Now it kept time with the beating of her heart, sending surges of pain up her thigh. It would have to be borne, just like everything else.

She'd left her packed bag by the cow's byre. She snatched it up and kept walking. She would not go see if he was sitting up yet or if he still sprawled there. Gillam did not need to see his father that way. Where to go, where to go? Which of her friends deserved the trouble that would go with her? Flee to Hilia, hope her husband would be home to keep Pell from killing her? Go to Serran's? No, the old woman would be frightened to death if Pell came shouting and breaking things.

In the end she followed the cliff-edge road and limped all the way into town, Gillam on her hip and Marmalade trailing after her and the hatchet clutched in her hand against her child's back. The promised rain began as she hiked, a gentle spring rain of small droplets. At the outskirts of town, the cat sat down. She glanced back at him. Rain glistened in drops on his whiskers. "Aren't you coming with us?"

Dogs. Big dogs require bigger dogs. You won't see me.

"I may not come back this way."

I'll follow. Or I won't.

"Very well." It was yet another thing she could not change. Eda bless and watch over him, she prayed silently. She paused to put the hatchet in her bag and then walked down the last hill and into the village. It seemed a quiet day. In the little harbor, only the small boats had set out to fish. The larger ones were waiting for a better tide. The little market was just starting to stir. She could smell the first bake of the day's bread on the rising wind. She glanced back the way she had come, but the cat was not to be seen. She had to believe he could take care of himself.

Before she reached the market street, the rain began in earnest with the rising wind tugging at her skirts. Her boy shivered in her arms and huddled into her. "Hungry, Mama," Gillam told her, and the fourth time he said it, he dissolved into helpless weeping. Her heart sank. She was hungry, too, but if she spent her coin on food now, what would they live on tomorrow? The rain was penetrating her clothing already.

She went to the tavern, the only one in the village, the one by the fishmonger's where she had first met Pell and been courted by him. Those days seemed like a song she had once heard, something about a foolish girl infatuated with a heartless man. It had been months since she had passed those doors, years since she had sat by the fire with a mug of Tamman's ale and sang choruses with a minstrel. For a moment, she recalled it all clearly. The fire was hot on her face and legs, and her back had been warm where she leaned on Pell. He didn't sing but had seemed proud that she did. All those times when she had defied her mother to be there with Pell, creeping from her bed quietly and sneaking off; how often had she lied for the sake of being with him?

It hurt to remember that deception.

Her mother had been so right about everything. She wished she could tell her that now.

She could barely bring herself to push open the tavern door and carry her child inside. It was darker than she remembered, but it smelled the same, of fish chowder and wood smoke and spilled beer and pipe smoke and hearth bread. There were few customers at that hour and she took Gillam to a table near the fire and set him down. The innkeeper himself came over and stared down at her in a peculiar way. Tamman's generous nature was reflected in his personal size. He looked from the door to her to the boy and then back again. His mouth moved as if he were chewing words, deciding to spit them out or swallow them. She spoke first.

"I've got a couple of copper shards. Can I have a bowl of chowder for the boy, and as much bread as that will buy?"

Tamman didn't budge from where he stood or change his gaze. He only opened his mouth and bellowed, "Sasho, chowder and bread for two!" Then he abruptly dropped down on the bench across the table from her. "Pell coming in?" he asked somberly.

A shudder passed through her. She hoped he hadn't seen it. "I . . . I don't know." She tried to sound calm.

Tamman nodded sagely. "Well, nothing against him or you, but I don't want trouble here. He was here last night, you know. That cross-the-bay woman, that Meddalee Morrany? She was here last night, waiting for Pell. She got pretty angry, sitting and waiting, but he finally got here, looking like something the cat dragged in. It wasn't coincidence, Rosemary. She was waiting for him." The innkeeper who had known her since she was a child looked into her tearless eyes, trying to see what his words meant to her. There was no malice in his look, only measurement. She blinked, trying to contain her thoughts. Tamman nodded to himself. "Yes. Those two had planned to meet here. And they sat in the corner there, by the back door, away from the fire and the crowd, and they talked for a long time." Tamman shook his head. "That woman's crazy. Her face was still bruised blue from the last beating that damn Pell gave her. Why she would come seeking that cruel bastard . . . Sorry. Forgot the boy was here. Sorry." He leaned his forearms on the table and it creaked.

"Never mind," she said quietly. Gillam was watching the fire and not paying attention to them. Sasho appeared with the food then, two brimming bowls that were dribbling white chowder down the sides and a napkin with three brown-crusted rolls on it. Gillam snatched at the bread before the serving lad could even set the food down. Her boy stuffed the corner of the roll in his mouth. "Gillam!" she cried, mortified, but the innkeeper put a large hand on her arm.

"Let the boy eat. A child that hungry shames us all. Go on, boy. There's a big bowl of chowder there for you, made this morning with fresh cream, fresh cod, and old onions. Go on."

"Let me break the bread for you while you try your soup," she suggested to her son quietly. Gillam did not wait to be urged again. Despite her anxiety, Rosemary's stomach growled loudly at the sight and smell of the hot food.

Tamman heard it. "Go on. You, too. What I got to say isn't pleasant, so you may as well hear it on a full stomach as not."

She nodded slowly as she took another of the rolls and tore off a bite of bread. It was fragrant and warm. She chewed it slowly, waiting in dread for whatever disaster was to befall her.

"Just as I was about to close for the night, who should come storming in but Meddalee's father. Morrany was furious with Pell for marking his daughter's face, and even angrier that she'd caught the cross bay ferry to come running after him. Made him even hotter to see those two all cozy with their heads together. Morrany spoke loud and plainer than any father should, saying if Pell wants to visit his daughter's bed, then he should marry her. And then he demanded to know where this grand fortune is that his grandfather was to bequeath to him, for he'd heard gossip the old man was dead for most of the winter, and if Pell was his chosen heir, well, where was his wealth, then?

"And you know Cham, who loves to sit and drink here more hours than he works in a day. Well, he was the one fool enough to stand and say that the old man had little enough, and most of what he had, he'd already left to Pell's bastard son after Pell abandoned the boy and his mother.

"Well, turns out Pell and Meddalee had never seen fit to tell Meddalee's father that bit of news. When her father started shouting at them both, saying he wouldn't be grandfather to fortuneless bastards, she started weeping and squawking that it wouldn't be like that, that Pell had come back to Cogsbay to fix things for them. And Rosemary?"

He cleared his throat and then said into her waiting silence, "That bastard as much as said, before everyone here, that he didn't believe that one was really his." The innkeeper tipped his head toward Gillam as if to be certain she understood his roundabout reference to her son. "When anyone who saw Pell grow up knows that the boy is an image of him when he was a lad." Then he looked down at his big hands on the edge of the table for a few moments. Perhaps he expected Rosemary to be shocked at the news. Or shamed. She was neither. His words confused her. She had been so sure that Gillam was why Pell had returned, that her boy was what he wanted.

She took a spoonful of the cooling chowder. Not even the taste of the warm rich chowder could chase the bitterness from her mouth. She met Tamman's gaze. "Pell's lies are none of my doing," she said quietly.

"More like what has been done to you," the innkeeper conceded. He looked at the fire, allowing her a few moments of quiet in which to eat.

"Thank you for telling me all this," she said at last. She had not asked him why, but he heard her question.

Tamman shifted on the bench. "Could be trouble is coming for you. That Meddalee is one determined woman. I've known her since she was a girl. Her parents used to send her here, clear across the bay, for her to stay with her cousins for the harvest. Rumor was that even then, they couldn't handle her. She's always been willful. She doesn't seem to care what Pell is, only that she thinks he ought to be hers, even if he slaps her, even if he's already got a son. Eda alone knows what Meddalee might do if she came out to your home. Be wary."

"If she wants Pell, she's welcome to him."

The innkeeper shook his blunt head. "Rosemary, you aren't hearing me. Her father was furious with her. Said that he wouldn't let Pell come back, that Pell was a penniless cad who would use her and leave her with a bastard just as he did to you. Morrany is a wealthy man, across the bay. Owns two ships and three warehouses. He wants his daughter to marry well, someone with property for his grandchildren to inherit, alongside his own wealth. Pell can't offer that. His father's debts are such that when he goes, there won't be two pence for his widow to rub together. His grandfather didn't have much; Soader gave the cottage to your lad, and his little house here in town went to clear his debts after he was gone. Eda bless the man, he was a good soul and shared what he had while he was alive. Everyone in the village knew that he slipped Pell's mother money whenever she asked; without him helping her, Pell's father would have beggared them long ago. And when Soader was gone, well, there wasn't anything left.

"So, think, girl. Your boy owns the only bit of land that might be an inheritance for Pell. Meddalee's a determined woman. What would she have to do to make that cottage and land Pell's?"

She furrowed her brow at him. The words came slowly. "Kill me? Kill . . ." She roved her glance over Gillam, unable to speak the words aloud.

Tamman nodded. "Now you understand." He looked away from her. "They sat together, away from the fire but close to the back door. I made more than one trip out to the garbage heap last night, dumping dregs and garbage. I overheard things, Rosemary." He looked at her directly. "Pell was talking, saying that he could fix it, that before summer was over, he'd have a place of his own and be free to marry her."

Gillam had finished his food and was looking with unabashed interest at hers. She slid the half-full bowl across the table to him. Suddenly her hunger was gone; fear filled her belly. What had Pell been shouting as he came down the hill? That she had stolen his inheritance? She tried to think as Pell would. He'd come back home to them and tried to make them believe it was good. Tried to get her to trust him. If it had worked, what would he have done next? Get rid of her first. A tumble down the cliff, or perhaps he would say the cow had trampled her. And then, well, a month or so later, tragedy would strike him again. His boy would die "of a cough" in his sleep. Or fall from the cliffs. Or wander off into the fens, never to be seen again. And the cottage would pass to him.

She looked at her boy spooning up mouthfuls of thick, rich chowder. A slow, cold anger rose in her. She'd been a fool. So blind. Gillam was the most precious thing in her life and she thought Pell had come back to take him from her.

He'd come back to destroy him. She thought suddenly of his knife. A gift. A very sharp knife. She suddenly knew who had given it to him.

"Will you be safe, Rosemary?"

The innkeeper's words called her gaze back to him. "I will," she said. Pell would not. Time to finish what she had left undone. She set her two coins on the edge of the table, but Tamman shook his head.

"Not this time, my dear. It's been too long since you patronized my place. And your coming here today saved me a hike around the cliffs to your cottage. Now. Where is Pell? Did he come home last night?"

She shook her head slowly and chose her words. "He never came into the cottage. I don't know where he is now." It was almost a truth. He had never reached the cottage door. And right now, he might have recovered and be on his way here. Or still lying behind the cow byre.

But the innkeeper only nodded as if that confirmed his guess. "Last night, Meddalee Morrany's father dragged her out of here. She was kicking and spitting and shrieking and trying her claws on his face. Pell stood and shouted that she was a woman grown, that her father had no right to force her to go home, but Morrany had the captain and the mate of one of his ships with him, and Pell daren't start a fight with any one of them, let alone three. He said, woman or no, she was acting like a spoiled child and so he would treat her. So, after a noisy shouting match outside, her father took her down to his ship. Said he was taking her back across the bay in the morning and that Pell would stay away if he knew what was good for him. But Pell's never known what was good for him. So I suspected that he'd follow and try to steal her back." Tamman nodded to himself and stood slowly. "Pell was pretty drunk when he left here. I didn't think he'd make it as far as your cottage even if he headed that way."

"He didn't," she said quietly. "Maybe he's sleeping it off somewhere. Maybe he went to his father's house."

"Or maybe he's looking for a way to get across the bay. Meddalee's father's boat is still tied up to the docks, waiting for the tide to be right. He might even be down there trying to weasel his way back into her father's favor."

"Maybe." But she knew Pell better than Tamman did. Perhaps at first, run off by Meddalee's father, he'd simply come home to her cottage as a place where he could go. But that wasn't what he'd intended this morning. He'd come back to the cottage, thinking to get rid of his inconvenient son. He'd come to kill Gillam. The cat had been right. And knowing that changed everything.

Everything.

The cat was right. She'd been a fool. Resolution as cold as iron stiffened her spine. She smiled at Tamman, a small cat's smile. "Well. We've errands to do, Gillam and I. Thank you for the chowder, Tamman, and for the warning. And you are right. It has been far too long since we've dropped in. Sometimes I forget that I do have friends."

And enemies. Sometimes she forgot that she might have enemies.

She looked at Gillam. "Is that better? Shall we go now?"

He nodded emphatically.

"The market stalls will be opening soon. Shall we go have a look?"

The boy's eyes flew wide. A trip to market was a rare thing for both of them. They lived mostly by barter and seldom used coin. He nodded avidly, and she bid Tamman farewell. Outside, the wind was blustering, but the rain had ceased. The clouds were being pushed aside from a bright blue sky.

The market in the little town was a tiny one, not more than a dozen shops and stalls and half of them seasonal. She was able to buy a short coil of sturdy line, a long slender boning knife, and then, because there was so little left of her money and life, she now knew, was an uncertain thing, a little packet of honey drops for the boy. He'd never had candy before and could scarcely bear to put even one of the bright-colored drops into his mouth. When she finally persuaded him to try a pale green one and saw his face light with surprise at the taste of honey and mint, she folded the packet up tight and put it into the bag. "Later, you can have more," she promised him, her mind full of possible plans.

They walked the cliff-top path home again. A quarter of the way back to the cottage, the cat suddenly appeared and trotted along at her heels alongside the boy. "Well, where have you been, Marmalade?" she asked him.

Rousing the bigger dogs. They sleep later than I thought.

"Don't the old wives tell us to let sleeping dogs lie?" she asked him and was rewarded only by a puzzled glance from Gillam. She said nothing to the cat of what she would do and felt no further brush of a feline mind against hers. That was just as well. What she would do, she would do, and it would be her own deed.

They reached the juncture in the path where a tiny trail wound down the grassy hillside to her cottage. She stood for a short time, looking down on it. Beyond it were the fens, a tapestry of grasses and ferns in a hundred different greens. No smoke rose from her cabin chimney. The cow had taken advantage of the open gate to lead her new calves out. The chickens scratched in the dooryard. All seemed calm.

Of Pell, there was no sign. He could be in hiding. He could be sleeping in the cabin. He might still be lying in the tall meadow grass behind the byre. She sighed. "I should have been certain of him when I had the chance," she said to no one. The cat lifted a paw and swiped it across his face, almost as if hiding a smile.

Gillam started down the path ahead of her. She called him back. She reached into the bag and gave him another honey drop, a yellow one. "You and Marmalade stay right here," she told him. "Sit down and see how long the candy lasts if you only suck on it." The novelty of the candy was enough to win her instant obedience. She put the little cloth bag in his hands. "When it's all gone, try a red one. When it's all gone, have a pink one. Suck on each one slowly. And wait for me to come back and ask you which one you liked best." Gillam's eyes were big as saucers at his good fortune. He found a rock jutting up in the grass by the trail and perched on it, sucking thoughtfully. The cat sat down beside him and curled his tail around his feet.

Luck.

"Thank you." She set her pack down beside them. She took only the rope and the skinning knife and the hatchet. She walked silently down the hill. It was impossible to disguise her approach to the cabin. It was a bare, broad hillside. She carried the bared knife gleaming in her hand.

She looked for him first in the cabin, but it was still and cold as a dead thing. She searched it well, even climbing up to peer into the loft and then looking under the bed. There was nowhere else in the cabin where a grown man could hide. She went out and about her small farmstead. The chickens scattered as she walked through the scratching, pecking flock but otherwise showed no alarm. The cow was grazing peacefully, her two red calves sleeping together. Pell was not hiding in her stall.

She glanced up the hillside. Gillam still perched on his rock. She could not see Marmalade. She waved at her son, and he waved back at her. Then, knife in one hand and hatchet in the other, she went behind the cowshed.

If Eda had blessed her, the man would be dead where he had fallen. But Eda was a goddess of light and life and fertility. One did not pray to her for a convenient death. Pell was not sprawled there. He was gone, and so was his knife.

And she suddenly saw her error. She lifted her skirts and ran, suddenly sure of her mistake. And as she rounded the byre, she saw Pell striding up to her boy.

"Well, what's that you have there, Gillam? Candy? Why don't you show me?"

His words just reached her ears. Pell was standing over the boy. "Gillam!" she shouted, a useless warning. What would she tell him to do? Run? He could not outrun a determined man. As Gillam turned, startled at her cry, Pell scooped him up. Scooped him up and began to run with him, up the path to the cliffs.

She screamed, a useless waste of her breath, and ran. Her heart was pounding so that it filled her ears, and then suddenly she realized that thundering sound was not her heart at all. Hoofbeats. Someone was riding a horse along the cliff trail. She lifted her panicked gaze and saw three mounted men galloping heedlessly on the cliff-side path.

"Stop him!" she shouted at them, helplessly, hopelessly. "Stop him! He means to kill the boy! Help me, please. Please!"

Did they even hear her breathless cries? She kept running and became aware of a tawny little shape that was leaping after Pell, catching at his legs and then falling back and racing after him again. Gillam had found his voice and was roaring with terror even as he clutched his bag of sweets. And Pell was getting ever closer to the cliff tops.

The three men all but rode him down. She cried out in horror as Pell flung her son at them and tried to run even as the men abandoned the stamping horses to chase after him. Gillam struck the ground hard and rolled away from them, and then lay, sprawled and still in the early spring sunlight.

"Gillam," she shrieked and ran to him. The horses, spooked by her cries, wheeled and ran back the way they had come. She cared nothing for them or for the struggling men by the cliff's edge. She reached her boy and scooped him up.

"Gillam, Gillam, are you all right?" she cried. She sank to the earth and gathered his little body into her arms. He seemed so small.

He took a shuddering breath and then sobbed out, "I wost my candy! I dwopped my candy!"

In her joy, she laughed aloud, and then, because of the hurt in his eyes that she laughed at his tragedy, she felt in the grass and came up with the little cloth sack. "No, you didn't lose them. See, here they are and just fine. Just fine."

He's gone now.

Marmalade had found them. He clambered into her lap with Gillam, and he hugged the cat tightly.

"Gone?" she asked in wonder. "Gone where?"

Gillam spoke the cat's thought aloud. "The bigger dogs chased him over the cliff's edge." He glanced back toward the returning men and observed sourly, "They took too long to get here. They were nearly too late."

SHE LET HIM keep the bag of candy and told him he might look at the new calves as long as he wanted if he sat on the top of the fence and did not go near them. The cat followed her as she walked toward the cottage. The three men were standing uncomfortably by the door. The oldest man leaned on a younger companion. "You are welcome to come in," she said quietly as she walked through them and into her cottage. They followed her, awkward and silent. "Sit down," she invited the older man.

His face was grayish with sorrow. He sat on her chair heavily and then lowered his face into his hands.

"I thought I knew him," he said quietly. "Three years he worked for me and courted my daughter. I thought I knew him. Never imagined he could do what he did."

"Pell ran off the cliff himself," one of the other men suddenly declared. "It was none of your doing, sir. He could have stood and explained himself and come back to town with us to tell his story to the council. He's the one that ran right off the cliff. If the tide had been in, he might have survived. But not that fall onto the rocks."

"It's as much as he deserved," the older man said quietly. "After what he did to my daughter. My pretty little Meddalee, flighty as a butterfly. She was thoughtless and willful true, but sweet Eda, she never deserved what he did to her."

"You're Meddalee's father?" Rosemary asked him quietly. She kept to herself her opinion of what Meddalee might deserve.

"He is." One of the other men answered for him. "And that bastard Pell killed his daughter last night. Must have crept on board and gone right to her room. Guess he thought that if he couldn't have her, no one would! When we went to wake her this morning, her own father found her there in her bed. Face all slashed to ribbons and her throat cut, neat as pie."

Light as a leaf, Marmalade floated to the sunny windowsill. He sank his claws deep into the wooden sill, stretched, and then sat. He lifted his paw to his mouth and began to wash.

"Shut up, Bell," barked the other man, and the talker fell silent. Meddalee's father groaned and hid his face deeper in his hands. "My little girl, my Meddalee," he murmured. Rosemary stared silently at her cat.

"Are you all right, miss?" the other man asked her. "He didn't hurt you, did he?"

She found her voice. She felt oddly calm as she gave them what he needed. "He threatened me. And came at me with that knife. It was a fancy one, made from Chalcedean steel, he said. He kept it sharp as a razor. But I think it was my boy he wanted to kill."

"Crazy," the first man muttered. "Man would have to be crazy to want to kill his own son."

She nodded silently.

"We should get back to town," the man named Bell suggested. "We need to tell the council what happened. And see to poor Meddalee." He looked suddenly at Rosemary. "You seen what happened, didn't you? How he broke from us and run right off the cliff?"

She hadn't, but it was a small lie to pay for peace. "I did. It was no one's fault, really."

"Sir, you think you can walk that far? Sir?" Meddalee's father slowly lifted his head. He nodded, and she almost felt sorry for the man as he left, leaning heavily on his captain's arm. She watched them make the slow climb to the cliff top and then stood watching as they followed the cliff-top path back toward town. Marmalade came out and wound around her ankles. She watched Gillam sitting on the top rail of the fence, blissfully pulling another candy from the pouch. "Red!" he called, holding it up for her to see, and she nodded.

She looked down at the cat. "Don't ever speak to me again. I don't want to know."

Marmalade didn't answer her. He sat down and began to clean his claws more carefully.